NEW YORK REVIEW BOOKS
CLASSICS

UNCERTAIN GLORY

JOAN SALES I VALLÈS (1912–1983) was born in Barcelona to a
Catalan family. In 1932, he earned a law degree from the University of
Barcelona and in 1933 married Maria Núria Folch. Their daughter,
Núria, was born the following year. At the outbreak of the Spanish
Civil War, Sales, who was a member of several regional anarchist and
Communist groups, fought for the Republican government on the
Madrid and Aragonese fronts before going into exile in France in
1939. He moved to Dominica in 1940, then Mexico in 1942, finally
returning to Catalonia in 1948. In 1955 he co-founded the publishing
house Club Editor, where he would edit and publish some of the most
important authors of twentieth-century Catalan literature, among
them Màrius Torres and Mercè Rodoreda, as well as his own work,
including a book of poems, *Viatge d'un moribund* (1952); a collection
of letters from his wartime and exile experiences, *Cartes a Màrius
Torres* (1976); and a Catalan translation of *The Brothers Karamazov*.
He died in Barcelona.

PETER BUSH is an award-winning translator who lives in Oxford.
Among his recent translations are Josep Pla's *The Gray Notebook*,
which won the 2014 Ramon Llull Prize for Literary Translation, and
Ramón del Valle-Inclán's *Tyrant Banderas* (both for NYRB Classics);
Emili Teixidor's *Black Bread*, Jorge Carrión's *Bookshops*, and Prudenci
Beltrana's *Josafat*.

JUAN GOYTISOLO (1931–2017) was born in Barcelona and was the
author of many novels, including *Marks of Identity*, *Count Julian*,
Juan the Landless, and *The Garden of Secrets*, as well as two volumes of
autobiography.

UNCERTAIN GLORY

JOAN SALES

Translated from the Catalan by
PETER BUSH

Foreword by
JUAN GOYTISOLO

NEW YORK REVIEW BOOKS

New York

THIS IS A NEW YORK REVIEW BOOK
PUBLISHED BY THE NEW YORK REVIEW OF BOOKS
435 Hudson Street, New York, NY 10014
www.nyrb.com

The translation of this work was supported by a grant from the Institut Ramon Llull

LLLL **institut**
ramon llull
Catalan Language and Culture

A catalog record for this book is available from the Library of Congress

ISBN 978-1-68137-180-1
Available as an electronic book; ISBN 978-1-68137-181-8

Printed in the United States of America on acid-free paper.
10 9 8 7 6 5 4 3 2 1

CONTENTS

A Confession by the Author

"The uncertain glory of an April day . . ." Every devotee of Shakespeare knows these words – and if I had to sum up my novel in a single line, I wouldn't use any other.

A moment comes in life when you feel that you are waking from a dream. Our youth is behind us. Of course, it could never last for all eternity, but what does "to be young" mean, in fact? "*Ma jeunesse ne fut qu'un ténébreux orage,*" writes Baudelaire; perhaps youth has never been anything but a gloomy storm streaked by lightning flashes of glory, of uncertain glory, on an April day.

A dark desire drives us on in those difficult, tortured years: we seek out, whether consciously or not, a glory that we can never define. We seek it out in many things, but particularly in love – and in war, if war crosses our path. That was how it was with my generation.

The thirst for glory, at certain moments in life, becomes painfully acute, all the more when the glory thirsted for is uncertain – I mean enigmatic. My novel attempts to capture, in some of its characters, a few of those moments. To what end? Others will be the judge of that.

But I know that he who has much loved will be much forgiven. In other times, there was greater fervour for St Dismas and St Mary Magdalene: there wasn't so much pedantry around and people didn't try to hide the passionate intensity we all carry within us under theses, messages and abstract theories.

We are sinners thirsting after glory. Because Thy Glory is our end.

JOAN SALES
Barcelona, December 1956

Truth against the red lie and the black

Juan Goytisolo

At the end of 1956, when I finally managed to fulfil my dream and leave the suffocating political, literary and moral atmosphere in Franco's Spain to find refuge in the freedom of Paris, my individual act of rupture soon took a more ambitious, less selfish turn.

By this I mean that my exile followed in the wake of the great poet Josep Palau i Fabre's, whose desire I shared to combat the castrating effects of Francoist censorship by trying to publish – as I was to continue to do through *Ruedo Ibérico* – books that the censors had banned.

Thanks to my companion Monique Lange, I assumed the responsibilities of Spanish reader at Gallimard, a task I carried out for more than ten years. This allowed me to give visibility in France to several writers in the Spanish language who, having been often forced to suffer the preventive surgery practised by the guardians of public morality in their own country, were finally allowed to publish their novels without suffering scissor cuts and amputation. Unsurprisingly, this earned me the hostility of Franco's regime, as well as a campaign of slander – of which I am duly proud – that lasted until the dictator died.

Reading the manuscript of *Incerta Glòria* that Joan Sales sent me was one of my most gratifying moments as a publisher's reader. Despite my as-yet-imperfect grasp of Catalan, I immediately realised it was a great novel, both because of the meticulous and complex way in which it was written and because of its original approach to its subject, the Spanish Civil War of 1936–9.

Written by an eyewitness from the camp of the defeated, it contained no political message and yielded no ground to glib partisan flag-waving. In its pages I found the same grief in the face of irremediable destruction that I had found in Luis Cernuda's book of poems *The Clouds*, a grief that avoided the rampant propaganda displayed by both camps – in the

9

mediocre, downright wretched novels and poetry by the poetasters of the Falange, and in the worthier efforts penned by republican and communist authors.

The duty of bearing witness to "the truth against the red lie and the black" – about which he subsequently writes in *El vent de la nit* (*The Wind in the Night*), a part added by the author as a sequel to the novel – gives Joan Sales the ethical rigour of someone who does not root his thinking in certainties but rather in lives exposed to the world's absurdity, its procession of blood, death and injustice.

The heroes of *Uncertain Glory* – volunteers and others fighting on the Aragon front – experience a situation that goes beyond them, making them pawns in a game they cannot control. Their suffering, doubts, heroic deeds and sacrifices embody "the uncertain glory of an April day" which gives the novel its title. Unlike the authors of most war novels, Joan Sales falls neither into the limiting trap of the melodramatic eyewitness account nor into lyrical rhapsodising. That is why the power of *Uncertain Glory* survives the test of time and why, when reading it today, one experiences the intensity that impelled it during the time of its writing.

The incomplete text I received contained paragraphs and passages that had not appeared in the Catalan edition at the time. Bernard Lesfargues translated them scrupulously into French and the novel received excellent reviews. My tiny struggle against Francoist censorship was thus happily rewarded, as it was again years later when Gallimard published *In Diamond Square* by Mercè Rodoreda. Both these authors are, in my opinion, the most striking writers of that sombre period of Catalan culture which ran from the end of the civil war to the death of Francoism. The present renaissance of narrative in the language forged by Ramon Llull would have been impossible without them.

JUAN GOYTISOLO
Marrakesh, June 2006

Publisher's note: The 1962 edition, to which Juan Goytisolo refers, is a much earlier translation than the considerably longer, definitive version published here. It carried the following dedication:

To Juan Goytisolo, who was a child.

Translator's Note

Joan Sales drew closely on his own experience of fighting in the Spanish Civil War when he began writing *Uncertain Glory* in 1948 in Barcelona, after nine years of exile in Haiti, the Dominican Republic and Mexico. The novel was first published in 1956 with the *nihil obstat* of the Archbishop of Barcelona. This was after Franco's censors had imposed a total ban on publication because it "expresses heretical ideas often in disgusting, obscene language". Sales continued to develop the novel and the definitive text – a much longer, more complex novel – became the fourth edition that appeared in 1971.

Joan Sales was a supporter of the Catalan Republican Generalitat and at the beginning of the war trained in its School for Officers; he was then sent to the fronts in Madrid and Aragon. In Madrid he was posted to the anarchist Durruti Column that had just killed all its officers for attempting to turn it into a regular army unit. Sales survived and continued with the Column in Xàtiva, and in Barcelona during the May events of 1937 which pitted anarchists against communists. His second posting was to the 30th Division, formerly the Macià-Companys Column, which was fully militarised and Catalan. It is life in this division that is reflected in the novel.

After the collapse of the Aragonese front in March 1938 Sales was arrested by the republican Servicio de Investigación Militar, the S.I.M. Nùria Folch i Pi, his wife, described the S.I.M. as "the local version of the G.P.U.". He was arrested for not naming two brothers who had not presented themselves to the army when called up. He awaited trial in the dungeons of Montjuïc and experienced at first hand prison life, the hunger and demoralisation in the city and the corruption of those in government: "And even so we must make a desperate effort to win this war; it's horrific to think how Catalonia will be treated if we leave," he wrote on 15 October, 1938. After being cleared, he was sent to an ex-communist column that put up final resistance to the fascists in the Balaguer bridgehead, and then to the army rearguard protecting the retreat of the defeated troops and the exodus of civilians. He would be one of the last to cross the frontier to France at the age of twenty-seven.

Anarchists had been at the forefront of the social revolution in Aragon and Catalonia, sparked off by the military uprising of 18 July, 1936 against the democratically elected government of the Second Republic. Factories were put under workers' control, peasants collectivised the land and popular militia were set up. At the same time, churches were burned, and priests, bankers and factory owners killed. As the war proceeded and Franco's crusade against "the liberal-Jewish-bolshevik-atheist-masonic conspiracy" received more support from Mussolini and Hitler, the republic turned to the Soviet Union and Stalin for help. This led to the growth of the Spanish Communist Party, the incorporation of the popular militia into a more formal institutional army, the arrival of the International Brigades and fierce conflict on the republican side between on the one hand anarchists and anti-Stalinists and on the other the supporters of the Communist Party. English readers are used to seeing these struggles through the eyes of Orwell or Hemingway. Joan Sales has created a distinctive tragicomic vision of life in the civil war in Aragon and Barcelona. His novel reminds us that many Catholics fought for the republic against Franco and for Catalan self-government, and that very little was as certain as the certainties of the ideologues.

Spanish anarchism was a mass movement that had its origins in the political and social struggles in the country from the time of the September Revolution of 1868. The struggles had climaxed in the Republican Federal Government of Pi i Margall in 1873. Bakunin's emissary Giuseppe Farinelli had arrived in Spain in 1868 and Bakunin's ideas soon found a following among landless workers in Andalusia as well as among workers in the textile factories of Catalonia. Anarchist philosophy was interpreted in various ways. It served as a set of ideas that led to the formation of trade unions such as the Confederación Nacional de Trabajo, which functioned to improve working conditions, shorten working hours and improve wages. There were also anarchists who were more interested in developing enlightened, rational, secular forms of education that might encompass vegetarianism, Esperanto and pacifism. The best known of these is Francesc Ferrer, founder of the Modern School to educate children in lay social ideas; he was arrested during the *Setmana Tràgica* and executed in Montjuïc on 13 October, 1909. Finally, there were direct-action anarchists like Santiago Salvador who threw a bomb into the stalls in the Liceu, the Barcelona opera house, killing twenty-three people in 1893.

In their early twenties when war breaks out, the novel's protagonists are all attracted at some stage to anarchism. Lluís, Soleràs and Trini are involved, long before 1936, in student protest circles which heatedly debated varieties of anarchism, Marxism and Freudianism in a tone anticipating the polemics of 1968. Trini's parents are utopian anarchist teachers. Her father is a pacifist opposed to anarchist involvement in the fighting. Like Sales, Lluís is first posted to take charge of anarchist militiamen; he then finds himself in a militarised battalion in a village on the Aragonese front that has been collectivised by anarchists. The villagers are frightened the new battalion may be like the anarchists; the battalion is frightened the anarchists might still be around. When showing Aragon and Barcelona, Sales re-creates the atmosphere of chaos, confusion and complexity in which people developed ways of life to cope with the devastations of war. Lluís and Soleràs are infatuated with the lady of the castle in Aragon whose husband was a fascist martyr; Trini turns to the Church and attends clandestine communions in city attics. Soldiers banter, play practical jokes and get drunk. The more intellectual protagonists engage in conversations full of savage humour about sex, God, death and war. All interact and coexist as best they can in the daily struggle to survive, whether scouring no-man's-land in Aragon for bottles of brandy or struggling from the Barceloneta with a sack of maggoty marrowfat peas.

Sales is a key writer in the development of Catalan as a modern literary language. His poetry and his letters to the poet Màrius Torres are unique parallel accounts of his experience of war and exile. He founded a publishing house, Club dels Novel·listes, later Club Editor, and published such writers as Rodoreda and Villalonga. He translated Dostoyevsky, Kazantzakis and Mauriac into Catalan. He was always sensitive to varieties of language as an expression of individuality and opposed to academic purists. I have tried to reflect this in the translation by using a variety of English that is non-standard as well as non-specific for the Aragonese villagers – who speak non-standard Spanish. I have also maintained the

Spanish and Catalan forms when both are used in conversations that in the original are bilingual – hence, "Lluís" (Catalan) and "Luis" as well as the diminutive "Luisico" (Spanish); and "carlà", "carlan" and "carlana" for the lord and lady of the castle. Some of the women in the village are bilingual because they have worked in service in Barcelona.

I would like to thank Joan Sales' grand-daughter, Maria Bohigas, for her constant encouragement and her mother, Núria Sales, for providing valuable clarification of certain references and pointing out distant resonances.

PETER BUSH
Barcelona, June 2014

Above all, one must adopt a doctor's precaution and never check a pulse before one is sure it is the patient's pulse and not one's own . . .

VIRGILIUS HAUFNIENSIS (Copenhagen 1844)

PART ONE

"What do you see?"
"I see," said Andrenio, "the same internecine wars two hundred years hence . . ."

GRACIÁN, *El Criticón*

I

Cito volat, aeterne pungit

CASTEL DE OLIVO, 19 JUNE

I am in excellent health, but as full of grumbles as a sickly child.

I can't tell you how much I have suffered serving in a division I loathed. I negotiate a different posting, arrive with high hopes . . . and everything collapses on me yet again.

I thought I would find Juli Soleràs here. They told me he was in the field hospital, either wounded or ill; but it turns out he's been discharged. And I've not seen a single familiar face among the thousands the phantasmagoria of war has paraded before my eyes from the day it broke out.

The lieutenant colonel commanding the First Brigade questioned me closely about why I'd taken so long: not surprising, given the time that had elapsed between the issue of my new posting and the day I joined them. He seemed happy with my straightforward explanation: an extremely sore throat. All the same, his touchy welcome needled me. Had I been hoping for greetings with open arms? We know nothing about other people, and couldn't care less; on the other hand, we expect them to know all there is to know about us. Our need to be understood is on a level with our reluctance to understand others.

Because – and I've no reason to conceal this from you – the people I now see around me leave me completely cold. If only I found them unpleasant!

Frankly, the lieutenant colonel had reason to be suspicious. A lieutenant who seeks a transfer from a unit on active service to another that's being reorganised and will remain weeks, if not months, far from the front line, could trigger barbed comments. People in these regular units cannot imagine the hellishness of brigades made up of gangs of escapees from prisons or lunatic asylums, led by raving visionaries. You need to live with them eleven months, as I just have.

I think of mules covered in festering sores, the telltale marks left by harnesses rubbing against their hide: the bitter resignation of gypsy mules that rivals the sky's when it confronts twilight. Day after day they drag their wandering tribe along endless trails, and never any hope of justice. Who will do justice by a gypsy mule? Posterity?

Life wears us down, as the harness wears down the mule's hide. To my horror I sometimes feel that these sores life inflicts on us will last as long as life itself – if not longer. My eleven months in hell . . .

It looks as if I'll be posted to the 4th Battalion, which they haven't even started organising. In the meantime I will continue to be bored out of my mind in this backwater. I have so much to tell you! I find writing these letters soothing, even though they will never reach you. You can't deny it: our family disgusts you as much as it does me, and you entered the Order of St John of God for the very reason I joined the ranks of the anarchists. Our uncle wasn't far wrong about that.

20 JUNE

When I got up, life seemed worth living again. Only because I have a little corner of this earth all to myself . . . They've billeted me in a farmhouse attic with a suntrap that looks out on land the glittering River Parral divides down the middle. The attic's under a tiled roof, and when I'm lying in bed I can see twisted reddish beams – of pine or juniper – and the reed roofing; you can see the tiles through the reed roofing. The floor isn't tiled, its timber gives when you walk over it. The walls bear traces of the many officers who've lodged here before me in the course of this year of war. I read "The village lasses are very pretty" written in pencil on the bedhead. A profound thought; I still haven't had time to check if it is as true as it is profound. All of the other scrawls dwell on the female element in the village, but few possess that lapidary quality. Some are illustrated by drawings so schematic that they look like maps of army manoeuvres.

In the end, it hardly matters. Every morning the June sun shines through the suntrap at the back of my bedroom and transfigures everything, bringing with it smells from the garden, of mown hay, fresh dung, and others I can't pin down. My attic space has a smell of its own; in better times it was a home to rabbits. Their stench lingers, but I don't dislike it; on the contrary, it keeps me company.

21 JUNE

I went to Parral del Río. They said I'd find Juli Soleràs there.

It's a small village devastated by the war where nobody lives anymore. The trenches and concrete machine-gun nests his company is manning are just outside. But he wasn't there and a lieutenant received me – the acting company captain. He's well into his forties, walks in ungainly hunting boots worthy of Tartarin de Tarascon, and never puts his S-shaped pipe down. His beady black eyes scrutinise you shiftily from beneath what you might call Mongolian lids, boring through to the marrow of your bones, while their owner, the "hail fellow well met" kind, puffs away without a care in the world.

"Are you a friend of his?"

"We've known each other for years. We went to secondary school together and then to university."

"I'm all for culture, that's for sure." He pronounces his S's with a strange lisp. He must have false teeth. "I like men with a profession. That's why I was happy to be appointed porter in the Science Faculty. I'd always been attracted to the sciences. You know, I'd just hit thirty-five, and that's no age to be staying on in the Foreign Legion. It's all very well for youngsters who want to get away from their mother's tit. As for me, I still bear the marks – those African lasses always leave you a little present to remember them by . . . but I shouldn't go on about myself, one should be more modest. Let's just agree that Africa is a filthy hole: no hygiene and no culture! Believe me, much better to get that porter's chair."

I'm inventing none of this: he spoke of his "professorship" with great aplomb and didn't bat an eyelid. The word sounded wonderfully soft through his false teeth, as if uttered through the beak of some waterfowl – if one such were able to articulate the word. Apparently, once he'd taken up his porter's chair he thought it would be opportune to "pay a pastoral visit" – his words – to all the villages and hamlets in the Vall d'Aran and seek out his first love – the reason why he hung up his habit, because, naturally, this exemplary life had begun in a seminary. Some seven years back, he'd taken his first strides thus along the road to culture and holy matrimony.

But I'd come to Parral del Río to find out about Soleràs, not to hear about the life and feats of Lieutenant Captain Picó.

"Soleràs? That's a long story. I wouldn't say he's been demoted, but he's such a strange character I can't trust him with any officer duties. I put him in charge of the company's accounts."

"The accounts?"

"Come with me to our pool and I'll tell you all about this mysterious business. The others will tell you eventually anyway. Everyone in the brigade is familiar with the story of *The Horns of Roland*."

As we chatted, we walked down to the River Parral which flows between three or four rows of ancient poplars. Lieutenant Captain Picó, being a stickler for hygiene and culture, has had a small reservoir built using sacks of clay. The water's dammed up and makes for quite a big swimming pool, at least two metres deep. "It is a hygiene installation," he explained. Twenty or so soldiers were sunbathing nearby, stark naked. When we showed up they stood to attention four rows deep – an astonishing, not to say grotesque, scene. Picó solemnly called the roll; one soldier was missing and he wanted to know why: "Gone to the brigade health unit, to get a wash down" – this machine-gun company wasn't assigned to a battalion and had to use the brigade's doctor. "At ease!" This order from their leader caused a couple of dozen Adams without a fig leaf between them to dive into the pool.

"If one didn't scare the living daylights out of them, most wouldn't wash in their whole filthy lives. I can read them like a book. And you can take your clothes off, no need to be coy." He was doing just that. "We don't worry about *loincloths* here. On the contrary, forget your shameful parts, we'd be shamefaced if we had none. I want to put an end to lice and pornographic novels – 'the two plagues of war', as Napoleon once put it."

We stretched out on the grass and sunbathed. He recounted what had transpired with Soleràs: "He was a highly cultured young man and that's why I was so keen for him to be in my company, but he was a dirty little sod. I don't remember him washing once in all the time he was here and there's no point issuing threats because you never know how people will react. He was in charge of a nest a long way from the others, but he's disorganised, he didn't attach the small warning bells to the wire. One misty night the enemy cut it through with pruning shears and launched a surprise attack in the early hours. Soleràs' soldiers panicked and fled, leaving him deserted. He may be short-sighted, but he shoots like an ace. He sat behind one of the machine guns and simply mowed down fascists. It was wonderful."

"By himself?"

"He had an aide, and two men servicing the gun. The ones who'd scattered filtered back, everything returned to normal, and I started my dispatch by recommending his promotion to lieutenant. Now listen to this: there was a second attack, his soldiers defended well, and this time it was Soleràs who left them high and dry!"

"What do you mean?"

"They searched high and low and finally tracked him down hours later to a hideout in a cave where he was reading a pornographic book that he quickly stuffed in his pocket."

"So how do you know it was pornographic?"

"By the saucy cover . . . the book is packed with dirty drawings. Besides there's not a soldier in this brigade who isn't familiar with *The Horns of Roland*. Some of them know it by heart! You get the idea . . . We should have executed him, but who'd have had the heart? First promote him, then execute him! I ask you! He's such a cultured young fellow . . ."

It's an eight-kilometre walk downhill from Parral del Río to Castel de Olivo, a beautiful riverside stroll. I was ecstatic in that silence and solitude. A quarter of an hour from the threshing floors on the outskirts of the village I sat under a huge walnut tree, perhaps the biggest I'd ever seen, and began eating its tasty walnuts. They were so fresh they stained my fingers yellow and suffused them with a bitter tang which reminded me of a medicinal substance – but what pleasure to feel nature's bitter medicine on one's fingers and in one's mouth.

Darkness was falling. An oriole sang, hidden in the walnut tree's thick foliage. I caught glimpses of the bird, a lightning flash of yellow. A toad poked its head out of the water and warily rehearsed the single note in its flute; a feathery canopy of reeds swayed in the sea breeze and Venus on the horizon was like the glass tear that baroque Sorrowing Virgins wear studded in their cheeks. But if you were hoping to find a baroque Paradise Lost in Castel de Olivo, you'd be disappointed. The landscapes of Lower Aragon look sentimental enough, but they aren't at all baroque; it's my first visit here and they strike me as very original. Against received opinion, I say they are completely different to those in Castile, where I've spent the best part of the last eleven months! At first I felt bewildered here, until I realised these landscapes belong not to space but to time; they aren't landscapes, they're simply moments in time. You must look at them as if you were looking at a moment – like staring a fleeting moment in the face.

When you've discovered their secrets, you wouldn't change them for any other in this world.

*

Soleràs is a very eccentric fellow. The story of the cave and *The Horns of Roland* didn't surprise me at all. It was even a disappointment. I was expecting a much bigger shock.

When we were in our last year at secondary school, he already seemed quite adult. I suspect he also didn't get on with his family; his lack of connection with them was one of the reasons why we fast became friends. What *was* his family, in the first place? A mystery! It amounted, possibly, to an old aunt; he always avoided the subject. As far as I remember, he never mentioned any other relative, man or woman. The old aunt was a spinster and saw visions: Saint Philomena appeared and spoke to her – in Spanish, naturally. I don't know exactly where he lived, I reckon he was ashamed to say. Why? His aunt must have been rich, because she paid for him to go on a luxury holiday to celebrate the end of his secondary schooling: Germany, Russia, Hungary, and Bulgaria. He chose those countries – not England, France, and Italy! He wanted countries where nobody ever went: he was the same with books – Schopenhauer, Nietzsche and Kirkegart – I don't know if he's spelt that way – authors I doubt anyone apart from him has ever had the patience to digest.

Anyway, why was he embarrassed about his aunt if he had a soft spot for way-out characters? He was the one who initiated me into the mysteries of spiritualism, theosophy, Freud, existentialism, surrealism, and anarchism; some of these things seemed new at the time. When we finished at secondary school, in 1928, Julio Soleràs was our fount of knowledge. He always told me that Marxism wasn't worth the candle, that it was simply commonplace: "Scant imagination," he would add, "never trust anyone who has no imagination: he will always bore you to tears." On the other hand, he was fascinated by sexual perversion. He knew individuals who were prey to various manias, and each time he discovered a new mania he experienced the euphoria of a collector who'd come across an unknown species.

Besides, as his visionary aunt never refused him money, he could smoke and drink hard, which crowned him with glory in our eyes when we were sixteen. To give himself airs he even wanted to have us believe he went to houses of ill repute and injected shots of morphine, but that was obviously ridiculous.

He introduced me to Trini's family: her schoolteaching parents, a brother studying chemistry, all anarchists. They lived in a dark and dismal flat on carrer de l'Hospital. The small reception room was papered a very depressing shade of ox blood. It had four Viennese rocking chairs and a small black table with a white marble top, and when more than four people came you had to sit on a sofa that doubled as Trini's bed because the flat was so tiny. The framed prints on the wall were really striking, particularly an allegory of the Federal Republic, with a photo of Pi i Margall in a Phrygian cap between two busty matrons, "Helvetia" and "America" respectively. They came from the heyday of Trini's grandfather, a lifelong federalist. I'd never been inside such a place before and I found these objects very novel and amusing. I think they amused Juli for the same reason.

TUESDAY, 22 JUNE

Talking about prints, I'm obsessed by one my landlady has on her dining-room wall. It's an etching and I think it must be from the beginning of the last century, and represents a Sorrowing Virgin – in fact a baroque Sorrowing Virgin with a large tear on each cheek and seven daggers stuck into her heart.

"People like looking at that print," my landlady remarked when serving me lunch. Although well into her forties, she is fair, plump and pink and was in service in Barcelona for many years; she speaks Catalan better than most of us. "'ave you never seen a Virgin Mary with these seven daggers? She's the Virgin of Olivel and 'ighly venerated in the district. People put their faith in 'er to 'elp solve their marriage problems and family squabbles . . ."

She sighed as she looked at her askance.

"All us women around 'ere 'ave daggers stuck in our 'earts. This is no life. Poor Virgin of Olivel! They didn't let 'er be. 'oo knows where she is now! I'd like to be out of 'ere too."

"Don't you like it here?"

"What can I say? There's no place like Barcelona. I really miss the time when I was a maid, us youngsters getting together on a Sunday afternoon, the lively sing-songs we 'ad . . . don't you remember the ones about Cat Fountain and Marieta Bright-eyes?"

She started off, I joined in the chorus and we both launched excitedly into

> *Walking about Cat Fountain and*
> *a girl, a girl . . .*

By the time we finished this silly song her eyes were all misty.

"But you're a landowner here," I interjected.

"Yes, of four little mudflats. Give me Barcelona any day. It's filthy and miserable 'ereabouts. You'll soon see. And I'm not the only one; all of us women who've been in service in Barcelona feel the same. The four of us. We even speak Catalan to each other. Would you believe that? Makes us feel we are reliving our youth."

"I reckon you must be exaggerating."

"You just wait until you've seen women 'aving to stand up to eat in these villages because only men are allowed to sit at the table, and a woman can't drink wine in the presence of a man, not even 'er 'usband . . ."

"Is that really true?"

"You bet it is. Ask your colleagues 'oo've been 'ere for months. When they first came they made themselves look ridiculous waiting for the women to sit before they started their lunch! If you invite a woman to sit it implies she's a . . ."

"Thanks for the tip-off. Every place has its can of worms."

"That's right, but the worst thing is the dirt. A woman who takes a bath gets a black mark, because in areas like this only whores wash. There was one, years ago, my age or perhaps a bit older, and she'd also been in service in Barcelona. She'd come up for the local fiestas to spend a few days with 'er parents. It was August, very 'ot, and she was covered in soot from the train when she arrived. She thought the clothes tub in the kitchen would be just the ticket. Didn't know what she'd done! 'er mother walks in, catches 'er curled up in the tub, grabs a stick and bang-bang smashes the tub to smithereens. 'er father was 'aving an afternoon nap – 'e goes by the nickname Turdy – so you can imagine what 'e's famed for. 'e 'ears the racket and leaves 'is bed. Know what 'e does? 'e curses 'is daughter and chucks 'er out of 'is 'ouse."

"Crikey! The villagers must have thought he'd gone crazy."

"The villagers? Guess 'ow they reacted: 'Hey, that Turdy's a real man, 'e don't truck no nonsense . . .'"

"And what became of this exemplary father?"

"'e volunteered . . . for the other side."

"What about the girl?"

"'er story would take too long, and what would be the point? She went back to Barcelona straight off, to the 'ouse where she was in service; later . . . people spread lots of gossip, but she's never been seen back in Castel de Olivo. She lives in another village: in Olivel de la Virgen, in fact," and she pointed to the print of the Virgin. I felt she was keeping quiet about important facts relating to Turdy's daughter, but at the end of the day was I really so interested in this tale of primitive custom?

The woman is probably partly right in what she says. I've witnessed a shocking spectacle: local girls sweating bare-breasted while reaping a field of barley under a blistering sun. I thought it must be down to the war, the lack of men, but far from it: there's been no levy yet, and very few youngsters are at the front, only men like Turdy who volunteered for the enemy side. It's worth noting that they don't call us republicans here but Catalans – "los catalanes"; so their feelings aren't shaped either way by what they think of Barcelona – if they have any coherent thoughts about Barcelona at all – but by whatever feelings Catalonia inspires. All this shocks the men who've just arrived, but it's true enough. As I was saying, the women reap because they always have; my landlady also told me that they thresh, harvest and collect manure. And these young lasses would be good-looking if toiling for hours under a boiling sun didn't shrivel them before time, let alone the filth . . . They are old by the time they reach twenty. Lots are fair and blue-eyed; around here there's an abundance of what they call the Nordic race.

Soleràs has also vanished from sight, like Turdy's daughter. And to think that I got myself assigned to this brigade to see him and be near a friend! I suspect he's avoiding me; if not, how come I can never find him?

WEDNESDAY, 23

He came to see me in my lodgings. And about time too!

Skinny, sallow, smooth-cheeked, short-sighted: the same old Soleràs. I got up from my chair to give him a hug, but after eyeing me suspiciously he merely snorted: "Nothing to get so excited about."

I told him I'd requested this posting so we could be together.

"Bah, you'll soon hate me, like everyone else. Nobody here can stand me, from the brigade commander to the lowliest trench fodder."

It was his usual deep bass voice, which sometimes sounds emphatic and declamatory – especially when he wants to pull someone's leg.

"I reckon you're my best friend."

"You know, I've come to say that you and I shouldn't be meeting up; it's ridiculous for us to meet. I heard you were looking for me. It's utterly stupid."

"Why so?"

"Simply because I'm your best friend."

He grinned as he said that – his favourite grin and cackle that bring to mind a broody hen.

"You'd like me to hate you, Juli," I told him, slightly put out by his riddles. "I don't understand why you're so keen for that to happen. Is this some new fad of yours?"

"My poor Lluís, if only you had a glimmering . . . I'm playing at staff sergeant. Do you know what a staff sergeant is? No, you don't have a clue. I didn't either before I got to be one. We're so in the dark about military palaver even though we've been up to our necks in this stuff for eleven months! A staff sergeant is . . . how should I put it? . . . a sort of grocer's assistant. Is this why we came to fight a war? I look after the bean count."

"I know all about that. I agree it's very peculiar."

"Did Picó tell you? That Picó's a very practical fellow! If you only knew how I despise practical men . . . They rule this world, and this world gets on my nerves. Hmm . . . Practical men! They don't understand if you wander off when it takes your fancy! Why should I have carried on there if it no longer interested me? Do we read the same novel twice? An emotional experience has no impact when repeated, the repetition makes it boring. There are, of course, exceptions, honourable ones. It's like Catalan grammar: one always writes *g* before *i* and *e* – with honourable exceptions, like Jehovà, Jesús and Jeremias."

"You're making excuses for yourself, as usual."

"When I was twelve years old my aunt took me to spend a summer in Godella, where she owns one of her properties. The place has a cave with stalactites and she was hoping it would send me into ecstasies. But I was already perfecting playing the elegant hypocrite, so with her I pretended boundless admiration for the stalactites and equally boundless admiration for the stalagmites. However, the railway track was what I really liked: I'd spend hours watching it! And I couldn't resist the temptation – though I modestly recognise it would have been much better for me if I had – to dig a hole between two sleepers, quite a shallow one, just enough to curl up in without my head sticking out above the slats. I expect you've guessed what I was after: I wanted to be curled up in there when the express came hurtling past – it doesn't stop in Godella. Feel it shoot over me! A few years later I discovered the same trick being played out in *Karamazov*, so you could accuse me of plagiarism, but I can assure you I hadn't read Dostoyevsky when I was twelve. Auntie had forced me to swallow Bossuet's *Funeral Orations* – 'forced' being the operative word as it was no pleasure. Besides, this trick with express trains is common enough, I've met so many people who've tried it over their age of innocence! I've met so many . . . it's so difficult to find a really original trick, something that's not already been done by thousands and thousands! Anyway, I'd feel the whole express hurtling over me. You see, that's what you call a strong emotion, though I'll be frank and admit it was missing an essential element. That necessary component of any emotion, you know, exists in seeing it reflected in another person's eyes. It's one of our greatest weaknesses – the fact that our emotions need an accomplice before they seem true. I wanted to take Nati there. Have I never spoken to you about her? She was twelve, like me, but what a fantastic twelve-year-old! Tall and dark, firm skin with a scent of warm straw . . . and that aggressive look in her eyes which comes when innocence combines with the most instinctive vitality. She was the daughter of Auntie's tenant farmers and had been born and brought up in Godella. At the time I don't think she'd ever been away from there. I managed to get her to accompany me and see how I crammed myself into that hole, how the express rushed over my head. Did she want to join me in there? The idea horrified her. 'Well,' I said, 'that's what it's all about, feeling horrified.' If only I could tell you of the delights that horror brings! . . . But what's in it for you if you only feel it by yourself? It was hopeless: she refused; and she smelled of recently mown grass . . . and those eyes of hers . . . As long as eyes like hers exist in this world, humanity won't tire of repeating what Adam and Eve got up to from the start. As I was saying: honourable exceptions, things worthy of indefinite repetition, for ever and ever, amen. I don't see war as anything of the kind; the first battle might seem novel, the second will perhaps pass muster, but when you've fought a number . . . Some aspects of war are so coarse your patience quickly runs out when they're endlessly repeated."

"Like what, for example?"

"My aide fell flat on his face once, while bringing me my canteen of coffee and rum; I need a canteen of coffee with lots of rum at times like that. All the coffee spilled and mixed with that idiot's blood – a wretched lad from Pobla de Lillet, one of those that sell cow's milk from their homes; they have a dairy on plaça del Pi. He'd been wounded, you know. Isn't that wonderful? War wounded; wounded at the front on active service; gloriously, heroically wounded! Then back in the rearguard one can tell one's best friend's wife – one's best friend being the one with the most gorgeous wife – 'They wounded me in such and such a skirmish. I was advancing with the standard . . .' You can boast with a clear conscience of how you were moving forward with the standard because those morons in the rearguard still think battles are fought this way. You could even tell them you were brandishing a sword on horseback, they'd believe anything – or act as if they do provided they aren't dragged off to take a close look. But the bullet from the Mauser had gone through poor Palaudàries' rump, and how do you tell your best friend's wife *that*? You might use euphemisms like 'bum cheeks', but you'd still sound stupid. As for me, I couldn't care a fuck! I prefer to scarper in such circumstances. I can't bear the sight of blood, it makes me vomit. Two soldiers had taken his trousers off and were trying to staunch the bleeding with a handful of grass. He was saying the Lord's Prayer at the top of his voice while crying out for his mother. His mother, I ask you! How did he expect her to turn up if she was selling milk in plaça del Pi? Let me say it again: the bullet had gone through his rump, so it wasn't a serious wound. But the blood was bubbling out so, it made me want to puke. A thousand times worse than with mummies! They're dry as a bone and don't remind you of anything as disgusting as blood. Mummies are a pleasant sight; I recommend a trip to the monastery in Olivel de la Virgen . . ."

"They say they found you hiding in a cave."

"Reading a lewd novel, right? I see this myth about me has reached even you. Well, not everyone can become a myth. Palaudàries, for example, will never turn into a myth however hard he tries, regardless of how much they turn his bum into a sieve."

"So isn't the book business true?"

"It wouldn't be the first myth to be a lie. I'd started it the day before and wanted to know how it ended. There are novels that can shock – I can pass it on to you."

"Thanks, but I'm not interested."

"You don't know what you're missing. It's the Gospel in this brigade! Everybody knows *The Horns of Roland*. Reading it, I've understood so much. You would too; you might even understand a few things about yourself, things you *should* understand."

"Such as?"

When I asked this, he stared hard at me with his myopic eyes – his outrageous vanity won't allow him to wear spectacles. He sighed "I sometimes wonder," then muttered between gritted teeth, "whether you're not cracked in the head. Such as! What the hell does it matter? Something! Anything! Understand!"

"So what do you get out of all this understanding?"

"It's obvious . . . it's obvious you've never tried a thing. And with so many things out there worth trying! For example, lying on the grass late on a midsummer afternoon, when the grass that's been frying the whole day gives off the bitter scent of a young country girl's armpit. Lying on your back late on an early August afternoon when Scorpio trails its endless tail across the horizon." His bass voice resonated like an orator's. "Scorpio! That's my favourite constellation. I'll let you in on a secret of mine: that tail rearing up, filled with poison, above the whole universe. We men lack such a thing, a tail like Scorpio's that can inject poison into the whole universe. Don't look at me like that! You know I'm right, and if we owned a tail like that our whole family could legitimately feel proud. But we don't, so we can only lie back, look up at the sky and . . . Vertical, in a raging temper! But it's pointing at you, at the middle of your face. Newton would say it's the result of the law of gravity; he can keep his manias, he can't see anything else and can't understand. This is what understanding is all about: about being hit by your own spit, hit by your own impotent sputum right between the eyes: to feel an intense and cold rage at our utter impotence."

"As if we'd said it's shit."

"Everything *is* shit, if you want to put it like that: obscene and macabre. Hey, Lluís, do you think you were born different from everyone else? Or that you won't end up like everyone else – an ineffable pile of shit? You're old enough to know: our obscene entrance and our macabre exit. Entrance gratis, and exit on a shovel. Believe me, it's worth letting loose a big gob of spit in a blind rage while there's still time. If he didn't know or couldn't do it better, why did he try?"

"Who are you talking about now?"

He stared at me in amazement, as if shocked by my blinkered petty-mindedness.

"You should do it for yourself . . . you're old enough . . . You really don't want to understand. Perhaps you feel happy with your lot, perhaps you feel you're at home in this world. Perhaps you've never felt a foreigner. Perhaps you live your life like so many other idiots; perhaps I'm the only one who lives life as if he were someone else, a life that doesn't fit, a life that feels alien."

"Juli, I sometimes get that feeling as well and I don't think it's at all odd. It's much more widespread than you think. We don't live our life; it's life that lives us. Life . . . It would be better not to worry so much. What difference did worrying ever make? Life is so lovely! It's an enigmatic mystery! Well, mystery always gives beauty an added attraction; we know that all too well. Like sadness. Isn't sad, mysterious beauty always fascinating? I too have my sad moments, Juli, and I try to experience them by myself."

A silence descended that he shattered with a cackle: "I expect Picó took you for a swim in his 'hygiene installation', as he calls it. He's so proud of it! He is a practical man, we won't deny that. And calloused in more than one respect."

In effect, I have to admit that the machine gunner Lieutenant Captain's calluses had caught my eye: six or seven on each foot, huge and hard.

"Why doesn't he have them removed?"

"Bah! You don't know him. Cruells did try once. Cruells is a nurse-cum-subaltern who hangs around the brigade, whom you'll bump into one of these days. He wanted to remove them using a new Gillette. 'Beat it!' he shrieked. 'I love my corns too much to do that.' We didn't get the better of him. We'd have had to pin him down by his arms, and, you know, cutting the corns off a man who's kicking his legs up . . ."

"I thought he was brave."

"I won't deny that. Once, we were being shelled by a battery of .28 calibre Schneiders; their artillery had honed their parallax and square roots so wonderfully the shrapnel hit the middle of our trenches. It was Picó who said, 'How beautiful!' It was rather disturbing, one has to say. At the time there was a young second lieutenant, a Vilaró, who'd just come out to the front. Picó was keeping an eye on him, because if he threw a wobbly the soldiers might scarper and it was only too obvious that Vilaró was getting nervous. All he ever did was look over his shoulder. Picó took out his false teeth, it's what he does in moments of supreme danger, put them in a glass of water and climbed onto the parapet. Without his dentures he's the spitting image of Voltaire. He walked to and fro over the sacks of earth, as if he were trying out some new shoes for the first time that might give him corns; he'd left the glass with his dentures on one of the sacks; a round of machine-gun fire smashed it to bits. The soldiers chuckled and winked in Vilaró's direction; he noticed and reacted: 'Do you think I can't do that?' He jumped up onto the parapet: shrapnel decapitated him just as he was about to speak. Perhaps it was no great loss; perhaps he'd have just said 'fuck' like so many other heroes. If you want to irritate Picó, talk to him about that incident. He knows that morally speaking he murdered that hapless fellow."

"Come on! How could he anticipate that . . ."

"It was entirely predictable. Picó is always lucky, he knows he is and plays with that. It was splashed all over poor Vilaró's face that he was quite the opposite: you could see it coming miles away that his number was up."

"Cut the crap and let the dead rest in peace."

"Let the dead rest in peace! They should be so lucky! I recommend a visit to the monastery in Olivel . . . As for the dentures, they turned up a long way from the trench; fortunately they were intact. I can tell you, I find Picó's false teeth much more macabre than the mummies in the monastery. This attic of yours is delightful on more than one count. I'd like to live here. You always have all the luck and end up with what I'd like. I'd have been delighted to have fetched up in an anarchist brigade made of escapees from the lunatic asylum – as you tell it; *this* brigade, on the other hand, is just humdrum. Order, hygiene and culture! However you did get . . . an attic like this, with the juices of a rabbit on heat thrown in . . ."

He scrutinised the little caricatures on the wall.

"Well, they're not bad, but they could be better. I find this brigade's lack of imagination quite appalling. When you leave Castel, I'll put in for this attic."

OLIVEL DE LA VIRGEN, SUNDAY, 4 JULY

We're now in this village, where we've been ordered to set up the brigade's 4th Battalion.

Only one small drawback: we had to take Olivel from the anarchists.

And who were the "we" who had to take it from the anarchists? On paper, the 4th Battalion; in fact, as the levied soldiers had yet to arrive, "we" were Commander Rosich – who was a loony – with his Ford and his chauffeur; Dr Puig, the medical officer; the nurse, a second lieutenant in the medical corps in his early twenties who I reckon must be Cruells because I think Soleràs told me about him in Castel de Olivo; four lieutenant fusiliers, one by the name of Gallart, a bar waiter in civilian life; and finally half a dozen infantry second lieutenants, including yours truly. A grand total of "eleven individuals and a chauffeur" – the description stuck, as coined by Dr Puig.

We drove off in the commander's car, a stupendous Ford. Those of us who could not fit inside hung on the running boards; one of the second lieutenants sat on the roof with a sub-machine gun between his legs. We'd hoisted the flag on the radiator. The road from Castel to Olivel is a cart track heading northwards for a dozen kilometres. The Ford cleared the gullies we encountered by being driven over a couple of planks we had brought for the purpose, which we kept placing on the track and then picking up. The officer with the sub-machine gun sang, laughed and cursed as if it were all one big variety show. He was short and skinny. He stared at me suddenly and shouted: "Hey, you! What's your trade?"

"You asking me? I've got a degree in law, but I've done other things."

"What does a degree in law mean?"

"It's like saying I am a solicitor."

"A solicitor! I'll shake on that! Almost the same as me."

"That is, defence lawyer?"

"No, a billboard man on the street."

At that point the village's threshing floors came into sight and we decided it would be prudent to leave the Ford, spread out and advance, pistols in hand, behind the palisades just in case the anarchists showed resistance. We later discovered they'd fled the previous day when they heard troops were on the way. On the other hand, the whole village *was* waiting for us: men, women and children, all thrilled to see us appear. The masses put roses in the buttonholes of our battle jackets. The role of hero is very gratifying when it comes so cheaply. There was a glitter in Commander Rosich's eyes. A middle-aged man gave him a hug; it turns out he is the mayor who was sent packing by the anarchists. He had suffered real torture hiding in the woods. The commander declared him reinstated forthwith: applause and hurrahs from the men, tears from the old dears, more roses in our buttonholes. The temptation was too great: the commander launched into the speech we were afraid was in the offing – this being a weakness of his.

The old dears dried their eyes on the corners of their black aprons. Meanwhile, the village children crowded around admiring our flashes and sparkling new battle jackets.

If I'm not mistaken, this is the village Soleràs had told me about – in veiled and mysterious terms, as I recall. My landlady in Castel had also put in a word about it when she told me about the Suffering Virgin; Soleràs spoke about mummies in a monastery. I could perhaps kill a few hours paying it a visit, if it really exists, for our stay here is quite soporific. The village, like all in this area, is a disaster; it comprises 280 buildings, what with houses, animal pens and a hundred threshing floors with their respective palisades. The church is brick-built, like the castle that looks down on the cluster of houses. The bricks have blackened over the centuries. The flies will not give us a minute's rest, especially at lunchtime; there are many more than in Castel, and that's saying something. It could hardly be otherwise given the quantity of manure – *manuwer*, say the friendly locals – piled up in the pens.

Before leaving Castel I tried to see Soleràs to say goodbye; a soldier in Supplies told me he had just been transferred to the brigade's Train Unit and he'd seen him getting into a lorry that morning to go off and join it. He could have put himself out to say goodbye. Bah, perhaps I shouldn't be so touchy.

The worst of it is that I miss him, because though I sometimes find his conversation irritating, it's always interesting. I remember one of his wisecracks from Castel de Olivo: "Seeing the brainless things we lot do, eunuchs have every right to feel superior; it's the same for you sceptics." I thought it quite intolerable for him to compare me to a eunuch, and yet . . . I'm sick to death of all these officers, especially the commander and the doctor, who spend their lives going from cellar to cellar tasting wine from the barrels and pronouncing their verdicts.

8 JULY

We are still doing nothing, just waiting for the recruits to arrive. We have already allotted officers to the future companies: I've got the 4th and my captain will be Lieutenant Gallart, the ex-waiter.

The village couldn't be more dismal: it's boxed in and you can't see it until you're inside. Its boundaries are extensive, it's mostly barren waste with the large olive trees that account for its name. From what people have told me, the monastery is a long way downstream. I go on long walks and sometimes sit at the foot of an olive tree and am so quiet the crows settle on the ground a few steps from me, as if I didn't exist. There are hundreds to keep me company. Bare mountains make up the backdrop and the district boundary. A cloud sometimes hangs over them: rock and cloud, permanence and evanescence. The cloud drifts by, looking splendid as it changes with the sunset; the rock stays the same. What are the rock and the cloud in our lives? Which is worth the most? Which part of us must remain unchangeable? Are we so sure it's more valuable than the part that leaves us at every moment? Or are we entirely ghostlike, clouds whose single hope is to live a moment of glory, one solitary moment, and then vanish?

All our instincts rebel against this idea. "I feel and experience that I am eternal", wrote Spinoza. I'm familiar with this quotation from Spinoza because of Soleràs. Who, besides him, would be capable of swallowing Spinoza? And how can one begin to explain the mysterious immensity of our desire? How do we even begin to explain that we feel this immense desire when we don't know why or what we desire?

Everything has an explanation – if we know how to seek it out; for example, this murder of crows that so intrigued me. Wandering at random around the area I suddenly found myself in the middle of a circle of lunar mountains. A most unusual sight: a kind of broad, deep, enigmatic lunar crater. The sun was low in the sky, its slanted light providing the extraterrestrial finishing touch. Not a single tree or bush, nothing but mineral and the play of shadow and light as raw as in the void between planets. It was fascinating. I walked to the crater's edge and looked down: a pile of bones solved the mystery. It's the charnel house, what they call the vulture trap.

There are more shepherds than farmhands in these parts, shepherds of sheep and goats. Into this they throw diseased animals that have perished. When a mule is sickly and the vet gives up hope, they don't wait for it to die, it would weigh too much. They drive it to the vulture trap, beating it all the way with a stick, and give it a shove. The mule falls in and if it is lucky dies there and then; naturally, it can take days. The crows and vultures are responsible for keeping the vulture trap clean, and it has to be said that they take their responsibility seriously: anything cleaner than those bare ivory white bones you could not find. *Ossa arida*, as some prophet or the other describes a great bone-strewn desert – human bones, of course, but what's the difference? That vulture trap impressed me greatly; the aridity of those bones gave me a huge thirst and reminded me of something Soleràs once said: "Huge thirst, a drop of water to quench it, and that sums it up; the infinitely large and the infinitely small. I don't know if you've heard of atoms . . ." "Sorry," I interrupted him bad-temperedly, "don't start on that nonsense. Atoms are a load of shit."

The dryness of the bones helped me understand the "huge thirst" that Soleràs was referring to. "I must live my life," I told myself, "live my life before my bones are cast into the bottomless vulture trap that awaits us all. I must live my life, but how do I do that? Live! A year at war, a year of no contact with women – and so few years! I must have used up more than a third of my quota already . . ."

One early evening I was standing at a particularly deserted crossroads for that time of day; I mean intensely deserted, you could feel the forlorn abandon. There was just one cloud, its flame so dull and wan it seemed made of basalt. Beauty is frightening; fortunately, it rarely crosses our path. On an evening like that – I've never seen such dramatic twilights outside Aragon – one feels alone before the universe, like a criminal before a court without appeal. What is the accusation? That we are so small, so petty and so ugly; the immensity judges and crushes us . . . I was so engrossed in my thoughts I didn't hear her footsteps; I didn't notice her presence until a severe, distant voice jolted me out of my reverie: "A good evening to you."

It was a woman with a child on one arm and another tucked in her skirt: a tall, well-built woman in widow's weeds who walked by without giving me a glance. She seemed surrounded by a kind of sorrowful aura as she walked slowly along the path, away from the sunset. Who was she? I'd never seen her in the village. When she went round a bend and out of sight I registered that she'd greeted me in Catalan. A Catalan woman in this village? A mystery: almost a hallucination.

15 JULY

The recruits have started to arrive. I am in charge of instructing these poor youngsters. I spend more time in the village and begin to get to know the houses and people.

I have still not identified the Suffering Virgin of Olivel – that is, the apparition from the other day. Or hallucination? Everything is possible.

As the village is enclosed in a deep ravine, the castle is all you see from a distance. You cannot see the huddle of houses until you're inside; if it is evening, you see the old dears by their doorways, sitting on stone benches and enjoying the cool. Dressed in black and chattering endlessly, they make you think of magpies. Seen in a snapshot like that, the village seems dirty and primitive.

The commander obliges us to give lectures to the recruits; not each officer to his own section, but each officer to the whole battalion.

We use the main hall in the castle as our base. That's how I managed to get a look inside: it's an old manor house that has been terribly neglected. It has a huge hall where the commander had a table placed on the dais: he sits and chairs while the officer stands and lectures.

Commander Rosich is short and fat, sallow and swarthy, with beady black eyes that are bright and sentimental. He'd be a lovely person if it weren't for his "imbibing" – "dribing and imbibing," he quips. I've already given my first lecture: "Machine guns must be set up on flat terrain." While I embroidered my subject – the advantages of skimming crossfire, etc. – I noted his beady eyes light up and glow like embers fanned by a breeze. I was using chalk and a blackboard that I'd improvised to explain the trigonometric principles of machine-gun fire with a curved trajectory when he suddenly stood up and hugged me in front of everyone.

"Such calculations bring glory upon our battalion!"

I confess I couldn't really fathom the reason for such an emotional outburst, even though I've always had a weak spot for sentimental types. That's why I finally managed to accept Ponsetti, the "billboard man on the street", a chatterbox. He's always hooked up with Captain Gallart, who is huge, naturally: tall and fat, ruddy and greedy, and rumbustious. My passionate love for tradition made me feel great respect for this couple, the tall fat man and the short thin man – as sentimental and boozy as the other couple, the commander and the doctor.

I've discovered a large pine grove quite close by, north of the village. In the heat of the day thousands of crickets buzz, the pine trees are tall and slender, their frayed tops let through a sun that scorches the earth. The air becomes saturated with the pungent sensuous smell of resin. I stretch out on a warm soft bed of pine needles and surrender to the sadness that attacks me in sudden bursts. Poor Soleràs, who thinks he is so unique: when, oh when did *I* live my life?

THURSDAY, 5 AUGUST

Teaching the recruits – things both theoretical and practical – takes up little of my time. So, apart from the days when I'm assigned guard duty, I have lots of time to fill. Ponsetti has joined the 4th Company; he and Gallart don't shift from the village, specifically not from the inn where there is a blonde, la Melitona, who makes them lose their marbles. Commander Rosich and Dr Puig are tipsy most days. The other lieutenants and adjutants don't move out of the village either: they're always after the young girls, the ones who put roses in our lapels the day we arrived.

Then there's Cruells, the nurse-cum-subaltern. He turns out to be a devotee of Baudelaire. He knows large chunks by heart, avoids wine and women – and dirty words: a *rara avis*! He comes for the occasional walk with me. Not very often: he must keep a firm grip on his work. Four hundred recruits are a lot and when they're not down with one thing they're down with another, generally venereal in origin. He is the baby of the battalion, barely twenty, and when he comes for a walk with me he brings along a kind of portable telescope or, perhaps more precisely, a "long-view eyeglass", the kind used by skippers in the last century, a good thirty centimetres long when extended. He says his aunt gave it to him for his twelfth birthday and he's kept it with him throughout the war; it takes up little space when collapsed – its sections slot inside each other. This instrument is much more powerful than my officer's binoculars, and when we go for a stroll together we linger until very late and he makes me take a look at Jupiter through his telescope: you can see the four "satellites of Galileo" quite clearly next to the planet, like four peas next to a plum, three on the left and one on the right. The day after, the one on the right has disappeared, and the day after that you see only two. Then you see all four once again, now two on the right and two on the left. He explained the reasons for these appearances and disappearances, as well as the different phases of Venus – which you can also see using his seafaring telescope – and much more besides; his head is as stuffed with facts about astronomy as mine is empty.

We'd take a nap in the pine grove, the castle looming in the background between the trunks of the pines. Don't imagine a feudal castle with battlements and barbicans: it's a square mass of blackish bricks. The village in its hollow is invisible from where we are. A question suddenly sprang to my lips: "So what did *you* do before the war?"

Half asleep, he looked at me through his tortoiseshell spectacles, which gave him at once the air of a benign owl and a decent person. He seemed to hesitate: "I'll tell you, but don't tell anyone else. I was a seminarist."

"A seminarist?"

It would never have struck me, but now it was clear as daylight. Why couldn't Cruells be a seminarist? Or rather, what else could he have ever been?

"And what are you intending to do after the war?"

"Finish my studies."

Days later Cruells gave us a real shock. Naturally, we have a contingent on guard duty at night – several soldiers under an officer doing his shift – which patrols the outskirts of the village. I wasn't on duty that night, it was an adjutant from the 2nd Company, and he filled me in on the juicy details. It must have been one in the morning, the village was asleep, there was no moonlight and the only sound was the hooting of an owl in the poplar tree by the fountain. Out of the blue the patrol spotted a man by the threshing ground on the edge of the village: it was a soldier taking aim with a weapon that, from a distance, looked like a 50 mm mortar. They were naturally alarmed, thinking he might be a fascist or an anarchist and that there might be others coming behind him to mount a surprise attack. Thank God the duty adjutant had the sangfroid to stop his men shooting their Mausers: it was Cruells with his telescope. His eyes were shut and he was sound asleep while walking along holding up his long-sighted eyeglass as if taking aim. He told me afterwards that he'd had other bouts of sleep-walking, though years ago. We asked Dr Puig whether sleepwalking was at all serious; he shrugged his shoulders and told us it wasn't and that nobody knows what causes it. Sometimes people never have repeat attacks, they are usually more common in adolescence – "Let's have no illusions, at the age of twenty Cruells is still an adolescent"; and, "At the end of the day, better not to harp on it; in any self-respecting brigade, and according to highly reliable statistics, for every attack of sleepwalking there are 463 of gonorrhoea."

On the days – that is, most days – when Cruells is on duty with the medical chest, I go out and about by myself. Now I have a horse and that's very useful for a *promeneur solitaire*. A lone walker can seem rather manic; on horseback, he earns general respect. Besides, with the horse, or rather the mare since it is female, I can go further: to the monastery, for example.

But I ought to explain things in the right order.

First: as a consequence of those theoretical and practical lectures of mine I've located my hallucination.

It turns out that the master of the castle, the *carlan* as the locals call him, was murdered by the anarchists. That isn't at all odd, naturally: it would have been odd if they hadn't. It seems he lived with a woman, and if she'd been legitimate they would have murdered her too and not thought twice about it, but this happened to be an instance of free love. So they not only did not kill her, they treated her with great respect as the lady of the castle and its estates. She's still living there with her two children. The old women in the village scornfully refer to her as the *carlana*, the lady of the castle, and affirm in their homespun Spanish that, as soon as the war is over, some distant cousins of the deceased, the only legal relatives he was known to have, will kick her out of the castle and off its land – "She and the couple of kids born on the wrong side of the blanket."

She leads a very secluded life and avoids seeing people. When the commander asked for use of the hall she immediately agreed, but when it's time for a lecture she locks herself out of sight with her two children.

I discovered she had a spare mare in her stables, the favourite steed of the deceased. Nobody rides her because nobody in the battalion or the village is keen on horse riding. I decided to ask if I could; she was doing nothing with the animal – the anarchists had tried to make her plough, to no avail – and she'd be just right for me and my solitary jaunts. The woman received me, standing in that same room where we gave our lectures.

In that guise, without the mysterious allure of twilight, she's a woman of around thirty-five, serious, distant and polite in manner. Her voice is a velvety contralto that sometimes vibrates with an almost imperceptible tremolo. I told her I was surprised that she spoke such good Catalan: "Don't be surprised. I've lived in Barcelona for so many years! I was fifteen when I went there. That was all I ever spoke with him and his mother. His mother was from Barcelona."

What she and the lord of the castle had done was so out of the way, I thought it best to carefully steer the conversation elsewhere: "I know there's a monastery within the village boundaries, some fifteen kilometres downstream."

"The monastery in Olivel, the Order of the Virgin of Mercy. The Virgin of Olivel was much revered in these parts. Many of us are named after her."

"Ah, so you must be Maria d'Olivel."

"Maria d'Olivel is my whole name, as written on the certificates of baptism. People usually call me Olivela."

I felt she seemed distant, if not absent; for a few seconds she looked as unreal as on that evening when I saw her silhouetted against the sunset along the solitary crossroads. Something about her hits you between the eyes: the mark of tragedy. There's no reason, of course, why a woman who's lived what she's had to live shouldn't bear the mark of tragedy. I've gathered she is from a family of modest means; being a kept woman placed her outside her class and family, at once above and below. Then the anarchist scoundrels murdered her *carlà* in front of her and their children . . . But that's not the root cause: the mark of tragedy comes from within, not from life. I tried to imagine what her loneliness must be like; she does have her children, but what kind of company do children ever provide?

"My first ride on Acorn will be to the monastery."

"Don't go there," she replied, looking me in the eye for the first time. "The anarchists sacked it after they murdered the friars. The Virgin has disappeared. It's terrifying. They disinterred . . ." The tremolo in her voice resounded like vibrato from the most bass string of a cello.

I could see the servant from the window – the only one still working for her – saddling Acorn at the entrance to the castle. She's a handsome mare, a roan with a small head and a large rump. She seemed happy to be out of her stable.

"Disinterred?"

"Deceased friars out of their niches . . . anarchists up to their usual tricks. Did you know that they executed all the day labourers? Four wretches, the poorest in the village, the friars paid them a day wage more out of charity than anything else. The poor fellows wore wooden clogs and they executed them for being fascists because they worked for the friars . . ."

A conversation with Soleràs suddenly came to mind. At the time, it hadn't struck me as important, having sounded like a caustic stream of incoherent nonsense. "These fools" – he was referring to Picó, the commander and the brigade in general – "these fools fail to appreciate the few original things that our country possesses. As soon as they come to a village they re-establish order. How vulgar! One must make the occasional sally to villages that 'our boys' haven't yet reached, where anarchism still rules the roost. I can breathe there! There's a monastery . . ." He put his fingertips in his mouth, as if relishing a parson's brandy snap. "I've spent long hours there in pure contemplation and, believe me, it was all fully warranted. Particularly one mummy, on the left, with the face of a crook . . . In whose name do they want to ban us from disinterring the dead, if that's what we feel like? In whose name? The men who did that were very likely idiots, but that's beside the point: perhaps it's all about proving you're a hundred per cent idiot. Not everyone can manage that! The intellect has been relegated to history as an antique that belongs to the eighteenth century; the future belongs to idiots!" "I can see," I retorted sarcastically, "that you're gearing up to conquer the future." "And why not? While we're about it, what's so particularly bad about digging out Virgin of the Mercy's friars rather than Egyptian pharaohs? Why do those who dug up Tutankhamen deserve more respect? Excavators, of whatever kind, are all looking for the same thing: they want to see the look on the face of a dead man who's had time to practise, who's devoted time to it, whether a few decades or a few millennia. Our era, which is idiotic in the extreme, has preferred to slash the veils that cover birth and death, the obscene and the macabre; if you haven't yet understood that, you've understood nothing about our era." I replied: "Do you think our era is important because we've tried to understand this?"

"Do you know Juli Soleràs?"

It was a banal question to pass the time of day – almost like my saying the weather was lovely: for how could she have come to know him? But this woman is one surprise after another, judging by the look on her face. "Yes . . . " she replied, after hesitating for a moment. "Why do you ask? Did he tell you about me?"

"Oh no, it was just an idle question. He told me about a monastery and some mummies, all quite vaguely, so he came to mind. He's a rather eccentric young man. He has an aunt who has visions, you know? I expect you've heard about Saint Philomena, though obviously that's of no particular interest to you. Was he really here when the anarchists were still around?"

"I got the impression that he and the anarchists were the best of friends. Can I ask a favour of you? Please never mention the fellow again."

Poor Soleràs, one can see how he is gifted at inspiring less than friendly reactions. People can't forgive him his haphazard conversations, so full of paradoxes and reticence. Trini and I are the only two who can tolerate him because we think he's amusing. We've known him for so long – ever since we were at secondary school! Later, when Trini and I started living together, he'd come and drink tea with us almost every afternoon, even when we did our military service – Trini and I had been headstrong enough to move in together before I was called up – and he and I both served over the same time as acting adjutants. He shouldn't have been drafted, they said he wasn't fit because he was so short-sighted – or at least that's what he told me. He asked for another test! And to think that so many do their best to be ruled unfit, while he moved heaven and earth to be recruited. Afterwards, in the barracks – we were fortunate to be sent to a regiment garrisoned in Barcelona – what he most enjoyed doing was jumping over the wall and going on a spree, especially if he was on duty. At our place, he always sat in the same chair; we felt he was like a peculiar yet familiar little bird whose rudeness one forgave because he was such good company.

Why did he come here and risk being executed by the anarchists? Was he practising being an idiot? "Nineteen-seventeen marked the beginning of a new Era, the Era of Idiots; blessed be the idiots for they shall become masters of the world . . ." – this was one of his "favourite prophecies". It goes without saying that prophesying was a weakness of his.

The river crosses the district from south-west to north-east. Over time it has opened up a deep, narrow gully with almost vertical sides, down which I rode Acorn from that day on and far into the distance. After watering the orchards of Olivel the river feeds the ponds of the old flour mills, one of which is still working. When I walked, this mill was the furthest I ever went; it is halfway to the monastery. The miller, a man in his fifties, lives there with a wife who is as dark as the flour they grind – and toothless. They have five or six children. They mill forty-five pecks a day, though not necessarily every day: sometimes the pond takes a whole day to replenish itself, depending on the water the river brings, and meanwhile they must rest. I like to watch them milling because I've never seen such an old mill work. They open up the millrace and the mill starts to turn, slowly; the hopper, which they call *lorenza*, is a large wooden funnel that's been broached very roughly; the grain pours out slowly and the millstone transforms it into coarse flour. Then the women of Olivel turn it into tasty brown bread. The village has three communal ovens for baking bread, and on the days they bake you can get the warm smell from afar, and the aroma of pine branches burning and freshly baked bread whets one's appetite.

The miller makes the most of the days of enforced rest to go hunting with his ferret. He complains about the lack of game: only hare are plentiful, but he loathes them from the day he caught one eating carrion. As for otter they interest him because of their valuable pelts. His ferret is scared of attacking them, though not of going for foxes. It catches them asleep in their dens – or *cado*, as they say around here – jumps on their backs and in a flash sinks its teeth into their jugular. It's a very agile male, its claws sharp as sewing needles. He has to carry it shut in its cage and handles it very gingerly because given the slightest chance it would sever his fingers. This fellow also told me about the monastery, the huge pine and fir forest that starts on the left of the river just before you get there and which, he says, extends for many leagues northwards, the direction in which you have to travel a long way before you come upon another village. A few friars, no more than two or three, succeeded in escaping through this forest. After you cross the monastery's estate the river runs out into a lake – or more precisely a great marsh – called the Cambronera, where you can hunt ducks and other migrating birds in winter.

I took advantage of the mill pond to go for a swim, much to the amazement of the miller, the miller's wife and the five or six little millers. They'd never seen a person dive and splash like a duck. They had some tame ducks: small, white, feathered with yellow beaks and legs that created a terrific din when I jumped in headfirst. After swimming a good half hour I'd stretch out on the grass to sunbathe. Sometimes I'd see vultures fly by overhead. They must come from a long way away, the bare mountains to the south, the Alcubierre range, or perhaps from even more distant peaks further south, hardly visible in my binoculars through the blue mist. With Cruells' telescope you could see the mountains were thickly wooded. As for the vultures, I'd seen, more than once, a pair flying fantastically high in the sky: I could calculate this roughly, thanks to the graduated lens of the binoculars and my idea of their possible wingspan, the female adult two and a half metres, broader than the male. I saw them glide across the firmament from one horizon to the other and not flex their wings for a second. The only explanation I can think of is that they let themselves be carried along on a current of air we can't feel at ground level. They sometimes describe concentric circles around the sun, like gigantic moths drawn to its still flame. Of course, they aren't flying around the sun; what can the sun matter to them? They're circling around the vulture trap. Each village has one.

The tracks alongside the river are good for riding. Acorn loves to gallop over the soft sandy soil. The way to the monastery sometimes disappears into the river bed; the mare's legs throw up a shower of minute drops of water where a rainbow shimmers. When evening falls and a breeze stirs you can hear birds chirping among the foliage of poplars, wild jasmine and honeysuckle: blackbirds, goldfinches, golden orioles and who knows what else. Far away, deep in the forest, a cuckoo calls out the time.

On my first day riding horseback I reached the monastery like a bedraggled hen. Acorn is a lovable beast: her large damp eyes are full of tender mystery, her tail and mane gleam darkly and almost drag along the ground as nobody bothers to trim them. But docile though she is, she can be nervous and whimsical. All was wonderful while we galloped over the sandy path, and she *was* delighted to be galloping after so many months shut in her stable. But when the path vanished into the river she suddenly knelt to splash and wallow in the cool water – leaving me as you can imagine.

The millers hardly give me a glance: their eyes are on my steed.

"Jesus! Ain't that Acorn?" asks the miller's wife, crossing herself.

"You know her?"

"Like my own child. Our dead lord's mare, may 'e be restin' in Glory. The whole of Olivel knows 'er."

And that was how we came to speak about her – they'd never mentioned her until then. We gradually slipped from mare to mistress; at first I thought the miller's wife wasn't daring to speak freely about her, though I guessed only too clearly from her reticence and half-mumbled words that she thought and knew a lot. Spurred on by my love of gossip, I urged her to confide: "The nasty vixen," she muttered between toothless gums, "should 'ave stayed in Barcelona with 'er own nasty brood. We can do without 'er sort roun' 'ere."

"What was she doing in Barcelona?"

"A maid. She worked for the old lady of the castle, who was still alive then. She were in service with them from when she were real young, no more'n fifteen."

A maid in service: that's why she got on so well with the lord of the castle's mother. Such a simple explanation, but I'd never have thought of it.

"Was she like other girls from hereabouts before she went to Barcelona?"

"No, she were always by 'erself and sad like a mopin' cat. I always said she weren't like us, we all follow in our dad's footsteps. Must 'ave got it from some place, if she were so stuck up. Graft an apricot tree an' git peaches as big as your fist."

"Shut up," interjected the miller, who I thought didn't quite share his wife's hatred of the mistress of the castle. "These be secrets only known to God. When she left the village, Olivela was just a snot-nosed little girl. No more than fifteen! The sparrow'awk was the master, may 'e rest in peace now 'e be dead, for 'e made the most of 'er innocence."

"Ah, 'er innocence, the poor wretch!" she rasped, scorning his compassionate tone. "When did *she* ever know what that was? We all got married for our innocence; we married for our honour, and not because we was 'ungry. But she and 'er witchy ways slipped into the castle, for bats like 'er always make their 'omes in old castles. That vixen's witchy ways made 'er the mistress o' the castle, and she ne'er 'ad to work in the 'arvest or pick grapes or collect shit up – none o' that. A laydee's life, lootenant, a grand lady's life: in the mornin' givin' meal to the pigs and maize to the chickins and in the evenin' a little walk in the orchard and before hittin' the hay a bath in warm water with 'er sweet-smellin' soap like a big sow . . ."

"Shut up, dear, shut up," her husband interrupted. "Don Luis likes his little baths too. Yer goin' to catch it comin' out with this muck, for God's sake."

I was more and more fascinated by the conversation and their picturesque Spanish – which always accompanies filth; so I kept egging her on to say more and kept my fingers in her mouth, as they say, to make her talk.

"When did she come back from Barcelona?"

"Well, the second the old laydee died, may she be in 'er glory," he explained, beating his wife to it. "Nobody in the village knew what 'ad 'appened."

"It were goin' on ten year ago," she added. "She 'ad such a big belly on 'er and that were the first sign we 'ad of 'er sinnin' bun in the oven. She gave birth in the castle, and two or three year later did it a secon' time."

"So was the *carlà* living with her?"

"Well, no, sir, 'e weren't, 'e lived in 'is 'ouse in Barcelona, but 'e'd often come."

"Our *carlán* was a lawyer," the miller pointed out, "and 'e 'ad 'is cases to deal with in Barcelona."

"And 'is luvvin' in Olivel," she added.

"Why didn't he marry her?"

"Crikey, Don Luis!" The miller's wife burst out laughing. "Since when 'ave lords of the castle and lawyers married shitty yokels?"

This bucket of mud was too much for me and I changed tack with the excuse that I wanted to get to the monastery.

The monastery was one of those big country houses that could have belonged to farmers or gentry, and in fact the friars did devote their time to agriculture. It was a large square house in the northern corner of a small valley planted out with vines and olive trees and encircled by a low range of barren mountains. One of the peaks is called Calvary and is distinguishable from its neighbours by the double row of cypresses that twist up to its top. It is a quiet, enclosed valley that seems shut in on itself and its aromas of thyme. Acorn takes from half an hour to three quarters to gallop to the monastery; since then, I've ridden that way often.

Now let me tell you what's inside. A large doorway that looks out onto an esplanade leads straight into a lofty, spacious church that could hold a thousand people standing. That first day I crossed the threshold rather apprehensively: something weighed heavy in the silence. It was a dry, hot morning and I'd tethered the mare to a solitary elm on the esplanade. I went in. My first impression was that it was pleasantly cool. On the way there I'd been dazzled by the cruel July Aragon sun which had seared my eyes as I galloped. In the cool half shadows, as if in a cellar, I could barely see a thing. My retinas gradually adapted and I began to make out the remains of baroque altars blackened by fire, heaps of books scattered around in a mess, candelabra that had been snapped and thrown to the ground, artificial flowers, an incense burner in one corner, a lectern in another. Right at the back, at the foot of the main altar, were objects I'd have assumed were friars if they hadn't been so still.

Several mummies had been extracted from the open niches, now emptied, in the wall behind the altar. They were arranged to create a strange tableau. Two were stationed by the foot of the altar, like a couple being married; one was adorned with a veil and a bouquet of artificial flowers. They leaned against each other so they didn't fall. A third was leaning upright against the altar, facing them, as if he were the priest officiating.

The others, up to fourteen, lean against the wall like guests at the wedding. One has lost his balance and lies on the ground. Another has a sly, crooked expression that sends an icy shiver through me, it's so bizarre.

They must be friars of the monastery, dead a very long time. Bits of their habit still stick to their skin. They are bone dry, as if made of parchment, which is explained by the dryness of the air in this country and by the niches being located at a considerable height inside thick stone walls. They are so strange, so still and so parched! My feeling of terror vanished. How could I be petrified when the main door was wide open behind me, and beyond that the glorious rays of the midday summer sun?

No longer terrified, I did feel a keen sense of strangeness still: those objects were simply incomprehensible. The idea of a mummy is too hard to grasp. We cannot imagine we'll become such an object someday, carried here and there, stiff and empty – emptied of what? Of soul, you will say; but whatever is *that*?

That must be momentous if its departure leads to such dramatic changes. What do I have in common with a mummy? Materially everything, yet in fact nothing at all.

And what does one make of this business of stationing them as if they were getting married? Obscene and macabre: they've grotesquely inserted a candle, maybe an Easter candle, into the bridegroom mummy. I'd like to meet the man who disinterred these mummies and make him tell all. Perhaps I'd get nothing out of him – they are all probably unaware of the symbolism they are putting into play. And as for us, what do we know of our instincts? Who has ever been *that* interested in the reproduction of the species . . . ? Who ever thinks about it when we're at it? Bah, nobody remembers, yet it is nevertheless what stirs us. Sex and death, the obscene and the macabre, two abysses that make you dizzy. I feel as if the macabre has ambushed me in this village: the vulture trap on one side, the monastery on the other. And as I face these mummies, which are so dry, the endless thirst which I felt near the vulture trap returns.

Live, live once and for all, enjoy it in one big gulp before you end up stiff for all eternity!

OLIVEL, 7 AUGUST

A stone staircase leads off from the church, its steps polished by feet that have climbed up over the years to the top floor, where the friars' cells are located. A large hallway at the top of the stairway is strewn with huge antiphonaries, their parchment pages enclosed between studded wooden covers. There are several abandoned harmoniums – the church doesn't have an organ – and heaps of books, mostly from the eighteenth century. I found a complete edition, an English first edition, of Cook's travels with engravings that reproduce the drawings made by the artist who sailed in his frigate. Just the thing for the long hours when I'm on guard duty in the village!

In one of the cells I found a four-volume treatise on the cultivation of flowers, also eighteenth century, with engravings, these having been hand-tinted with watercolours, re-creating the colours of each species with great precision and verve. The flower of the pomegranate is a glorious red – and brought the mistress of the castle to mind. Why? What kind of glory? Glorious sin or glorious tragedy? How melodramatic, my God! *The uncertain glory of an April day*? It's strange, but she gave a start when I told her I was intending to visit the monastery. "Keep away from that place . . . the Virgin's gone . . . it's terrifying." She too must have been terrifying years ago; beauty is terrifying when it reaches a certain level; hers is stylised and terrifying even now. Lots of women are attractive, but few are beautiful. I'm unlikely ever to meet another who will make me think of Michelangelo's *La Notte* the way she does. She has that disagreeable effect on me that small men must experience when talking to tall women, yet I am taller than her – I've worked that out on the sly. I'm a good six inches taller.

*Piaceme il sonno e più l'esser de sasso**

---

* Sales' adaptation of a line by Michelangelo – 'I like sleep, even more being of stone' – that the sculptor/poet wrote in response to praise of his *La Notte*, a tall, sleeping nude.

Why do I spend so much time thinking about this woman? Because I'm bored out of my mind in this back of beyond! How old is she? Ten years older than me? She gives the impression that she's faded more than her age warrants, and that's natural enough given the horrors she has seen. That isn't what is extraordinary. What is extraordinary is how this premature withering, tinged with melancholy, actually enhances her.

Another cell has a small cupboard set in the thick wall that opens onto the outside but can be opened from the inside as well. I could hear a kind of humming, like the sound of wheat running through a sieve; I heard it from a distance, then right next to me, almost inside my ear. I decided to open the cupboard door. The cupboard was made of worm-eaten wood and measured no more than ten centimetres square. Here was the key to the mystery: it was a hollow space purpose built for bees to make their hives. The little beasts carry on working, indifferent to our ups and downs, without a care in the world – and the cupboard is full of honey! Their buzzing, now I know it's them, keeps me company over the long hours I spend in the monastery.

The next-door cell holds more surprises: a cramped spiral staircase, also concealed within the thick central wall, which goes up to a small attic that houses a pigeon loft.

The pigeons also carry on without a care in the world; several females are brooding. They've become wild. When they hear my steps the males fly off; the females look at me in fear but don't move from their nest boxes.

I then explored underground, discovering a huge cellar: the monastery's main product was wine. The miller had told me how the anarchists started sacking the cellar – with a drunken binge on claret and Maccabeus, the two varieties of wine the friars produced. But it appears to have been an orderly binge: the barrels are still in perfect shape and almost full; so they seem to have inspired more respect than the niches. One barrel is enormous: a hogshead, which they call "vessel" in Catalonia, with a capacity for tonnes, as if it were a barge. It is made of oak, its history inscribed on its front with a shield and a date: 1585.

I wish my imagination could reconstruct that long hot night at the end of July last year. An orgy of wine, blood and mummies scorched by the dog days of summer. Were women involved? The miller assures me they were not. Well, the detail of the Easter candle . . . it had struck me as a female idea, the wit of some lusty woman.

The miller is trenchant. The murderers were seven strangers who constituted the "committee". They dragged along half a dozen wretches from the village to help disinter the mummies. "Six poor fellows . . . we in the village know the lot." "Do they still live there?" "Yes, you bet, but don't give them away; all they did was dig out the dead."

The miller saw them coming and going from the mill, that was the route from village to monastery along the gully, and there wasn't a woman among them. What's more, and I find this really intriguing, he says they simply placed the deceased against the wall under the niches. He's very surprised by what I tell him about the wedding scene.

"But they weren't like that, I tell you, lootenant. They never were!"

"Are you sure you really remember?"

"The last time I was there, some four months ago, they weren't like you say, Don Luisico, but as *I* told you: lined up against the wall. I'm telling you straight, lootenant!"

"And what about the Easter candle?" He looked at me with eyes as big as oranges. He didn't understand. When he did, he burst out laughing: "Crikey, whoever did that is a filthy fellow! But they didn't, I swear they didn't, lootenant. I can tell 'oo they are, but don't you give them away. One's Pachorro, the 'unchback, who lives near the fountain; the other, el Restituto, ain't quite right in the 'ead."

I should pay the six of them a visit to see if I can get to the bottom of this.

On one of my first visits – I'd go every day, it was a constant lure – I was brought to a halt in the doorway by the din emanating from the cells. Cheerful out-of-tune notes from flutes, violins, double bass, mixed up with childish voices and laughter and footsteps so light they seemed like wings in flight. What was all that about? I went cautiously up the stairs: I wouldn't have been surprised to find a swarm of cherubim having fun. It was a band of shepherd boys from the area who'd shut their goats in the monastery stable so they could come up and play the harmoniums. The sight of me created panic. They were hilarious as they ran off in their big straw hats, their velvet breeches reaching below their knees, and I was dumbstruck for quite some time.

I took food with me so I didn't have to return to Olivel at midday and thus had time to investigate the piles of books calmly and methodically. Most were theological and many were in Latin, but there were also lots I found very interesting; that's where I found the *Criticón*, a first edition in fact, that later helped me kill so many hours on night-time guard duty. When I felt hungry I went down to the cellar to eat lunch. It's deep and gloomy; I have to grope my way down well-worn millstone steps. As your foot seeks out the next step, wave after wave of cool air hits you with an aroma of wine. Once among the casks, I lit a small oil lamp that I had to hand, and I ate; I couldn't have done that upstairs, where the presence of the mummies hung so heavy in the air. The coolness of the cellar and the smell of wine is refreshing. The flickering oil lamp projects shadows from the barrels on walls built from crudely hewn ashlars that are draped with thick cobwebs, some perhaps hundreds of years old. The claret was cold, very dry and fragrant, and tasted slightly of flintstone and sulphur. This was presumably on account of the sulphur matches or straws with which they will have fumigated the insides of the empty casks before transferring the new wine, according to the practice of the best wine growers; the Maccabeus was more like syrup and left a mellow taste between palate and tongue. I blew out the lamp with a puff and retraced my steps. I had to cross the church once more and walk to the cells with the largest heaps of antique books.

On one of these many afternoons, more embroiled than usual in my inspection of abandoned books, I came across an edition of Petrarch's sonnets printed by Elzevir and a seventeenth-century *Summa Theologica* with some outstanding vignettes. I was looking at them when a very loud clap of thunder interrupted my thoughts. I looked up at the window: the sky was darkening in sudden waves, as if a scene changer were switching off the lights behind a backcloth of clouds. Another thunderclap, this time cracked and hollow, broke over the monastery and I felt the lightning must have made a direct hit on the belfry, which had no bell within it.

A deathly glimmer gave the landscape the strangest pallor. The inside of the monastery was in darkness; lightning and thunder ran into each other. The lightning seemed to illuminate the interior more sharply than it did the landscape, presumably because the objects inside were closer to my eyes, but the final effect filled me with anguish. On nights when a dry storm, the most unnerving of all, is raging, I see the Earth more clearly than the sky; the sky is black and stifling, while a faint glow hovers above the Earth. This anguish we bear must be prompted by the feeling that the universe enclosing us is all shadows: shadows beyond.

A summer deluge began and the rain took a great weight off my shoulders: a dry storm is frustrating. The downpour lashed the great roof of the monastery, which resounded like an empty box.

I had to go back to the village, but first I had to get through the church. I walked back, staring hard at the square of brightness that was the open doorway ahead. I was halfway down the nave when the two sides of the door began to swing on their hinges and shut with a moan that rang around the vaults. The shadows had turned to total darkness and I was trapped inside. I was alone with the mummies.

Know what I did? I crossed myself and prayed the Lord's Prayer: there's nothing like terror to bring us to our knees. A draught had shut the door, I opened it easily. Outside it was raining cats and dogs. I ran to the elm tree: Acorn had gone. A piece of the reins hanging there said it all: scared by the thunder, the animal had snapped the thongs and made its escape.

Within a second I was drenched as thoroughly as if I'd fallen to the bottom of a pond. What could I do? Go back in and spend the night in one of the cells? Not likely: I would be too terrified. It would be madness to think of reaching the village without my mare, but I could try to make it as far as the mill.

I was a long way from the monastery when I realised that the Parral wasn't the usual brook but a great river swelling by the minute. I couldn't walk any further along the gully. I would have to scramble up and spend the night in the open on the slope. Upon reaching the top I spotted a small light – the light from a fairy tale! I made my way through the undergrowth and a blinding curtain of water and finally reached the mysterious brightness, where I found the miller, the miller's wife and their five or six little millers.

With the aid of an axe they had improvised a small shack from trunks of juniper, with a roof made of branches of rosemary and lentiscus. The wife was crying, her children huddled against her, the oldest staring at her with serious, dark eyes, while the young ones slept. The miller made room for me: "Don Luisico, see what a sad, wretched mess we're in."

"My mill's dead an' gone!" she wailed. "My litt'l chicks are dead that allus laid me eggs! The sow we bought is dead, and we fed 'er on such lurvely slops!"

He stared at the bottom of the ravine as if looking for the remains of his mill in the pitch dark.

"There's another mill in the district, upstream from the village. If only they'd rent it to us, but for note until we mill our first flour . . ."

"Whose is it?"

"It's the dead *carlán*'s, may he rest in Glory. You get on well with the mistress, I mean Olivela, you could . . ."

"Don't yer think for one minute, lootenant," she spoke as she stopped crying, "that I wish 'er ill; I didn't mean anything 'orrible when I spoke about 'er afore."

At least better think that now.

Before daylight broke we started our retreat along the ridge. We found the locals out in the street in Olivel: the women screaming and moaning and the men silent. The downpour had swept away their plots of land. Their harvests of hemp and corn were completely ruined. The poor folk's last hope lay with the saffron that grows on the dry lands outside the ravine, this being the crop that brings most money in good years.

Old Olegària – the old dear in the house where I'm lodged – was upset, wondering what might have become of me. I've yet to tell you about this coarse old woman who, with the best intentions in the world, cooks me dishes from hell; they are exactly the same as those she cooked for her grandson. I'll tell you about him some other day.

I'd received a letter from Trini: "Your little boy is insatiable when it comes to fairy stories. He asks for more, for yet another. 'Father used to tell me more,' he protests, and even adds, 'Father's were better.' I've started telling him stories about wicked stepmothers and he loves them. He opens eyes as big as oranges when he's listening and finds it hard to understand the father's role in the stories: what did the boy's father do? To soothe him, I say that the stepmother would beat the father too . . ."

Old Olegària knows as much about the state of my boy as I do. She's illiterate – all the women in the village are – but she always knows when a letter is from Trini by the envelope.

Naturally she thinks we are husband and wife. I see no need to enlighten her, as it would be beyond her. She waits for me to finish reading before asking me for the latest news about Ramonet, taking a lively interest in him – as if she knew no other children.

She is quite ancient and lives with her only daughter, also a widow, who looks as if she's past fifty. The dishes they cook for me deserve a term: they are horrific. One Sunday they wanted to give me chicken for a treat. They still haven't mastered the art of roasting in these parts. They drown the chicken in a saucepan filled to the top with oil and then boil it. When I take my first bite, I grimace with the shock of tasting so much oil.

"Isn't the chicken cooked properly? Don't you think it's got enough oil?" She told me the village had given me up for dead when they saw the mare ride up by itself with its reins snapped.

"So where is Acorn now?"

"In 'er castle, Don Luisico, like a flash! Don' need no 'elp to get to 'er manger. 'er does that by instinct. Beasts 'ave a character of their own."

Quite unawares, she had defined herself perfectly. Old Olegària is so much a beast and a character!

OLIVEL DE LA VIRGEN, SUNDAY, 8 AUGUST

The Parral is bubbling cheerfully along its usual course, as if it had never gone crazy. The saffron crop on the dry lands looks better than for many a year and the farmers are hoping it will make up for the loss of their hemp and corn harvests.

News from the battalion: we now have a machine-gun company. I was crossing the main street yesterday when I saw an officer well past forty, stout, in hunting boots, with a huge S-shaped pipe in his mouth. His little bright sly Mongolian eyes reminded me of someone, though I couldn't think who.

"It's Picó. Don't you remember me? We went for a swim together . . ."

"So what brings you to Olivel?"

"They've put us together with your battalion." He puffed on his pipe as he closed his little eyes, "And have you been in touch with Soleràs?"

"No, I've not seen him since."

"He's a cultured young man, but the filthiest in the brigade. We were camping out in the open in January. We slept in heaps of three or four, with all our blankets on top. The officers made separate piles, naturally; one must avoid being too familiar with the troops. Can you believe it, he was too much for me because he stank like a billy goat! 'Hey, lad, I'd rather you didn't sleep with us.' He was forced to sleep by himself, out in the open, in temperatures of six or seven below. You know what he did? He stretched out under the dung from the company's mules. Then there was a heavy snowfall: 'That Soleràs,' we said, 'on his tod and with just one blanket will be frozen as stiff as a mummy.' In the morning he assured us he'd been sweating the whole night long."

"I bet he had. Covered by mule turds with a foot of snow would be like sleeping under four eiderdowns! It wasn't such a bad idea."

"What can I say? I'd prefer frostbite and gangrene. Culture's all very well, but without hygiene . . ."

Today I made the obligatory visit to the *carlana* to apologise for what had happened to the mare. I mentioned the millers: "I've no worries about renting them the Albernes mill. I'd like to help them."

I'm writing this in my bedroom, that is, from old Olegària's grandson's. I've taken to it, though not to the grandson, whom I've yet to meet. This is a square whitewashed room with eight gnarled reddish juniper beams in a ceiling still reeking of resin. A west-facing window overlooks the main village square. An iron bedstead painted a pale red, a reed chair and pine table comprise all the furniture. For one's "hygiene", as Picó would say, there is a hand basin, that is, a washbowl on an iron tripod; old Olegària keeps an eye out so I always have a clean towel and a square of bitter almond soap that perfumes the whole room. See what an improvement this is on Castel de Olivo! I write with the light from the rump end of a candle listening to crickets through an open window. The air's warm and I'm starting to feel sleepy. I can hear the voices of Gallart and Ponsetti who are crossing the main square. They must be on their way to Melitona's tavern. While they stay there into the early hours, I'll be sleeping soundly in bed – which is the best place to be at night. The mattress sags in the middle. Initially, it irritated me so much I couldn't get to sleep. Now I've become so used to it that I would miss it: it's become familiar and keeps me company. And old Olegària's grandson must be missing it right now . . .

I'm falling asleep and thinking about my conversation with the *carlana* as if I'd dreamed it.

"Have you known the miller and his wife very long?"

"All my life. We're from the same village."

"Of course, from Olivel."

"No, not Olivel. Castel de Olivo."

"You aren't from Olivel?"

"Santiaga and I are first cousins. Some years ago, when her husband was looking for a mill, she asked Enric for ours. But Enric knew she was gossiping about me, so he refused to rent it to them. I'm not spiteful and should help a cousin if I can."

It's odd the miller's wife hadn't told me they were related. Does she find it embarrassing? Or . . . doesn't she really believe it to be true? "If she's turned out so stuck up, must 'ave been some graft or other" – obviously only a hypothesis, but hypotheses could take us a long way . . .

"The Albernes mill pond holds double what the other can take. We used it to water our cultivated plots. If they want, I'll rent them the land as well so they can get the benefit of both."

I wasn't really interested in what she was saying; it was as if she were talking about things very remote: Santiaga and the Albernes mill. I was listening not to the words but to her voice. I've woken up some nights with a start, thinking I could hear her voice in my sleep, warm and voluptuous like perfume, serious and thoughtful like a solemn promise . . .

OLIVEL, 10 AUGUST

I spent yesterday in Castel de Olivo. They'd summoned me from brigade headquarters to draw up an indictment: something as complicated as it was trifling. If you only knew how I hate drawing up indictments. I did all I could to postpone it.

I reached Olivel after midnight. I had walked because Acorn still remembers her drenching and won't budge from her stable, where she's well wrapped up in burlap sacking. The shortcut from Castel de Olivo runs alongside a broad, barren valley with healthy marshlands beyond. Hundreds, if not thousands, of toads of different kinds live in the valley – big, medium and small. Each lent its distinct, clear, precise note to the chorus: a magic trill of tinkling glass bells. The moonless night made every one of its stars twinkle – as distinct, clear and precise as these notes. I'd been walking for an hour and a half with a similar distance to go and sat down there, completely entranced by the wizardry of the desert, the toads and the night. Sagittarius was flourishing its bow of stars at the very heart of the Milky Way, where it becomes as dense as a cloud of diamond dust. I shivered from time to time, feeling the night-time breeze, or terror, and I thought of her and her voice and told myself: She is the first real woman I've ever met.

The world is so lovely, yet we turn our backs on it to manufacture private sordid little hells . . . Poor Soleràs! "The hell I'm manufacturing for my own private use is so cramped," he'd said, "there's no room for anyone else." Why does he avoid me, the only person in the brigade who likes him?

I found him in Castel de Olivo.

I decided to pay my old landlady a visit: "You're back? That friend of yours is sleeping up in the attic."

"Soleràs?"

It must have been gone two and he was having a snooze. I walked slowly upstairs to give him a surprise. The attic still silently exhaled the stench of rabbits I knew so well and the shutters were closed. He turned over in his bed. I couldn't see him, I was still blinded coming in from the light, but I heard him whisper sarcastically: "And what are *you* doing here?"

I told him how I'd been summoned to draw up an indictment – "as they might have summoned you," I added, "given that you too have a law degree."

"If I'd known you were coming to Olivel today, I'd have left for Mont-forte."

"Thanks very much. We've not seen each other for two months."

"If you had a clearer idea of things, you wouldn't *want* to see me."

"A clearer idea of what?"

"Lluís, you and I should hate each other."

"Why should I hate you? Because of your so-called perversions? I've known you far too long. You like to act the cynic and I know the story by heart. It's like water off a duck's back. Your vices are imaginary. You're hypocritical when it comes to vice: that's your only virtue. All that morphine business was complete nonsense. I expect you were really drinking lime infusions."

"I'm not prepared to tolerate your insults," he growled.

"I've even reached the point of doubting your aunt ever had any visions."

"Do you doubt the existence of Saint Philomena?"

"Her existence is one thing . . ."

"To exist or not to exist, *that is the question.* One doesn't get the aunt one asks for, you know; in fact, we get the aunts we deserve. And what about the Innocents?"

"What Innocents?"

"Do you also doubt the existence of the Holy Innocents?" His bass voice was becoming more emphatic. "Do you deny the existence of the *llufa*?* So many people carry them quite unawares; very important individuals, great men, sublime men," and he laughed unpleasantly. "They don't realise and never will; they forget they have a behind, they are so sublime! They don't even believe in *llufas.* They are sceptics, didn't you know, and sceptics are duty-bound not to believe in anything. However, they do believe in themselves and their own importance; Satan, with his fine sense of humour, has stuck his *llufa* on them. A little portable hell embedded just where they can't see it. And I'm not only referring to jet-black sceptics; there are light-pink sceptics who are even more startling. They don't believe in hell, they are so angelical: innocent lilies! It happens particularly with certain ladies; ladies from the best families, didn't you know, frightful ladies, ladies who go to Saint Vicenç de Paül's lectures. They don't believe in the *llufa* but carry it embedded in their behinds!

* *Llufa* is both a fart and the card or material hung on the backs of unsuspecting people on the Day of the Holy Innocents, 28 December.

A portable little hell. As they are ladies of such good breeding, I take particular note. They worry a lot about their faces, but their face is their least interesting feature, indeed, quite the contrary."

"And why can't you stop spouting this nonsense?"

He gave me a withering glance: "I suppose you *have* heard of Easter candles."

"Easter candles?"

He pointed to the wall full of little figures and stupid graffiti. I had opened the shutters to let in some light and fresh air.

"Let us imagine you're right, that my vices are purely imaginary," he went on, as I inspected the wall: it had new drawings which I was sure weren't there when I had the attic. "I'll add another adjective: solitary. What an association of adjectives to toy with! A good association of adjectives is a good enough start. Let's imagine that I hid from everyone simply to take lime infusions . . ."

There evidently were new drawings; one, especially, was very striking. It portrayed a kind of procession of men or women – it was impossible to tell which because their creator had sketched them very roughly. What was striking was that they were each carrying a big candle, lit and dripping molten wax, and a *llufa* on their back.

"I don't know if you have ever noticed that the Easter candle is lit on glorious Holy Saturday and extinguished on Ascension Thursday, then see you again next year! We all live in the hope that it will be lit again come glorious Holy Saturday, that is, at the beginning of spring. But there will be a year when it won't happen. A year when spring won't return. Have you never thought how April, that month of uncertain glory, escapes our grasp? And uncertain or not, it is the only glory. So, back to our Easter candles . . ."

"Let Easter candles be. I'm an unbeliever but I respect sacred things."

"I'm the complete reverse. I believe. If I didn't, why would I take pleasure in mocking them? If only I could stop believing! How I envy you people who don't believe or think you don't believe! You, for example, are the luckiest of the lucky. When faith might be a nuisance and get in the way, you lose sight of it; when you need it, it comes back. Don't deny that's your technique. A technique that couldn't be bettered! On the other hand, I work the opposite way: faith blocks my path when I'd prefer to forget it and doesn't come when I call on it."

"Do you really think this makes the slightest impression on me? We who don't have any faith wish we did, but the contrary . . . to have faith and wish we didn't . . . would be absurd . . ."

"Exactly. The absurd has sunk its teeth into us, and we find evil attractive. We've been granted so little time to do all the evil we'd like to! We'd do much more, but alas, we don't have the time. Conversely, do you think doing evil is as easy as some people believe? Not just any old evil, but the evil one really wants to commit, because, you know, doing evil that doesn't appeal is of no interest . . . That's the evil to cap all evils, being able to do what is of no interest at all, while in the meantime life rushes by. April is rushing from us, believe me, and this blasted war will spoil it for us. It may last a long time, long enough to bugger us all. You lack imagination; you think this is a summer shower that catches you unawares and that a good thyme broth will shortly appear, a soup steaming by the hearth after you've changed your socks and shirt. You'll be in time for your good thyme broth! Nausea is what will appear, or perhaps you didn't hear the news? Are you certain that word means nothing to you?"

He said all this without getting out of bed. Then stretched out an arm and took his canteen from the reed chair that doubled as his bedside table.

"Would you like a swig? It's cognac. I mean that, it's cognac, not rotgut. And fascist cognac into the bargain! The genuine article from Andalusia! A bottle that has survived . . ."

He drank from the spout, wiped his lips and got back again on his high horse.

"You still haven't told me how you reacted to the Easter candle in the monastery in Olivel. There's something quite remarkable in Olivel apart from the mummies. I suppose you must have noticed."

"What do you mean?"

"The *carlana*. Don't miss out on her. She's remarkable on more than one score . . . but what's wrong?"

"Nothing's wrong, don't be such an idiot."

"It's common knowledge that the *carlana* . . ."

"That the *carlana* what?"

"Lets you ride her horse. She wouldn't let me."

"So now you're spying on what I do?"

"You surely realise that news of one's friends circulates in a brigade. I know that you go to the monastery every day and mount the lady's beast; don't be offended, I do mean her horse. I even know that you spend your time salvaging antique books and other portable items of value. I shall reassure you by saying that this is all deemed praiseworthy. Your battalion commander has told the brigade commander as much, praising your attachment to culture to the skies. Everybody in this brigade is in favour of culture and hygiene; it's not like the 'flatfooted' brigade. The whole weight of the brigade is behind your culture and behind you putting a little order into that 'historic building' – the whole brigade knows it is 'historic' – with a view to returning it to the Friars of the Virgin of Mercy in good shape when circumstances allow. Know what I mean by circumstances, right?"

"Like a book, but no need to be reticent. I find your reticence irritating."

"So much in life is irritating and we must learn to put up with it . . . Religion, for example, as we've mentioned friars and monasteries; religion slots perfectly into this conversation. Why do we find religion so irritating? If it were false, we wouldn't, it would be great fun. It's irksome when they poke our sores – the sore that runs the most. And don't be under any illusion, their aim is deliberate and that's why they irritate. We'd all like to do the same, with great gusto, but we can't; April is disappearing fast. They do us and undo us and never ask our opinion. Who? Why? 'Young fellow, you just mind your own business.' Fine, if you want to hide the who and the why from us, why not the how as well? Godella is a wonderful estate and the dog days there set me up a secret rendezvous with the most obscure dreams, a rendezvous soaked with salt-laden scents. The sea is nearby. Naturally, my aunt forbade me to go. I was forced to swim hiding from her, not on the beach that you could see from the house but on a cove where you could swim in the nude. My aunt refused to buy me swimming trunks.

"And it was in that cove that . . . I was twelve at the time. I heard voices before I got there; two voices, a woman's and a man's, foreigners. I've always found foreigners intriguing. I hid among the reeds and fennel in order to spy on them. He was blonde, with a deep tan, and had clearly been sunbathing a lot; tall, broad shouldered, with hair so thick on his chest it ruffled his shirt, hair that glinted like gold on his chocolate skin. He laughed loudly, showing splendid white teeth that gleamed quite offensively, the kind only perfect savages sport. As you know, I've had bad teeth from the age of twelve . . . They'd just landed in a motorboat they'd moored on the beach. They were foreigners, I didn't understand a word they said, and that's why foreigners have always intrigued me – because I don't understand them – so I hung on and spied on them. My nose was full of the scent of fennel scorched by the August sun and they were laughing and chatting. I wanted to know what foreigners do. People who speak so strangely must also do strange things, or so I thought. She seemed much bigger than him: one of those well-fed mature Nordic women who are apparently made of a hard elastic substance like solid rubber. They came to the cove every morning in their boat and did so throughout that summer; I'd hear the hum of the motor from Godella and run to my hideout. One day I found a dead donkey that had been abandoned by gypsies halfway along the path. From that moment on I found the donkey more interesting than the foreigners. It didn't smell the first day, and I'd even say it lay there in a civilised fashion; only a hint on its lips, a cynical expression, as if it had a hidden agenda, betrayed the fact that it held a surprise in store. It was planning – as later developments would testify – to stink to high heaven. The day after it was so swollen it was barely recognisable; I suspected the village butcher of being responsible. The butcher inflated kid goats before skinning them because he said it was easier once they were blown up; that butcher – Pancras by name, for your information – would inflate them through their behinds, using a reed. I was fascinated by my donkey's swollen paunch and punctured him with the needle-sharp point of a marine bulrush. I extracted the reed and the little hole hissed like a mouth full of saliva as the donkey deflated gradually, like a tyre. Its stink filled the air . . . and I fled. It was unbearable. I fled to my hideout by the cove. The foreigners were there and the man was laughing more outrageously than ever, flashing his savage's teeth. I threw up. I threw up like a god lamenting his creation. You don't believe me, as always; you think I invented all this. Well, not one bit: I did throw up. Like so many people, you think we only came into this world to drink lime infusions. Well no, I'm not inventing a thing; I threw up. I must have told Nati: 'There are foreigners on that cove who say very curious things you can't understand, and there's a dead donkey as well . . . They do even stranger things and the donkey swells up and deflates.' She refused to go; she was more scared by the foreigners and the donkey than by the railway line. I tell you, I'm not fibbing; I speak with my hand on my heart . . . I went every day, expecting the spectacle of putrefaction to begin, but it didn't. The foreigners stopped coming towards the end of September and the donkey couldn't make its mind up. I was intrigued and poked it with a stick; an army of rats was scurrying inside its parchmented skin. They'd made a hole in its belly and eaten its insides while respecting its skin, its appearance. I find this respect for appearances that one sees throughout nature quite peculiar, this need to respect appearances and hide away on a solitary cove . . . You refuse to believe me, you never have, yet you don't want to mistrust me. I hope you don't think I find it pleasurable to inspire so little mistrust and to have suffered toothache from the age of twelve . . . They do and undo us, they inflate and deflate us, there's nothing a child likes more than this double mystery: how they both do and undo us. Not that they ask us for our opinion: 'You just mind your own business.'"

"Have you finished?"

"I have for the moment. I felt inspired, Lluís, and had to make the most of you being here to listen. I've occasionally tried to speak to myself, I mean out loud; but it's demoralising. You fantasise about my vices, Lluís; they're neither as imaginary as you think, nor as solitary. No, solitude isn't my strong point. I need accomplices, you understand? I get demoralised speaking out loud to myself; I need an accomplice to listen in. It's like the love that we all know as a crime, but its most unpleasant feature is that we can't perpetrate love without having an accomplice."

"You're being really stupid."

"No, I'm not. Baudelaire, your beloved Baudelaire, said that first! But didn't you know that there are people who maintain the universe inflates and deflates like a bellows? That's right, I said 'the universe', why stare at me like that? It inflates, then deflates, and for ever and ever, amen. But why don't we speak of things that affect us more immediately? I don't know if you've heard that some tins of condensed milk . . . the El Pagès brand to be precise . . . have gone missing."

"From Supplies? The indictment I have to draw up is all about these missing tins. I've deferred it for lack of information. I also find acting the role of prosecutor most annoying."

He glanced at me in a curious, mocking manner, that short-sighted, spectacle-less stare of his; he grinned and chuckled sarcastically: "What a coincidence! It's a small world. You should know that the person stealing these tins of El Pagès is yours truly. What a pity you have postponed the indictment! I steal from soldiers on the front line to give to whores in the rearguard. Ever since they assigned me to the Train Corps I go to the rearguard every so often in a truck. If only you knew what they can give you in exchange for a tin of milk! Some of them have children . . . It's so sad when a child dies from the lack of a tin of El Pagès milk . . . You see, a mother's milk is a very sensitive thing, and they're not rough children, born anyhow. Perhaps you'll still have time to reverse the postponement and try me. A summary judgement will do: we are troops on a war footing, after all. An execution would break this enervating boredom and the whole brigade would give you a vote of thanks."

Naturally I didn't believe a word of all this. He says these things to arouse admiration or to shock. I knew his routine by heart.

"You are as incapable of stealing a tin of El Pagès as you are of spearing a dead donkey with the point of a marine bulrush and all the other crazy things you've just mentioned."

"As you like, Lluís, you play it your way. You are missing out on a splendid opportunity to . . . rid yourself of your 'best friend'. It's odd you don't see that. Perhaps you'd get it if you read *The Horns of Roland*. Or the article on 'The Bicycle' in the *Espasa Encyclopedia*. What a great book that is! One of the greatest books ever written; at least nobody disputes that, though that's another story."

When I reached Olivel, everyone was asleep. There was no light in any window. The streets were deserted. Even so, I found Captain Gallart and his inseparable Ponsetti in the square.

I couldn't think what that pair were hiding up their sleeves, whether they were after a girl or a wine cellar – or both things at once. It was obvious from the sight and smell of them that they were tipsier than usual: "Nobody understands us! You heard!" trumpeted the "Publicist of the public highway" with the rhetorical glee of someone on carrer Pelayo extolling the virtues of a pen or an umbrella. "Right, nobody understands us!" Gallart repeated. "We desperately need another guitar." "It's the 'flatfooted' brigade . . ." moaned Ponsetti. The only thing I managed to get clarity on was that their guitar had disappeared and they suspected that the "flatfooted" brigade – our neighbour and rival – had nicked it from them; I also thought I'd fathomed that there was a new development in the battalion it would be worth digging out.

II

Old Olegària was waiting up for me. She'd decided against going to bed so as not to leave me with a cold dinner; because these fine people, who eat such horrific muck, get the shakes at the very thought of eating cold food. I scolded her. I said it really didn't matter if one ate one's supper cold, or even if one ate no supper at all; that it might even be good for the health and that in any case it didn't do hers any good to stay awake into the early hours.

She looked at me, nodding her head, not at all convinced: "I always think of our boy, out in this war like you people."

Naturally, this wasn't the first time she'd talked to me about her grandson. I was already familiar with some of his traits and with her firm beliefs: "When I lodge a soldier, I always think I 'ave to treat 'im like they'll be treating our boy." But I'd always assumed he must be serving in a republican unit.

Early that morning, while I ate the dinner she'd reheated, as she stood and watched me I asked her about her grandson, including the unit he belonged to. The poor woman didn't know what to say, she couldn't tell a regiment from a battalion, but the word "regiment" caught my attention as there are none on our side. I finally grasped that he was serving in an enemy unit. She could hardly tell the difference: she thinks "we're all tarred with the same brush", and maybe she's right.

Her grandson is one Antonio López Fernández. She's shown me photos of him dressed in uniform or his Sunday best: these people wouldn't be photographed in their everyday clothes even under threat of death. Our Antonio López Fernández has a stiff air about him and a look in his eyes that doesn't match the constrained smile on his lips. They've been retouched – you can see the lines of his eyebrows and hair have been shaded in with charcoal. Old Olegària has hung them in her bedroom in frames painted purple. One deserves a special mention: it is the inevitable First Communion photo of Antonio López Fernández dressed as a sailor boy with a girl next to him who's around the same age – ten or twelve –

clothed as a bride. But a bride from the past century, both incredibly provincial and unfashionable.

"Dear Olegària, I didn't know you had a granddaughter."

"She's my sister, not my granddaughter."

"Your sister? And the same age as your grandson?"

"She were, when she 'ad 'er first communion, but then the poor little thing died . . . That must be some sixty-odd years ago. You know I once lodged a lady 'ere, as I do you now, and she were a real lady, Don Luisico, she were the village schoolteacher. When she moved to another village, she gave me that frame unpainted; and I asked the photographer who came every year at First Communion time: 'why don't you put my grandson and little sister, may she rest in peace, in the same picture and make the most of this pretty frame?' He asked me for a 'undred pesetas to do that little job that you couldn't do with a needle and thread. So they're together and I always think I'm seeing 'em 'ere and now: it's lovely, ain't it? These photographers are real devils when it comes to making big lovely photos; for one 'undred pesetas all told . . ."

A good waste of a hundred pesetas, but I wasn't going to tell her that. On the other hand, she's not the village record holder for stupid photos. The mayor – the one Commander Rosich restored to his post – has hung on his dining-room wall the X-ray they took of his stomach when they had to operate on a tumour. The tumour turned out to be benign but the X-ray is as repulsive as if it were cancerous. The fellow framed it and is very proud; he tells everyone that "the photo cost me a good thirty napoleons." Perhaps this could be the source of some deep philosophical thinking: what if the mayor was right? Why should the photo of our face be worth more than one of our stomach?

I went to the castle. Acorn is recovering, is hungry again, so the servant said, and he's removed the burlap sacking as she was too hot. The mistress received me for the first time not in the main hall but in the wing where she lives. As it's a huge castle and she doesn't have staff, it has shrunk in effect to a few small indispensable rooms with a good outlook. I was really curious to see that part of the building so zealously locked and off limits to all of us.

They are rooms with windows that face cheerfully south over the village. They gave a view of all the roofs and their light-grey tiles spotted with rust-coloured lichen; a belfry built of blackish bricks rises above the sea of roofs. If you look up, you can see the castle barbican jutting out sharply, with a mass of swallows and swifts' nests. I counted at least fifty. The mud they are made of has a hard surface; they say that these birds return year after year, if they can, to the same nests, in need of only slight repair, and quite possibly some nests are as old as the roof.

This part of the castle confounded all my expectations. It's not that I was expecting to discover the distasteful, strident luxury that's evoked by the idea of "a maid bumped up to a lady", since that had never occurred to me when thinking about her: even so, I was surprised by the extreme simplicity.

These are interiors that wouldn't be out of place in a monastery. The small sitting room where she welcomed me also acts as the dining room; it leads to a spacious bedroom furnished with an iron bed, a pair of reed chairs and a Queen Isabel *secrétaire*. I could see all this clearly because the door was wide open. The kitchen must be on one side of the dining room-cum-lounge – the door was closed – and the children's bedroom on the other. The walls are simply whitewashed, the floor tiles are quite ordinary and embellished with red oxide.

She sat me in a friar's chair; between us was a round, smallish walnut wood table where they must eat. We naturally talked about the millers, since they were the reason for my visit.

"They came yesterday and we reached an agreement. They will move into Albernes tomorrow."

"We can assume Santiaga will stop her nasty gossip."

"The wretched woman started blubbering. She's not evil, just foolish. They do more harm in these villages from foolishness than spite."

I told her about the rumours that were rife in the battalion: "We'll probably be leaving Olivel. This is the longest I've been in the same village since the war started."

"Poor things, it's quite natural for you to want some peace and quiet, but Olivel is so small, so dirty, so wretched, so closed in . . ."

Silence descended. She was looking towards the open window. We could hear the mewling swifts flying busily to and from their nests and she suddenly burst out laughing as she repeated: "So wretched, so closed in."

I was upset by her laughter and interrupted her on a sour note: "Yes, Olivel is sad. And so are you. But possibly it's the sadness I find so attractive. I found Olivel oppressive the first few days, but now I can say that I'd not change its barren wastes and bare mountains for anywhere in the world. There's nothing quite like sadness that is so calm and measured; open to the sky, these extensive deserts dotted by a few hermitages on humps of yellow clay with a few cypress trees . . ."

"How can you like this kind of countryside?"

"The same way I like a sad melody, November twilights . . . or a woman with a past to her."

She'd stopped laughing and grinned at me sarcastically.

"We peasant women don't notice such things. We've more down-to-earth matters on our mind: whether the sow is fattening, the hens are laying, the tomatoes are ripening in the orchard, or the food in the larder will last to the next pig slaughter . . . Why think about anything else? The past . . . If you let yourself be carried away by a few memories and sadness, you start to feel distressed straightaway. The past is so strange, if you begin digging around! I was at that stage, did this or that, how could I have? What became of whatever we said, did or thought years ago? I lived in Barcelona for many years and I understand you; you see I can follow the thread of what you say. But believe me: a woman with a past is a spent cartridge; and if you missed your target, patience be thy name. When a woman has a past, she is irremediably old. I am old and my life is a failure and that's that. Don't try to find heavenly music or November twilights; don't raise your hopes."

That morning the late summer sun shone diagonally through the window, glinting on the murky mirror in the cornucopia on the wall. As she moved her head, the rays reflected on the light chestnut hemp-like hair she wore in a short thick plait. As she spoke, she sewed a patch on short trousers that no doubt belonged to her younger boy. They, her children, never spend the morning with her; they're always running around and about. I got up to leave. I'd have liked to say something but I felt I couldn't respond to what she'd just said, the words wouldn't come: "God knows," I muttered, "that no other woman . . ."

I don't know what else I said, if I did say anything.

"Thanks, you are very kind," she replied naturally, not looking up from her sewing. "You were brought up in Barcelona and people there pay attention to women of my age; I'm familiar with that way of life. And although I know you only say that as a compliment, kind words are always appreciated."

"You think I only said that as a compliment?"

I defended myself with real feeling and yet I hadn't realised what I'd said. She looked up rather suspiciously: "Of course, as a compliment. Why else would you say something like that?"

She stared at me as if trying to discern my motives. I knew I had to desist; besides, I found her eyes so distracting: her eyes, I could see, weren't black, as I'd imagined them, from close up they were dark grey and flashed fiercely.

"You're very young," she said slowly, no doubt aware I was embarrassed, and looking towards the window; once again her voice became deep and remote as on that evening by the crossroads, against the sunset. "You're very young. I could be your mother."

"Don't be so ridiculous. I have a four-year-old son and I am almost thirty."

The lie came of its own accord, effortlessly. Months ago I'd made it to twenty-five; is it so far out to say "almost thirty"?

"And how old do you think I am?"

She hesitated for a moment and didn't give me time to reply, whispering: "I'm over forty."

Once again I had the unpleasant feeling of being a small man talking to a tall woman. She went back to mending the patch with her needle: "You're a polite young man and know how to treat a woman properly. It's a real pity you have few opportunities in these back-of-beyond villages to show off your manners. Some might even take them amiss."

"Please don't continue in this vein or you'll depress me. I think you must have mistaken me for someone else."

"For someone else? Who do you mean?"

"I'm not referring to anyone in particular. I really am not. I'm not polite, quite the contrary, I've been dragging myself around the war fronts for the last year. You can be as off-putting as you like, Olivela, but I . . ."

"You people are really peculiar. Don't you see that? What do you want from me? Before you came, I was living a quiet life in this big old castle, a ruin inside a ruin. The anarchists saw that more clearly than you lot; they dubbed me 'the old girl in the big pile'. And I didn't find that upsetting; that way they left me in peace in my little corner. They respected me."

"I'd be very upset if you thought I didn't respect you."

"I didn't mean that," and for the first time I thought I detected warmth and even gratitude in her tone of voice and the luminous way she looked up at me from her sewing.

"I'd be very upset, believe me, Olivela, as I am when you address me as one of the crowd, as if I were only an ordinary fellow from the battalion, just one of many lodging in this village who'll be off God knows where tomorrow."

"I didn't mean that. I didn't mean the battalion. I was referring to Soleràs."

"Soleràs? You told me never to mention him again."

"Yes, better not. You're right, much better."

A heavy silence descended.

"So let's not," I interjected. "That's enough for today," I added, taking advantage of that lull to withdraw discreetly. "You should see you have a good friend in me, ready to help in any way."

That banal sentiment, voiced for want of anything better to say, provoked quite an unexpected reaction. She looked at me silently, as if I'd given her an idea. "Are you really ready to help? For example, if I asked a favour of you – something you could do – a small favour that would be important to me . . ."

"Don't doubt for one second; for you, I would —"

"Really," she interrupted me now, "you people are the masters of the village as Olivel now falls within the domain of the front and is subject to military jurisdiction. If you wanted, you could take the castle and its land, the Albernes mill and the mare and even the few pieces of furniture I have here. You could also do quite the opposite. The small favour I would ask, not now but in due course, would be very easy for you, as you are a lawyer. We'll talk about it another time."

"Why not now?"

"Because you're in a state. Look how your hands are shaking."

She gave me that steely-grey stare. "What do you want of me?" I thought and then realised she could ask the same question of me, but she'd returned to the patch she'd dropped on her lap and was no longer looking at me. She was quietly continuing with her darning after she'd threaded the needle and cut the surplus thread with her teeth. It was then I realised that the atmosphere around her smelled distinctly of lovingly starched ironed linen that had been put away with lavender in an ancient cedar or walnut chest. Afterwards, when I was walking down the staircase – the only thing in the castle made of quarried stone – the cool air from the ground floor that smelled of cellars, straw, pine and juniper blotted out that aroma of white linen and bridal chests.

Today old Olegària cooked *mortajo* for my lunch. It is the regional dish *par excellence*. Horrendous, of course, though you have to act as if it were the ambrosia of the gods.

It consists of sheep's belly stuffed with the unfortunate beast's entrails, sewn up and boiled for hours and hours. When they serve it and slit it open, vapour hisses out as if it were a steam engine: a reek of warm offal that would dampen the spirits of the cockiest cove. No need to add that the stench attracts battalions and brigades of flies.

11 AUGUST

I was returning to the village after one of my strolls to the monastery. When I walked past an outlying house I heard a violin playing. Something by Chopin, but did Chopin write solo pieces for the violin? At any rate, it was beautifully played, with infinite sensitivity. It was dusk and the music seemed to meld into the glow, the scents and the exquisite dying fall of twilight. The dog days are dying too; every year when the dog days die, something dies within us. That downpour delivered the mortal blow, and I have to sleep under a blanket on the odd night. But who the devil was playing that violin?

I asked the nurse, who looked at me in astonishment: "Didn't you know? It's the doctor."

"Is there a doctor in the village?"

"You know, the battalion doctor, Dr Puig. Where've you been? On the moon? He plays the violin like an angel."

"That drunkard? I thought he was only interested in wine barrels."

"Well, you're wrong. He is a very sensitive fellow."

"You'd like me to believe he drinks to forget."

"And why not? There are sayings that start to sound like clichés precisely because they speak to real situations."

"Bah . . . what about the commander?"

"The finest person imaginable."

"Nobody will dispute that, Cruells. What I wanted to know is whether he too drinks to forget."

"You can be sure of that; everyone who drinks does so to forget."

"To forget what?"

"They don't usually remember."

He said that in all seriousness. His tortoiseshell spectacles made him look more owlish than ever while he tried to persuade me that the doctor, the commander, Gallart, Ponsetti, all those "still on the baby's teat" – so says the commander – drink wine to drown their feeling of emptiness, "the first step to religion".

"As much as to say," I retorted, "that they take it on the totter."

"You give the impression," he persisted, "that you don't feel any inner void, that, as yet, you never have."

"You mean you'd like me to get drunk?"

"Just forget it."

*

I received a letter from Trini, and it made me think about my conversation with Cruells. "I am sure you'll understand one day; till now you have fled from happiness as if it horrifies you . . ." "If you like, we could start afresh, despite being apart, despite the bad times you've put me through . . ." "You still refuse to accept that I exist. I don't mean you don't love me, but you carry on as if I don't exist. Sorry to speak to you like this but there are times when I can't stand it any longer and need to let off steam. It may not hurt you to feel alone in the world, or at least so far you've not realised that's the case; I, on the contrary, can't bear it. You've not written to me in a whole month . . ."

A month . . . It must be about that.

Ramon, I vaguely suspect that I'm a complete scoundrel. Much more so than the lieutenant doctor, who at least plays the violin. Even Soleràs seems a saint by comparison. You know nothing about my life since you left. Even a man's entry into the Order of St John of God can harm someone else! You left me alone in that house . . . Do you remember that double bed on which we slept when we were children? I'd sometimes wake up with a start and grab the tail of your nightshirt to get over my fear of the dark. If only you knew how often I've felt nostalgic for the tail of your nightshirt! You told me stories about Father; you'd known him personally, you knew the details of his death in Africa, you spoke plainly and simply, like someone going about an everyday task. Did you never suspect that when you left you made me desolate, feeling as if I was lost in the middle of a forest? Nobody since has spoken to me about Father except in roundabout ways, random words that meant very little and were hurtful. And Julieta scared me, with those eyes I thought were sucking me dry and her vampire mouth that I felt all of a sudden one evening in the garden where we still played with her, Josep Maria and friends from school. Josep Maria, our cousin, the poor fatty with the fluty voice, I don't think he noticed how the atmosphere in the garden got so heavy when darkness fell; I'd at least like to do him the honour of thinking he didn't notice, since one of those involved was Julieta, his sister. I couldn't stand Julieta; I couldn't stand her at the time, when we were fourteen, because I found her so scatterbrained that she grated on my nerves. And then that kiss on the lips I wasn't expecting . . . It is strange how a kiss – such a trifle – can make such an impact when we are in the process of abandoning childhood. As far as I was concerned it was the revelation of an aspect of life that I still feel is repugnant: female sensuality.

I think sensual women are quite monstrous.

All that seems like a thousand years ago, but it's only ten or twelve! How can we change so much in such a short time? Trini, on the other hand, acts as if she never experienced any turbulent transition, that she went imperceptibly from childhood to young womanliness. The sect her family belonged to published a newssheet, *La barrinada*, perhaps the only anarchist newspaper published in Catalan. I even wrote for it and sold it on the streets with Soleràs and Trini, though I never read it. Conversely, I never failed to post it to our uncle every week and that was really all about shocking him with the idea that I'd become an anarchist. One day, when we'd finished lunch and were chatting over coffee, he told me to come and see him that evening in his office.

You must remember only too well the depressing black leather chairs and that bust of Dante on the filing cabinet. Uncle was busy with his accountant and I had to wait a long time in one of those chairs trying to imagine what the connection was between Dante and the manufacture of pasta for soups. The accountant left and Uncle eventually looked up, glancing at me half pityingly, half mockingly. He extracted a newspaper from his inside pocket; it was, of course, the latest issue of *La barrinada*, where they'd published an article by me.

"Do you think you've kept me awake at night? I expect you wrote the phrase 'the pig getting fat' with me in mind. One day you'll be ashamed you signed these articles with every one of your names like a little innocent. Did you never think that, as your guardian, I could send you to a reformatory . . . ?"

That word came wrapped in a heavenly halo: I'd be a martyr in Trini's eyes. Uncle Eusebi went on and I now realise he only mentioned the reformatory to frighten me, but at the time I thought he really meant it. He kept breaking off the conversation to scrutinise papers, figures or telegrams his employees brought in: "Next week we have a meeting with the management committee for shareholders. I must balance the books and prepare a report . . ."

Yet another employee came in with a telegram; he gave it a glance and put it on his desk: "Another telegram from Madrid . . . Alright, let's get back to you. I know that you go for long solitary walks with an anarchist girl. Is it free love? Not a bad thing at all. I mean, it wouldn't be if you weren't a fool. How do I know? You must understand that, as your guardian, I have a man I trust keeping an eye on you. I'd be held responsible for anything that might happen to you, and you haven't yet grasped that this free love lark would be great fun if it didn't have any fallout. A fool, that's right; this young girl . . ."

He opened a letter that had just arrived with a pair of scissors: "Bah, the correspondent from Caracas . . . Free love will work wonders for you if you don't watch out. My dear nephew, in a word, I have very little time to devote to you. I want to get a vote of confidence from the shareholders in order to expand the firm; it's well on its way, you know, but I must draw up a convincing report, weigh my words carefully, check the figures." He lit up a cigar, sprawled back in his armchair and closed his blank business-man's eyes. "I really don't have time to devote to you and it's a pity you make me waste it on stuff and nonsense, when here," and he waved vaguely in the direction of his letters and telegrams, "hundreds of thousands of pesetas are at stake. I'll be brief and to the point: I was intending to send you to a boarding school to save you from a disastrous marriage, which is what free love usually leads to, but I consulted Father Gallifa and he didn't agree. He says that if I shut you up, I'll spoil everything. He thinks," and Uncle Eusebi laughed as if he found it a really amusing idea, "that you are more Christian than the lot of us, him included."

Father Gallifa! I'd completely forgotten that old Jesuit. Ramon, do you remember those "talks" he'd give us every Sunday after mass, in the church of San Lluís de Gonzaga, the poor fellow's boring "talks"? To be frank, I felt disappointed: I wasn't going to be a martyr and there would be no reformatory. But the mention of Father Gallifa did make an impact. I went to see him as soon as I left that office; the monastery on carrer de Casp was only round the corner . . . He saw me in his cell, which smelled like the typical cramped space that's never properly aired, what you called "the odour of sanctity" when you still allowed yourself to crack that kind of joke. Everything was exactly the same as when you and I used to go there: the small table, the reed chair, the little iron bedstead that was practically a child's. He sat on the chair and told me to sit on the bed and I thought how he'd aged since the last time we met.

"I've not come to listen to any sermons," I said, "but to thank you."

"I'm not interested in your thanks, keep them to yourself. I'd only ask you to listen to me for a short while, not long, as I know you've always found me a bore."

He said that with a kind of inferiority complex I found disarming. He was like a poor uncle asking for a big handout from his rich, important nephew.

"You may not have grasped that I too am a bit of an anarchist." He smiled as if he'd cracked a joke. "The social encyclicals from the popes —"

"Father Gallifa," I interjected, "if only you knew how all that business about the industrial revolution, the proletariat, surplus value, a planned economy, leaves me completely cold . . ."

"So you aren't an anarchist?"

"How do I know? What does being an anarchist mean? If only one could know what one is, or what one wants. What if I told you I couldn't care a fig about all that . . . Anarchism! What if I told you it all came from some witty remark Soleràs made, that essentially all he ever wants is a good time . . ."

The expression in Father Gallifa's tiny tired, bloodshot eyes switched from one of surprise to shock, and from shock to sadness, "Poor Lluís . . . now you've got this far, for whatever reason – who is this Soleràs? A friend of yours? – you should take a moment to think these matters through. You frighten me, Lluís, not because you are an anarchist, but because you aren't anarchist enough. I mean you should take it in good faith, good faith can save lots of things. Anarchism has lots of excellent points, if you know how to pick and choose . . ."

I burst out laughing. I found that apologia *manqué* for anarchism from the lips of a Jesuit so absurd. He smiled vaguely and for a second his expression was that of a blind man – that blind man who begged alms on the corner by the church of Bethlehem.

"Your uncle told me about a student girl you go for long walks with. I only know what he's told me, that she's an anarchist and that she has evil ideas. Do you know what I think? Love her, but with all your soul; love her as much as you can. If you can't believe in anything else, at least believe in anarchism. The important thing is to believe and to love if you believe in something; if you love with all your heart you'll eventually come to the right path."

He looked at me again with that tired, imploring, sad expression.

"Lluís, are you sure you love her, that you won't leave her?"

Back on the street, I was only ashamed of the fact that I'd cried. I was thinking about Trini's family, about the *La barrinada* group: "Luckily they'll never find out." What about Trini? I shall never tell her about this stupid exchange!

The next day we went for a walk in the Ciutadella Park. We sat on a bench under the leafless limes, not far from General Prim's equestrian statue. The park was damp, cold and empty; the smell of rotten leaves wafted through the air on a melancholy breeze. I felt old: I'd just celebrated my twentieth birthday.

"I will do what I feel like doing. They'll have to accept that."

But a sarcastic little voice within me whispered: what about Father Gallifa? I told her the Jesuit had spoken in my favour without going into detail; but what with one thing and another, everything came out as if I'd been talking to myself. I think that happened because she was listening so attentively; she was sixteen at the time. And I came out with what I'd wanted to hide from her: that I had cried at the end of the meeting.

"You see, I acted like a coward, or worse, like an idiot."

Trini said nothing. And then I told her about you, Ramon, because if she'd ever heard people talking about the Jesuits – and you can imagine the tone of voice – she'd never heard of St John of God. She said nothing and listened to me intently. I'd not yet mentioned you to her, isn't that unforgivable? Ramon, if you'd seen her eyes – they aren't pretty eyes, they're homely and round and a dull shade of green, though they look at you with such childish naïveté, ready to swallow whatever is good, noble and generous . . .

III

Six bulls limped out,
all six were lame,
that's why churches
were set aflame.
                    – Popular song, 1835

13 AUGUST

Captain Picó has organised a "republic", that is, a group of officers who dine together. It is the second to be organised in Olivel; a few days ago the commander and the doctor founded the first with Captain Gallart and the Publicist in support.

The great Picó has hoisted the anti-alcohol banner and as he is a pipe smoker the pipe has become the symbol of the new brotherhood, as against the "republic of the baby's bottle". The ex-porter has discovered a chef from the Hotel Colón among the machine gunners who rejoices in the name of Pepet – like so many other misunderstood geniuses – and is a silent, solemn man. Poor old Olegària can't compete with a rare bird like him, so I was quick to join the "republic of the pipe". I hardly need add that the nurse has also rallied to the pipe's cause along with two lieutenant gunners: we could have constituted a republic as ideal as Plato's if it weren't for a last-minute intruder. Like all intruders, at first he seemed to be the brightest pearl imaginable.

This new hero in the army of Catalonia arrived in Olivel a couple of weeks ago. We thought he'd come to organise the battalion's Communications section, as that was what the commander kept asking the brigade for: he was the Communications lieutenant we needed. The commander, who was floating adrift on hot air, didn't bother to look at his papers; it was enough to know he bore the Catalan surname of Rebull. He arrived in shirtsleeves, without stripes but clenching a big pipe between teeth gleaming white, as if advertising toothpaste. His shirt was spotless, his teeth amazing and, even better, he came haloed with the reputation for culture that is the hallmark of all Communications officers. "A true man of the world," as the commander put it.

Picó was as quiet as a cat burglar, but he'd already put all his pieces into play to prevent this outrageous pearl from joining the "republic of the baby's bottle". Right now, we'd happily hand over our acquisition. He turned out to be a poet. He recites verse from his own pen, and may they string us all up if we understand one jot. When we're having lunch he tells us we are prosaic, that times have moved on since Baudelaire and that we don't "experience the feminine". He also reckons we don't know how to smoke a pipe and gives us encyclopaedic instructions on the subject. But worst of all, he was never a Communications officer: he is . . . a political commissar!

When we finally got that out of him, there was consternation all round.

It's not that he's a communist – he doesn't even make it to socialist. What generated consternation was the threat of a fresh political barrage – new courses in republican education, lessons in rights and civic duties – and in effect he took no time at all to summon the whole battalion, commander, officers, petty officers and the ranks, to the castle's baronial hall to harangue us with the most pedantic speechifying on the subject of fascism and republicanism. Halfway through his speech, as we were dropping off, the commander stood up, livid, waving his arm, and exclaimed, "They are the baddies and we are the goodies and that's all there is to it! We know that by now, no need to tell us, we're fed up of being told, so start acting as a Communications officer if you don't want us to make your life a misery. If you don't know how, learn!"

There's another new, more interesting development in the battalion: it turns out that Cruells also knows Father Gallifa and calls him "Dr" Gallifa. In retrospect it's not really surprising that we both knew him but hadn't met each other, though it seemed like an extraordinary coincidence at the time. He told me things I didn't know: that, at the time of the laws against the Company of Jesus, Gallifa was forced to leave the monastery and go to live with a brother who owns land on Plana de Vic, or les Guilleries, and lives in a very old flat on riera del Pi. He says he lived there as a lay chaplain and came to the seminary as a teacher, and that's how he got to know him and why he always calls him "Dr". "Dr" Gallifa strikes me as very odd! I also find it hard to imagine him outside his cell. Ever since he found out that I know him, Cruells never stops talking to me about him.

"But he's so interesting," he assures me, astounded that I found his Sunday "talks" in the church of San Lluís de Gonzaga so boring.

The days and weeks seem long as if they are really dragging and I try to find distraction in battalion gossip, but there are moments when I feel absent, in a void, as if I've been struck on the head and am floating in a state of semi-consciousness. A letter from the *carlana* is obsessing me. This woman is disconcerting: she's sent me a letter when I live just round the corner! The battalion postman delivered it to me; it was franked in Mora de Albullones – I haven't a clue where this village is. Who can have posted it there? It isn't dated or signed and the style is so ambiguous I didn't understand a word. She listed the names of the murdered friars. "These were the ones who were definitely murdered, the ones whose corpses were found." And she reminded me of that famous favour she'd mentioned the other day: "It will be so easy for you." So easy . . . to start with, I hardly know what it's all about. I still go to the monastery almost every day, I inspect the piles of books; I look through documents in the sacristy and the cells. It's like looking for a needle in a haystack. Such a large monastery, sacked, ravaged, burned and finally abandoned to the elements for months and months . . . Worst of all she forbade me from going to see her until I'd found this certificate: "Don't try, I won't see you." Her ban upset me to the point of making me lose all sense of what's ridiculous: I wrote to her – I don't know what I wrote! I was drunk, but on what? Is this what they call passion? At any rate, it was something I'd not felt till then. I don't know what value a feeling like this has; I'm not really bothered either. All I know is that the sting of desire is so great that even if she caused me more torture, I'd still want to feel that sting, and even more intensely . . .

I was in the sacristy in the monastery and the air seemed heavy and dank like stagnant water; I felt absent from the world, as if adrift. The sacristy smells of fine wood, of ancient cedar wood, a dry, rather bitter smell: a smell . . . like hers. She has some grey hair, perhaps four strands; I've counted four. I'd got close to her and smelled the cedar scent of her hair; and those four shocking, shameless threads shone like the ones spiders spin in the night that you find in the early morning thanks to drops of dew the sun hasn't yet evaporated. Fragile, delicate, early morning cobwebs are so brittle, but those four strands . . . She'd turned round to take an item of clothing from the table and I was tempted to kiss her on the neck, under the ear. I didn't, and still regret it; my lips would have felt her throbbing blood – blood that must be a warm rich red. She'd have turned brusquely and I'd have seen an expression of huge surprise in her eyes – that she would probably have faked – because she must know I'd take the wrong step one day . . . The smell in the sacristy comes, of course, from the large empty cedar-wood cupboard where they must have stored the items and clothes the priests wore. The sacristy looks straight over the main altar, next to the epistle side. In my search for the mysterious certificate I'd examined every inch of that enormous cupboard, and when I turned round, almost fainting from the smell of cedar and incense, I saw the bride and bridegroom, the only two I could see through the narrow sacristy door.

Is this what she will become one day? Will the rich, warm pomegranate flower, the scent of cedar and incense in her hair be reduced to this stiff, incomprehensible stillness? A kind of robotic action led me out of the sacristy and I found myself face to face with the sly crook that seemed to look into space like someone in on a grotesque secret and pretending. It's an odd fact that they weren't accustomed to closing eyes in this monastery; they look at us and don't see us . . . And the snarling face of that sly crook was there, opposite me, so stiff; I remembered Soleràs, and the things he'd told me that seemed crazy now took on some meaning. Because the mummy stood between my thirst and the forbidden font; not the one I could see here, but mine, the one I will become. And hers . . . A feeling of quiet disdain propelled me towards that cynical face, my mouth filled with saliva . . .

14 AUGUST

Picó has just discovered that Rebull is not only a political commissar rather than a Communications officer, but that he's come from the "flatfooted" brigade to boot. He was their company commissar; now they've promoted him to battalion commissar and landed him on us. The party he represents has also been clarified: the Left Federal Nationalist Party of the Ampurdan. However incredible it may seem – and what can we think of as incredible after what we've seen and still see? – of the hundreds of parties that exist to sour our lives there is one that actually carries such a name.

As for the "flatfooted" brigade, I should perhaps tell you about this renowned unit that's a constant topic of conversation here. It's the second brigade in the division – ours is the first. They say, and as I wasn't there I wouldn't put my hand in the fire, that its commander excused them from involvement in the last round of military operations, "it being the case", he stated in his communiqué, "that most of the recruits who have joined us are flatfooted despite all the medical checks, and they won't withstand a long march." At the present time, this brigade covers the section of the front to our south. As I've gradually discovered, a fierce rivalry has existed between them and us from the beginning of the war and it's mainly to do with political squabbles: they are more hot-headed than we are.

Ever since we've had a political commissar, the commander has been trying to put the fear of death in him by stressing his idea of "restoring order in the monastery".

"Our brigade fights for hygiene and culture; it's not like the 'flatfooted' kind," he says, looking askance at the commissar. "The day will come when we must reinstate the hallowed mummies" – his actual words – "in their niches, with a proper, solemn ceremony: a culture without funerals isn't worth its salt. We should be discussing right now which funeral march would be most fitting, just as it would be an excellent idea if the same people who disinterred them buried them as a way of absolving themselves in respect of the deceased, because even if they are deceased they still deserve our respect."

Needless to say, political commissar Rebull has to act as if he enthusiastically supports the idea. The funeral march has led to endless arguments, and I should tell you we now have a drum and bugle band, hence these frays. We don't have any accompanying instruments as yet, but we do have drums and bugles. The little detail of the funeral march is the reason why we haven't yet staged the ceremony. It turns out that, in his heyday in the Foreign Legion, Picó had been trombonist under the flag for a few weeks. Not that he knows his scales, because he doesn't have a clue;

however, he played by ear the "Death of Åse" from *Peer Gynt*, and that fills him with legitimate pride. He often hums it to us after a meal so we don't doubt his past musical triumphs. As for the commander, he's a fanatical Wagnerian and is pushing for Siegfried's funeral march. It's been left to Dr Puig to arbitrate: he likes an easy life and washes his hands. He assures us that of the poor lot on offer he prefers Verdi to Wagner: "At least he had more of a sense of humour." On the days when the band is rehearsing he puts the sickroom under lock and key and closes the shutters so as not to hear. Inside he plays Chopin's funeral march on the violin.

16 AUGUST

As the annual fiestas in Olivel were yesterday, we'd invited the commander and doctor to lunch in our republic. They came at one on the dot, winking at each other. What were they hatching? Picó kept his eye on them throughout lunch and never lifted his foot off the pedal; the great Picó had also invented a device to frighten off the flies: "a practical man", as Soleràs had told me. It comprises a real table-sized fan that hangs from the ceiling and a frame, made from four sticks of bamboo, which gives it the necessary tautness. The end of the long piece of string that dangles through a small pulley is attached to a pedal. Seated like a patriarch at the head of the table, Picó works the pedal and the fan scatters the clouds of flies. Before he came up with his brilliant invention they dropped into our stew by the fistful.

General conversation. The doctor tells us he'd been summoned to the castle in Olivo the day before by the brigade's Health section: "The Health section captain had received a circular from the Army Corps. And it was very alarming too. Just imagine that there is a unit in our division, the 'flat-footed' brigade to be precise . . ."

A sideways glance at the political commissar, a wink in the direction of the commander, a small cough: "Well, doctor, sir," responds the commissar, "what were you saying about the sadly famous 'flatfooted' brigade?"

"*Mictionis caerulea* . . . a most rare disease! For the moment, it's the only known case, but it is one hell of a case! The patient was in no pain, felt wonderfully well; 'nobody could have anticipated such behaviour', in the words of one Dostoyevsky. Early one morning, two days ago, when he wakes up and realises his uniform is too tight, he tries to put it on but can't, he's swollen up during the night! He can't do his buttons up; he needs a good extra seven or eight centimetres for the buttons of his fly – Gentlemen, I say 'fly' because that is the *mot juste* – to reach the corresponding holes . . . It isn't forbidden to talk of flies in this brigade, I presume? As for his urine, well, it comes out blue; it is blue, and keep this in mind, because blue urine is the inevitable symptom. The death agony begins within a few hours and is horrifically painful . . ."

"What terrible symptoms!" exclaims the commander. "But what else can one expect from the 'flatfooted' brigade? I'd always suspected it was plagued. What do you reckon, Rebull? In your status as political commissar, you must surely have swallowed the *Complete Works of Hegel*."

"Hegel went out of fashion some time ago," the commissar pontificated; and for the moment nothing more was said on the subject of the lethal *Mictionis caerulea* because the conversation turned to the influence in Marx's *Capital* that can be traced to Hegel, a subtle philosophical matter that, as you can imagine, hardly sparks off our passionate interest.

Today – naturally – a Rebull in pyjamas appeared at break of day in the battalion's sickroom, pale, out of sorts and sweating blood.

"The poor fellow," Cruells told me, "was a sorry sight. I accompanied him back to his bedroom; the water in his glass, on his bedside table, still bore traces of cerulean, a harmless substance that gives urine a blue colour. And it was obvious someone had unravelled and then re-sewn his trouser fly, and very poorly, that's for sure . . ."

17 AUGUST

One evening I found myself back at the crossroads where I saw her for the first time; it was less than two months and it already seems like an eternity. Two months can plumb the same depths as two thousand years. That evening two months ago feels as distant as the world's first dawn and the memory of her appearance as deeply submerged as memories of my remote past.

I stayed there well into the night. A nocturnal bird – perhaps a nightjar – was gliding rather than flying above the ground. It suddenly landed in the middle of the path, as if waiting for me, and when I got nearer it quickly took flight again, silent as a moth. The heat of the day was rapidly fading and the breeze brought a bitter forest-like smell that made me think of her hair. While glimmers of light remained I felt like a bow drawn painfully tight and had a splitting headache; as darkness descended a weight seemed to be lifted from my shoulders, as if the bowstring had slackened.

After supper I went out to enjoy the cool in the streets. Gallart was standing under the boarding house window with a guitar. Where can he have got that?

"Melitona, should I sing you a romantic song from my neck of the woods?"

And he started crooning a profoundly melancholy ditty:

> We want bread and olive oil,
> bread and olive oil we want . . .

18 AUGUST

I went to the Albernes mill to see how those good folk were getting on. The mill looks more like a castle than the castle itself; the walls of the dam were built from limestone ashlars that five centuries of sun have gilded – I say "five centuries" because of the date above the entrance. The millers' house that backs onto the dam, also built of limestone ashlars, is only broken by a mullioned window and an arched doorway. In the front is a large kitchen garden with a fountain half hidden under a thick, tangled vine. Water spurts from a greenish bronze pipe into a red rustic jasper basin, the edges of which have been worn away by the many animal snouts that have drunk there and the many pitchers rested there. I gather that until the Parliament of Cadiz abolished seigneurial rights small farmers within the castle's jurisdiction were obliged to bring their wheat to be milled here.

The millers welcomed me with great glee and told me "the laydee" was upstairs, "by the water wheel". I wasn't expecting to find her here and didn't dare go up.

"The laydee will be upset if you don't say 'ello . . ."

They were so keen to do the right thing by the "laydee" and for me to do likewise! Of course, they didn't know she had forbidden me to go near her and I could hardly explain that now. They pointed to a steep, narrow path that climbed from the orchard to the top behind the pond.

It is a pretty place and as well kept as a garden: the pond, the "water wheel", with a reflection of a large weeping willow on this side and a little juniper wood at the back, halfway up the slope. The children were swimming and she was keeping an eye on them, sitting on a rock in the shade of the weeping willow.

She didn't notice me because her back was turned to me. She was using the time to mend a garment and was slightly stooped over her sewing. Her two children were screaming hysterically and splashing. Their little bodies covered in pearls of water glinted like copper and the sunbeams filtering through the weeping willow's leaves wove rainbows on the water they splashed up.

I drew nearer, treading on the soft grass along the edge of the irrigation channel that bubbled and gurgled along.

"Good afternoon. I didn't expect to find you in Albernes."

She turned round, astonished.

"You? Here?"

Her shadowy eyes seemed to be saying, "I wasn't expecting to see you so soon."

"Have you brought the certificate?" she whispered when I sat down next to her, visibly making sure the children didn't hear. The certificate? My mind went blank; what with that night-time forest smell and the lightning flashes from her eyes . . .

"Why don't you give me an answer?"

"What?" I replied like an idiot.

The certificate? Which certificate? The night-time forest scent she gave off, her eyes blinding me . . .

"I've searched everywhere." I had to make an effort to concentrate my mind. "I've found nothing that looks remotely like a certificate. Believe me, I'm really sorry. Couldn't you give me more precise indications? You can't imagine the number of books and papers strewn around in one great mess."

Her steely look went from surprise to stupefaction, from stupefaction to sarcasm, then to a mixture of pity and contempt. She responded with a resigned sigh, "I see I can't rely on you."

"But you didn't give me the faintest idea where I might find this document," and once again I had that unpleasant feeling of speaking to a taller woman.

"If you make no effort to understand . . . How can you expect me to be understanding towards you, if you aren't with me?"

Her mocking glance had turned into a glint charged by confused promises and blurred complicity. My head went into a spin.

"I do understand you. I'm beginning to understand you. You're made of ice, and precisely because you're made of ice . . ."

"Don't go down that path. For the moment I'm only interested in the certificate. The future of my children depends on it. So please leave now; we've said all we had to say. You're a polite, well-bred young man; in that respect I trust you entirely. You won't betray a poor woman."

A poor woman? Anything but! I'm writing in my bedroom – the one that belongs to the grandson of old Olegària, that Antonio López Fernández I've never met and probably never will. The setting sun filters one last vinous beam through a crack in the shutter and comes to rest on her letter. A letter written on lined paper, the sort maids in service once used; her writing reveals a hand that's not accustomed to writing: large, misshapen letters, committed to paper slowly, one by one. But it was never a letter sent by a poor woman! The spelling mistakes on my table silently exhale the cool clean scent of freshly mown grass.

IV

Eppur si muove.

19 AUGUST

Our eyes sometimes have quite inexplicable lapses. For example, how can I have possibly walked past the cell with the bees so often and not noticed the words inscribed in charcoal on the wall? They're even in huge letters: *Eppur si muove.*

Eppur si muove. Did the anarchists write that to indicate that they were avenging the memory of Galileo? I doubt the anarchists on the Olivel de la Virgen's committee had ever heard of Galileo or had a clue about astronomical matters. So then, who was amusing himself embellishing the wall with this erudite quotation? I'm at a loss.

The most extraordinary side to this is that there was a volume beneath the inscription I'd never seen before either – and yet it was very visible, by itself, away from the heaps of books, its studded wooden covers filled with parchment. On the spine, handwritten in Gothic script, it reads: *Book of the Deceased*. There are entries for the deaths of friars from 1605 to the very eve of the cataclysm: indeed it seems there was even a death by natural causes on 17 July, 1936. Oh happy days in a past when friars died of natural causes!

How could I not have noticed such a large tome?

The pages are blank after that last entry – about halfway through the volume – and I'd never have thought to look further if there hadn't been a strip of red card sticking out near the back. I opened the volume there and found a different frontispiece, "Booke of Holies Matrimonies in which will be wrytten those contracted by the devoute in the church in the monasterie of Our Lady of Mercie of Olibel with the permission of the Ordinarie and seal of the reverend priests of the parish. Anno Domini 1613."

My pulse beat like a hammer on an anvil. I suddenly realised the following: The Virgin of Olivel – as my landlady in Castel de Olivo had told me – is much revered in the district and is the patron of happy marriages;

it is, in miniature, our Montserrat.* From devotion rather than pious belief some couples sought permission to marry there rather than in the parish of the bride, as laid down by canonical law. The friars kept a register of these marriages that were, in fact, few: fifty-seven from the first they had noted in the year 1613.

20 AUGUST

I am invited to dine at the "republic of the baby's bottle". Afterwards, when the rest were drinking their coffee, the commander took me off to his bedroom. "Listen, Lluís," he put his finger on his lips, signalling he was about to reveal a deep secret: his binges usually start like this. "I must tell you about some of the mysteries in my life, terrible mysteries! If the 'flat-footed' brigade . . ."

He staggered over to the door, closed it cautiously and then looked under his bed and each chair in case a spy from the rival brigade was hiding there; finally, reassured on that front, he stretched out on his mattress. All that without letting go of a barn owl he'd "fished", as he put it, the previous night from its nest in an olive grove.

"You know it's an owl of my vintage, but it catches incredibly huge numbers of flies. I don't know if I'll be able to keep it. This lot," he gestured vaguely towards the dining room, "are a bunch of drunks; they go from one drunken binge to another like butterflies flitting from one flower to another. In a moment you'll hear them spitting their coffee out. Don't tell anyone," and he put his finger back on his lips, "but I filled the sugar bowl with salt."

"Commander, I know mysteries much more terrible than yours."

"More terrible? Where are they? Under the bed?"

"Nothing like that. In the monastery in Olivel."

"The mummies!" He stared at me, his eyes bulging out of their sockets.

"They aren't mummies, Commander; luckily they are alive and healthy – two children who love each other."

* The Black Virgin kept in the monastery in the mountains of Montserrat and a symbol of Catalan nationalism.

"I don't like stories about mummies, Lluís . . ."

It was hard to channel him where I wanted him to go. I thought if I managed to get him to mount his horse, a ride in the open air would help clear away his drunkenness. It suited me fine if he was a bit tipsy, but not that much.

"Commander, whether these children have a father or not depends on you . . . Imagine Marieta . . . without a father . . ."

His dark beady eyes looked me up and down and quickly began to fill with tears. "Marieta doesn't want them to kill her dad. She really doesn't!"

"Well, boots on, Commander. Let's not waste another second."

I pulled them on him; he let me do that as docilely as could be while he kept a tight hold on the owl. In the dining room they were spitting out their coffee and splitting their sides laughing, and didn't notice when we left.

The commander's horse, which he rarely rides, is as fleet of foot as Acorn; we galloped the whole way. Once we were in the sacristy he sat down on the floor because he couldn't stand up straight; "I'll teach the band a really funereal march because one shouldn't make fun of the dead. Who does Picó think he is? I'm the commander, not him."

"Absolutely right, but listen . . ."

The wine made him belch, a huge, resounding, lengthy, modulated belch: afterwards he seemed calmer, as if that magnificent belch had cleared his brain.

"I'm all for Wagner, you know. I want funeral marches that are the real thing, the ones that speak to the depths of my soul. Ah, there are so many mummies . . ."

It was now or never: "Commander, the register of deaths and marriages is in this cupboard. I've found a very important entry among the latter. I beg you to pay close attention. The future of two innocent children is at stake."

It made a much greater impression than I had anticipated: he read and reread the last entry in the register and tears the size of chickpeas rolled down his cheeks.

"And to think that the old women in Olivel, those magpies, call them bastards . . . So why doesn't the lady of the castle protest?"

"She's afraid people won't believe her; and also because of the purely religious nature of the wedding. Just think, Commander, the anarchists have been here and we don't have such a wonderful reputation. We aren't exactly thought of as Jesuits."

"One of these days I'll line up the battalion and they'll say the rosary to a man. Who the hell do they think they are?"

"Yes, Commander, we all know you're a champion of order and culture, but all the same they dumped a political commissar on us, and worse still, he's from the 'flatfooted' brigade. With one stroke they dragged our prestige through the mud."

"I'll scare him so much he'll beat it like crazy! You just watch, Lluís, see me get on with it. I'm your father, for heaven's sake, I'm the battalion commander! I watch over you. I was the one, you know, who unpicked and re-sewed his trousers, when he was asleep. The doctor wanted to help but he was too drunk and couldn't thread the needle however much he screwed his eyes up. It was left to me to perform that delicate sewing operation."

"While we wait for the commissar to clear off from the battalion, and he'll take his time because he's like a pot of glue, we must carry out this righteous deed. Why didn't the lady of the castle say something? Just think for a moment how the friar superior and the other four friars who were witnesses were murdered the following day, and she may not be aware that the friar superior wrote this entry in the register before he was murdered. She knows that not one friar escaped alive."

"But some did escape through the woods, everyone agrees on that."

"Yes, Commander. I'd also clung to hopes that one of the signatories of the register was among them. But they are all dead, dead as doornails: I've checked that. The villagers identified the corpses."

"The friars who survived could make a declaration to the effect that the marriage took place, even if they didn't sign the register."

"The marriage took place after the survivors fled. As regards the people who were still in the monastery, just remember that the anarchists executed even the day labourers – three or four men, the poorest in the village the friars paid out of charity. They were so poor they wore wooden clogs . . ."

This gave him a real jolt: his eyes glinted with energy.

"How do you know? Were you there?"

"The *carlana* told me. I know every detail because of her. The anarchist committee assassinated the parish priest; the *carlà* was afraid, rightly, that he would meet the same fate. He thought of escaping; but foreseeing the risk that he might be killed if he failed, his conscience began to stir. He decided to marry the mother of his children before fleeing. It was impossible to do so in Olivel, since they'd killed the parish priest, so the monastery was his only option. The members of the committee were all from elsewhere and hadn't yet realised it existed; the villagers kept quiet about it because they loved the friars. That same night the castle lord saddled Acorn and went there secretly with his lady riding behind. The younger friars had fled: the friar superior and the remaining four were about to. In the circumstances, the marriage was held *in articulo mortis*. They rode back equally secretly to Olivel and the *carlà* was preparing to make his escape, after leaving her in the castle, when the seven anarchists arrived . . ."

The commander listened excitedly: "So, naturally, no-one knows apart from her. They're all dead . . . What does one do in a case like this? You're a lawyer, Lluís; you must know the tricks of the trade; advise me. We must make ripples with this one, show we're not a bunch of Jesuit-eaters like the 'flatfooted' brigade. Back in Barcelona, I have a blessing from the pope *in articulo mortis* . . ."

"We'll start by taking statements from the witnesses."

"Witnesses? Didn't you just say they were all dead and mummified?"

"The men who raided the niches may know something. We'll get them to sing."

Once we were at H.Q. he handed me my appointment as a prosecutor. I saw those six fellows; six wretches willing to declare anything under the sun provided we didn't execute them. They *always* think we want to execute them. They came to H.Q., one after the other, cowering like beaten dogs. The file fattened. They sat down and signed an impressively endless rubric. I don't think they understood a word; they felt too happy they weren't being executed to ask for explanations.

Restituto, who's not quite all there in the head, had got tangled up with a double mattress that his wife had tied him to with a rope round his body. You could only see his head and feet. All Olivel came to their windows to stare: "What the hell's up with you, Restituto?" "Crikey, that should silence the bullets!"

I returned to old Olegària's really late. She can't go to bed until I'm back, even though she's not cooking my supper anymore. She sat in a low chair by the fire for it gets cold at night; poor summer, your glory is uncertain too . . . I sat down next to her – as I did to have my breakfast before the "republic of the pipe" was founded. In the early days the old girl gave me ridiculous things for breakfast, like jerky soaked in vinegar or salted herrings with hot pepper, while I'm the sort who can at most down toast dunked in white coffee. She thinks milk is for the ailing; and as for toast, "Joshua! What a waste of bread!" And she'd make the sign of the cross watching me stick a slice over the embers on the end of a fork. Toasting something as hallowed as bread . . . what a sacrilege! I also had to brew my own coffee; she didn't know what coffee was and once when she took a sip she spat it out like poison.

"Old Olegària, what can you tell me about the lady of the castle?"

"She's no laydee, Don Luisico. The 'ole village knows 'oo she is."

"The village could be wrong."

"How could the 'ole village be wrong? She's from Castel, from the Turdy 'ousehold, that's what they call 'er father."

"I know, old Olegària. Santiaga told me. Even if she hadn't, I'd have guessed that Turdy's daughter and the lady of the castle were one and the same. Some things hit you in the face: the loose ends tie up of their own accord. Poor lady of the castle . . ."

"Poor laydee my backside! If you'd have met the laydee 'oo's deceased, may she rest in peace, now she was a real laydee. We'd all line up by the spot where the boundary cross used to be and welcome 'er when she came to Olivel. She'd ride up real laydee-like in 'er trap, pulled by a mule. I can see it now, a gleaming dapple grey, stuffed with carob beans, treated better than any pope. May she rest in Glory now."

"The lady or the mule?"

"When she died she didn't know she'd get grandchildren from the servant. I mean the old laydee of the castle, and it do seem like only yesser'day when the rumour went the rounds: 'The laydee's 'ad a stroke.' She lived stuck in that wheelchair, poor thing, and 'er son mekkin' 'er a granny behin' 'er back. That vixen turned up the summer after she died; in the family way, and all eyes were on 'er belly. The wimmin were gossipin' about note else."

"I can imagine."

"The village lads were up in arms at the shame of it and daubed the castle doors early the next morning."

"What do you mean? Daubed with what?"

"Well, what d'yer think?"

"What animals!" and to think that Trini and Ramonet, in these people's eyes . . . "My God, what animals!"

"The lord of the castle was furious when 'e saw it. 'e bid the people what done the daubin' to do the cleanin'. As 'e gave them day wages now and then, they 'ad to obey."

"And he was right, only piglets . . ."

"Piglets are women who don't 'ave any shame. Wimmin around 'ere don' live in sin, thanks be to God."

"There are children, dear old Olegària, and they're not to blame. They're innocent."

"Innocent they ain't. They are bastards."

No point arguing, logic isn't her strong point. I try to get my way by another route.

"Dear old Olegària, you love your grandson."

"Joshua! Don' I do right?"

"If your son-in-law had married your daughter in untoward circumstances, before he died, and the marriage had remained a secret, your grandson would be a bastard, as they say in this village, and he couldn't be called Antonio López Fernández, just plain Antonio Fernández."

Her bleary eyes regarded me blankly. How could her grandson be a bastard? How could he not be a López? Some things require . . . too much imagination . . . !

The fire was gradually dying in the hearth and in the dim glow old Olegària, mouth gaping wide, looked like a witch; she stared at me taken aback, almost in a state of shock, as I told her my version of the facts. It's very late and I can sleep peacefully: now my version, on old Olegària's lips, will run through the village like a dose of salts. And the night-time breeze blows through my open window, bringing the song of the crickets and soaked in the scents of the death throes of summer.

21 AUGUST

A new development in the battalion. The commander received an order from the head of the brigade to have our battalion ready tomorrow. He'll be coming to make an inspection. Nerves, panic and frantic activity; we've spent the day drilling. Recent recruits are poorly prepared and it's our fault: we've pathetically wasted our time on the "baby's bottle", "pipe" and other foolishness. Even today, despite the panic, Gallart and Rebull have been up in arms: they've been swearing and cursing, and all because of Melitona, the blonde innkeeper. Picó had to sort them out: "What the hell has she done to make you so crazy?"

Obese, red in the face and sweating, Gallart tried to find excuses: "Well, haven't you noticed the stir she causes when she walks up and down her tavern? She's no tambourine shaker, more a brigade drum major!"

"If that's the case," Picó declared philosophically, "you have my permission to crack that nut together in peace."

Each company drilled separately, ours on the threshing ground. But how can you teach in a day what we should have taught those soldiers over many weeks?

It's late and I'm exhausted. Because of this furore there's been not a whisper in the battalion about the news of the day in the village. Old Olegària was saying: "To think how the kids chucked stones at them and we old 'uns said 'the bastards deserve it'! And now it turns out the poor littl'uns aren't bastards after all . . ."

22 AUGUST

Our day of triumph. The head of the brigade congratulated Commander Rosich: "I congratulate you, I congratulate captains and officers and congratulate N.C.O.s and troops; you are a battalion that's fit to engage in combat. Our brigade can be proud of you and the neighbouring brigade quite envious . . ."

The review took place on the esplanade in front of the monastery, the only space in the whole area where a battalion could be put through its paces. And our commander decided to choose that moment as an opportunity to give the friars a solemn burial. When would he have another such solemn occasion, with the whole battalion on parade in the presence of the head of the brigade and his chief of staff? The locals from Olivel took up their positions on the hillocks; Calvary was like an anthill. The mayor was in his Sunday best and a sight for sore eyes: black silk sash, black silk scarf round his head, brand-new rope and a tasselled walking stick. The day was as still as can be.

The head of brigade is a tall, stout lieutenant colonel in his sixties, an affable, courteous fellow with one distinguishing feature: he lost all his hair in his youth as a result of some illness – the whole brigade could tell you which – and wears a wig and painted eyebrows. This makes him look like a Japanese doll, a giant one, of course. Would you believe it? Catching a "walloping" bug gave him cachet in the eyes of the whole brigade – officers, N.C.O.s, the rank-and-file. "He's a real man!" "He's got balls!" His car glinted by the monastery door; next to it, our commander's vehicle, his blessed Ford, seemed a poor relation. The whole battalion had had to clean up the track with picks and spades so the whole length was wide enough to take a car, otherwise two of them would never have made it.

So much life and energy on that esplanade and inside it was so stiff and still . . . The battalion went through the motions to drum rolls and cornet blasts. I looked at my men, thinking: "What on earth have I ever taught them?"

Attention! The recruits stopped dead at the signal from the bugle. An unruly silence settled over the locals. The six idiots from the anarchist committee were sitting behind the mayor and they too were wearing their Sunday best. They stared at the Japanese doll with his medals and stripes with the eyes of hake unable to comprehend how they'd been hauled out of the water. The Japanese doll yawned and passed a handkerchief over his mouth in an elegant, half-hearted flourish. The moment had come. The moment to restore to mystery what belongs to mystery, to extend the veil once more and cover over what's macabre, as if it were obscene.

The half dozen hake slid the mummies back into their niches in sight of the battalion and the village – "*coram exercitu populoque*", said the Publicist, who'd clearly also spent time in a seminary. The battalion band struck up the "Death of Åse" and we initiates cast sideways glances at Picó, who was puffing away. He's not a man to become vain in victory.

The Japanese doll kept yawning as the six hake closed up the niches guided by a building worker. The fact is the operation was endless, and thus tedious. The last brick was finally laid and people started to disperse when Rebull, in his capacity as political commissar, felt duty-bound to give us a speech: "From this moment onwards, the intellect, that is culture, will float for ever over these corpses, because hygiene and culture are inseparable from a democracy that is liberal, radical and federal, but can never be clerical. No, my friends, no, my brothers, no, my companions, no, my comrades, let nobody be mistaken: we are not clerical, but we *are* liberal, radical and federal . . . and *we* are the pillars of these social ideals . . ."

Nobody was listening; the villagers barely understood Catalan and we'd had enough of his litanies. And this is what our commander said: "Would the political commissar please stop haranguing us and let us get on with the war in peace."

The brigade has decided to post guards by the entrance until such time as the monastery is restored to its rightful owners, the Order of the Merciful Virgin. The lieutenant colonel whispered to the commander, but loud enough for the officers to hear: "The flatfooted lot could never have put on such a splendidly orchestrated performance. They don't know what hygiene and culture are . . ." We felt flattered and laughed as he winked at us and hugged the commander before getting into his car. When he drove off, the troops and locals applauded as one. We're agreed that our lieutenant colonel is a most delightful man. "Just imagine, he's from Manlleu," said Gallart, who declares he knows that for sure.

Privately, when we were having supper in our republic, Picó explained the mystery of the funeral march: "Our battalion is like a married couple: he's the commander but I wear the trousers."

The success of our enterprise has taken us by surprise: the mayor and justice of the peace say that they already knew, that they had heard it from the lips of the lord of the castle. The commander has taken it on board and keeps asking for fresh statements. The mayor and the justice of the peace soon fattened the folder, quickly followed by the councillors and bailiff. The municipal secretary was the only one to be churlish; apparently he's a man of advanced ideas and very opposed to religious marriages, particularly when they are *in articulo mortis*, but the commander had a solo session with him, and when he emerged from the exchange he signed on the line just like the others.

I was keen to obtain this unanimous statement from the great and the good in the municipality, bailiff and town clerk included, because, in the prevailing climate, a merely religious marriage ran the risk of lacking a legal basis. All the loose ends were tied, everything was as planned: we had a marriage in canon and civil law.

Old Olegària was the biggest surprise of all; she also said she knew! I mean, that she'd known all the time. My head went into a spin and I asked her how come: "Well, the whole village knew," she replied. In the end, they'll convince even yours truly; how does the adage go, *vox populi vox Dei?*

I went up to the castle. I was received in the diner cum sitting room and the minute I walked in I noticed something new: a snapshot beneath the cornucopia. A man in his late forties: a plump, ordinary face, with bushy eyebrows over half-wily, half-simple eyes. I'd have mistaken him for a grocer whose corner shop was raking it in.

"My husband, may he rest in peace."

She said "husband" quite naturally. She was wearing a black silk bodice I'd not seen before with an enamelled gold and diamond brooch at her breast.

"He gave it to me as a present on my saint's day. I didn't ever dare wear it."

"It really suits you."

Her eyes were radiant with gratitude. Her children's bedroom door was open; I'd never seen inside before. It's very cheerful, gleaming white, reddish exposed beams – probably juniper; a trousseau chest by the wall, natural pine wood, without cornices or mouldings as is the style hereabouts, where it is still a common piece of furniture. A reed chair on either side of the chest; the two small iron bedsteads, painted pale red, are in a small alcove separated from the rest of the room by a very plain archway; the eiderdowns are cretonne with big red and white stripes, like the curtain hanging from the arch. There is a hand basin between the beds identical to the one I have at old Olegària's. A scent of lavender, of bitter almond soap, of linen sheets that have been stored with quince and apples wafted through the open door; bright, cheerful and simplicity itself.

"I'm so grateful. Thanks to you they'll have a name and status. You've worked wonders."

I looked at the two little beds and thought: it didn't strike me I was doing it for them.

"I'm delighted I could do it for you. Now we can call you 'the lady of the castle'."

"I couldn't care less. I wanted it for their sake."

"I didn't do it for them. I would be a hypocrite if I pretended I did. You know very well —"

"I'm so grateful." She cut me off with those quietly murmured words. She bowed her head and her eyes that were darker and brighter than ever looked at me askance. What did that look mean? I soaked it up silently, not daring to venture into the no man's land that lay between us. Yes, we were like two enemies barely separated by a scrap of no man's land overtaken by a heavy silence. She suddenly looked up and out of the window that was wide open as usual. Swallows flew to and fro; their mewling didn't reach that no man's land – it belonged to the outside world.

"I'd like to ask you something, Don Lluís."

I was upset by her "Don" – that was so unexpected.

"I don't address you as 'Donya Olivela'."

"Quite right: it doesn't fit. One must be born with that 'Don'. Your face says it: you come from the breed of gentlemen. Don't try to deny that. It's obvious, stronger than anything else. Experience has taught me that. I'd like to ask if I need to do anything else to ensure my children's inheritance."

"You need to legalise everything with a notary and take it to a court of justice. The nearest is two hundred metres from the front, but who knows where the nearest notary might be?"

More silence. I looked at her. She was staring vaguely into space, as if absorbed by something she couldn't find the words for. She was breathing deeply; with each intake she seemed to breathe in all the air in Olivel, air drenched in memories for her. A smell of fresh bread wafted in on a breeze from the three communal bakeries and mingled with smells of straw, sheep and basil – there's not a window sill in Olivel, big or small, that doesn't have its pot of basil to ward off the flies. Each smell must arouse in her an upsurge of faded emotions like the flocks of birds that fly up and scatter when people walk by, those preparing to migrate in the autumn. I said nothing. I waited for the magic word that would open up that inner world, so closed and forbidden, which made my head spin. She was equally silent; the magic word wouldn't be forthcoming.

"Olivela, you promised that you would read my letter if I found the marriage certificate . . ."

She stirred from her thoughts, as if rudely awoken, and gave me a look of surprise: "Yes, don't imagine I've forgotten. I read your letter and *naturally* I am grateful to you for your kindness."

The *naturally* was a scalpel that sliced through my heart.

"You are so kind," she continued, looking back out of the window. "I don't know if I can thank you for everything you've done. I would hate you to think I am ungrateful!"

"You don't need to thank me for anything. I'm not kind. What I —"

"I'd ask you for two days to think it over quietly. You must understand that with all this emotional turmoil I've only been in a fit state to think about my children. Put yourself in my shoes. Their lives were being decided. When Santiaga brought me the news, I fainted. I'd never fainted before. I'm sure I'll never faint again. You can't imagine how I was at my wits' end waiting on those decisions. It was all or nothing! No, you can't. In your letter, you tell me things, private things I'd never have told anyone, you know? Don't be upset if I say that I don't like these sorts of confession.

I can't relate to things like that. Believe me, they aren't things you tell other people."

"I would tell *you* everything, even my saddest inner secrets. I want you to grasp how much you —"

"Please stop." Her icy glance was more forbidding than her words. "Stop being so foolish and listen. As you've revealed such private matters in your letter, I'll match them with some of mine. Then you might understand me just a little. No, don't be under any illusion, you understand nothing! You've mistaken me for somebody else. I've felt that right from the start. I was born in Castel de Olivo; my father is a landless farmhand, one of the poorest in the district. I've not seen him for years. And don't want to. On the other hand, he no longer lives in Castel: he's in enemy territory."

"I know all about that. They told me in Castel when I was far from ever thinking that I'd get to know you, that one day you —"

"Do you know they call my father Turdy?"

"Yes, of course, I know all about that."

"A ridiculous business. Tragedies *are* ridiculous. It's not the poverty. Why should I worry if my father is poor? Nor am I embarrassed by his nickname, and I'd have good reason, don't you think? I've never done anything to hide it. No, it's something else. The rudeness and lack of sympathy . . . It's all very well to say that you should resign yourself to being the child of the parents you've got; that's very easy when, like you, one is a Don Lluís de Broca i de Ruscalleda."

"Not true," and I repressed a sad smile. "I'm not a 'de Ruscalleda', on the contrary, I'm 'Ruscalleda's Son, Fine Pasta for Soup'. If I told you . . . it would take too long. You fantasise about my family! I'm an orphan; I never knew my father or mother. And I've suffered more than my fair share of rudeness and lack of sympathy from my uncle . . ."

"Whatever you say, it's not the same. I don't know your uncle, but I'm sure he washes and doesn't swear and drink. Though I often wonder if some people are alcoholics, even though they don't drink, because my father doesn't drink, I can assure you. He doesn't have that excuse. He's not a drunkard. So let's forget all this. Tragedies are ridiculous and that's why sensible people avoid them. You're a qualified lawyer, an infantry aide-de-camp and perhaps other things not on file; I expect your wife has studied too, can play the piano . . . The piano! Can you believe I sometimes dream I'm playing one! Of course, I don't know my scales. I learned to read with the real lady of the castle; I find it hard to call her my mother-in-law. The good lady died never suspecting that's what she would end up being . . . She treated me very well: she taught me to sew, to embroider, to read, to write, to cook, even to speak, because I spoke the hotchpotch they speak in these villages . . ."

She was becoming animated, and her eyes sparkled in a way I didn't recognise. The wind from the past seemed to kindle a flame hidden beneath the ash.

"The lady played the piano very well; a strange, different music. I loved to listen to her. I'd be in my little room darning or ironing, and she'd play in the sitting room. She did once tell me what the music was; some strange names . . . I thought they were from another world. I'd so like to hear them again! I'd so like to! But in these villages . . . Don't think I didn't ever ask her to teach me! She didn't scold me; she was very good about it. 'Olivela, what use would the piano be to you? It's not for you; you learn what will be useful to you and don't crave other things.' She was right. Why would a servant want to learn to play the piano? And she couldn't ever suspect I could be somebody else. Poor Donya Gaietana, she was such a good person. If she had had the least suspicion, she'd have died from the shock. The poor woman started to grow old but she was never begrudging. One summer she gave me a week's holiday so I could be in Castel de Olivo for the annual festival. I was fifteen. I'd not seen my parents for two years. I went full of expectation. I loved my parents, can you believe that?"

"Everybody loves their parents until the contrary is proven. I, for example, am crazy about mine, though that doesn't stop me from some-times thinking: would that still be the case if I'd known them?"

"Do you know what it feels like to walk into the house where you were born so full of expectation and find . . .? Bah, tragedy's ridiculous. I don't want to play the victim. People have insulted and scorned me: when I came pregnant to Olivel, they even daubed the doors with —"

"Yes, I know."

"Well, can you believe that I prefer it if they hate me? Pity revolts me. It's a cowardly way people have invented to express their contempt and at the same time feel good. I prefer them to spit in your face, daub your doors with . . ."

I was shocked to see her so uncontrolled. She always kept her feelings on a tight rein.

"You're so young. When you reach my age, you'll realise that loneliness is our daily bread, out-and-out loneliness." Her magnificent contralto voice, fired by passion, made her tremolo resonate even more deeply. "And we should face up to it, see it as it is. Listen, please; don't interrupt. I know you won't understand, but so what. Why should you? I couldn't care less. I want to tell you everything. I feel you've created a fantasy around me, and I'd like to tell you that we women don't like that sort of thing. We don't like being seen as angels; it's uncomfortable and an imposition."

"I don't exactly see you as an angel."

"A vampire, then? Worse still. That would be even more disappointing."

"Neither vampire nor angel."

"A maid in service?" Her eyes flashed sarcastically. "Who managed to make it to mistress of the castle by the riskiest of routes?"

She stopped looking at me; there was a horrible silence that went on and on. I'd hit bull's eye, and finding her sore spot gave me tremendous pleasure. Perhaps passion is a cruel mystery. No pleasure can be compared to making one's idol suffer so we can wreak revenge for the way she inspires adoration!

She looked into the distance and started to speak slowly, whispering as if talking to herself: "What could I do to haul myself out of the pit? I had to return to Barcelona; where else could I go? The lady of the castle acted in an understanding way – provided distances were maintained. She welcomed and consoled me. Enric was twenty years older, a difference that seemed huge at the time; to begin with, I didn't understand his insinuations, the words he whispered in my ear, in the passageway. I should add that he seemed even older, because he was so fat, and premature baldness made him look highly respectable. What's more, the poor fellow was shy. The lady, when we spoke about my position, always said the same: 'In the end, Olivela, if your parents don't want you, I do: we are a Christian family and, thanks to God, an old-fashioned family.' Poor lady! She was more innocent than I was. She'd give me Sunday afternoons off, provided I spent them in a nunnery on carrer de Consell de Cent. I can see it now: the Convent for Domestic Servants. I'll not a hide a thing: the nuns treated me very well and they would have been delighted to take me as a novice. I could have been a nun in that convent, it was friendly, welcoming, clean and spacious. The Mother Superior liked me a lot. I didn't know which way to go. I couldn't see what would be best. If the master, that is, Enric, had been young and handsome, I'd have become a nun."

"I'm not sure I understood. Haven't you got that the wrong way round?"

"Wrong way round? Why?" She glared at me, surprised by my question. "If Enric had been young and handsome, I could only have hoped for a short-lived, trifling affair, the sort you don't even tell your friends about because they're pointless. Fortunately, he was fat and bald, much shorter than me and, most importantly, was already my father's age. He was my father's age but wasn't my father, and that was the big difference!"

"What was the difference?"

She looked at me as if she'd suddenly remembered she wasn't alone, that I was listening. She paused.

"I'll tell you the truth. I don't want you to think that I hated my father because he was poor." She was getting highly emotional again. "I've never told anyone, you will be the first and the last. I'd be upset if you . . . particularly you . . . I've never worried what others might think about me, but you're not like anyone else. I was hurt by what you said. Don't ever think that again, I'm not an evil woman." She was being so emotional now I thought she would burst into tears. "I'm just unfortunate, believe me."

"I believe you."

More silence. She was visibly trying to calm down. I thought: What if she really isn't evil? So what? What exactly is an evil woman? A woman who goes to your head? But what if it's no fault of hers?

"Of course, you've heard the story of the laundry tub; a very silly story. And you believed it, like everybody else. Like Donya Gaietana, like Enric even . . . It's so easy to blindly believe a story is true when it's so silly and so idiotic! My father never threw me out of the house. I left of my own accord. And I didn't even dry myself, because I *was* having a wash in the tub. I left dressed in whatever I could grab. I bolted. I needed to escape! I shouldn't say this, but my father always had a brutish face; usually though – how can I put it – it was the face of a tame brute. I'd never seen the expression he had that day; I don't want to see such a face ever again, anything but that! I let out a horrible shriek and ran off, knocking the tub over."

Silence descended again, and was nastier than ever. I looked at the ground.

"If only you knew how that wild face comes back to me . . ."

There was a shift: her contralto voice assumed its normal tone: "Enric, on the other hand, was never frightening. He seemed defenceless . . . He could seem a bit disgusting, because he was sickly: he'd had an unruly youth. He could offer me security and a quiet life. Wasn't it natural for me to do my sums? I thought that if I could get some leverage on him, I felt that would be easy enough, one day when his mother was dead I'd persuade him to marry me. I was wrong. 'Are you mad? You want me to marry Turdy's daughter? No chance!' 'They know nothing about all that in Barcelona,' I insisted. 'Everything comes out sooner or later.' And I couldn't budge him. I had no choice but to play for all I could get, especially now I was past thirty; I couldn't waste any more of my years. I'd already wasted too many!"

She spoke as if she were talking to herself, as if she'd blocked me out.

"I engineered it so his precautions failed. Such pathetic precautions! My God, isn't it pitiful? To think that's why men say and even do such horrible things . . . Well, they don't really; they think twice first. Once I was sure I was pregnant, I begged him to do the right thing by his son, and I played the religious card. I was certain of victory and was wrong yet again: 'Do you want to make me the laughing stock of all Barcelona? Me marry the servant!'

"I looked askance at his corner-shop grocer's face – no debts, no debtors, so smug and sly. No credit today, none tomorrow. This was Don Enrique de Alfoz Penyarrostra, lord of Olivel castle and prince of Aragon, as they call him in the papers I've just found."

"This fellow must have made you suffer a lot."

"Suffer?" and she looked at me so strangely again. Her contralto voice seemed distant and veiled, her tremolo fading as if far away or in a twilight zone, like that 'good afternoon to you' at the crossroads. "Please don't question me about my feelings for him. Why are men always so keen to find out this kind of secret? If you only knew how I hate being asked questions . . . Be satisfied with what I've told you, which is far too much. Think how you know all about my biggest secret, the secret between you and me, our secret – that my children will never find out!"

She looked at me knowingly, darkly, with more than a hint of mischief.

"Olivela . . ." I drew nearer to her, could see her four grey hairs, the fragile threads of a cobweb. "I'd like there to be not just one secret between us, but every possible secret, life and death secrets . . ."

The hint of mischief disappeared and gave way to a different, lucid gaze I'd never seen before, as if she were penetrating deep into my soul. I kept moving closer, could hear her breath, but that soon passed and her gaze assumed its usual slant. "No . . ." said her distant voice. "That would be too lovely. There are things that would be so good if they weren't so bad . . ."

"We could be happy just letting ourselves be swept along by the tide . . . a moment like that can transfigure a lifetime!" I didn't know what I was saying. "Why waste time on thoughts that only kill off the only thing that matters? We're linked to each other, let's be damned together. This lunacy alone makes it worthwhile!"

"Please," she really seemed scared and to be asking for mercy, "calm down. Can't you see you're taking advantage of my situation? Can't you see it's an appalling temptation . . . ? Nobody has ever loved me and now you speak to me as nobody ever has; now, when I thought I was an old failure, on the shelf for ever . . . when I wasn't expecting anything else from this world!"

"We have met, thanks to this blessed war," and I didn't know what I was doing but she stopped me. She made another of her disconcerting shifts and said, in the most matter-of-fact tone: "Come back the day after tomorrow and we'll talk about this." She shook my hands as if we'd been having a banal exchange about the weather or business: only a damp, grateful gleam deep in her eyes gave a different meaning to her gesture and words.

She acts innately like *une grande dame*: she knows how to assert her authority effortlessly, *comme allant de soi*. It's in her blood. Santiaga's hypothesis . . . In the end, after the stupid bathtub incident, wouldn't what Santiaga suspects be an infinitely better explanation?

24 AUGUST

There are repeated rumours of large-scale manoeuvres; the battalion will leave Olivel, probably for good. From my bedroom I can hear the sing-song voice of Captain Gallart booming out in the village square; the Publicist is accompanying him on that cracked guitar. It is a monotonous, mournful, enervating song, grimly cloying, like thick, sweet liquor, and underlined by the South American accent that Gallart thinks fitting:

> I lurved a girl in Olivel
> she didn't lurve me at all.

Referring to Melitona, naturally.

25 AUGUST

Our marching orders arrived early this morning. Destination unknown; we'll find out when we get there.

I went up to the castle. She was sitting in a low chair by the foot of the window, making lace.

"We're leaving the day after tomorrow."

"You poor things, off into the wilderness yet again . . ." She smiled and handed me a letter. "Here's your letter. Please burn it. I know you'd be all anxious in the future, wondering whether I kept it."

I didn't understand. I didn't know what she was talking about. A letter? A letter from me? What letter? I suddenly remembered. And I knew what she meant.

I knew what the gesture of giving it back was all about: "But . . . do you realise what it means if we leave? Do you realise we may never see each other again?"

"I wish you good luck."

"Ever again . . . do you know what 'ever again' means?"

"Shush, I beg you . . ."

"For you I have . . ."

"Shush or lower your voice, the children are here, they're still asleep."

"I could be in prison . . . and I have a son! Or haven't you grasped the seriousness of what you made me do?"

"I'm only too clear. Please calm down. I'm very grateful and will be as long as I live."

"What do I care about your gratitude?"

My hands were shaking. I must have looked absurd. If only I could find a sore spot, as I did the other day, and snap her out of her annoying complacency . . . I watched a chasm open up between a frantically passionate man and an ice-cold woman that invites one to act absurdly. I could see the abyss and took a step forward. I knelt by her side.

"Calm down. You're really agitated. You don't know what you're doing. If my children were to walk in now . . ."

I kissed her hands like a fool: "I do know what I'm doing. We are free; you are a widow . . ."

"But you aren't."

"I'm not married, as I told you in my letter."

"You're hallucinating. You don't know what you're saying. You'll regret this when you get over all the excitement. Would you leave your wife to marry someone . . . like me?"

She gripped her lace-making cushion between her knees. It shook under the impact of her loud laughter. How could she laugh like that? I felt like the most wretched man on earth.

"Whatever you say, you love your wife; all men love their wives, never mind the nonsense they dream up. Even Enric loved me, in his way; he was terribly bored, but he couldn't have lived without me."

"Don't compare me to him. We have nothing in common!"

"Meaning what? Why don't you marry Trini? Why don't you do right by your son? You men are all the same! It's us women who aren't at all alike."

"So which sort are you? A woman who coldly calculates everything, who's never swayed by feeling!"

"Get up for heaven's sake. The children will wake any moment now! You'd be horrified if you could see yourself in a mirror! You look so stupid."

"And why shouldn't we look stupid once in a while?"

"If you don't get up, I will. It's disgusting to see such a well-bred young man like you behaving so brainlessly."

It's easy to fall on your knees before a woman who has gone to your head, the difficult bit is getting back up on your feet.

"Now sit and listen." I obeyed like a puppet. "Put yourself in my shoes. How can you expect me to ruin everything I've set up just to please you? The best for me now would be if people stopped talking about me, if they left me in peace in my lair and forgot all about me. You did me a great favour. Don't destroy all your good work for a passing infatuation. Can't you understand? Don't you remember how I told you I was old enough to be your mother? If you were a widower and sixty, with six or seven children from his first marriage still on his hands, I might think you meant it and weren't raving. Leave your wife for me! Admit that such foolishness had never occurred to you till now and that when you recall this incident in the future you'll simply be embarrassed by what you said."

"You're a woman with a heart of ice. You guessed the impact you were having on me from the start and knew you could profit from it. You're incapable of love!"

"I love my children. Who do you want me to love? Every officer in the army of Catalonia who happens to pass through Olivel?"

"Who's thinking about any army or Catalonia? Is that all I am to you, just another officer passing through?"

"No. You are no old run-of-the-mill officer," and her expression was full of gratitude once again; a tear glinted in her eye but came to nothing. "I realised that from the start, Lluís. But you find it so hard to understand! Believe me, apart from my children, I've never loved anyone as much as I've loved you."

"You're lying."

"Believe me, Lluís. Why won't you believe me? Why won't you trust me? Why do you find it so hard to understand? An intelligent, well-bred young man like you . . . It's so simple! You'll find this incredible but I am really happy in this castle."

"You are —"

"Shush and listen. I am happy. You could only bring me more misery. I've had enough of that, and I don't feel like any more! I don't like feeling miserable and I say that because some people seem to enjoy it. I'm too aware of the ridiculous side of misery. And you shouldn't deceive yourself: you don't like tragedies either, you too are afraid of looking silly. Yes, you are."

"How can you say you are happy?"

"Why can't I? I love this castle. You said I'm incapable of love. What would you think if I told you I was deeply in love with this castle? This big country house smell," her expression became as serene and distant as ever, "the smell of well-being, of wardrobes full of linen," her eyes looked beyond the window, lost in the distance, as if she were dreaming aloud, "the smell of a fine house, of large rooms with high ceilings, of fine wood and linen . . . Naturally, you're not familiar with the reek of what's rancid and mouldy; maybe for a few days or hours, when you were in transit, but not for a whole lifetime! There's nothing like a large, antique sweet-smelling walnut wardrobe full of linen that is clean, dry, starched, folded . . . a smell of lavender and warm bread . . . Winter in this country is so long . . . The north wind blasts and howls eternally, the water freezes in hand basins in bedrooms. If you don't have a cellar, a pantry, a barn, firewood piled high outside the castle entrance and large wardrobes full of white bedding for the winter . . . Because it's not like Barcelona, here we don't wash clothes every three or four days or every week. As we do our washing in the river, we can't wash clothes in the winter. Here we do two washes in the whole year, at the beginning of spring and autumn. We load it onto one or two carts and take it to the river where village women are paid to wash the lot. They do nothing else for one or two weeks. You must think we have lots of clean clothes in a self-respecting house to do things this way! Well, we change ours every two or three days and pile the dirty clothes in an attic until the day for the big wash comes. I should tell you that we use ash from the hearth to make bleach, old-fashioned style. You can't imagine what it's like when the north wind starts to howl, believe me, it howls like a dying animal and makes your heart shrivel . . ."

"But in Barcelona . . ."

"I'd feel buried alive in a flat in Barcelona, as if I were back in my father's house. The time spent in Barcelona seemed so long from the very moment the lady of the castle told me to pack cases! I was frantic to come back to the castle. This castle . . . which I love much more than if I'd been born here; I love it as if I'd died here! I would feel so lonely without it to keep me company . . . Some feelings are so strange, you can't explain them because the words don't exist. This castle's rooms are so vast, its lands so extensive. I love nothing so much as to walk and wander across these expanses, particularly at twilight; I often take the children with me. That evening when we first saw each other, that you remind me of so often, I'd just walked the length of the Coma Fonda – don't be surprised by its name, a lot of land and areas within the district boundaries have Catalan names. And the Coma Fonda is but one of the farms that belong to the castle . . . I often take my children, but I prefer to go by myself, as I did before . . . long before . . . You need to experience the north wind howling through this village from early December to early April to understand these peculiar feelings of mine. Some feelings are so peculiar . . . as if one were remembering things from before one was born . . ."

What a great actor she could have been!, I thought; what a great actress! From the very first she's been performing a role for me, and so naturally! So easily she doesn't notice she's doing it! And her voice is such a help! What a contralto! The Liceu would collapse under the applause.

"It's been a pleasure to talk to you about these peculiar things," she continued. "That's why I shall always be grateful to you and love you, because you're the only person with whom that's been possible. How can I ever think you are just like all the others? When I can speak to you about that and you coax from me things that are so hard to express . . . There are stretches of land within the boundaries of Olivel that make me feel as if I'd lived many happy, solitary hours there, but when? I first came to Olivel when I was eight years old; they hired the girls in Castel for the grape harvest, to pick olives and harvest saffron. When the day's work was done I'd leave the gang and go for a stroll by myself across the castle lands. At dusk, a scent rises from the earth like the music the lady used to play, a scent from another world, and I felt I'd known that twilight scent for a long time, but how long? How long, for heaven's sake? Remember . . . remember what? What does it mean to remember? I have so little interest in the memories of my life, the life of a day labourer, of a maid in service, of a friendly village that once daubed her doors with . . . But there are other memories, another past . . . How could you expect me to leave this castle? They've told me so many stories about the place; they've told me it was so ancient . . . I was really drawn to it when I came from Castel with the gang of day labourers and saw it in the distance – and I was always the first to see it on the horizon, silhouetted against the sky. If only you understood . . . I could have found love, whatever you think; when I talk to you like this, I realise I could have found love, Lluís, and passionate love at that. Believe me, Lluís, I could; I could have loved Enric, but he hated this castle, he hated these lands. He wasn't happy here; when he was here, he only thought about Barcelona. After Donya Gaietana died, he even thought of selling up: 'This land isn't profitable: I could reinvest the capital in something productive.' Enric wasn't the type to strive to build a business; he only killed time in Barcelona. He'd go for a stroll in the port to see the steamers that had docked, or go to the Llotja and listen to the wholesalers raising or lowering the price of corn or barley, or wander off to plaça Reial to listen to the cheapjacks. He spent hours in the Liceu café where he met a man from Reus, an expert in manufacturing socks, who needed a partner with capital. If in the end he didn't sell up in order to finance a sock factory, it was because the poor fellow lacked energy and commitment . . . He was also shy. Just imagine how he spent his time in Olivel in the cellar, by himself in the dark, sitting hour after hour in the gloom, doing nothing. He hated the castle and its lands, yet I'd have loved him, yes, I would; believe me, I'd have loved him if he'd acted like the heir to these lands, the lord of the castle and master of the village. I'd even have understood if he'd not wanted to marry me; I'd have forgiven him that. The *carlà* of Olivel . . . But he thought that was a joke: 'Nobody in Barcelona knows what a *carlà* is. There's no point putting it on your visiting card. If you try to explain what it is, you look even more absurd. On the other hand, a manufacturer . . .' He also said that castles and *carlans* were past history. So why didn't he marry me? What was stopping him? If he wasn't the *carlà* . . . and he acted as if he wasn't! He didn't do anything the *carlans*

117

who preceded him did. As soon as Donya Gaietana was buried he sent the poor people who lived in the castle off to a workhouse in Saragossa. Of course, you don't know about this: previously, the poor in the boundaries of Olivel didn't have to go to the hospice because the castle took them in, the *carlans* looked after them. The 'soup kitchen' still exists where they ate lunch and supper; the fire has not been lit there once since Donya Gaietana died. He even got rid of the 'village barrel' – that was a big cask in the entrance, under the staircase arch, it was always full of wine anyone could come in and drink. In those days the castle gates were never closed night or day. Naturally, all the villagers blame me for these changes. After all, there are so few poor in a village like Olivel, where everyone has their house and strip of land! The odd cripple or childless widow . . . It cost so little to look after them! Why send them to the hospice far from everything that was their life? 'All that belongs to the past,' he'd say; but if all that was past history, what was stopping him from marrying me?"

I saw hatred for the first time in her eyes, a fire that diminished all other feelings, just as red makes all other colours turn pale.

"The castle . . . I could tell you so many strange stories about the place! But Enric acted as if he'd forgotten everything about it. One evening, Enriquet, who must have been four or five, came down from the attic with a baby owl. 'Put it back in its hole,' I told him. 'If you do, you'll find a coin.' I knew nothing about the coin, not even where the owl's nest was. It was a gold *unça*: the first I'd ever seen. I could tell you such strange stories . . . There was a face with a wig. One night . . . Why should I tell you? What would it mean to you? I love this castle; it's a source of great joy for me to think that my children were born and bred here. What do I care what it cost me to get here? I'd like to know how old these *unças* are? Are they from the grandparents' time? Or are they older than that? The great-great grandparents? It's all so very old! So very ancient! One can't keep track and it keeps you company. It keeps you company to think the great-great grandparents lived here, and that the grandchildren of the grandchildren will still live here. We are so puny. Children, grandchildren, great-grand-children, that's real might. Everything doesn't end with death! My God, don't let death be the end, or we'd be so petty. Children, grandchildren, great-grandchildren: they're born here and grow up here. The castle will always be full of memories for them. After I put them to bed, I go for a prowl round the castle every night. It's not because I'm afraid of thieves because there aren't any around here. I do that because I like to. Everything keeps me company: the mare kicking in the stable, the sow grunting, a mouse coming and going in the attic, even a woodworm gnawing in a beam. I like to see geckos on the wall, and I'm pleased to know there's an owls' nest in a hole in the attic and that the eaves are full of swifts and martins' nests . . . So much good company, so much life! A big house like this is like a frigate of stone, people and animals all on board, all sailing together in this huge ship that seems still but is moving across the ocean of time. If you only knew how depressed I was by the flat in Barcelona: it was so tiny, so dead and empty, no swallows' nests, no owls' nests, no cellars and no attics. Somebody in Barcelona once asked me if I wasn't afraid of ghosts at night in such a rambling, solitary mansion. Ghosts? Believe me, if I found one on my night-time jaunt round the house, I'd welcome him as a brother. When I came to live here after the old *carlana* died, I found a cradle in one of the attics that from its shape looked like a coffin, though the head was too high. They still use this style of cradle in poor houses in the area: they are made of pine, though the head isn't higher than the sides. That one was made from very beautiful shiny wood and smelled wonderful; the head bore the family coat of arms, an olive tree beneath a cross. Enric told me it was his grandfather's cradle. I brought it down for Enriquet and sent the modern effort with metal bars up to the attic. I liked the other one because generations of children in the family had slept in it, it was like the cradles the poor use today except for its scent and coat of arms. I also liked its coffin shape . . . Oh to be born in this castle, to die in this castle, to sink your roots deep in this land like an olive tree! I should like Enriquet to belong to this land and never think of selling the castle. I wouldn't like him to marry anybody but a woman of his rank, from a house with a coat of arms above the door. There is one in Castel that belongs to the baroness who has a daughter his age. Now they are far away, abroad. The baroness is a widow; recently the family has had lots of worries, has had to mortgage farms, but it is such fine stock! As ancient as ours . . . If they didn't have almost everything mortgaged, I might not have thought of this possibility; I wouldn't have dared. In no way do I want my Enriquet to marry someone ordinary! He comes from this family, from this castle, from this land . . ."

"This is why you wanted the castle, the lands . . . For this and nothing else. You —"

"If I were as you imagine me, I'd not be wishing you good luck."

"What do you mean?"

"You know my secret. You will all leave the day after tomorrow, many will never return again, to Olivel or anywhere. You could be one of them. In your case, I could feel that a weight has been lifted from my shoulders. I can assure you it's not like that. I swear to God I want you to be lucky. Believe me, love your wife and marry her as soon as you can. Don't you realise how difficult it is for a single mother? And then you say you've nothing in common with Enric!"

"Don't keep on. The two situations are quite dissimilar. If Trini and I haven't married, it has to do with our ideas."

"Say what you like; everything boils down to ideas, if that's what you mean. Believe me, the end result is the same. I'm fond of you and prefer not to know why you might do something so stupid. I'd feel remorse for the rest of my life! Marry Trini and forget these crazy things that will lead to nothing useful."

Nothing useful! Her cold words were what hurt most, but there she was, opposite me, her lace-making cushion between her knees; indifferent, magnificent and monstrous like life itself. I remembered a scene I'd witnessed not long ago in a field of stubble on the village outskirts. I was stretched out under an olive tree, trying to nap in the open air in that heat; a praying mantis was advancing through the truncated ears of wheat. It was the giant kind that usually appears after the dog days of summer, an extremely elegant greenish grey, and finger length. Like a stylised body, it gracefully swayed its small head on top of a short, slender thorax that contrasted with its huge abdomen. It advanced slightly, then stooped and looked back, as if something had caught its attention: another, smaller praying mantis, drawing closer with trepidation. I grasped what it was about: the former was the female, the latter the male, and I remembered reading something about that years ago. The male spread its wings with a kind of shudder and mounted her between his legs. I watched the scene with that mixture of curiosity and horror the mystery of life's renewal provokes. The business went on and on, a good hour had passed and the pigmy was still on the giant. It shuddered almost imperceptibly, as if in ecstasy. I had lit my pipe and was eager, watch in hand, to time how long that ceremony lasted when a Soleràs boutade came to mind: "Love is sublime for the doer and obscene for the observer." The half hours and quarters of an hour went by. The shudders and shaking continued. I tired of looking at them and went for a walk. I returned to my observatory two hours later: the couple was still at it. The male still seemed to be in ecstasy on top of her, but he'd lost his head. She'd turned her graceful little head round and was gradually devouring him and it was impossible to say whether those last shudders were caused by pleasure, terror, or both things at once.

She suddenly focused her eyes on me; they glinted with that damp, flickering light, a moonbeam to transfigure the depths of an underwater landscape.

"You're wrong if you think I am horribly cold and ungrateful," she remarked, as if reading my thoughts. "I don't want to judge you as you judge me, superficially and reluctant to understand, for I'd form a very poor opinion of you. You must have done all this, not for my children – or for me, if you like, more generously – but with the single aim of getting me to . . . How cheap that would be, for heaven's sake! Can't you see that? I prefer to think it was an attack of lunacy, that you don't know what you're saying and never wrote me that letter, or ever said what you did. I prefer to think you wanted to help me, to give my children a name and status. I'd like to repay you, don't you see that? I'm not ungrateful, believe me. You have a son. If I could do anything for him as you did for mine . . ."

"I repeat: the situations are different. I'm annoyed you keep insisting. I've recognised him. I've made a will in his favour. It's all by the book and planned. Don't compare . . . it's depressing," and out of the corner of my eye I looked at the sly grocer on the wall.

"Life takes such funny turns! Who knows if one day . . . Although you may never need me, don't ever hesitate for a second. I'm in your debt; I'll repay you in the same coin, whenever it's appropriate."

The light dampened and flickered more intensely: for a moment I thought it coalesced into a tear. Her usual cold, steely, distant look suddenly reappeared.

V

. . . la griffe effroyable de Dieu

SIERRA CALVA, 28 AUGUST

Back to a life of wandering, marching by night and hiding by day. I hear my captain's deep, liquor-fired voice from his hovel:

> I lurved a girl in Olivel
> she didn't lurve me at all.

Olivel de la Virgen is over and done. It's one more village sinking into a past of fantasy. Where are the roses the girls put in our lapels the day we arrived? Those dark red roses – "the colour of the cape of the *Ecce homo . . .*" They all came in their Sunday best with the mayor and the whole council to implore us not to leave; they were afraid that if we went the anarchists would come back. The commander sweated blood to get them to understand that whether we stayed or left didn't depend on us.

"Aren't you happy in Olivel?" they kept asking.

And old Olegària? Tears the size of chickpeas rolled down from her bloodshot, bleary little eyes. Gallart was there. When the last threshing floors had vanished from sight, he confessed to me: "The saliva stuck in my throat."

We take up positions on the crest of mountains as bare as the palm of a hand. The steppes extend before us. I can see the zigzag lines of enemy trenches through my binoculars. La Pobla de Ladron lies behind them.

The main engagement has started fourteen kilometres to our east. Two divisions attack the town of Xilte, quite unknown earlier but now key because it represents an advanced enemy mountain stronghold. La Pobla de Ladron is right on the col and that's why it's so vital we take it. Our division advances in a pincer formation: our brigade on the left, and the "flat feet" on the right.

Dawn breaks. Quite unannounced, a line of small cloudlets silently rises from the ground beyond the enemy trench, between it and the outlying houses of La Pobla. I focus my binoculars. Another equally silent and unexpected line springs up right at that moment, but beyond the trench, between it and the barbed wire. The blasts from the first explosions reach me now. They took fifteen seconds. About five kilometres, I calculate. It's less in fact: I can't have noted the two reference points on my stopwatch at all exactly. To hell with precision, I'm no artillery officer. A third salvo sends up a string of white mushrooms from the same trench, replicating its zigzags. "A lovely sight," Picó would say. He professes unbounded admiration for gunners and their trigonometry. Ever since our batteries scored a direct hit, they continue bombing with such continuous fire that the rounds run into each other. I didn't know that our attack on La Pobla de Ladron was to start today; it is the most concentrated burst of artillery fire I've seen from our side since this war began. If they can sustain this pace for an hour, that is, if the guns are up to it, not a soul will be left alive.

The first ray of sunlight slants across the trench and gives me an unusually precise view through my binoculars.

The enemy abandons its trench. They are civil guards: the sun glints on their three-cornered patent leather helmets. Redoubtable civil guards in those three-cornered helmets! But what are they doing? They leave the trench where the grenades keep exploding. They leave their lair but don't flee to La Pobla, quite the reverse. They go over the top and lie between the parapet and the barbed wire. Dead still in front of the trench, evenly spaced out, you'd think they were crocodiles drowsing along a river bank. The batteries should be warned, they are wasting ammunition on futile salvos: they are bombing an empty trench. They should shorten their aim; a few more metres this way and they'd blow them to smithereens. Damned three-cornered hats! I couldn't phone the observation point and it's too late now. Our infantry is already dipping towards the wire and the batteries had to hold their fire. The guards return to the trench all at once. I can now hear their insect, metallic voice, the rat-a-tat of their machine guns. Our men fall among the wire.

I don't want to watch. I go back to the hovel.

I write by the fireside. The mornings are cold in these desolate heights. I'm accompanied by the dull slurp of the campaign soup that will be our breakfast. The officers' republics are no more; we all eat the same from the brigadier to the most recent recruit. Hallowed equality endowed by army soup!

SIERRA CALVA, 31 AUGUST

The 4th Company is being held in reserve along these heights while the others attack La Pobla de Ladron. Yesterday the enemy finally abandoned the trenches ravaged by shells and barricaded themselves in houses in the village.

Artillery and air power must have destroyed them. Now I can only see master walls through my binoculars; the empty interiors are visible through the shapeless holes that once were windows. There's nothing inside and they remind me of the mummies in Olivel.

Night is falling. Until a moment ago you could hear the woodpecker tapping in the pine grove, followed by complete quiet. The occasional crackle of irregular mortar fire and crickets.

Apparently the "flatfooted" brigade has just taken the last bastions of La Pobla de Ladron, those the enemy has abandoned. All in all, the "flat feet" have performed magnificently. But don't go telling our men that.

SIERRA CALVA, 1 SEPTEMBER

We're still being held in reserve. The other companies are in combat past La Pobla, to the northeast; the enemy has begun a ferocious counterattack. Softened by distance, the concert of mortar blasts and machine-gun fire sounds like a stew bubbling on a slow fire.

Every night we three lieutenants repair to the captain's hovel, located in the centre of our position that's three kilometres long. We tell stories; Gallart's are inexhaustible. His forte is stories of unrequited love, including the tale of Melitona; if we are to believe him, he has lived a lifetime as a misunderstood lover, a tragic case of misfortune that only a great poet of the Romantic era could have rivalled, though, so he says, the most dramatic disappointments he'd experienced so far pale in comparison with what he suffered at the hands of Melitona: "She used to knock me silly, that lass wields a hell of punch; makes you see stars!" His duel with Commissar Rebull is another bewildering epic, even if they never came to blows. If only one could say the same of all epics!

These moonless nights on a bare mountain are wonderful. Through the dry desert air the stars seem like the brightest of eyes giving us the wisest of looks. I know my constellations and spend hours each night tracking the paths the planets take. Cruells taught me the little I know; at first I was at a complete loss. When I walk back to my hovel all alone, just before dawn breaks, that strange peace fills me with wonder. Men stopped killing themselves some time ago: one can only hear the distant whisper of the night-time breeze and the hoots of mountain owls that seem to mock our sad victories.

SIERRA CALVA, 2 SEPTEMBER

I, who never dream, have had a dream.

It was like an ancient ruined temple on a rocky crag. Someone was walking through the shadowy darkness inside and I could hear the sea swell with the even panting of a sleeping animal. The man walking towards me wore a kind of soutane, his eyes were open but could see nothing. He was looking through a portable telescope but he was sleepwalking. There was a mass of suitcases and huge trunks, double basses, pianos and mummies. The somnambulist with the telescope kept moving across all that, never stumbling though all was invisible to him; Soleràs and other familiar faces were among the mummies; some I now don't recognise that in my dream seemed strangely familiar. These mummies were as silent as the cases and the trunks; that silence, like the silence of the big suitcases, was disturbing because who knows what they hid? They watched me walk past and didn't look at me or budge though they were making a supreme effort to tell me something: they all wanted to say the same thing. They couldn't; they couldn't speak. The high altar gleamed in the background. The sleepwalker went over and looked at the presiding image through his telescope. It was a Virgin, perhaps a Virgin of Sorrows? Lots of things were stuck into her, but they were bayonets, not daggers. Dressed in stiff silk, she was like one more mummy, so still and so yellow, and the somnambulist walked over to her but never got that far. His soutane kept growing and he was dragging a huge black tail behind him. I felt confused and terrified and wanted to pray, but my voice couldn't get through my gullet: I was another mummy without a voice, lost among the others, among the suitcases and the trunks. My voice couldn't be heard, as if a hand were strangling me, and the idol's eyes shone in the dark like a cat's. The sides of the temple now sank into the ground. It was like a cavern or a tunnel full of cobwebs and bats that hung downwards in thick bunches. Then the somnambulist made a strange gesture, as if to strike someone with the telescope – or was it an iron bar and no longer a telescope? – someone moving in the darkness – a terrible, hard blow to the skull, someone moving and moaning in the shadows . . .

I woke up mid-dream with a start. In that haze I possessed the lucidity they say belongs to the dying. You float between reality and the beyond and see so clearly. Now I understand nothing in my dream. I only remember it was fascinating, nasty, feverish and sinister – and yet seemed so full of meaning.

SIERRA CALVA, 3 SEPTEMBER

As night fell I was patrolling the three kilometres of bare mountain occupied by the 4th Company: guard duty. I glimpsed a man in the half dark on one of the parapets, tall and lean with his back to me. His clothes, so different to ours, caught the eye: velvet trousers, the shiniest high leather boots with silvery spurs. He was in shirt sleeves, but his shirt was sky blue, not khaki. A sky-blue shirt here? I have seen the most peculiar garb in this long year at war, but a sky-blue shirt beats the lot.

Leaning over the parapet, as if it were a balcony, the stranger was looking at the plain that spreads outwards from the skirts of the Sierra Calva, now flooded by shadows. He seemed lost in his dreams. The splash-splash stew sound of guns was still audible in the distance, hand grenades and machine guns interrupted now and then by the more bass note of a mortar; all with that dying lilt of battles late in the evening, as if overcome by sleep.

He turned round when I shouted "Who goes there?" It was Soleràs. I took him to my hovel for a cognac. I was cold and astonished to come across him in these peaks. And we chatted until just before dawn. We chatted the whole night.

He told me so many things . . . He says he is tired of the Train Corps, of Supplies and chickpeas: "If you only knew the fantastic amounts of chickpeas the idiots in this brigade get through . . ." He'd asked the division to send him to any of the artillery companies, "even the flatfooted brigade".

"As long as it's not yours. I never want to be under your orders! Though in the end so what? That might be a brilliant idea: in the ranks under your command!"

"And what brings you to Sierra Calva?"

"I came for the views. You get a glorious view of the battle from here: the enemy positions and ours, the troop movements, the flight paths of the .85 mortars – just like an eighteenth-century engraving: the wretches taking part see nothing. They can't see the wood for the trees and at the same time have far too many other things on their minds."

"And how come your extraordinary outfit?"

"Bah, one of my bright ideas. I often go to the rear with the Supplies lorry, as I think you know, and with a flashy uniform and a few tales of battle they take you for a hero. I keep quiet about the chickpeas – and why not? Conversely, with a few tins of El Pagès milk . . ."

"You're crazy."

Silence. We were stretched out at the back of the hovel, next to the fire; I had lit an oil lamp on a hook. In the darkness the dim flickering glow illumined the twisted trunks that supported the ceiling of branches and packed earth. Field mice ran to and fro across the ceiling during the night, attracted by the crumbs and other leftovers from our meals. The cold wind blew through the cracks. A mouse sent the occasional cloud of dust over us; the lamp wick crackled.

"Crazy . . . and why not?" he retorted, wiping the cognac from his lips.

"Women always think I'm a man who is 'different from the rest'. And they tell me their secrets; they think I'm pure," and he laughed – his unpleasant hen's cackle – staring me in the eye. "And to think that Saint Philomena appears in person to my aunt and she doesn't bat an eyelid . . ."

"You're crazier then ever, Juli. What's the point of all this idiocy?"

"You're so naïve. You admire me, you have no choice, and I can tell you quite frankly that I couldn't care less about your admiration. You and I shouldn't see each other again. Why do you find that so difficult to grasp, Lluís?"

"This time you came to see me."

"Yes, true enough. This time I took the initiative. There must be one almighty motive, believe me, or I wouldn't be here. Let's think what it might be. Why did I come? It's so difficult to work out what the motive is when it's so powerful. Sorry to disappoint you, but we have no idea what the powerful motives driving us are all about. Maybe I've come precisely because I shouldn't have; precisely because we shouldn't meet up. According to crime novels – that's all I've been reading for some time as I know *The Horns of Roland* off by heart – criminals will return to the scene of the crime; they find it hard to keep away from the victim's corpse. Maybe you're a corpse, maybe I am . . ."

"I'm a corpse? You know I won't tolerate people being rude."

"I'm not asking you to. I've not come to ask you to tolerate anything at all; on the contrary, I'd ask you not to. A barrier's been erected between us, Lluís, can't you see? A barrier. You aren't a corpse, nothing like, but I can talk to you about corpses; you're one of the few people I can talk frankly to. The macabre is banned from conversation, as are obscenities. The beginning and the end: totally banned from conversation! But I can talk to you about them as naturally as I might speak about the weather; you're one of the few people who will listen, so why deny it? Understand? But to get back to what I was saying. What do you think of women who sell themselves, or, rather, rent themselves out? All told, for a very modest price; some are so modest! Some would follow you to the ends of the earth for a tin of El Pagès milk! But they are so terribly passive . . . it's like lying with a mummy, don't you think? I sometimes wake up from a deep sleep and think with a jolt: I'm clasping a mummy for eternity . . . We can deny the existence of heaven, even laugh about it as if we were at a Sunday theatre show performed by amateur Daughters of Maria. As for hell, nobody is going to doubt that it exists. It follows us everywhere, like shit that's stuck to our shoes."

"Theology isn't my strong point," I replied, "but I imagine that if there is another life, justice there must be severe. If we all acted like you, if we poked our worst sores . . . with your cynical bad taste, don't you think we'd all end up as neurotic as you? Stop dwelling on the idea that you are more perverse than anyone else, can't you see the crazy pride inspiring you to think that? We all come from mud, Juli; we're all stuck in a sea of mud up to our necks. I've done things that . . . I'm sure you've never sunk so low! We just have to make an effort to stop the mud reaching eye level. At least let's keep our eyes out of the mud! Our eyes at least! I must be able to see the stars . . ."

"You are so very inspired today," he broke in sarcastically, with that operatic bass of his. He took another swig from the flask. "But what do you know about the stars? Does Cruells get you to look at them through his telescope? Bah, so stupid . . . Cruells is a mere sleepwalker and if he goes on wasting his time on the stars he'll never make it to bishop. On the other hand, what would the stars give to be like us? Back to what I was saying. Women never get you wrong: they know at a glance you are a man like any other. But I . . . 'I can talk to you like a brother . . . ' They're so silly! Since when could one ever speak to one's brother?"

The murmur from the distant battle ebbed; a bare night, no moon, nothing. He kept sipping his cognac, staring short-sightedly at the tin cup from time to time, without his glasses, like a rare species of animal.

"And they like confiding! When they start, they go on and on, nobody understands the poor things! They feel an imperious need to be understood . . . They drown you in such dross, if you let them!"

I listened silently to his rambling monologue, trying to guess where it would lead.

"So it seems I'm a gifted listener. You, on the other hand, don't understand them, you get straight to the point. You don't waste time listening. You just go for it. The oddest thing is that we like the same kind of women."

"Please, Juli, can you stop the flow of rubbish? The same kind of women?"

"Don't look so daft – you look like the Economics professor. You were suggesting as much only a moment ago: 'I've done things that . . .' I know perfectly well what you have done."

"What do you mean?"

"Your latest fling."

"What fling?"

"The *carlana*, of course. While we're about it, let me congratulate you: what a woman! Fantastic . . . Worth a few lines from Baudelaire:

> *Ce qu'il faut à ce coeur profond comme un abîme*
> *C'est vous, Lady Macbeth, âme puissante au crime . . .*

"You know, there was never anything between us. You must find these fantasies in your novels about —"

"About what?"

"About whores?"

He stared at me in that short-sighted, lucid yet mocking way of his that made the colour come to my cheeks. And he drawled, in his best bass voice, keeping his eyes glued on me: "*Eppur si muove.*"

I wanted the ground to open beneath my feet. My hands were shaking, my face was on fire. He had stopped staring at me and was taking a long swig straight from the flask.

"Spell out what you're thinking." I stammered. "I expect it's more slander."

"Call it what you want. Don't try to make me believe that you manufacture marriage certificates . . . free of charge. You must agree that register worked a treat! And you still say I'm not a good friend, that I'm not generous, that I refuse to help a friend who can't get himself out of a huge mess . . . and so discreetly; I realise you'd not worked out that it was me. I could have sold it to you: supply and demand; do you remember our Economics professor? A total fool unable to see anything beyond supply and demand! But I'm a fool too, even if I haven't yet earned myself a chair in pedantry: thinking my forte was canon law, and marriages *in articulo mortis* in particular . . . Such a balls-up! The association of the two things has always fascinated me, death and the nuptial night, the macabre and the obscene . . . So you'd think the idea of the wedding *in extremis* must have come from me; well, it didn't. It was hers. When I met her, she'd got it all worked out. She'd never crammed canon law into her head, but she's as clever as they come. I've even suspected that . . ." He looked at me as if he was wondering whether to say it, "And why not? She was a real rogue; and if you start to hypothesise . . ."

"I can't think what you are suggesting."

"The *carlà* was the last to be assassinated. Why did they leave him for dessert? He was a completely grey person: let's be clear about that, a simpleton, incapable of formulating a single idea. I don't think he even made it to be a Carlist, you know. Why would the anarchists have such a big grudge against him? The idea of murdering him could well have been suggested by —"

"Suggested by?!"

"The *carlana*. You've experienced her, she has a gift for suggesting and fascinating —"

"I will never believe such a thing!" Then I remembered my praying mantis pair.

"So much the worse for you. You imagine her as much less of a literary character than she is. I tell you, you don't have a clue. *Âme puissante au crime* . . . She is extraordinarily literary! And wasted on you . . . It is really true when they say 'God gives beans to those who have no teeth'."

"If you understood her mind so well, how come you didn't fake the certificate?"

"Your idea, like so many good ideas, has one ever so small drawback: you don't see that it was impractical. You forget that Olivel was anarchist territory; if I infiltrated, I did so clandestinely, without a uniform. Strictly incognito, we could say. It was difficult to set up a marriage *in articulo mortis* in anarchist territory. How would you get the anarchist committee – remember, the mayor and councillors have vanished into thin air – to recognise the signatures of friars and the act as valid? After suggesting the idea to – and, let me repeat, the *carlana* is wonderfully gifted at suggesting things for other people to do – she beat a retreat. She hesitated. 'No, I can't. It would be a forgery!' She spoke as if *I* had suggested it to her. She'd simply realised it was unviable while the anarchist committee was in Olivel. Qualms of conscience come when we know we'll lose everything if we throw them overboard. She was simply sublime the last time I saw her: 'You mistook me for someone else. You ought to know I'm not interested in forging documents, let alone your propositions.'"

"What propositions?"

"What do you think? Exactly what she suggested to you: with the small difference that she said 'yes' to you. Agh," he sighed and paused. "Have you forgotten your penal law? Dishonest propositions . . . She's very sensitive to dirt – I don't know if you ever noticed: she's a woman who is spotlessly clean, that is, who has no feeling. Because feelings always come with a spot of dirt or two, or filth, you won't deny. I was dirty in her eyes, fantastically dirty. I could see the mixture of fear and disgust in her eyes. It's difficult to provoke disgust, believe me; it's hard to sustain a conversation and guide it where you want it to go without being interrupted! One day I asked her about the deceased's favourite sexual perversions; it would be quite odd if a dead man like him had never practised some sexual perversion . . ."

"Juli, you are a moron . . ."

"Thanks. Perhaps you don't realise I could report you as a forger and you'd get years inside."

"You do what you think fit. Just think of the children: you'd make bastards of them again."

"So you did it for them, did you? The poor little orphans. So sublime, Lluís, I congratulate you."

"Don't be such a fool and give me a straight answer: do you have it in you to report me?"

"I already have."

Silence. My hand was trembling and making its own way to my back pocket, but I remembered it wasn't loaded, I always carried it unloaded. He calmly swigged cognac from the flask.

"I've reported you, Lluís, not to any judge, but to your wife. I've described your splendid goings-on with the most literary lady roundabout with a wealth of gory detail."

"You're so stupid. It's not any of Trini's business."

"Perhaps you are the stupid one. Do you really think it's not any of her business? Do you think you can leave a woman all alone because she's yours and she'll just make do? The poor things then complain their husbands don't understand them and have every right to complain that he's been cuckolded in the end.

I grabbed the flask and threw it at his face. The cognac poured down his cheeks and all over that sky-blue shirt. He didn't lose his temper, just wiped it with a handkerchief and went on: "You think I'm intolerable and you're the one that's intolerable. One can't tell you anything!"

LA POBLA DE LADRON, 19 SEPTEMBER

We're all poor sleepwalking wretches and have had two weeks of macabre fantasy . . .

The 4th Company left its reserve positions because of violent enemy counterattacks. We've lost a lot of men.

We've been given a short break back in La Pobla, which is being hit by mortars and howitzers and even stray machine-gun fire. Their aeroplanes shit on us two or three times a day; we've guards on watch at the top of the belfry who sound the alarm by shouting out: "They're shitting on us!" Because they only sound the alarm when they see actual bombs dropping from the aeroplanes; if they had to shout whenever a little squadron flew over we'd never leave our cave.

Our cave is the cellar of the only house still standing, a freestone, probably fifteenth-century, house. An underground cellar with stone vaults; the bombings resound there like a prophet's voice in the catacombs and the clouds of dust coming down the spiral stairs make us all cough.

All that remains of La Pobla is this house and the ruins of the church; the rest is rubble. The high street is strewn with parchments and ancient title deeds; a bomb exploded in the parish archive and blew it up. I don't always go down to the cave when the alarm sounds, because you grow tired of doing so; I sometimes prefer to watch the aircraft unloading. They look like insects in flight laying their long thin eggs. Sometimes I pass the time investigating ancient title deeds; it's strange how in the fifteenth and even in the early sixteenth century they still wrote in a mixture of Catalan and Aragonese.

I've lived the last two weeks as if under the influence of an overdose of cocaine. I felt on a strange high. I now know we retook La Pobla, and that the enemy launched a counteroffensive; the only souls we found alive were the lice. Incredible amounts! We scratch like mad.

Could I give you a coherent account of what happened in those two weeks? No. Battles leave no memories. You say and do things as if dictated to by someone else. I vaguely remember I was on the move – and that's all.

I remember an esplanade: was it stubble or barren land? The enemy had set up their machine guns as if they'd attended my lecture in Olivel: their lines of fire came at belly level. It was impossible to advance. And we'd been ordered to advance – without cover: we had no tanks.

Gallart led the company and was the first to fall; the Publicist soon after. I remember the lavender bending in the wind; every now and then a stem split in the middle as if cut by an invisible sickle. The recruits were in tears; it was the first time they'd looked war in the face. The other officer, a Miralles, fell, and I was now alone leading the three sections. Barely half the company had survived; we retreated into a wood of pines and juniper.

Hand grenades and mortar bombs fell among the pines but it was an oasis of peace compared to the esplanade. We had a problem with our wounded. We could hear them shrieking; some tried to shout and their voices turned into a sob like the last cry of a rooster being beheaded. We'd lost touch with the battalion. There was another stretch of barren land behind the woods, an open, treeless expanse that was also under machine-gun fire. The recruits realised we'd abandoned our wounded – we couldn't risk retrieving them. We'd lose more than we'd rescue. I was at a loss: how could I restore contact with our commander?

That was on my mind when I saw an officer with a handful of soldiers crawling over the barren land behind us to dodge the bullets. They were also trailing something behind them. Commissar Rebull was bringing us the telephone wire.

You see, the commander had got his way and turned him into a Communications officer! Incredibly, when he was sent to work with our battalion, that Communications officer hadn't yet arrived from Army H.Q. Here was Rebull acting as best he could as that non-existing officer: he successfully advanced beneath a constant stream of machine-gun bullets that hummed like swarms of mosquitoes. He was sweating blood. I remembered the stupid jokes we played on him in Olivel; now I could have cried as I watched him grafting so hard. I couldn't repress the temptation to give him a big hug. He looked at me in amazement, clenching his pipe between his teeth, as if he found my outburst out of place and tawdry. He handed me the field telephone. Commander Rosich was at the other end of the line: "At your orders, Commander. Captain Gallart is dead: we're afraid the other two lieutenants were killed as well. We can no longer hear their voices. I've taken charge of the company."

"Don't move from the woods. I'll send a couple of .85 mortars to shut up those blasted machine guns."

"We've got wounded, Commander, bleeding to death out in that open country."

"Don't try anything before the mortars reach you or that will be the end of the 4th Company, the only one left! The mortars will be there in no time. Remember my barn owl? He's dead too!"

We hid in that wood for several days. Despite the mortars, hostile machine-gun fire caught us whenever we tried to make a foray. We'd used up our provisions and water.

I remember our last desperate sortie like a hallucination.

The recruits followed us as if they were in a trance. All I could think was: quick march! I could hear the machine guns as if I were in Uncle Eusebi's office when the four typists were all in action. Naturally, I heard them in front. Then I suddenly started hearing fire from behind: were we caught between two lines of fire? The others made a different noise: screeching partridges rather than tapping typewriters. It was clearly a different model of gun. They were ours.

We even heard snatches come and go on the wind of that lame rhyming hymn Picó invented and forced his men to sing:

> The machine-gun singing
> death bringing
> to the fatchas . . .

Our two mortars weren't off target. We were beneath the parabola drawn by their bombs and I have to say they were dead on target; they were falling, almost plumb, on the machine-gun nests the "fatchas" had set up – whoever made that word up? It's what they're always called at the front! And the recruits kept following me; some fell, the others paid no notice.

They advanced as if in a dream . . . What's this? What do you think it is? Barbed wire! How did we get here so quickly?

The mortars had blown up some of the stakes; we worked hard widening the gaps with the butts of our rifles – in a mad rush, otherwise nobody would live to tell the tale. Now we're between the barbed wire fence and the trench. A hundred steps and we'll be there! A hundred steps stooping low and running fast if we want to get there alive.

"They're surrendering!" I hear the cry go up to my left.

I can see a tall thin man dressed in rags, covered in dust, with a two-week beard, standing on the parapet. A tramp, I think. What the hell's a tramp doing on that parapet?

Something glints on the torn sleeve of his shirt; it's an adjutant. He crosses his arms as if he wants to give us a hug.

"Stop firing! They're surrendering!" I hear hoarse voices shouting. It's my men.

It's a pity a moment like this takes longer to tell than to live. We're all brothers! Stop firing! Let's stop killing each other! Let's stop being such savages! This is a lovely moment . . . Perhaps we're in Heaven? Perhaps we're dead and that fatcha dressed in rags is our welcoming angel?

The tattered angel is winking at his men hidden out of sight in the trench. I watch him through my binoculars. And on the sly he's signalling to them with his right hand, as if he were conducting an orchestra. What's the symphony he wants them to play? No doubt something in our honour. The "Death of Åse"? I see through him as if I could read inside his head. Get your hand grenades ready and when they come to give us a hug . . .

It's an old trick we've often played in similar circumstances. My men throw down their rifles in order to scramble up and embrace them, on a crazy high. I suddenly remember they are raw recruits unfamiliar with these ploys.

"It's a trap!" – but they don't hear. A noisy mêlée: they seem bewitched by the loving welcome they've been offered. For God's sake, how can this desire to be brotherly run so deep? How can we let it get a hold and kill us by the dozen . . . ? "Idiots!" I bawl again, but my voice disappears in the fracas. As if it has a mind of its own, my hand goes into my back pocket and I find my pistol between my fingers, as if it had been born there. I take careful aim; the man on the parapet is waving his arms in my glinting sights. I press gently, voluptuously; the trigger makes a small, ridiculous noise. I remember it's unloaded.

A dead soldier lay four steps away. I vaguely recall that his name was Esplugues and that he came from Arbeca. I pick up his rifle. Or maybe his name was Arbeca and he came from Esplugues; what's it matter? Hardly urgent now. I feel a wonderful kick from the rifle and the tattered angel falls on his face like a marionette.

My men have got it at last; got it totally! They attack and massacre with their blades. They sink their machetes into every belly, even the bellies of those who kneel and beg for mercy. My shouts disappear into the air: "What are you doing, you animals? Let them be! No more killing!"

Now, at least, that they're all dead, they can't kill any more. Our mouths are covered in sores. Thirst is real torture! Picó manages to send us one of his mules with a wineskin of water. We drink as if we've got dropsy. It's hot and muddy and we think it's the best water we've ever drunk.

How quiet it seems once we've had our fill of water! We don't dare look each other in the eye, as if from now on we'll harbour a shameful secret. Can we ever look ourselves in the face again?

More days of battles and trenches. It turns out that, unlike us, the enemy had dug out three lines of trenches at different levels up the hill. It was so demoralising to take out one, only to find another a few hundred metres further on. Everything we'd done was to no avail; we had to attack again.

I remember a wood that burned at three corners after an aircraft dropped phosphorus bombs. We couldn't get out: it was an island in flames surrounded by a swirling sea of machine-gun fire. We ate half-burnt bread. The acrid smell of that wood stuck to me; it often comes back to me, as do the sad, obscene songs the recruits sang.

We slept as best we could in a shallow pit we each made with our small hammer. What peaceful nights! Looking at the sky, listening to the odd stray bullet whistle by, and above the stars of Cygnus or the Northern Cross that Cruells had taught me to see and recognise. When I looked at the starry cross I thought of you, Ramon, and I thought of Trini and our son, and fell asleep saying the Lord's Prayer. The four staves of that cross were such good company, twinkling in the depths of infinity! We're in such a bad state, for God's sake. We need company so badly!

21 SEPTEMBER

I have one real worry: I searched the pockets of their dead second lieutenant, as per our orders. I can tell you it's the most unpleasant part of one's duties. But it has to be done: you never know what you may find among the documents of an enemy officer. This fellow only had letters on him from a girl who spoke of getting married once the war was over. Four letters tucked into one envelope, the only one there was and without which I wouldn't be in the quandary I'm in now. It said he was Antonio López Fernández.

Dear old Olegària never said her grandson was a second lieutenant, but perhaps he'd earned his flashes only recently. She had only very sporadic news from him through the International Red Cross . . .

I prefer to think it must be pure coincidence: so many people go by those names!

I've not told you the worst: the day after, when we went to put the dead in a grave, I found he'd been mutilated. They had ripped his trousers open with a knife . . . I'd like to identify the coward who did it and execute him in front of the company.

22 SEPTEMBER

I'm worried by that episode. War is such an unpleasant thing. If only one bore a grudge against those one kills! Or perhaps it is best as it is; we'll all die one day, war or no war; the worst isn't the fact that we kill each other but the hatred. Let's kill each other, given that it is our duty, but without the hatred. It's what Soleràs said once: let's kill each other like good brothers.

I'm not sure what I should do: write to the girl? Her name and address are on the back of the envelope: Irene Natalia Royo Jalón. It's strange, given that j and i are the same letter in Latin, so her initials would make up I.N.R.I.

And what would I write? "Dear Miss, I'm pleased to inform you that I've just killed your fiancé . . ."? That's ridiculous. Best forget it. And it would be so difficult to get a letter to her! Via the International Red Cross, obviously, or an embassy. "Miss, I'm very sad to bring you the news of your fiancé's heroic death: standing on the parapet as we were advancing . . ."? I don't have to say I did it. "We buried him with all honours, as such a brave enemy deserved . . . "? What about the mutilation? Shut up! If only I could find the scoundrel . . . It could well be a soldier by the name of Pàmies who looks the part: he has such a stupid crooked expression on his face, the look of a dog that's been beaten, a sly grin like that mummy in the monastery, but I can hardly execute a man simply because I don't like his face!

I can't execute him; it's not customary to execute mummies. The quartermaster came to say it was time for grub: the men lined up in front of a big sooty black tin stew pot, in tatters, hair tousled, as black as the pot; not to mention the two-week stiff stubbly beards. Fortunately we couldn't see our own faces and it was frightening to think how we must smell, though luckily we could no longer smell a thing. But at least our eyes shone, our eyes looked and saw and dreamed . . . of a life that's on the boil and isn't mutilated, awaiting us at the end of the war beyond all the wretchedness: our dreams stay firm in spite of everything. A double line! They obeyed my order, mechanically; they all gripped a tin plate, the plate that is never washed – it's hard enough to find water to drink – and imprints its rancid taste on everything we put there. I reviewed my soldiers. I walked past each and every one, looked into their eyes, read their dreams: maybe a woman or a child, maybe a farmhouse with a barn, in the Vallès or on the plain of Urgell, or maybe a tiny flat in Gràcia or the Barceloneta, maybe a kiss that was never given and that might have turned the world upside down . . . Finally, I come to eyes without dreams, those belonging to the mummy: the crook's eyes that believe in nothing. My mouth filled with saliva as it did then but this time the gob of spit silently hit that face and slid slowly between the bristles like a fat worm. Pàmies didn't flinch. The other soldiers' eyes were full of their own dreams, of the pot sending a vertical stream of steam up to the sky, as when Abel was sacrificed and everywhere stank of wool: the eternal mutton that Supplies served up. Almighty God, why did you allow Cain's seed to survive in this land?

I find it really difficult to believe that the dead lieutenant is old Olegària's grandson. She'd not told me that he was courting; of course, he could have met that Irene in fascist territory, after he'd passed over to their side: that Irene comes from far away. You can draw little out of the four letters: that the girl's quite "uncultured", as Picó would say, and little besides. There's a "yer ever luvvin'" that is absolutely genuine. Though that's a very general complaint: didn't Juliet our cousin once write "my deerest Lluís I adoor yer"?

FALGUERA DE LOS CABEZOS, SATURDAY, 9 OCTOBER

The area we've taken with many losses was a bare plain, grey as a basin of porridge, surrounded by equally bare mountains. Their peaks are geometrical, pyramids and truncated cones: at sunrise and sunset, the oblique light hit them and projected stark, angular shadows so it looked like the vulture trap in Olivel. It had a charm of its own: geometry is pure, mineral is clean; life is dirty. Xilte and La Pobla de Ladron were far behind us and we were roaming with the remnants of the battalion between what looked like craters on the moon. We were now an advanced contingent in enemy territory.

Once, we were totally isolated and had not eaten or drunk for two days. We set up in the shadow of a hill safe from gunfire; every approach was covered by artillery and machine gunners in trenches. Two from Supplies managed to slip away with a mule along a deep gully trail; when they came back, a grenade blew up a few feet from the animal and its belly opened up like a big flower. Three days later, its scent reached us on the breeze. Wasn't its silence cynical? Why couldn't we be a bunch of stony-faced statues?

Now we're a long way from that plain. The enemy is surrendering the wide open countryside rather than fighting us for the saddle of the hill, as we thought they would. A long valley, two to seven kilometres across, lies between them and us: no man's land. The four or five little villages are intact but deserted.

Los Cabezos is a cool, leafy mountain range covered in pine trees, dotted with springs and brooks. The shepherd's hut where I've established myself is next to a brook and I wash in a pool deep enough for the water to come up to my collarbone. The foliage of elms and poplars has a thousand hues, yellowy green to reddish purple, and the stream carves out luxuriant meadows here and there. Cows and goats come to graze from the villages behind us, where life has returned to normal soon after a new front was established. I don't think they are at all worried that the front protecting them now fights under a different flag. Didn't dear old Olegària often say "We're all tarred with the same brush"?

The land is more pastoral than arable; there are no plantations, and the sound of tinkling bells is so pleasant after weeks of only hearing the rat-a-tat of machine guns and explosions of mortars. The goatherds sell us goat's milk that otherwise they'd throw away since people around here won't drink it. The goats belong to a mountain breed, they have long silky wool and graceful horns.

Every day at sunset the woodpecker's powerful, insistent cry echoes down the wooded ravines. With a bit of imagination it sounds like a neigh and that explains why the locals call it "horse". It is the bird's farewell to the dying day; then you hear only the cries of mountain and barn owls and the cackling night jay.

However, the woodpecker's farewell isn't gloomy but energetic, confident, cheerful. One evening I was by myself among the pines; I'd stretched out on a bed of pine to smoke and dream. I was so quiet the woodpecker didn't notice me as its beak busily hit a tree trunk and its taps echoed round the countryside. The rays of the sun filtering through foliage glinted on its feathers now and then: a deep red, green and yellow flash of lightning spotted black and white. It must be a male, brightly coloured and as big as a turtle dove. Clinging to the trunk with its claws, it was working at something important because I drew near and it wasn't distracted. When it finally was, rather than flying off, the woodpecker went to the other side of the tree and poked its head out to keep an eye on me. I walked round too, and it repeated its manoeuvre, as if playing hide and seek. Its head kept poking into sight and I found its beady, suspicious little eyes very funny. I tried to catch it but it took flight and screeched, as if to warn the whole forest.

From the top of Cabezo Mayor you could on very calm days make out a bluish line on the misty horizon, far to the northeast. Sometimes I would sit on a high rock and spend hours trying to encompass the stillness of that perpetual snow. My heart kept telling me it was our country's advance guard. I've been away for almost eighteen months, eighteen months without seeing Trini and my boy. I've not missed them till now. Why the change? I feel strangely heavy in my chest – no, not in my chest, in my stomach. As if I'd eaten meat that had gone off, that upsets your insides until you vomit.

The nurse comes to see me occasionally, always with his telescope. We look at Venus, that shines like a trembling tear until long after sunset: it's now enjoying its "maximum length", Cruells explained. His is an extending navy telescope from the nineteenth century – maybe I've already described it to you? – of the kind with sections that slot back into each other; once it's collapsed back it's barely ten centimetres long and when extended it's more than a metre. On evenings like these, Venus seems like a thin, fragile strip of new moon. Our observatory is that high rock, where the tops of the trees don't obstruct our view of the sky.

One evening, when we were sitting on that famous rock and amusing ourselves looking through his telescope at the craters and seas on the waxing moon, he suddenly asked if I was feeling unwell.

"I'm just about right. Why do you ask?"

"You look yellowish, as if something hadn't gone down too well."

I gave him a look of surprise: "I've had that feeling for some time. Something's weighing on me inside. It's probably stuff and nonsense, but my stomach really hurts. Where do you puke up stuff and nonsense? Can you give me confession?"

He shook his head gravely.

"I've not been ordained."

"That's irrelevant. I need you to listen. Who can I talk to, if not you? I don't know whether I believe or not and perhaps it doesn't really matter – it comes and goes with the moon. However, I do feel this heaviness in my stomach. I am sure of that."

I told him about the second lieutenant and didn't miss out the detail of his mutilation: "I won't regain my peace of mind until I've executed the scoundrel who —"

"How would that solve anything?" he said, shaking his head. "He's dead now, forget it. You did your duty, as he did his; pray for his soul and don't give it another thought, I beg you. War is war."

"And what if he was old Olegària's grandson?"

"Unlikely. It would be too much of a coincidence. Old Olegària's grandson wasn't well enough educated to be a second lieutenant. He's probably illiterate."

"That may very well be, but this is much, much worse than the poor dead, mutilated second lieutenant. In the end it's the usual story: the obscene and the macabre. The mutilation may be a ritual that comes down to us from pre-historical times, perpetuated over the centuries; Melo gives examples in his history of the war of the Segadors: some of Goya's etchings from the war against France show such cases. How can these rituals pass from one war to another if they are sometimes centuries apart and the culprits haven't a clue about history? It's not passed down by tradition; it is born instinctively. What instincts do we have? What are they, for God's sake? You are right: better not think about it. And in the end, the adjutant got what was coming to him! What the fuck was he doing, standing up on the parapet? Couldn't he see it would all end badly? No, other things are tying my stomach in knots. It's not the dead adjutant. I'm an adjutant too. I'll be dead one of these days. He'd have killed me if I'd not killed him: we are quits. *Requiescat in pace*. To hell with him."

Cruells' lips were moving imperceptibly.

"Don't pray now; don't be a fool. You'll have time enough for that. Now listen to me."

And I rolled off all my dealings with the *carlana*, not sparing him a single detail.

"You see how far I've sunk. I can tell you now, the forgery doesn't worry me at all; I keep thinking about poor, resigned Trini . . . And I left her all alone to cope by herself. I've carried on my life as if she didn't exist. My life or whose? It's true that she and I have advanced ideas, that the idea of not being married by the Church or by civil law was something that came from both of us, possibly more from her side, as she's from an anarchist family; advanced ideas . . . If I told you . . . Is that any reason to abandon a young woman and disappear into thin air? Is that what

144

advanced ideas are all about? I told the *carlana* that I'd be prepared to leave Trini for her . . ."

"To leave Trini? I don't imagine you'd ever have done that."

"At that particular moment . . . Afterwards, obviously, I'd have pulled my hair out but then I didn't know what I was doing or saying. Clearly, you've never been there and find it hard to understand. If you don't up the ante, they don't take any notice. They don't want half-baked passions: it's sublime and crazy or . . . They have an extraordinary refined sensitivity when it comes to perceiving emotions, if you don't go full out, might as well not bother! They are astonishing, Cruells, much superior to us! If you suggest staking all, life and death, well-being and peace, they'll follow you to the ends of the earth; they are astonishing, Cruells! Why should we think it so strange we like women if they are a thousand times superior to us?"

"You speak as if this little affair weren't the first."

"The first? Please, Cruells, you're forgetting I wasn't a seminarist. The first! Bah, if we had to drag out my past affairs . . . it would be never-ending! On the other hand, it's been a long time and I'd probably not remember some by now. They belong to the pre-war period and a lot of water has passed under the bridge! I have duly repented: please, let's not rake up stuff I've put behind me. Only one very occasionally comes back to mind and the fact is I got myself into such a tangle . . . my God, what a tangle that was. Naturally, Trini never suspected anything. Perhaps the worst of it is when you get into a mess and can't find a way out, can't seek relief from the only person in the world who can help you get rid of that burden, namely your own wife. You're so isolated . . . Then I'd never thought of confessing, as I am now to you. I went through a very bad period, I can tell you. She was a divorcée with a couple of children and had to maintain herself because her husband had vanished. She'd had the bright idea of marrying a South American, who as his name suggests disappeared without trace when she found she was pregnant for a second time. She performed bit parts in a music hall on carrer Nou de La Rambla to keep herself and her children, and lived in a boarding house on carrer del Carme. She was dark-skinned and stunning, waist-length black hair and eyes straight out of *A Thousand and One Nights*, but she was so stupid . . . so stupid, for God's sake! She devoured cheap novelettes and listened to melodramas on the radio; she soaked them up like the Bible and quoted whole sentences at you in conversation; how could one ever resist such wisdom? I remember she once said to me word for word: 'Love is male; but passion is female', and she always quoted this stuff in Spanish because she saw herself as a passionate soul and perhaps was. The drawback was that she acted like that with all and sundry. If I were to tell you the sordid situations I got into that I managed to tolerate because I didn't have the strength to break with that fool! I was hooked, unable to give her up like a coke addict; it lasted for months. I felt tarnished, destroyed, as if I'd fallen to the bottom of a pit and would never have the strength to drag myself out – where'd I ever find a helping hand? The only person who could have helped at the time was Trini and I couldn't say a word to her! They were months I spent in hell. I felt as if I'd lost contact with Trini and everyone, as if they'd shut themselves off from me. Sensual women repel me, they always have, and that woman was no exception; how could I explain the enigma that you can be so hooked on a woman and yet think she's dreadful? Yet, she was still a thousand times better than I am; a thousand times more generous, more accepting. But why are we talking about her now? That seems like a dream now. I can't think how that hapless woman could have dominated me as she did for four or five months of my life . . ."

"Poor Lluís," was Cruells' only comment.

"However, I was never attached to any of them as I was to the *carlana*, I can tell you; none could rival the *carlana*! Of course, it must be because the *carlana* snubbed me. What an impregnable castle! And if you'd seen me acting the fool . . . Isn't that another ploy that passion likes to use – there's nothing we desire more than what we're refused? The *carlana* is worth not a thousand, but six thousand times more than me, even if what Soleràs suspected were true; and that's only a hypothesis, right? After all, the *carlà* was a perfect idiot, the most loathsome variety, a timid idiot. She was looking after herself and that's natural enough. She was taking advantage of my stupidity to resolve the inheritance for her children. She even gave me good advice – can you believe that? I don't think any man can ever have found himself in a more ridiculous position! 'Marry Trini, forget madness that never leads to anything useful.' That's a good piece of common-sense advice, don't you think? That at least is beyond dispute . . . except that advice was the last thing I was after, but . . . better forget all that. I made a real fool of myself. Don't you go gossiping and saying the certificate is fake out of some scruples of conscience. You'd do a really bad turn to her two kids – they're completely innocent."

"Poor Trini," he muttered. "Will you marry her soon?"

"Marry? How? Via the Church? Neither of us believes. Via civil law? Why should we believe in the State any more than in the Church?"

Cruells looked at me seriously through his spectacles, nodding silently as I spoke; the telescope lay neglected on the top of a rock. He glanced at his watch: "I must go. Dr Puig is expecting me at Battalion H.Q. It's a two-hour trek along a bad path. You're more in the right than you think; marriage is a sacrament or if not, what is it? I must be going before it gets dark . . ."

"Don't start sermonising; sermons are unhelpful, they're like grub up, the same for everybody when we each feel our own particular grief is unique and non-transferable. Don't do a Father Gallifa, who spoiled everything with his sermons, whose eyes said it all. What do we mean when we say 'sacrament'? I know it's not just the ceremony, no need to tell me that; I passed canonical law with flying colours and I know that Adam and Eve didn't have a ceremony. They went straight to the point. However, how does one know there is a sacrament? How does one know a man and woman are Adam and Eve and made for each other? Wait, listen to me, it won't be dark for some time. Let's use the *carlà* as an example The *carlà*! A rascal and a fool! Did you know he wanted to sell the castle and its lands to build a sock factory? Not for him to run, of course. He'd found an industrial partner, a man from Reus who was promising him fantastic profits if he risked half a million pesetas: 'There's nothing like socks,' he apparently told him. 'Every day more are worn out; as people walk further, their feet sweat more.' But let's leave the socks in peace, we were talking about marriage. If the *carlà* had married someone else with all due ceremony, which of the two would now be Eve to that Adam in God's eyes?"

"God knows, no man. But your Eve is Trini and you know that's the truth. Do you know what that heavy feeling is in your stomach? It's the claw of God. Baudelaire was such a great poet!"

I'd have liked to shout "Come back and tell me about the claw of God," but he was already off along the goats' trail and soon disappeared among the kermes oaks and junipers.

FALGUERA DE LOS CABEZOS, SUNDAY, 10 OCTOBER

Depending on which way the wind blows, we hear a bell chiming in bursts, God knows from which small village . . . From enemy territory, that's for sure, since no bells are left in ours, but it's such good company! I am happy: I dreamed about Trini! Would you believe that it's the first time? A pity the dream was so incoherent, but I could see her so clearly, smiling at me, tears glinting in her eyes, the eyes of an ingenuous but understanding child.

And this Sunday morning, listening to the distant sound of a church bell, stretched out under a pine tree, enjoying the mellow mid-October sun, I began to think how we three – her, the child and I – could be so happy in this birthing shed. . . And why not? With a cow and a few goats, far away from everyone, people would let us enjoy a quiet life! The chimes of the anonymous bell melded now and then with the bells of the cows and goats and I kept thinking that everything would be so lovely if life were so simple.

But many have thought these thoughts before me and many will after me . . . So lovely if it were so simple . . . We should start by being ourselves, by being solid as statues and dumping the appalling tangles we weave unawares. The desolate plains of La Pobla de Ladron only tell the seasons from the temperature: an oven in summer and the North Pole in winter. The vegetation stays the same all year round. It's so pleasant to be in a quite different area and face to face with living nature, even if it's dying. To see foliage that's turned yellow or reddish, autumn hard at work from the inside, and the woods now full of mushrooms. My aide picks me a pannier every day; we eat them grilled. He once even brought me wild honeycombs. His arms and face were terribly swollen but he assured me he wasn't in pain: evidently, when you reach a good level of stings they no longer hurt. The honey was slightly bitter, but delicious all the same. We have even better desserts: bunches of alcoholic, juicy grapes from vines abandoned in no man's land.

The locals look horrified when they see us eating mushrooms. "That's goats' food," they mutter in disgust; yet they eat such wonderful rubbish like their *mortajo* as if it were the best thing ever. Nor could you persuade them to drink a glass of milk: "That's for the poorly. It gives us a belly ache."

The sound of our steps through the wood sends lots of thrushes flying up – and that species of bird with such an amazingly crossed beak, I think they're called crossbills. Vultures fly high in the sky on their way to the plains of Xilte and La Pobla de Ladron, the scene of recent battles; I imagine they can't tell the difference between a battlefield and a vulture trap. At the same height or even higher we see storks beginning to migrate southwards. They are the first to migrate, winter's advance party.

You feel how peaceful life is after those weeks of madness. I've kept hold of one habit: I can't go to sleep without first saying the Lord's Prayer looking up at the Cross of the Cgynus. "Pick up your cross and follow me" – didn't your God say something of that sort, Ramon? Of all that crowd of gods I'm only interested in one, the one who became man: why should the others interest us if they've never taken an interest in us? If God exists, he must have become man. Why would he not have done such a thing? How could he have left us so alone with that horrible thing they call intellect – lucidity in the face of the nothingness, a meaningless glimmer lost in the eternal and endless darkness around us? If it were so, if we were alone, when we gaze up at the night sky the space between the stars would freeze us to death: the terror of empty space, unimaginable cold, eternal shadows, the universe's incomprehensible backcloth.

Why then does the sight of the sky at night soothe us, keep us company, fill us with confidence? Why? Who keeps us company? Who?

So many things exist without rhyme or reason, and what if God didn't exist?

FALGUERA DE LOS CABEZOS, MONDAY, 11 OCTOBER

My promotion to lieutenant has just arrived from the ministry. The document specifies: "as captain responsible for hardware". The commander came personally to my birthing shed: he had a hangover like the good old times in Olivel. He gave me a really tight, emotional hug, as if they'd promoted me to Marshal of the Holy Empire. I pointed out that the battalion has no support fire – those .85 mortars belonged to the other brigade and they took them when the operations were over.

"Don't you worry, Lluís. I'll buy you some soon!"

For the moment, as we have no support artillery, I remain in command of what's left of the 4th Company. Every night I do a tour of our positions and once that's over I sit in a solitary spot and seek out the Cross of the Cygnus. It's become a real obsession! What is a cross? A simple artefact that genius in ancient times managed to invent; an artefact to prolong death agonies . . . A horrible invention. "Pick up your cross and follow me." So, is suffering the only path?

VI
Alas, so fleeting . . .

OLIVEL DE LA VIRGEN, 15 OCTOBER

Back in Olivel, with a raging temperature: 40°. A laryngitis caught among the icy peaks of Los Cabezos. They'd given us collective permission to regroup and organise in Olivel – 150 men left from 500 – while we waited for new recruits to arrive; it was a miserable return. In rags, shoes split, eaten alive by lice, many with scabies – and the day we arrived was overcast and depressing, dark at noon as if it were already night-time. How different from the day we first arrived here!

I was back in my old bed: the familiar mattress gave me a friendly welcome! And what if he really was that second lieutenant? Don't think about it; don't torture yourself; it can't be reversed. The bedroom has its usual bitter almond smell. Picó, Cruells, the commander and the doctor came for a chat around my bed and I thought how strange they seemed four months ago when I met them for the first time in Castel de Olivo. Now we're like a family. The doctor gave me some kind of pill which reduced my temperature considerably. Dear old Olegària stuck her oar in: out of sight of the doctor, she prepared me herbal infusions that had to be drunk very hot. She even greased my back with marinated tomatoes. She wouldn't have slept peacefully without applying a cure she says is infallible against sore throats, and besides, what harm could it do? It was no hardship being greased like that and if it made her so happy . . .

Every step she takes on my behalf makes her think another old lady is doing the same for her grandson, wherever he may be. Her grandson . . . Maybe if I just came out with it, the doubts would be cleared up: it would become clear her grandson has never been a second lieutenant and has never courted any Irene. Whenever I'm about to mention him, a knot forms in my throat; I've only dared to ask her the date when she received her last letter in the hope that it is recent. Unfortunately it dates back to well before the fighting in Xilte – she only receives letters every three or four months and it's all very complicated. We can't even know where he was then, because the enemy camp has established a norm, which we should also adopt, forbidding soldiers from saying where they are in their letters.

One evening, while we were chatting, a soldier came from chief of staff with marching orders he'd just received from the brigade. We weren't expecting it, our new recruits hadn't arrived and the battalion was as depleted as when they withdrew it from the front to regroup. It was an urgent order from Divisional H.Q. The enemy had launched a counter-offensive. We had to be in the theatre of operations before dawn; the division was concentrating all its forces there, however decimated. I'd stay in Olivel alone with my raging temperature and sore throat.

People didn't seem at all enthusiastic – quite the contrary: "At this rate, nobody will be left to do a tally." "And to think that the 'flatfooted' ... ?" Picó took my pouch and the commander my mackintosh, on the sly. They thought I was out for the count, but I watched them out of the corner of my eye. What could I say? I don't need them and they are sure my things bring "good luck". They'd never have picked up poor Gallart's cape! I've survived the lot without a scratch and now have a wonderfully sore throat: so much good luck is, evidently, down to my pouch and my mackintosh. But when I caught the doctor, after he'd given me my Pyramidon – that's what my pills are called apparently – also sticking my pipe in his pocket, I simply had to say: "*Tu quoque?*"

"You know, Lluís, just because I have a degree in medicine it doesn't mean I don't have as many complexes as everybody else."

Only Cruells remained and he looked at me in silence with those soothing, owlish eyes of his, as if he was sad to leave.

"You'll be left by yourself in Olivel."

"Yes, Cruells, and I'd not like to lie to you: I am pleased. So much war is exhausting."

"I'm afraid for you. Relapses are dangerous."

"You mean my laryngitis?"

"You know what I mean."

"You're wrong. I'm cured. After so many nights with the Cross of Cygnus for a roof! I prayed a lot, Cruells, though you won't believe me."

"And why wouldn't I?"

"You know – and don't laugh – I even prayed in those battles. Curled up in a hollow, wrapped in the mackintosh the commander has just swiped, trying to get to sleep, listening to the whistle of stray bullets, I stared up at that starry cross and said: 'I'm an animal, Lord: an animal! Uncle Eusebi is worth a thousand times more, the *carlana* too. I can't be sure about the *carlà*, but who knows . . . They're all better than me, God. Have mercy on me, even if I'm the worst animal there is left on this earth.'"

"One prays for what one can, not what one wants," replied Cruells, as serious as ever.

I miss the battalion. It's the first time I've been by myself since I joined. I don't have a temperature today and I'd have left the house if the sky hadn't been so grey and rainy – that's even more depressing in a village so closed in upon itself. Old Olegària looks after me as if I were the apple of her eye: chicken broth, cups of oregano with rum and sugar, fresh goat's milk. She insists her grandson must have laryngitis like me: laryngitis! That poor dead, mutilated second lieutenant . . .

From my bedroom I hear the shouts of children playing in the square despite the rain. I miss the battalion as one of these youngsters would miss the others if they shut him up by himself. "I'm the *carlán*, you must obey me," I hear one shout. I look through the half closed shutters: isn't that the *carlana*'s older boy? Enriquet . . . When she was pregnant with that snotty kid, the village lads daubed shit on her doors to the village's general approval and with the old women's special blessing. The other children didn't want to play with him: now they look at him with respect. They obey him. And how! He kicks one who was being stupid – and they all think that is right and proper . . .

16 OCTOBER

I went out. It's strange that the *carlana* hadn't deigned to ask after me in all this time. I don't mean she should have come in person, but she could have sent her servant. She may be afraid of getting involved, or perhaps I'm of no concern now. I'm an orange she's squeezed dry.

I went for a stroll around the outskirts of the village. Along the banks of the River Parral the leaves on the poplar trees are yellow and red and falling. The river carries more water than it did when I rode on Acorn.

What's happened to that horse? Has she forgotten me too?

Now it's all silent in the pine grove where the crickets sang and it doesn't give off that resin smell: the dampness from the earth is everywhere. It's starting to be cold. I'm missing the mackintosh those fools stole from me.

The neighbours are busy with an excellent saffron harvest. The village streets seem carpeted with petals: the river sweeps huge quantities downstream. Their scent isn't so strong, but it's similar to the scent of roses and is in every doorway. Old and young, men and women, are sitting on low chairs between big panniers. They take the flowers from one, pull out the red pistils, place them in the other pannier and throw away the purple petals that are no use. Then they roast the pistils and the dry dust left is the saffron that's worth its weight in gold: the true wealth of Olivel.

When I sit down in a field by the river I watch thousands and thousands of petals float by: there are so many that in places they completely cover the river to very strange effect: a river of purple.

In the end the saffron scent becomes an obsession; I really don't know why but it makes me think of her.

After lunch, old Olegària left me alone in the house; she had to go to water her allotment, or she'd lose her turn until the next week. The water from the river is severely rationed.

It was the opportunity I'd so been waiting for. My bedroom is on the ground floor; hers is on the floor above. I went up like a thief. The door was only pulled to: the smell of a room where someone sleeps and is never aired hit me in the face like bad breath. It was pitch dark inside; old Olegària only opens her shutters in special circumstances, like that one time. I'd never have thought I'd come back one day by myself and on the sly . . . I groped my way to the window. What would I say if she came in unexpectedly? I'd not tell her the truth; let her think I was stealing, whatever, no matter.

I leaned on her bed. It has five woollen mattresses, as double beds do in these parts.

I sank into it as if it were a cloud because they're shapeless, not reinforced. Old Olegària had been to Barcelona once in her life; she had to consult an eye specialist as cataracts were forming. Her only precise memory is of the mattress there: "Crikey, how can they sleep on something so stiff?"

The photos stared at me from their purple frames. The fixed smile, the staged expression, the charcoal hair and eyelashes . . . Then, all of a sudden – you idiot! What made *you* of all people stand on top of the sandbag parapet?

Didn't that second lieutenant also have a deep wrinkle to the left of his mouth, an early sign that something was wrong with his liver? Bah, in the end we all look alike. When two people look alike, there's always one who looks more alike than the other. What does looking alike mean? What does having something wrong with your liver mean? A man who'd just been shot from a range of thirty feet, who may have been hit in the liver, could be forgiven for looking as if there was something wrong with his liver. In such a situation, who wouldn't look poorly?

This bedroom really reeks, worse than Father Gallifa's cell, and that's saying something. And what guarantee is there that those photos, which have been so retouched, give any idea of his real appearance? Particularly this one, when he's taking first communion at the same time as his grandmother, I mean his grandmother's sister – thanks to the good works and grace of a portrait photographer who thus earned himself a hundred pesetas. A hundred pesetas! The wretched swindler! And this horrible frame, a present from a *Doña* . . . "A real *Doña*, Don Luisico, because she was the village schoolmistress." Can you expect anything but toil and trouble from such people?

OLIVEL, 17

The weather is still so dismal that I went to the tavern rather than for a stroll. Melitona was going to and fro, as busy as usual. And poor Gallart abandoned on that barren waste . . . A strange reaction on the part of the commissar, he refused to set foot in that inn when he returned to Olivel. "It wouldn't be right in Gallart's absence."

The commander wrote: "Don't move from Olivel. These operations have been a disaster. Wait for us. We won't be long."

Is there something in the Olivel air that goes to the head? Why do I always feel so well here? The afternoon's thousand hues, the migrating birds, the falling leaves, the water bubbling in the brook, all seem to say: "Don't waste the best years of your life, you won't live twice, your seconds are ticking on towards the void like the saffron petals the Parral is sweeping away . . . and those seconds could be wonderful!" I would give everything for a moment of glory.

I was twenty-six the day before yesterday: I just remembered. And a wave of melancholy flowed over me like a forgotten melody. Like a piece of music that was perhaps wonderful but we didn't notice when we were listening and now we notice, we've forgotten . . . O God, where do the years we've lived disappear to?

This morning, without realising, instinctively, I found myself walking up the slope to the castle. Fortunately, I stopped halfway: where am I going? Why would I go to say hello to her? What would I say?

OLIVEL, 18

I climbed up to the castle.

Her servant took me to the attics I'd never seen before. There are eight or nine huge attics, separated by the top of the building's master walls. The sharply sloping ceilings are the underside of the roof, the supporting beams of which are eye-catching. Where did they find such gigantic trees? They must be ancient walnut trees, like the ones along the banks of the Parral, that seem to touch heaven with their crests and hell with their roots.

There are lots of swallows' nests among these enormous beams, and in both north- and south-facing attics, nests different from the ones you see under the roof eaves; I gather they are made by different varieties of swallow. However, the swallows have now left both kinds of nests, though the geckos are still running around. In the odd wall – and they aren't plastered – you see the holes where barn owls must make their nests. The floor isn't tiled and shakes underfoot. There's a lot of old junk piled up in each corner: an antique dealer would find more than one piece of interest. Worm-eaten walnut-wood chests, some with Gothic lids, escritoires with drawers missing, friars' chairs with broken legs, extraordinary baroque braziers, tools you can't put a name or use to. Three paintings caught my attention: they were stacked facing the wall so only the back of the canvas was visible, they were large and punctured in various places.

She was in the smallest, south-facing attic. There was no junk, but cages of rabbits and hens and a small pigeon loft, as well as a reed fence on a pair of damaged boxes, and a mat with figs covered in flour drying in the sun.

She was sitting on a low chair, busy with saffron like everyone else; the children also have their little chairs and corresponding couple of panniers, and were concentrating hard, doing what she was doing. There and then a ray of sun slipped through a gap in the clouds, seemed to quiver full of invisible droplets until it came to rest on the head of the younger boy. I hadn't realised he was so fair: he gleamed like old gold on the altarpiece.

She told me to sit on another chair, not taking her eyes off her work. Pleasant and polite, and that was it. I couldn't think what to say: I asked her what the three paintings were about.

"Enric's grandparents. The anarchists amused themselves firing their pistols at them. I brought them up to the attic because I felt they were giving me the evil eye."

"Can I take a look?"

Three equestrian portraits that, apart from belonging to past eras – one corresponding to each ancestor – are quite undistinguished, third-class provincial paintings of the sort you can't see improving with age because the years make them darker and harder to see. I calculate that they represented, respectively, the grandfather, great-grandfather and great-great-grandfather of the deceased Enric, judging by the style of clothes from one to the next. All were dressed in their best and mounted stiffly on their steeds, looking straight ahead without a hint of irony, their left hands on the hilts of their swords and their right on the reins. Their blank stares are made of the same stuff as old Olegària's grandson, and, just as the latter's absence of irony is accompanied by an impressive good faith, the three equestrian portraits have the same half-foolish, half-crafty eyes that so enliven the photographs of their descendant. All three naturally carry the same knightly shield under the legs of mounts that are prancing spiritedly: a silvery olive tree in a field of green, unless I'm a complete dunce at heraldry. The *carlana*'s children don't have a grocer's beady eyes; they don't resemble these people in the least . . . or the *carlà*!

I think the shield is missing its motto: "No credit today, tomorrow maybe."

"You should have them restored someday. They are your children's forebears, after all."

"Yes, of course, I'll bear it in mind."

She pulled out the pistils with a light touch and around her the uneven attic floor was strewn with petals; the scent seemed to come not from the plucked petals but from her. Stooped over her work, she had no eyes for me. I looked at her in silence.

"Holy Maria of Olivel . . .," I muttered. Then I was silent again. What else could I have said? Pray for us?

She raised her eyes, they flickered with that shadowy light I knew so well.

"Did you say something?" Her contralto voice rang out naturally, with none of the tremolo that used to knock me out. Or had I dreamed that tremolo? Could that voice ever have quivered?

"Yes, but I don't know what. I think it was to do with the saffron flowers. Or perhaps the praying mantis. I don't know if you've ever read a book called *The Wonders of Instinct* by Fabre from Provence; it's very interesting. I found it a pleasant surprise years ago. I was fourteen or fifteen, just imagine."

"I thought you mentioned our local Virgin."

"Yes, her too, and why not? We could also mix in the local Virgin, since you bear her name. Maria d'Olivel, Olivela, so much work simply to profit from those minute pistils! And these pretty, scented petals are simply thrown away; the river's full of them and looks purple from a distance."

"They're good for nothing," and she turned her gaze back on her work, never resting her fingers.

"Agreed, they're good for nothing. Instincts are a wonderful thing but in the end what use are they? What use would life be if we lost the only thing of any value?"

"What are you talking about now?"

"How do I know? One can dream up so many hypotheses! Some

people dream them up without thinking, Santiaga, for example . . ."

She looked at me as if she were thinking: he's got a screw loose. If we're going to dream up hypotheses, why doesn't Soleràs take his further? Those children who are so fair, those big eyes – their mother's. There is a sure way to make certain precautions fail, but then there are so many possible hypotheses: this could be never-ending. For example, what if the *carlà* and the *carlana* turned out to be brother and sister and were quite unaware of the fact? And why not? There's been a graft from somebody, God knows who. But then they'd bear a slight or strong resemblance; the children would have something of the deceased, who must have been their uncle . . .

Strangest of all, the fact that she'd brought those splendid children into the world was what most attracted me to her. A dark instinct stirred inside me, perhaps more vegetable than animal, spurring the spread of powerful and dominating life, like one of those walnut trees on the banks of the River Parral with fantastic roots, to spread a race of gods: *Eritis sicut dii*, our most secret desire, the uncertain glory for which Adam exchanged the quiet, certain glory of Paradise. The wonders of instinct, I thought: the female, once inseminated, devours the male who is good for nothing, then denies herself until she dies for a posterity she will never know: everything for posterity! We are nothing; posterity is all. However, what is posterity? A pack of fools like us. And insects are basically as foolish as we are.

Perhaps when the deceased was alive there were precautions that were worth defying. But now . . . now she is free . . . and she doesn't have to trick anyone . . . what would be the point . . . ?

"They are good for nothing," I repeated. "They protect these red pistils. Once the pistils are gone, what use are they?"

"That's right," and she nimbly carried on with her work, almost completely ignoring me.

"You know what I'm referring to?"

"No, I can't think what you're talking about."

"Do you know what a praying mantis is? It's an insect that's noteworthy for several reasons."

"We call them 'nuns' around here. There are lots in the stubble when it gets really hot. People say that if a child loses his way in the fields, he has only to ask a nun the way; the insect will put its hands together in prayer and point him in the right direction."

"That's another hypothesis. If we start, believe me, we'll never finish! Just listen to what I wanted to tell you: isn't it a pity to throw such pretty flowers away? It's fine to keep the pistils, I won't deny that, but it's cruel to throw away the petals . . ."

"What would we do with them? They don't serve any useful purpose."

"No useful purpose like a woman who has brought children into the world. I don't mean that children don't deserve respect, children when they're 'home-produced', as our commander says. However, must we renounce love and glory? Believe me, Olivela, utility isn't everything! We mustn't be like insects."

"Which insects?"

"The nun, for example. Obviously you haven't a clue what I'm talking about. The nun has habits – how can I put it? – that one shouldn't recommend. Yet will you believe me if I say there are times I feel exasperated and envy the male who's been devoured? At least he had his moment of glory, however uncertain. An instant, but think how long it lasted! To be envied! Why live longer? Such a moment is worth an eternity."

"I haven't seen a nun in a long time," she said as naturally as a great actress. "When we were little, we searched for them in the stubble, held their tails between our fingers and said, 'Join your hands together.' And they did. My God, how the years have flown by . . . We also went tadpole fishing in the river and kept them in jam jars until they turned into frogs."

"There are so many possible hypotheses! Olivela, you're the one person in the world to make me imagine so many. You mention tadpoles that change into frogs if they don't fall by the wayside. It's called metamorphosis. And some turn into toads and others into salamanders, because the world is as full of metamorphoses as it is of hypotheses. You meet such hypotheses as you travel the world: Turdy, for example, poor Turdy . . ."

"Say what you think. Are you worried you might offend me?"

"Turdy was never your father! Some things hit you between the eyes.

A toady tadpole inevitably leads to a toad."

"Don't think that hadn't already occurred to me . . . You won't believe how often I've thought that and wished it were true, for my sake and his. Especially his. It would so much better for him . . ."

"Yes, Olivela. What about the other one . . ."

"Which other one?"

"The other idiot, the shy, polite kind. The well-mannered idiot. Don Enrique de Alfoz i Penyarrostra . . . that tame Roland! If we could start hypothesising about him, we'd never finish. Agh, the gap in the roof lets a cold breeze in . . ."

Her eyes flashed blindingly like lightning: "We're at cross purposes," she interrupted me. "I'm sorry. Why do you find it so hard to understand?"

"To understand what?"

"My position. I'm only interested in my children." She returned to her work.

The hesitant ray of sun, with its burden of raindrops, now settled on the head of her elder son: "I'm the *carlán,* you must obey me", and he too gleamed like old gold. Both were separating out the pistils, intently, quickly. The swallows' nests were so silent!

OLIVEL, 19

An unexpected visit. Soleràs.

He turned up at old Olegària's place: "I heard you were ill. I'm glad you're feeling better."

I told him to sit on the only chair. I was lying on my bed.

"You're a lucky man. Wonderful laryngitis allows you to live like a king . . . and in the village where you have your bit on the side . . ."

He took off his leather blouson and dropped it on the floor.

"I don't have a bit on the side, here or anywhere. Please don't start on your usual rude nonsense. Do want a smoke? They stole my pipe and pouch, but there's a small packet there and paper to roll."

"I'd be more grateful for a glass of cognac."

The republic of the baby's bottle fellows had left me one of fire-water, which, according to them, the doctor included, is the best cure for laryngitis. He poured himself almost a full cup – my tin cup – and put his feet on the table, stretching and yawning.

"You and I should have words, Lluís, and not about your bits on the side who don't interest me. You can preserve them in aspic. Frankly it's a side of life that does nothing for me either way. At the end of the day, if you give it a little thought, all a man and woman do when they kiss is to bring together the top ends of their digestive tubes."

"Is that what you call philosophy?"

"Yes, the cheapest kind, that's within the range of any intellect, like yours now."

He laughed with that unpleasant cluck of his while taking a long swig from the cup.

"It will make you ill, Juli, it's firewater."

"We should talk seriously, Lluís. Don't you think that *Macabre Wedding* would be a good title for a novel? One I'll write someday; for the moment I've got a title. A super-pornographic effort worthy of our times! What if I were to tell you that the idea for that monastery wedding was inspired by you . . . and Trini. Or do you deny that you're like a couple of mummies doing your double act?"

"I repeat, watch what you're saying. You could make me lose my temper like last time."

"Poor Trini! You can't forgive her for remaining faithful: "*Et lire la secrète horreur du dévouement . . .*""

"Have you come to sermonise?"

"No, Lluís. I've yet to scale such heights. You can take it easy. I came to tell you that you and I will never be notaries. Notaries! Is it possible that you and I ever prepared for the entrance exams? Those cramming sessions we had with the *Digest*, the *Book of Decrees* . . . A waste of time, Lluís! Not to mention the *Pandects*. Yuck! Who now remembers the *Pandects*? We've had a taste of glory that leaves an aftertaste to make one hate the *Book of Decrees*, the *Pandects*, the *Digest* and even Papinian's *Definitions*. We've been a-wandering, we've done this and that, we are free, we have acted like men and we've acted like wild beasts . . . how can anyone now ever become a notary? War is the bit on the side that poisons your blood for ever; anything else pales in comparison. Just think for a moment, why do we still read the *Divine Comedy*? Supposing, that is, we do still read it, and I have to say that it's a book I've read with even more enjoyment after *The Horns of Roland*. Because only one like it has been written in three thousand years while so much other nonsense has been poured out – oceans of tedium! But only one *Divine Comedy*! So then, if one is written every three thousand years, that means three thousand *Divine Comedies* would take three thousand times three thousand: however little trigonometry or algebra you know, you can work that sum out. And the years just fly by; it seems that only yesterday the diplodocus and prehistoric sloths were wandering on God's earth . . . and two hundred million centuries have whizzed by! So poor Dante will end up stashed away in huge attics full of books as good as his that nobody reads: who could read so many million works of genius? Human memory couldn't retain the names of the thirty or thirty-five million Dantes who will have accumulated, even though this planet of ours, that's noteworthy for various reasons, may endure a reasonably long time, astronomically speaking, provided it doesn't pop like a fart – a not entirely impossible outcome. That's why I have decided not to write *Macabre Wedding* and have given up the idea of being the next Dante."

"Fascinating, but I don't understand why you've come to Olivel to give me this piece of news. You may have something in common with Dante – but do I?"

"Perhaps you aspired not to be a Dante but to be a notary. Though for every Dante there've been approximately four billion six hundred thousand million plus notaries."

"I see you've done your sums."

"I made that calculation on a night when I couldn't get to sleep. If you can't get to sleep, do what I do: count up how many notaries there have been, are and will ever be on this wonderful planet from the first specimen you can recall. You go to sleep quicker counting notaries than sheep or goats. Bah, notaries create so many clouds of dust! You could count the stars in the sky or the grains of sand by the sea quicker! I've always suspected that Abraham took up the wrong profession: he should have been a notary. Read up on his purchase of Machpelah's grotto, that big cavern where he wanted to bury his wife; read it and you'll see he bought it for four hundred shekels of silver – *Genesis*, XXIII, verses 7 to 20 – and while you're about it you'll see you couldn't cobble together a better contract of sale and purchase. He was a great notary! Believe me, Lluís."

"So what?"

"Believe me, Lluís, the things men try to substitute for the only real glory that exists are fake and ridiculous. Literary glory? Idiotic and dead on the page . . . Be one book among millions, one mummy among millions, and may your plaster bust find display space on the filing cabinet in the offices of 'Ruscalleda's Son, Fine Pasta for Soups'."

"So what is 'real' glory?"

"Love and war, killing and its opposite! That's the only one, but I've suffered from the most terrible toothache ever since my tender childhood . . ."

"Love and war, killing and its opposite! Don't think you're the first to say that! Maybe you were. These things pall, they are too familiar . . ."

"Of course they do. Glory palls, lasts for a moment. But what a moment it is! We all live for that moment . . . Marriage? Whoever mentioned marriage? Forget it! In fact I came to tell you just that . . . No, don't count on me! Forget marriage! Marriage is their favourite sacrament, the poor little things, much more so than baptism! But not mine! I wanted *un grand amour*. Who doesn't aspire to be the lead in a great love affair? A great love affair, I mean, forget marriage! Don't even toy with the idea; that's what I came to tell you."

"To tell me! You should realise . . . What can you tell me?"

"It's odd you don't get it. If I carried on like you, I'd be married with kids before I noticed; but I won't, right? Don't fob me off with any of that nonsense. A great love affair, maybe, that's always entertaining, but you can forget marriage! Particularly if you have to take other people's children on board . . . Ugh, that would be the last straw. Children, as the commander well said, must be one's own crop. Maybe even love and war, killing and its opposite, providing it only lasts for a moment. By the by, did you know that I've never killed anyone?"

"Picó told me you fought like a tiger."

"With the machine gun? That's not killing, that's dispatching. I mean kill personally, for personal motives, someone you've got a grudge against.

Your best friend, for example. Killing him with the same relish, the same relish with which one . . . because killing and *that* are equivalents."

"Bah, as I said before, if you think you made that discovery —"

"I've not discovered anything, right? Nor would I want to."

"Glad to hear it."

"To discover something would be to triumph, and only fools triumph, people who don't aspire to the unattainable. I came in fact to tell you that the only love that interests me is a love that is unattainable, so forget marriage! The only thing possible is the unattainable; make a note of that, it's probably my motto for my life. I would so like to kill! Not with a machine gun but with my hands: to squeeze a quivering neck until it's strangled . . . I've got decent biceps, you know, I'm all sinews and muscles! You don't believe me, you never have, you've never deigned to mistrust me, but I am capable of killing! Just with my hands, you know. You've always thought me a weakling. You are as stupid as that lieutenant colonel . . ."

"Which lieutenant colonel?"

"The one in the Military Health division, who wanted to reject me as useless because I was pigeon-chested."

"You always told me it was because you were short-sighted."

"The fools! You people don't realise that there are two kinds of muscle, the ones you see and the ones you don't. That foreigner, for example, who was so tall and broad-shouldered, with a chest like a horse, so spectacular! I could have floored him if I'd wanted to: there are supple muscles that are invisible . . ." With that Soleràs rolled up a sleeve and showed me his long, skinny, shapeless arm. "With one punch, I'd . . ."

"Poor Juli, you've always had this mania. You know that a kid would knock you to the ground in no time. Forget the invisible muscles that only exist in your imagination. You've got much more important qualities! I'm surprised you're still so worried about muscles. I hope you wouldn't change your lot for a stevedore's."

"You bet I would," he replied, taken aback. "Why wouldn't I? That foreigner was probably one. He was so bronzed and blonde – don't you reckon he might have been a stevedore from the Cristiania jetties? With a splendid set of teeth only Africans usually have . . . You can't imagine the toothache I've suffered from childhood! There are Swedish millionairesses who can afford these caprices: she was much taller than him, a well-preserved, mature Nordic wonder. He was twenty years younger and she was maybe fifty. A magnificent couple! There will always be couples like that with a motorboat who think they've discovered a completely deserted cove, a cove where they can frolic like two horses! And a young twelve-year-old will always be hiding among the fennel wanting to throw up at the sight . . . Don't be under any illusions, there are no solitary coves: everything we do in secret is watched by innocent eyes that don't miss a trick. So I'm short-sighted, am I? Don't make me laugh. If only! Not seeing beyond the end of my nose . . . like all you people. Do you think seeing inside everything is great fun? I'll give you an example that you might find enlightening. The *carlana* is a fantastic dame, like that Swedish woman; Lluís, when you look at the *carlana* —"

"Please could we let that business be?"

"It's only an example. What do you see when you look at her? Her eyes, her hair, her mouth; you don't go beyond the surface. What would you see if you had Roentgen rays? Her brain, her sinews, her larynx, her lungs."

"If we saw that, we'd find no woman attractive."

"How do you know? Lungs can be wonderful. The *carlana*'s, for example, or that Swede's. As for livers, this kind of dame has a great liver. Like a sunbeam! A delicious purple with rainbow hues . . . What a pity I don't paint! I'd paint you my vision of the *carlana* or the Swede and it would knock you out. What wenches! They're bursting with health to give away or sell. Fantastic endocrine glands that charge up their powerful femininity! Conversely, I must confess, alas, that my endocrine glands are —"

"Leave your glands in peace, all this is stuff and nonsense."

"Stuff and nonsense? They were cavorting in the sand and neighing like horses . . . And I threw up. I would have liked to strangle that moron and the other morons like him scattered throughout the world!"

He stopped and stared at me with his short-sighted eyes and began to laugh silently: "I don't envy you these dames, Lluís. I really don't. I don't envy you them! I aspired much higher. But that's life: it's good to repent since that way you get two returns on your time, first sinning and then repenting. Repentance strings it out . . . sins have such short lives! On the other hand, repenting because you've not sinned is a barren exercise that brings no satisfaction! Happy the man who can weep copiously over copious sins! It's like rain on a field that's been covered in manure: the harvest is splendid! In contrast, I'm such thin land, and always parched! You won't believe that Saint Philomena appears to my aunt just as you won't believe that I was the one stealing tins of El Pagès milk from the Supplies store. *Eppur si muove.* What if I were to say you'll soon be convinced? Very soon: you won't take long at all. The minute I leave your bedroom. I refer to the tins of milk, not to Saint Philomena; you'll have to take my word on her. My aunt has an iron constitution, which she attributes to her style of life and above all to the special protection she receives from Saint Philomena. I'll tell you a thing or two about her style of life that she reckons is so healthy. It's all to do with Saint Philomena. My aunt once had the flu, like yours, with a raging temperature. As she'd never suffered from anything, that temperature of 40° was a noteworthy event; it was, one could say, a crucial turning point in her life, because, apart from that flu, nothing out of the ordinary had ever happened to her. Well, one night when she was feverish and couldn't get to sleep Saint Philomena appeared to her and said: 'Don't be afraid, I will save you.' And why was Saint Philomena speaking in Spanish? I haven't a clue, ask my aunt. Because Catalan wasn't yet an official language, I imagine – it was during the Dictatorship."

"We've got no hope if even the saints in the world beyond —"

"And my aunt is no fan of Spanish, you know? On the contrary, she's always had a weak spot for Don Carles and the Carlist Holy Tradition. However, do you think I came here just to tell you about my aunt? If we start to reminisce about life under the Dictator, it will be never-ending! We met then, during the Dictatorship, at the end of secondary school. You must remember that we started at university together in 1929. And we set off those fantastic shenanigans in December 1930, if I remember correctly, do you remember? Trini was with us: you'd only just met her; we climbed up onto the roof of the university to hoist that flag, the Federal Republican flag. We argued so much about which flag to hoist! Some wanted it black, others red, others red and black, others republican – though strange to say, at the time, nobody knew what a republican flag was; it's curious how we never went for the simplest idea, the hoisting of the Catalan flag – that was the one we all knew and the one that represented everybody.

"There was a vote and the federal flag won out. Fresh problems: what *was* the federal flag? We had to ask Trini's father; and, following instructions from her father, Trini patched it together using different materials. It had red, yellow and purple stripes and a sea blue triangle dotted with white stars; we cut these out from untrimmed paper with scissors and stuck them on with starch paste. That bloody flag was so much hard work! The stars set off more arguments; how many should there be? One for every state in the federation, but who knew how many there should be? When in doubt, no half measures, so we stuck on a lot, fifteen or sixteen to make everybody happy! Then came the practical problem of putting it in place on the sly; I wrapped it round me like a sash under my overcoat – I was well and truly stuffed! It's the only time I've drawn attention to myself because of the huge size of my paunch. And finally, off we went to hoist the flag! Lluís, do you remember how we crawled over those creaking roofs, you in front, Trini in the middle and me bringing up the rear? All those arguments, all that work and effort, all that crawling over the roofs of the university, so passers-by could look up from the square in amazement and ask: 'What's got into the students now? Why on earth are they raising the flag of the United States?'"

"Is that what the passers-by said? News to me!"

"You're always in a dream, Lluís! What did you expect them to say? What reactions do you think you get if you hoist flags that not even your mother would recognise?"

"I do remember you found a drum of oil somewhere and were desperate to set fire to the library. I stopped you in your tracks."

"You've always been one for culture. Do you think it would have been any great loss if the university library had gone up in flames? But I've something else on my mind I'd like to broach before we lose sight of one another for ever. It's this: do we remain the same throughout our lives? Do you feel you have anything in common with the six-year-old child you were twenty years ago? When you're eighty – and it will happen – will you feel anything in common with the Lluís of today? Who are we really? Do think on it awhile; make the effort: a stone is always itself, its substance never changes, however many centuries and millennia go by, but we . . . until eternity changes us into ourselves . . . Our cells are constantly renewing;

we lose old ones and acquire new ones; at our age now we probably retain not even a molecule of what we were when at the breast. So are we only a form that's always changing, with matter going in and out like the water of a river? A form where matter settles like the rats inside that donkey; in that case, the great law of the universe should be: 'Keep up appearances! Nothing else counts.' And who moulds this non-material form? The space that surrounds and limits us? No, don't blame poor space! It has a different task! Is it time? What else? Space and time, what a pair they make! I tell you if you start thinking this over, you'll soon get a migraine: there is no solution. I'd like to know, say, who the scoundrel is who moulded my shape and gave me this feeble, myopic mug that belongs to an introverted schizophrenic. Do you think it's nice to have a mug like mine? You, of course . . . let me finish, don't interrupt. Do you think it right I should have to bother about your hang-ups? I've made up my mind on that front! No more hang-ups and no more *tête-à-têtes*! I'm up to here with the lot of you, with you, Trini . . ."

"Trini?"

"Yes, Trini, why do you look at me like that? Your wife is very special, Lluís. If anything happens to me, people will think it's to do with her."

"I think you're off your head. Whatever is going to happen to you? What's Trini got to do with it?"

"I knew you were thick, but not so . . . Don't you know these women still read the Romantics, Schiller, and that other fellow, Goethe? Goethe, how awful! If you want to believe me, Lluís, stop reading *Elective Affinities*, and try the entry on 'The Bicycle' in the *Espasa Encyclopaedia* and you'll get a better hold on all this: 'It must be pointed out that this type of very modern vehicle is for one person to ride and even two, but never three: it is very dangerous.'"

"Bicycles have never interested me."

"There are dames around . . . And I don't mean your wife, God preserve me from them, or even the *carlana*. You never visited my home; you can't imagine what an aunt like mine is like. You'd never have appreciated that stink: the smell of that peculiar secret life. I lived it for years and years, years without end, maybe three or four centuries. Because, believe me, it's not easy to put a date to an aunt like mine. Generally speaking, other aunts belong to the seventeenth century, long before the French Revolution, but mine is well in advance of her era and talks about the French Revolution as if it had already taken place. She tells you about Marie Antoinette as she'd tell you about a sister-in-law she can't stand or bear to see, but who is still family. Sometimes, on the other hand, she sinks into the shadows of a shapeless past, retreats into historical periods that are difficult to define. At such times you could speak to her not about Marie Antoinette but about Tutankhamen in person and she would look at you blankly, like Stone Age Man, incapable of suspecting that he was *the dawn of humanity*. And, my God, what a dawn that was; and what humanity! In any case, the stench in the flat dates from 1699: not a year more or less. Because you have an uncle who's tight-fisted, you think you're the misunderstood nephew *par excellence*; don't count on it. You could swagger and post him *La barrinada*; as for poor me . . . don't think I didn't try it . . . Don't be such an innocent; all us nephews have had the same idea. But we don't have the same aunt. She'd sit in her Louis Philippe armchair, put on her spectacles and . . . not a peep! Until a few months after receiving her weekly *La barrinada* she deigned to make a comment: 'I can't think who sends me this very peculiar magazine that is always mentioning this Bakunin. It must be the Oratory Brothers.'"

"There are the strangest aunts . . ."

"If you only knew . . . One year, when by chance three young men who were family acquaintances got married a few months apart, Auntie concluded: 'I find that boys are marrying more than girls.' And then, when remarking the odd behaviour of relatives: 'These people do everything back to front.' I could tell you a thing or two! I'd never finish. And I could tell you so much about that flat . . . It was a tiny flat, in the topmost street in Sant Pere. The windows have to be closed all year round, with the shutters down and the curtains pulled to because Auntie suffers from agoraphobia and heliophobia. I should add that she never left her bedroom in Godella, where we spent our summers, and that it was always in darkness: I hardly need say she never set foot on to the beach. The only thing that ever caught her interest – in the outside world, I mean – was that cave with the stalactites; I sometimes think it's strange that stalactites didn't form in that flat in the topmost street in Sant Pere. A flat of the kind, I can say, that is really to my taste; it makes you feel like Tutankhamen, you know, like a properly mummified pharaoh deep down in his crypt: in other words, like a fish in its swim. I've lived there for years without end, for centuries, so I know what I'm talking about. Auntie can't tolerate electricity – she's never once been inside a tram – so the flat still has gaslight. A smell of vintage 1899 gas blends in with vintage 1699 molecules and gives off a unique spicy *je ne sais quoi*: the Cancan meets Jansenism! As for the walls . . . they don't exist! They're completely covered by paintings; loathsome paintings of saints, male and female, naturally, of souls in Purgatory, the death of the righteous and the death of sinners; even one of all the monarchs of Europe. From before the 1914 war, obviously: a mass of monarchs shuddering around poor François Joseph with his fantastic side whiskers, as if he were that gang's patriarch. And then family portraits, lots of family portraits: ugly, disgusting faces, of people yours truly somehow owes his existence to. Frightful faces that look unnervingly like mine! Auntie sleeps in an interior windowless room, like so many in nineteenth-century buildings. She only gets air from a door that leads straight into the tiniest lobby, one by one and a half metres. Remember that fact because it's really important: Auntie sleeps a metre and a half away from the front door since her bedhead abuts onto the partition wall between the lobby and her bedroom. That means it's not easy to open the front door without her noticing; she's got sharp hearing and sleeps lightly like all money-and-mania-ridden old women. Well, I did. As you see me here, I've gone in and out in the early hours and she's not noticed. She wouldn't let me go out at night, not until I was call-up age. And I'm grateful for that: going out at night wouldn't have been so much fun if it hadn't been forbidden fruit. The bliss of hypocrisy; but let's be clear on that: one hundred per cent hypocrisy. There are those who are hypocritical when practising virtue and sincere when practising vice, when it's really about being a full-time hypocrite, about always leading a double life. You may find that difficult to grasp, but it's very simple . . . I slept at the other end of the flat and walked barefoot along the passage in total darkness, guessing where I was by the number of footsteps I'd taken so as not to bump into the furniture. I opened the door incredibly patiently, and off I went, at one or two, off to the *barri xino*. Why the *barri xino*, you may ask. Isn't the *barri xino* terrifically old hat? Well, yes, it is, about as old hat as you can get; as old hat as the class struggle and the emancipation of the proletarian masses! That's what attracted me there. I've now shown you how much I liked vice when I'm basically as devout as a pilgrim and have often wanted to join the Oratory Order. I can see from the look on your face that you can't make head or tail of it . . . It's simple enough. Be patient.

"If I could only get you to grasp the pleasures of phantasmagoria! To be and not to be at the same time – poor Shakespeare; to be oneself and another: to be and not to exist, to exist and not to be, all at the same time! A split personality, total escapism, the heady feeling that you can only lead a double life! I won't attempt to describe the knocking shop, which was like they all are: sordid, stale-smelling and dank, inhabited by the three or four same old whores – morphine addicts in their fifties. And, naturally, a print of Our Lady of Lourdes on the wall. All these knocking shops are the same. Now and then a pervert would drop in and enliven the place a bit. If it hadn't been for the print tacked to the wall, I might have mistaken that den for a little corner of hell: it was a cheap-rate little hell: a hell for all pockets. The most disgusting anisette was on offer, distilled from wood, I expect; you could buy morphine and cocaine at a bargain price and people came out with the most wonderful obscenities and didn't bat an eyelid. At the time you refused to accept that I visited such places; you always suspected that I went off for secret lime infusions, blessed at most with a few drops of El Mono anisette; *eppur si muove*, you know? I was sixteen and already fed up with all that. In a minute I'll tell you the only thing that interested me in all that. I'd come home between five and six in the morning with a skinful and desperate to . . . I hung on because that was the best part. I hung on because there's nothing like being desperate to do . . . whatever! When I was a boy I hung on and didn't drink because of the joy water gives when you are really parched. Maybe pleasure is only grief in reverse; maybe pleasure *par excellence* is grief that's been mysteriously turned on its head. However, to return to my thread. When the night watchman opened the door to the street, I was so desperate I had to make a supreme effort not to piss in my pants. The fellow gave me a lit candle, something they still did in my neighbourhood, and locked the door, leaving me inside, gripping my candle and desperate, a desperation spiralling into the acute phase, the unbearable phase: you know, after lots of glasses of anisette, lots. I reached the landing on the second floor in an extreme state of tension, about to explode. I hadn't mentioned that Auntie rented a second-floor flat – the house is hers – to a highly respectable family: a notary, would you believe? And the notary had a daughter who was almost fourteen at the time; an angelically rosy-cheeked girl. With two plaits of dark hair, bright eyes and tall and thin as Desdemona. By her side Nati would have seemed an animal – remember Nati, the tenant farmers' daughter. Where's your little packet then?"

After rolling a little cigarette he continued his soliloquy: "Both Auntie and the notary had got it into their heads that it would be a tremendous idea to marry us off: when we came of age, obviously. First I had to finish my degree; by then I'd have started with the notary as a clerk and studied for the entrance exams, and once over that hurdle . . . off to the parish church! But, you know, didn't I say we'd never make it to notary? It was a tremendous idea, except they'd not taken me into account. There I was in front of their door, gripping the candle in one hand and unbuttoning my fly with the other. I stood there for a few seconds feeling it like a pistol, holding on in one last supreme effort to test my strength of will, because, as Dale Carnegie says, you need strength of will to triumph in this world. What's that? Do you think it odd that I've done Carnegie? I've done it all, I tell you! I've even done Bossuet's *Funeral Sermons*! And to be frank, there's one book that's a sight more deadening and that's *Das Kapital*. I think I'm the only person in the entire world who's swallowed that whole! In German too! Hey, and I didn't do that to cover myself in glory. Marxists . . . mmm . . . are only Hegelians, left-wing Hegelians; that is, they've taken the imagination out of Hegel. And, believe me, don't ever trust people who don't have imagination. I've told you that more than once. They are terrifying! There can be no sense of humour without imagination. In the same way that they would chop the heads off half of humanity to force *Das Kapital* on every infant class, the day they feel like a scrap of exhaustive erudition. Lluís, it's a real shame you've never believed in my gifts as a prophet – a real shame! Up to now you had to be a Krausist* if you wanted to be appointed to a solid, permanent university post in pedantry; so here's another prophesy: the day will come when all pedants will be Marxists. Now, where were we? Ah, yes, Carnegie? Strength of will? Yes, strength of will! I was telling you about how I was exercising my strength of will in front of the door to that notary's second-floor flat. When I had tested out my maximum level of strength of will, I finally released a violent stream of piss, aiming at the crack under the door so it hit their lobby. I wished I'd had reserves of pee to flood the whole flat, including the bedroom where that innocent lily must have been dreaming of meringues and angel cake: oh to flood out notaries in the whole wide world! Well, that's me. But I was soon empty, horrifyingly empty with a feeling of such impotence . . . I walked up to our flat, second door on the fourth floor, a desperate failure, feeling terribly sad, melancholy eating me alive. I was sixteen: the age for such things."

He sighed deeply, as if he'd just spun me a tale of adolescent love and despair. I was so beside myself after listening to that lunatic, brainless deluge I was at a loss for words.

"After that experience, you can imagine how I react to any prospect of marriage, however remote it may seem. I piss on matrimony and have done from the age of sweet sixteen! Ah, we'd be well out of it! Not me, not likely! One night, when I'd come back from an expedition to the *barri xino*, I was in bed and saw a luminous vision in the darkness. It wasn't very big, not a dozen centimetres all told, and glowed dimly, barely visible. It was like a nun in a white habit, completely one-dimensional, with no bodily presence, the strangest thing! Saint Philomena, I thought, terrified. I told you there was no electric lighting in the flat: I'd have had to get out of bed to light the gas and was too scared. I put my head under the sheets but couldn't get to sleep. Finally, daylight came! I took my head out and look: there, nailed to the wall, was a print and naturally it was Saint Philomena. A phosphorescent print: one of Auntie's brainwaves. She had found out

---

* In 1843 the liberal government sent Julián Sanz del Río to Germany to study German philosophy as a step to combat Spain's intellectual isolation. He brought back the philosophy of Karl Krause, a minor German idealist/pantheist and "*krausismo*" became a major influence in Spanish liberal thought – the main source of the pedagogy of Giner de los Ríos, founder of the Institución Libre de Enseñanza in Madrid.

about my night-time sorties and had thought to edify me with the luminous print trick. She never said anything, then or ever; she said all she had to say with that simple appearance put in by Saint Philomena. The day after, the print was gone, she'd spirited back to her bedroom. No explanation; not a word on the subject. Then one day she let slip after lunch: 'The notaries on the first floor . . . are so worried about what keeps happening. It's a real mystery . . . Maybe you won't do it again.'"

He poured a last cup of firewater.

"I came to say goodbye, Lluís."

"Are you changing brigades?"

"Well . . ."

"You're not off to join the flat feet, I suppose?"

"You got that mania too?"

"No, I saw them in action in the last round of operations. They're like us, when all's said and done. They got the same or a bigger bashing than we did. Have they sorted out your new posting in the division?"

"Maybe . . . And I thought I ought to give you these letters. I'd been holding on to them . . . like an idiot. I'm an idiot too: much more of one than you are when I try. I just put on a front as best I can. I don't want to hold on to them any longer. You keep them. But don't look at them now. You'll have plenty of time when I'm far away . . . I'm off. I don't want to act the fool again. Goodbye."

OLIVEL, 20

Ramon, I wish you were here by my side . . . and I'd cry, cry for hours on end! These letters were from my wife to Soleràs . . . How could I ever have suspected? I'd so abandoned her . . . I've read them driven by morbid curiosity. This is worse than any battle on a desert plain.

PART TWO

Le malheur est ridicule.
SIMONE WEIL

26 DECEMBER 1936

My dear Juli, Christmas was so dismal yesterday! I was by myself with the boy and he was grouching all the time asking for his father. "Have you forgotten Father is off fighting a war?" "Well, I want to fight as well." Lluís and his son are so alike it makes me laugh: the same mannerisms, the same way they curl up in bed. If you only knew how lonely I feel . . . I really write to receive your replies; your letters keep me company. He writes so little!

Yesterday, Christmas Day, we had nougat and champagne. At least these are in plentiful supply in Barcelona – I expect because all the factories making nougat and champagne are in republican territory. I tried to celebrate as cheerfully as I could pretend in front of the boy, but I kept remembering the 26 July when Lluís left. A summer storm rattled the metal roof of the estació de França, the stink of wet earth melded into the smell of steam from the trains. I could have cried when he hugged me: tears at moments like that bring relief, but . . . I knew how much he hated tears! Sentimentality, as he calls it, puts him in a foul mood. I'm sorry to be seeking comfort from you – who else can I turn to? If only you knew how lonely I feel, how lonely I have felt over these last five endless months . . .

2 FEBRUARY 1937

When I got home four letters were waiting for me, two from you and two from Lluís, who gave excellent news that dispelled the anguish that's been dragging me down. I only feel sad now when I think how far away he is on the Madrid front . . .

I'm sad though pleasantly so because – how can I put this? – my memories and hopes have been given a boost. The happy memories of our first moments together: Lluís doesn't realise that he has a natural gift when it comes to winning people's affections; his son has inherited this and that makes me glad. My lack of such a gift has made me suffer terribly. I have many reasons to feel hopeful. His last letter is full of affection: he seems to miss me and begin to see how much we mean to each other. The miracle will happen. I believe blindly that it will and you, who've been like a brother to him and to me, must have helped it on its way hugely. Don't deny it. I imagine you'll do all you can to influence him, to bring him back to me. Obviously you'll never say as much: you're too sensitive. Unfortunately very few men are like you: we women are intuitive and rarely get it wrong when we put our trust in someone.

A little excitement in our lives: as the boy often gets a sore throat – another thing he's inherited from his father – I decided to have his tonsils removed. Lluís has always refused to do this but I didn't want our little one to suffer from sore throats for the rest of his life when it's so easy to cure. The operation was quick, though he experienced a highly unpleasant couple of moments. Particularly the second tonsil; the first caught him completely unawares. He'd learned his lesson, kept his mouth shut tight and lashed out at the dentist.

Now it's over and done with and I'm happy. One less thing on my mind.

I'm thrilled about these letters from Lluís! And about yours too, naturally. Thank you for your soothing words that I don't need now, thanks to God. They reach me when I feel the whole world has been given a fresh lick of paint.

3 MARCH

How can you doubt that your letters really keep me company? Especially now I've not heard from Lluís for weeks and weeks . . . He'd given me such high hopes! His last letter was yet another string of short sentences . . .

If I didn't have yours, I'd feel so alone in this world! I'm not like Lluís, who can get along by himself in life; loneliness saps my spirits.

It isn't that Lluís has taken a dislike to me; that's not what I meant at all! I know only too well that he needs me and that he will realise it one of these days. Eventually he'll see that life is only tolerable if you share it with someone else; otherwise, you only experience a scary sensation of walking in the wilderness! One day he'll realise we all need a helping hand along the way. Otherwise, we are so lost . . . he *will* realise that eventually. If I can't sustain this hope, how would I survive?

I'm writing to you and gazing at the wonderful pile of El Pagès tinned milk in the middle of the drawing room. Yes, I've had fun removing them from their crates and building a pyramid. The five empty wooden crates are still there next to the pyramid in the middle of the room where you left them after unloading the lorry. I should put them in the cellar but I'm reluctant to – the wretched crates are such good company!

You made me so happy when you turned up out of the blue like that! After not seeing you for so long! How long had it been? I couldn't tell you! From when the war started, that now feels like the beginning of the world. Barely nine months, nine months like an eternity!

I'm sure he could get away if he wanted. You managed it. And he is my husband and Ramonet's father . . . He does send me his wages as an adjutant at the front every month. He keeps very little back for himself, but why has he never tried to come and see us?

I can imagine what a sacrifice it must have been to bring these five crates of tinned milk. You wouldn't admit it but I'm sure they were your daily ration that you've been hoarding over weeks and months. They'll do us such a power of good! I didn't know where to go to get milk for the boy; it's one problem after another here. Lluís could never tolerate listening to problems on the home front, or what these hard times mean for us women. I'm sitting in my favourite armchair, next to the window that overlooks the garden, gazing at that pyramid of tins, and I feel so happy, so delighted to be well provided for, and tears stream down my cheeks. It's a quiet sob, like a spring shower, like the fine drizzle rustling the new leaves on the lime tree.

What a pity you were here for such a short time. We had so much to talk about after all these months! So much, Juli . . . You left almost as soon as you'd unloaded the crates! Can you believe that the pyramid of tins I've had such fun building is as high as a Christmas tree? I'm even thinking of decorating it with candles!

12 APRIL

Poor Juli: I'm so lonely that I cling to your letters; they're all I have to keep me company! I've kept every one you've written and reread them from time to time. You've written me many more than he has; the difference between your pile and his – I've kept every one – is astonishing! He's not written for a month: a whole month and not a single line!

You must rid yourself of this depressing view of yourself – why should you put off women? After all you've the one quality we all appreciate: sensitivity. You think of everything, you can always imagine yourself in someone else's shoes, you know how to keep us company when we need it and how to vanish when you're in the way. Why do you say you'll never find a woman to love you? I'm sure you will one of these days. You are just the person to make a woman happy: you'll make a lovely husband, a model husband and an ideal father! I've seen that with Ramonet: he thinks the world of you. He remembers every single story you told him when you came to our place before the war as well as the one you told him on the evening of your surprise visit with the tinned milk, the one about "the three wise men of Piteus". I can't think how often I've told him it again, he liked it so much. He laughs himself silly!

That night you were quite shocked that I went to mass: you asked me why and I promised I'd tell you. Yes, Juli, I owe you this explanation because you were the first person to take me to a mass, something I thought quite ridiculous. If I go now, it's because of you.

Do you remember? It was in Santa Maria del Mar, a long time before war broke out. How could we have imagined then that Santa Maria del Mar would be burned down like every other church in Catalonia? You and I went up and down those streets and side streets on the pretext that we were selling *La barrinada*. Lluís hadn't yet joined our group and I didn't even know him, but you and I were already taking long walks around old

Barcelona with a bundle of copies of *La barrinada* under our arms. We'd come out on the small plaça de Santa Maria; it must have been eleven. All of a sudden you said, "Let's go in." And we did.

Once inside I knelt down next to you, simply because I saw you do that. I'd never been inside a church before. It was all new to me. You were kneeling by my side, holding your head between your hands; then I realised you'd been crying and I felt vaguely annoyed: what was your playacting about now? What was the point? How distant that all seems now! How time has passed! It must be at least seven or eight years ago and it's just a distant blur. I'd passed my entrance exam to the science faculty and was mad about geology: I'd never remotely felt religion could be of any interest. In my family there'd always been a great respect for the positive sciences and a complete indifference to what they called "metaphysics". We thought that sooner or later the positive sciences would rationalise the whole of society, namely the scientific organisation of anarchy: anarchy was for us the logical consequence of the positive sciences and we were in no doubt about it. You can imagine how shocking we found your barbed comments: I remember how you shocked us when you said, "It's obvious that once we know the exact age of the fossilised *os Bertran** of a diplodocus, within a margin of under six minutes and three seconds, we'll all become brothers and sisters."

Why did you say such things? Didn't you see that making fun of science was sacrilege in our eyes? Or were you perfectly aware of that? When you said all those things you made us feel you weren't one of us, that you were paying us a visit like one of the foreign tourists who came to our country – before the war! – to look for what was "typical", basically because they thought our country was picturesque, when it's the most ordinary, banal place as far as we are concerned. One night you even went so far as to suggest we should hold all our meetings in the dark and set up a "spiritualist chain". You couldn't have suggested anything more shocking, given what our views were.

The few times you talked to me about Christianity had a similar impact as your "spiritualist chain" and that's why I felt so uncomfortable leaving

* An imaginary backbone that was supposed to bring on laziness, invented by Joan Amades, an apothecary in Barcelona, who also thought up the necessary healing ointment.

Santa Maria del Mar after I noticed you'd been crying. I'd found the ceremony mechanical, boring, and devoid of meaning . . . "But what about the Gregorian chant . . . ?" you replied. If only you'd known how bored I'd been, not to mention the carnival costumes . . . I knew, because I'd read about it, that Christians think the host is transformed into Jesus Christ when consecrated by the priest, but what most caught my attention was how long the priest took, as if he were playing with the host, like a cat with a mouse. In the meantime, you'd knelt next to me, hiding your face behind your hands, and I wanted to roar with laughter at the idea of the cat playing with a mouse before eating it.

And now I go to mass every Sunday!

Well, not every Sunday. It's difficult to find one. A mass is now as clandestine as our meetings used to be, and that's why Uncle Eusebio – I'll tell you about this someday – when he found out that I was going, exclaimed: "Clandestine masses? They must be like a cell meeting!" And my father, who also knows I go, thinks that in my case it's all about the spirit of contradiction: "You're a real daughter of mine," he says, "always going against the tide! But isn't going to mass taking it too far?"

I owe you an explanation, because if I go to mass it's because of you, although I find that hard to explain even to myself! It's both very simple and very complicated . . . Too simple to express in words! One day I'll tell you the events and circumstances that led me there but I'm not in the mood today. It's been so long since I received a letter from him! Do you remember that day when you brought me a bunch of hyacinths? No, I don't expect you do – I do and I'll never forget it! Lluís was so surprised that he asked you, "Where are you going with that?" He hadn't remembered it was my saint's day. If only you knew how the scent of those hyacinths has stuck in my mind. It often drifts back to me. It's strange how scents leave such precise memories that are quite beyond words.

If you only knew how lonely I feel at times! You'll say I have the boy. True, but children don't keep you company; on the contrary, we adults must keep them company. I could try to distract myself, but what good would that do? Escapism is so tedious. Better to stay at home and wallow in sadness, a feeling which taken calmly can be almost as soothing as an April shower. If we knew how to make the most of our sadness, we might realise that the only happiness possible in this world is the sorrow of quiet resignation. But there are times when sorrow shows its most repugnant side; there are times when it's not even sadness, when it's only emptiness, aridity, tedium, and then . . . Even so, escapism is even emptier and more arid; it empties and deadens whatever it touches. Forgive me yet again for recounting all my sorrows. You're compassion personified, my true brother. After all, what do I have in common with Llibert, apart from the fact that we happen to be the offspring of the same father and mother?

16 APRIL

The other day I was talking to you about escapism and don't think I did so lightly: people have never been as frantic about finding distraction as they are now. It's depressing; you see such sights . . . Cinema queues have never been so long since the war started. I don't go, because I've always found films incredibly boring. However, I do something similar: I read more and more books about geology. I'd come to hate studying just after getting married – if one can use that word in my case – and I'm now getting back into it in order not to feel so alone and empty.

The daily newspapers are always full of battles, attacks and counter-attacks, dead and wounded, positions lost and won; you adapt to everything and end up not taking a blind bit of notice. The butchering has been going on for nine months now and people queue outside cinemas. The more savage the film, the better. And I understand: can you believe that I find fossilised molluscs from the Carboniferous Period more interesting than dispatches from the front?

At night, now, when Ramonet and the maid are asleep, I sit in my usual armchair with my book open on the table in the dim lamplight and distract myself as best I can, like everyone else. I'm not any better than they are – on the contrary: could anything be more absurd in these tragic times than finding fascination in the fossilised bones of an unknown species of squid that lived five hundred million years ago? That's much more absurd than going to the cinema. Sometimes, when I'm alone like this at night, I think I can see that face again: those eyes, that mouth gaping in horror. I never told you or Lluís about that. I didn't so as not to depress you, but so many months have gone by . . . It was early morning on 1 August: you and Lluís had been at the front for a week. That last night in July was horribly hot; the dog days were oppressive in Barcelona and I couldn't get to sleep. I heard three short shots ring out on the plot of wasteland behind our house just before dawn. I'd nodded off in my chair and woke up with a start. You people at the front don't see the horrors in the rearguard, and just as well; we hear gunfire every night in Barcelona, though I had never heard anything so close to home. I went out. It was a few minutes to four, dawn was faintly breaking over the port.

He was very old and his soutane had turned green from wear, it was patched and mended. His eyes and mouth were open wide. I was terrified and screamed and called to our maid. She ran down in her nightshirt looking exhausted and some neighbours came who'd heard my scream and the three pistol shots. The magistrate on duty finally arrived at six when the sun was high in the sky and a few flies, the fat golden green variety, were strolling over the lips and nose of that stiff scarecrow who'd met his end near us. "We get them early every morning," the magistrate said, "a few more or a few less depending on the day, but always a lot." "So what can we do to stop this butchery?" "Next to nothing," he replied. "The authorities can't cope." "Who is he?" I asked. "A poor village priest," the magistrate replied, "I'm sure of that. Marauding gangs of hotheads go round the villages burning churches and murdering priests and they often bring them back to Barcelona to kill . . . We find them early every morning," he repeated.

A week later, quite unexpectedly I found myself attending a clandestine mass.

An old friend of the family lives in a flat on carrer de l'Arc del Teatre, a woman who is getting on, the widow of a print worker who'd been a close friend of Father's. She hasn't any children, so lives by herself and earns a living doing housework. I'd had to take her a bread voucher that my brother Llibert – it's amazing how his pockets seem full of them – had got for her, after bread disappeared from Barcelona as quickly as silver coins and everyone was chasing vouchers. Three weeks after the war started, a baguette became a thing of the past.

I climbed up to the eighth floor where she lives to give her that bit of cheer: a bread voucher! After she'd hugged me very emotionally she suddenly said: "Come up to the attic with me." I followed her up. I hadn't noticed it was Sunday. I had no idea what to expect: we found a dozen or so people in the attic, almost all women. It was stiflingly hot because the ceiling was very low and immediately beneath the roof terrace. I had only been to one other mass, with you in Santa Maria del Mar, and this one was quite different. Why had that widow decided to say "Come with me" when she knew I wasn't a Catholic?

The few pieces of furniture were very battered. A small, unsteady, chipped chest of drawers they'd put on a little dais acted as an altar, one of those black chests with a white marble top every household used to own and that now seem so tawdry and old fashioned. The strangest thing was the old man officiating: he was the living image of the murdered priest.

If the anarchist's widow had whispered in my ear "He's an apostle, apostle so and so", she probably wouldn't have taken me by surprise: everything was so unexpected! An ordinary apostle, of course, the most ordinary of the twelve. He must have been eighty and wore an old work-man's clothes, patched velvet trousers, a smock and rope sandals. He'd put a chasuble over them, and his trouser legs peeping out from underneath looked ridiculous. His actions were weary, as if his body had run out of strength: when he kneeled, he flopped down like a sack of something and the sound of his knees made the legs of the little dais rattle. When he turned round to bless us his expression reminded me of the murdered man's bulging eyes . . . What an expression, my God! How can they say the soul is invisible?

I went on other Sundays, perhaps just to poke my nose in, perhaps it was my way of protesting – though nobody would ever find out and it would serve no purpose – against the "priest hunt" that was at its height across the country. I'd have liked that old man to preach a sermon, to say something to us, but he never did. "He says he doesn't know how," the widow told me. "He said he did when he was young but now he's old he's realised he has nothing interesting to say, that he's always been a bore talking, and that, anyway, we already know what he might say as well as he does." He did once utter or rather mumble a few words. "My children," he said, "look how the Church has returned to the catacombs. Jesus is showing us his face covered in blood and spittle as when Pilate said: *Ecce homo*."

He never said another word. And then one Sunday, it was the beginning of November by now, the widow said there would be no mass, there would be no more because the old man had disappeared. We don't even know his name; we've had no more news of him. I shall never forget his exhausted, imploring expression. Sometimes, quite unawares, instinctively, I put my faith in him, I pray to him. You'll think me ridiculous praying to someone who may still be alive, but when I remember a face like his I feel there's nothing separating this world from the next.

18 APRIL

I've received the letter in which you ask me for more detail about what you call my "conversion", possibly with a touch of sarcasm. My "conversion", as you call it, is no such thing, it's much vaguer and more nebulous. The letter I sent you two days ago gave you an inkling and perhaps there's no point adding anything; as far as geology goes, you'll recall I'd given that up when Lluís and I started living together. He was always cursing the bourgeoisie, though we lived comfortably on his dividends from "Ruscalleda's Son" – where he never deigned to set foot since he had always thought manufacturing soup pasta was stupid and the pits. I had no need to earn money and as Ramonet had come into this world very quickly – only three weeks after we'd started living together – I simply spent my time looking after the house.

However, this wasn't the real reason why I hated geology, though that's what I told you and him. I hated life as such and hid it from you both. I felt overwhelmed by disillusion a few months after coming to live in this mansion. You know the house is his, that he inherited it from his mother: what I possibly never told you is that Lluís, immediately upon coming of age, assigned it to me and Ramonet at the notary's, with the single condition that the legacy would be extended to other children if we had any. You see, Lluís has this generous side, though he'd already started suffering those attacks of silence that could last for days. You often came to spend the afternoon with us and your visits were the only thing in the world I had to look forward to. He also brightened up when you came. Once, we were drinking our eleventh or twelfth cup of tea, the rays of the winter sun were shining diagonally through the window and the wood stove, full of holm oak shavings, was glowing red and spitting. As usual, we'd been talking about fifty thousand things, jumping from one to another: life and death, spiritualism and magic, the mating habits of scorpions and burial rites in Papua New Guinea. Silence fell. You broke it and summed up the conversation with what seemed like a casual remark: "It's obvious: we come from the obscene and are on our way to the macabre."

You like these boutades and don't realise how hurtful your words can be. Words we let slip, not thinking they may open up a pit beneath other people's feet, a bottomless abyss, or that others may suffer from vertigo. You like to walk along these precipices that make my head spin! It was when I began to think everything was pointless, whether studying Carboniferous Age molluscs or bringing children into the world, from the moment it seemed the world didn't or couldn't have any end or point to it. It was just one sprawling suburb – a suburb, but in which city? – a chaotic space criss-crossed by dead rail tracks and bristling with posts that supported cobwebs of cables, and all to no purpose, an appallingly grey area fenced in by two interminable walls: the obscene on one side and the macabre on the other. What sense could anything have, if everything was reducible to this?

If you only knew how lonely I felt then, especially when Lluís was at home; yes, especially when he was by my side. Much lonelier than I feel now, I can tell you, now he's far away and can't crush me with his silences.

19 APRIL

I'm so ashamed I wrote you that letter yesterday. You know, when I got back from the post office I found two from Lluís the postman had slipped under the door.

Two letters that were so loving and so sad you can't imagine how much they moved me. He says he misses me, that we will start a new life when peacetime comes and that the war has helped him understand how much we're made for each other. He asks me to forgive the things he did in the past and put my trust in him for the future. How could I deny him that?

Lluís really knows how to find the words to make me cry and forget ... A couple of loving letters from him and here I am surrendering abjectly yet again – and not for the first time! I'm such a walkover! Lluís has a natural gift when it comes to finding forgiveness, it's so natural he's quite unaware of it, doesn't even notice. If he did, he'd be such an actor! Such a performer! But he's not, he does it spontaneously when he acts ... His son has inherited this gift along with many others; if you could only see how he wheedles forgiveness from me after a tantrum, and he's good at throwing them! He is such an adept and then all of a sudden he'll decide to stop playing up and be as nice as pie, and he's good at that too!

The postman came back later that afternoon to bring me the money from payments that had been delayed: three months of an adjutant's pay plus the extra bonuses for being in action that add up to more than his pay. It was a big wad of notes. I felt so happy that this morning I couldn't resist the temptation to buy a Queen Isabel *secrétaire* I'd seen days ago in a hotel sale; street porters have just carried it here. I've put it in the drawing room and hung above it that portrait in oils of his great-grandfather, the colonel in the First Carlist War, the one you said was a spitting image of our boy. I hadn't told you I'd found a gilt frame in an antique shop on carrer de la Palla that was just the right size, shape and style, so I've now framed the great-grandfather we were keeping in a drawer until we'd found the right frame. It's an old gold oval frame and the painting looks very decorative on the wall. He certainly does resemble the boy: I was scrutinising the portrait and the boy just now and imagining Ramonet with those huge side whiskers and the big red beret. It's so comical: if only you knew what my family thought about Carlists! And about colonels!

Ramonet has turned out a real Brocà; these Brocàs have war in their blood: he won't shut up, is always nagging me to let him go to war with his father. The more he does that, the more like Lluís he becomes ... and I just feel more childish and older by the day. Both at the same time. I'm twenty-one now; it was my birthday yesterday. I've come of age ...

Yes, Juli, I've been baptised; didn't I tell you? I'm sorry, I've been so frantic I don't remember when I last wrote you or what I said – was it two weeks ago? I only remember it was before your second visit, as unexpected as your first . . . However, to be frank, despite what you said on that long night that was so . . . short, for heaven's sake, I wasn't by any means convinced. You made it out to be very important, but I . . . I felt fine as I was; I was happy to be more or less vaguely Christian. I found it hard to decide to do something just to please you.

I've finally done it and, to tell you the truth, I feel exactly the same as I did before. I'm writing from my armchair by the window and every now and then I look at the pyramid of tinned milk that's really shrunk. You had no reason to apologise for not bringing more on your last visit, as I can imagine you can't do that very often and, on the other hand, I have enough to be going on with. I was so happy to see you so unexpectedly! The night passed so quickly talking to you . . . I remember everything you said: I keep pondering over your words and sink deep into my armchair as my grand-mother does into hers. Now, right now, quite frankly, I feel rather annoyed that I yielded to your pressure: how can a person as intelligent as you think that such an external rite like baptism can be so important? Yes, I know all about sacraments and the grace infusing them . . . I reckon the only sacrament I'm struck by is marriage!

And when I say marriage is a "sacrament" I mean what the theologians say; I'm not referring to the ceremony, whether it is religious or civil, which I know isn't strictly necessary. I mean the union of a man and a woman with a view to permanent bonding and the transmission of life: if that wasn't a sacrament, what would it be? It would be a gross obscenity, the mere thought of which sends a shiver down my spine!

As for baptism . . . what can I say? Is there anyone who can still believe in anything so idiotic – that by splashing a few drops of water on some-one's head and muttering a few magic words we manage to save a soul that would otherwise be condemned . . . ? I'm sorry, but I must speak as I feel.

I know you'll tell me that this isn't what one must believe; that many people who have been baptised will be condemned and many who've not will be saved, because the designs of God are inscrutable, etc., etc., etc. That's all very well, but what then is the point of baptism? If I've had it done, it was because you were so insistent and for no other reason, I can assure you.

From my armchair, through the open window I can see the lime tree glinting with new pale green leaves full of silvery reflections and I remember the worst days when I hated everything, absolutely everything, even this poor lime tree! That was when your boutade – "We come from the obscene and are on our way to the macabre" – was always hammering in my brain. Ramonet wasn't walking yet, only crawling over the drawing-room carpet, and I looked at him as if he were a kitten and wondered what right I had to give him a life that can only end in death; this life that is only one long death agony without hope. Nevertheless, I loved my son, of course I did; I was crazy about my boy, but wasn't that another of nature's tricks, like the one impelling us to perform the act that transmits life? Would we be so amused if we brought them into the world as they will become later, like my grandmother, for example? It was November and there were no leaves on the lime tree the gardener had pruned back to almost a bare trunk. And the lime tree seemed as idiotic as everything else; every year the same performance, losing its leaves, growing new ones, and to what end? What was the point? It was as ridiculous as Lluís' beard. I would hear him every morning because he's much more of an early riser than me. He liked to shave, not in the bathroom but in the bedroom sink, so I'd be half asleep listening to him scraping away at his beard with a razor. As ridiculous as the beard they shave every morning, that grows back again, day in day out! Everything in this world was endless, senseless, monotonous repetition. That was when I began to loathe geology which, more than anything else, cynically strips bare the interminable, futile succession of identical acts, the appalling monotony of layer upon layer of sediment, each representing tens or hundreds of thousands of years, one settling on another until they are several kilometres thick: the abyss of time that is beyond our understanding and brings on nausea . . . And the trunk of that lime tree was an obscene pole being poked into my brain and provoking a headache worse than any migraine! It stood there, against the light. Fortunately, that November is now quite distant. Time dragged so slowly it seemed to come to a halt, its slowness crushing me the way Lluís' silences did once. When I was a child, time had seemed like a magician! As far back as I can remember I had loved the passing of time: I loved the traces it left, and the past itself. Sometimes, when wandering down the byways of old Barcelona where I was born and where my parents have always lived, I'd be entranced by an old doorway with a date – 1653, 1521 – I would count the years that had gone by since people like us had built those arches and stones which accompanied me through life. The older they were the more companionable they seemed. Then, when I was older, I was attracted to geology because it gave me a great sense of security with its sedimentary rocks that count the centuries in their millions. It's strange: if I strain my memory, I find I've savoured the ineffable pleasure of having a past from the age of four or five. It's hard to understand, but that's how it is: a four- or five-year-old already has a past that's like an abyss.

Around that mid November, when time had stood still and seemed like a hand that was strangling me, my mother paid a visit one afternoon. I could barely follow the thread of what she was saying: I was living as if I didn't belong to this world, as if my links with the world outside had been severed and were impossible to re-establish. She talked and talked, as she always does, telling me lots of things I couldn't hear. Some words suddenly surfaced from her endless chatter and sounded like the distant rumble of a waterfall: Mother was telling me about an incident that had created a stir down the whole of carrer de l'Hospital. A neighbour had thrown herself and her newborn child from her eighth-floor flat: "A young, perfectly normal neighbour; you know, we all have neighbours like her. And she seemed so happy to be expecting a child: it was her first. Nobody understands it." "It's obvious enough!" I exclaimed. Mother looked at me as if I'd gone crazy, then nodded and changed the subject. Why am I telling you all this? Because it happened soon after you gave me – also for my saint's day – the Gospels in a single volume. I've kept it on my desk ever since. It's still got the bookmark between the pages where you'd put it: when I opened it there I found the famous passage where Jesus says we have to eat his flesh and drink his blood. All his disciples abandon him when they hear him say something so monstrous and the apostles who are still hesitant start to leave as well. Only Simon stays. Jesus asks him, "Will you also abandon me?" And you had underlined Simon's reply in red. "If I don't follow You, whom will I follow?" I looked through the whole volume, I was curious to see whether you'd underlined any other passages, but you hadn't. Only this one! And on the blank endpapers you'd written: "The Cross or the Absurd".

The Cross or the Absurd . . .

A few days later, I was coming back from the market by tram. In one of those rare coincidences in a city as big as Barcelona, I saw Lluís standing on a street corner surrounded by people. It was dark but he was under a street lamp and the gaslight had made him luminous. I was sitting by the window, looking out but not seeing a thing; raindrops streamed down the glass like tears and beyond them was a chaotic jumble of cars, trams, and people rushing along the pavements of the Rambla under their umbrellas – I was coming from the Boqueria market – while the central path was almost deserted under the bare branches of the plane trees. The rain glinted on the oilskin covers the stallholders had placed over their newspaper displays. And there he was on the corner, surrounded by people; he and I were going through one of our worst spells and hadn't spoken to each other for days . . . And there he was on the corner of carrer del Carme, waiting to cross the road, like everybody else. The rain soaked his hair and trickled down his cheeks; as usual, he didn't have a hat or umbrella. He looked so anonymous in the crowd on that dark, rainy November afternoon in Barcelona; so anonymous . . . A person is never so alone as when seen in a crowd; his eyes stared blankly; he was ill-shaven and that was unlike him, or perhaps it was already late in the day and he'd shaved early that morning, and the shadow was back. I could see him through the glass misted by rain but he couldn't see me; for a moment I thought he was crying but he wasn't: it was the rain dripping from his hair. His eyes seemed enormous against his motionless face – the fact that they were so blank made them looked even more desperate. I'd never seen him look like that; I'd have liked to alight from the tram, which had stopped for a moment, and run after him so we could cry together; I'd help him bear the burden that was oppressing him, even if I couldn't fathom what it was. But the tram started off and once I was home and by myself in my bedroom I lay in bed and sobbed and sobbed thinking how one day some tram or other would start off and an even mistier window would separate us for ever. I'd see him and he wouldn't see me, and couldn't see me ever again. I'd see him looking lonelier, more anonymous than ever among the jostling, indifferent crowd, more at a loss than ever . . . and he wouldn't, couldn't see me however much he wanted to, now when it was too late! I cried on and on, stupidly, feeling pity for him and for myself; afterwards, as after a heavy downpour, my sky suddenly cleared and I no longer hated Lluís, I felt sorry for him.

No, Juli, it's not that Lluís can't stand me. Don't start on that again. It's not what I told you the other night; it's not that at all! I know only too well that he needs me although he doesn't realise he does. He finds people who wish him well irritating. It's a psychological mechanism that's so stupid I took ages to see through it. I suffered a lot before I did. Lluís is terribly hard on people who love him – on his uncle, for example. I'll tell you about that some other day. Lluís is so contradictory, I often can't follow him. He kept talking about his brother Ramon, for example; you know he worshipped him but he'd never taken me to meet him. When I asked him to, he'd say, "You'd faint, you'd not stand it, you'd be really shocked." I couldn't persuade him and he kept talking about him in a way one can only describe as devotion. Lluís thinks he is a non-believer, naturally; a non-believer, I ask you! He can act like a monster and often has towards me, quite unawares, but a non-believer . . .

One day, he finally took me to the Order of St John of God and I met his famous brother Ramon. We could hardly talk to him. He was feeding some mentally deficient folk who were grunting and slavering; ten or twelve quite adult defectives, between twenty and forty years of age, a very distressing sight – and he fed them and wiped away their drool as if that was the most natural thing in the world, as I did with Ramon when he was eleven months . . . While he was giving spoonfuls of soup to one, another peed in his trousers, and Lluís, who was visibly upset, tugged my arm and said, "Let's go. Who can live with such a spectacle?" The scene stuck in my mind for days and on the odd night I'd dream of the mentally ill – I, who never dream. The things I tell you! Just let me add, by way of conclusion, that a few weeks later I was sitting in my armchair by the window as usual. It was a bright December evening and I was watching the evening star descend into the horizon: it twinkled for a moment before setting. Shocked and bewildered, I thought I could see the face of that man who'd peed in his trousers and at the same time I heard a distant voice saying: "The obscene and the macabre, the Cross or the Absurd." I was trying to understand how a moment earlier the evening star had been around, twinkling so brightly, and was now gone, as if it had never existed! A moment can be so long when it separates what is no longer from what still is . . . and the past from a moment ago is as past as a moment from a million centuries ago! Who can ever grasp this? And I suddenly thought of the stupid bare trunk of the lime tree I could see against the sunset, I thought I could see a branch growing across that obscene, macabre trunk . . . something to cling to! "The Cross or the Absurd", I repeated to myself, still not understanding what was happening. No, please don't make fun of me: I'm not trying to say I had a vision like your aunt; no Saint Philomenas! Please, no more Saint Philomenas! It was then I understood your words: the Cross or the Absurd; and I understood that ancient line, *O Crux, ave, spes unica.*

I beg you not to make fun of me. Perhaps you've sometimes thought my letters trite: it would be a poor world if we couldn't be trite now and then! If only you knew how consoling it is to have a friend you can tell everything that's going through your mind, however silly . . . You've seen how I spend hours writing to you; obviously I could burn these letters but I'd rather not. After all I write to communicate with someone. Could that be anyone but you?

7 MAY

You ask me for details of my baptism; it's curious how you think it's so important when I don't oblige. If only you knew how meaningless and external the ceremony seemed; it left me feeling quite cold . . . As I didn't know where to turn, and you'd been so insistent, I mentioned it to the widow of the anarchist; since the Jesuit disappeared – she told me that, in effect, he was a Jesuit – they'd stopped holding mass in her attic, but she knew of another house where they held one almost every Sunday. A place where she's done lots of housework for years and is completely trusted.

It was a house on a side street in Sant Just that from the outside looked as grey and old as any other in the neighbourhood . . . Inside was another matter . . . I thought I was seeing visions! I'd never been in a house like that. It's really strange the anarchists haven't requisitioned it yet; maybe it hasn't occurred to them that the most diehard aristocrats own houses in old neighbourhoods. And it's also very strange so many of them still live in Barcelona and have been able to survive the horrors.

When the anarchist's widow, Ramonet and I arrived, a group of twenty-five to thirty mostly middle-aged ladies were waiting for us. I was surprised there were so many and felt inhibited, especially when Ramonet started playing up and saying he wanted to go home; and the more they fussed over him the more he hid his head in my skirt. Then, as often happens, he suddenly stopped being naughty and decided to be good as gold, to the great excitement of all those ladies fighting over him. While we waited for the priest and the godfather who still hadn't come, I took a good look at that drawing room: it was huge, with a high ceiling, the biggest I could remember seeing. Naturally, the windows and doors were shut, and they'd even drawn the thick green damask curtains so nothing would be heard outside. A huge rock-crystal chandelier with twenty or thirty wax candles illuminated and perfumed the whole room. When the lady of the house saw the surprise on my face she said they only lit them on special occasions: "Today is one such occasion," she told me, smiling most pleasantly. On the walls large gilt-framed mirrors alternated with period paintings –"by El Vigatà"* the lady said – and the ceiling was decorated with frescoes that I thought represented the "Judgement of Paris" or some other piece of mythological nonsense. In each corner of the room was a chaise longue with four armchairs, all antique, made from solid mahogany and upholstered in dark red velvet. A large carved walnut double door occupied the middle of one wall, two wide windows the one opposite and two large chests of drawers the centre of each of the others. Each chest must have been worth a fortune. They had such elegant lines, with delicate filigree and sculpted silver handles; you could spend hours if not days treasuring them. The most beautiful feature of all was the amount of space

* Marià Colomer i Parès (1743–1831), a painter from the town of Vic.

left, so much bare, empty wall by each chest, window and walnut double door: what bliss – large white walls are so restful on the eyes!

They'd placed a *guéridon* in the middle of the room under the chandelier and on it a kind of solid-silver basin: "an antique wash basin, that belongs to the family," the mistress of the house told me, eager to placate my nosiness. I gathered it was necessary for the ceremony they were about to enact; I'd no idea how a baptism was performed – I'd never seen one. I've said that all the ladies were on the old side, fifty plus, though there was a young blonde who I assumed was the lady's daughter-in-law. She started to talk to me so enthusiastically about my decision, even though I didn't think it was such a big step and didn't know what to say in reply. The priest finally arrived in a rush, as if very short of time; he too was young, around thirty, freshly shaven, dressed like a worker, impeccably so, and acted confidently and quickly. Hand on heart, I took an immediate dislike to him! To temper my hostility I told myself he was risking his life to exercise his ministry and that all those women were in danger too. The godfather was taking his time arriving and the priest kept looking impatiently at his watch: he stretched his arm out brusquely, holding it up to his eyes, even to his ear, as if afraid it had stopped: he was obviously worried by the time he was wasting on our behalf. The godfather finally turned up. He was a most courteous, shy, affable, little old man who was delighted to see all the ladies. He kissed some on the hand. I'd have preferred the godmother to be the anarchist's widow, but they'd planned everything and it was to be the lady of the house. It would have seemed very rude to try to unpick all that. Besides, I was feeling more and more as though I couldn't care less about these preambles that seemed to make no sense.

"Well, now we are all here," said the priest, raising his voice and immediately silencing the ladies' chatter. He'd donned a white alb the lady of the house had taken from one of the chests, and the ceremony began. Its only charm was the fact that it was clandestine. The priest kept explaining the meaning of everything he was doing and the more he explained the less sense I thought it made. It would probably be better to say nothing and just use the minimum words necessary; the more they say, the more they undermine the whole ceremony. Ramonet found everything very entertaining, but I thought it was drawn out and boring! The priest had a sternly energetic face and all that grim energy – so much conviction! – riled me. He spoke with a self-assurance that annoyed me: how can such obscure things be so clear? How can he be so sure, so convinced? In contrast, the other priest, the old man, the Jesuit in the attic on carrer de l'Arc del Teatre, hadn't seemed sure about anything very much! He was every inch a decrepit, down-at-heel apostle with little conviction and a whole lot of faith . . .

If the old Jesuit from the attic on l'Arc del Teatre had baptised me, I think I'd have felt stirred within myself. I remembered the first mass the old man had said in that sordid space – where he'd lived in hiding, the anarchist's widow subsequently told me – it turned out she'd hidden him there. I gradually learned all this later. The memory of that mass reminded me of the stiflingly hot and horrible summer when they were hunting down priests throughout Catalonia. But this priest had said mass so simply, as if it were an everyday act . . . Swarms of flies flew in through the wide-open skylights and a few were always crawling over his upper lip that was covered in beads of sweat. He did nothing to frighten them away and I thought I could see the other face, the murdered priest's, that other face with those other flies. If he'd baptised me . . . why did I never think of it when he was among us?

I could see . . . Here and now . . .

The priest sprinkled me and the boy from a silver conch shell they'd also taken from the chest of drawers; they had everything in that house. The owner finally decided to show me an eighteenth-century "baptismal dress" that had been worn from the time of the Archduke and was still being worn by all the children in the household: "because in this house," she told me, "we are, naturally, supporters of the Austrias." It was a sumptuous garment made from extraordinarily intricate lace, though it was hardly suitable in our present circumstances: Ramonet couldn't wear that garment made for a newborn babe and I even less so. "You should think," the lady continued, "how it was used to baptise the nephew of the prince of Darmstadt, who was born in Barcelona during the siege of 1714, and we were his godparents too." If I'd taken her literally, I ought to have imagined that lady and her father-in-law – it turned out that the old man was her father-in-law – as being over two hundred years old.

The marquis – one of the other ladies whispered to me that he was the Marquis of X, and if I write "X" it's not out of any wish to imitate tear-jerking novels or to avoid compromising you should this letter fall into the wrong hands, but simply because I don't remember the full title she mentioned – seemed old but not that old, and was really charming. He was such an attentive, unpretentious man with a childish sparkle of hope in his eyes! "He's almost ninety," added the same lady who'd whispered that he was the Marquis of X, "and he refused to flee abroad. He's always been a great eccentric." He heard her and retorted with a laugh: "At my age, one would rather die at home than live among strangers."

I've just realised that since I'm telling you about real ladies and a real marquis, you may be imagining they were dressed as such, but nothing could be further from the truth. They were disguised as proletarians like everyone else in Barcelona – apart from my father: he has not only refused to give up his usual jacket and tie, but now, ever since the revolution, wears a hat too, when previously he'd never worn anything on his head. "The revolutionary carnival," as he calls it, makes him furious. Strangely, it is immediately obvious that these people are well-to-do. Perhaps it's the fact that they exaggerate their proletarian garb and it doesn't seem quite right, or perhaps it's the way they walk, move and speak – that is, never like labourers, though they are all disguised as labourers: as if they didn't suspect that there are other kinds of workers, better-off workers who dress as smartly as the next man. After the ceremony the lady of the house served a snack. A servant – also dressed like a labourer – brought in chairs that he placed in a circle around the *guéridon* and people chatted. The priest took another look at his watch, said he must be off soon and that in the meantime he would make a start on registering the baptisms. He extracted a book from under his smock, where I discovered he'd been making a note of all the baptisms he'd carried out since the Church has been forced to go underground. He asked the lady of the house for two sheets of uncut paper in order to prepare our certificates. He was only doing his duty, and putting his life in so much danger to boot, but I'd had enough! – this paperwork was out of place, it seemed so much stupid red tape! Then a small detail made me see it differently.

The priest wrote on Ramonet's certificate of baptism: "Ramon de

Brocà i Milmany, natural child of Lluís de Brocà i Ruscalleda and of Trinitat Milmany i Catassús . . ." You can imagine how the word "natural" seemed like a stab in the back! It made no odds that it was what they had called *me*; I'm so used to seeing "natural daughter" on my documents . . . I asked them why it couldn't just be "son", without going into detail: "No, senyora, we're obliged to put that." "But it's not his fault he is illegitimate, is it?" "He isn't illegitimate," the priest replied, as if shocked by that word, and then he told me that "natural" had no pejorative connotations, as if all children were illegitimate apart from adopted offspring, and that natural children became legitimate when their parents married. "Unlike illegitimate ones," he continued, "who are procreated by parents who can't marry." You, as a lawyer, must be laughing at my total ignorance, but I think this must confuse lots of people. "Now, of course," added the priest, "we all," and he pointed to the congregation seated on the circle of chairs, "we all hope that as soon as your . . . husband returns to Barcelona, you will make your union legitimate with a proper church marriage." I realised he thought we'd had a civil wedding and I was quick to tell him we hadn't, that we weren't married at all. "As far as we are concerned," he went on, "it makes no difference whether you are or aren't. We believe there is no marriage without the sacrament."

And what if I told you, Juli, that I agree . . . how could a marriage not be a sacrament? But I couldn't take it any further; however much I agreed – at least to an extent, though he was blind to it – with much that he was saying, I really didn't like the priest. His aplomb, his conviction, his energetic expression and gestures . . . the way he continually looked at his watch, making us feel we were wasting his precious time!

In the meantime the maid had brought in a large tray of toast she left on the *guéridon*: it was solid silver like the basin he'd used for the baptism; the plates they then handed round were Sèvres china with gold trim. The beautiful crockery contrasted with what was served up on them: small pieces of toast made from thinly sliced rationed bread with thinly spread dripping. They were freshly toasted and warm and the whole gathering said they were delicious.

"Who'd have thought the time would come," said one of the ladies, "when we would put dripping on our toast rather than butter."

"And we're lucky to have that," said another.

"We received this yesterday," interjected the lady of the house, "from my brother-in-law via the General Consulate of Great Britain. I don't know how we would manage without the parcels of groceries he sends us."

"A few weeks ago," added another of the congregation, "we got a dozen tins of corned beef from an uncle in New York, also via the General Consulate – of the United States. Before the war we'd never heard of corned beef and if anyone had ever told us such a thing as tinned meat existed we'd have fainted with disgust."

"Yet corned beef is so tasty," sighed the lady of the house. "There were so many delicious things we never suspected the existence of. After the war I think I'll continue to use dripping instead of butter and corned beef rather than roast beef. I've never known anything so tasty!"

Then they served tea: in Barcelona you can find as much tea as you want because so few people drink it. Sugar has disappeared completely, but the lady of the house had procured several kilos of sugar from London along with the dripping, and the sweet tea tasted so good, as it did when we drank it together! At home I drink as much tea as ever, but without sugar – I think the saccharine some people substitute for sugar is disgusting.

Toast with dripping and tea with sugar were, of course, special treats – all in honour of this baptism that the assembled ladies apparently considered a historic event. I was reluctant to think it so important. I didn't believe it was so out of the ordinary and then concluded from the comments they made that they felt it was more a victory than an event. What the young blonde said made me suspect they were interpreting my decision as a sign that I was finally admitting that *they* were right. When I realised this, it struck me as comic, because I felt as alien in their midst as I might have with a tribe from Papua. When I said how strange it was that there was only one man among so many women, the young blonde looked astonished. "All the men have fled the red zone, didn't you know, except for Grandfather who has always embodied the spirit of contradiction. Just imagine that when everyone was republican, he was a monarchist and now everyone is —"

"Now that everyone is fascist," he countered affably, "I'm still the incorrigible liberal I've always been, you mean?"

And he addressed me with a childlike smile I found quite disarming: "Senyora . . . or senyoreta, since according to the reverend, we can't accept that you were married if you only had a civil —"

"Not even that," I insisted.

"The reverend has already said that it makes no difference. Can you believe that for the first time in my life I regret not having any talents? Yes, I've never been worried by my scant talents. Our Lord gave me some, but now I would like to be as gifted as Stendhal so I could write a novel that I'd entitle *Neither the Red nor the Black*."

"Don't take any notice . . . Grandfather has always been rather . . . special," said the young blonde, and I realised she called him "Grandfather" because the marquis was her husband's grandfather. "Would you believe he even refuses to listen to Radio Sevilla? And if we tell him what we learn from its broadcasts, it leaves him cold."

"Whichever side wins, I'm a loser," he muttered, still smiling at me. Then he looked down, as if afflicted by a sudden wave of melancholy.

"But, Grandfather, when our boys are risking their lives on the field of battle . . . Don't you think, senyora," she added, turning to me, "that in the circumstances within which we're facing this, indifference is suicidal?"

When I heard her say "our boys" with reference to the other side and in a tone which took for granted that I was one of "theirs", I stared in bewilderment at the anarchist's widow. In effect they'd seated her within their circle of chairs and were giving her dreadfully patronising glances from time to time; she seemed so happy to be there with all those rich ladies, not seeming to grasp any hidden agenda behind what they were saying. She does their housework, I thought, and is happy because for once in her life they've allowed her to sit next to them. I understood at once – when she saw I was looking at her, she looked at me with a big smile and misty eyes – that what was making her so happy and so adrift from our conversation was the fact that Ramonet and I had been baptised, and I immediately understood she was worth more than any of us! The priest kept glancing at his watch while taking slices of toast from the tray; the young blonde was excitedly talking about "our boys" and referring to the day – it wasn't far off, according to her – when they'd be here. I listened to her and thought: who does she think I am? At that point I interrupted her to say I'd been baptised on advice from a "red" officer and I underlined my point by staring her in the eye: "An out-and-out red."

She had used that absurd adjective to describe you republican fighters. The marquis gave me an amused, very supportive look, whereas I thought the priest had been stunned by my outburst. In any case the conversation tailed off, the priest took the opportunity to say goodbye, "horrified by how quickly time passes", the lady of the house accompanied him to the front door and the meeting dispersed.

There was one final incident: I was going out, holding Ramonet's hand, and followed by the anarchist's wife across the passage from the drawing room to the front door, which is so dark and covered by a very thick carpet that I stumbled on the edge of it and fell head over heels.

When I was back in the street and the fresh air, I felt a huge weight had been lifted from my shoulders. Why should I conceal this from you? It all felt like one big misunderstanding. And left a bad taste in my mouth.

The only thing that I felt resembled that "supernatural happiness" which books of religion talk about came a few days afterwards when I saw how our baptism shocked my mother. I relished a wicked pleasure quite mercilessly against her and shamelessly confess it now. I even began to suspect that, deep down, I'd decided to take that step more for the joy of annoying her than because of your insistence. The wickedness we hide within us is terrifying.

13 MAY

You ask how that conversation went with my mother: "It must have been dramatic," you say, and as you put it that way . . . Yes, it was, if not worse.

I now feel I couldn't live seventeen days in that flat on carrer de l'Hospital where I'd lived the first seventeen years of my life. Her constant presence would make it unbearable: her presence alone is a real deadweight. I don't know how to say this: my mother is the kind of person you hear even when they say nothing. They cannot and refuse to be unnoticed. My mother . . . it's sad when one can't love one's own mother! We carry so much wickedness within us, and mine started long ago! I didn't like her when I was a young child. She always behaved as if she preferred Llibert, which is natural enough: they are so alike . . . They both see the world in the same way, as the most delicious cake they're not allowed to sink their teeth into; all they worry about is finding some way to get a bite. They are so different from poor Father, who has always regarded the proletariat with such tender good faith. Years ago he was offered the editorship of a commercial magazine: his experience as a journalist on *La barrinada* would have served him well and he could have earned a decent wage. He refused the opportunity . . . he has no interest in earning a good wage! He wants to live the life of a proletarian; he would never move from that flat on carrer de l'Hospital for a better place, as Llibert now says he should; if Father had to live somewhere else, if they moved him from his beloved flat, it would kill him.

Yes, I went to the flat. I climbed those stairs that were divided into ramps, joined on each landing and then separated out again: wasted space that could have been used by the flats. With four flats on each landing . . . The walls on the stairs were still flaking, there were more damp patches and more pencil or charcoal scrawls than ever. I remember how you called it "graffiti" and told me it would be valuable if one wanted to study the psychology of the masses. I remember how you'd even started to collect it. You'd see many more now: a few months of war has led to an explosion of political and obscene graffiti. As for that wrought-iron banister which you thought so fantastically baroque, if not a masterpiece, it's being eaten away by rust since nobody gives it a layer of paint; put your hand on it and it comes off all red. The house is a hundred years old; you must remember the date above the door onto the street: 1837. Romanticism . . . Did they spend all their money on staircases in those days? The banister handrail from the bottom to the second floor is made of beaten copper and shines like gold: it is the only thing the concierge cleans. Let the copper shine, the rest can go to hell. The steps also mark out sharp class differences: they are marble as far as the first floor, then they're ordinary tiles with a wooden lip, the tiles and wood worn out by use. A hundred years of feet tramping and stamping up and down . . . So many feet go up and down this staircase, almost as many as walk down the street, for heaven's sake! Almost as many as walk up and down carrer de l'Hospital, a gorge that's always flooded with water. And the streams of humanity can be so wretched! Clearly, a hundred years ago the various classes lived in the same buildings and the difference was marked out by the floor. The poorer you were, the closer you lived to heaven. As I remember it, apart from the first floor – with only one door, behind which a doctor has always lived and had his surgery – starting with the second, which had four doors, to the seventh, where we lived, it was all worn out. That kiosk owner is still in the entrance, the same fellow who has really built up his business: as well as newspapers and magazines he now stocks popular fiction, not to sell but to loan out. For ten cèntims he lets you have one for a whole week and he has a lot of local customers. As I walked up, I passed fifty or so people coming down, and I'm not exaggerating, I counted them, forty-nine all told. Apart from the first floor, there are six levels with four flats apiece: 6 x 4 = 24 families. And they're not small families; ours with only five members is an exception. As I went upstairs I heard Policàrpia screeching, fourth floor first door, she who spends her day arguing through the window with the woman from the fifth floor second door. To think how many years I heard her shouting and hardly noticed; now she'd give me such a migraine my head would explode.

How easily we become addicted to calm and quiet, white walls, space, and a few items of individually chosen furniture! That heap of ridiculous furniture, umbrella stands, sideboards, dressing tables, chairs with cardboard imitation-leather seats lining the passageway ready to trip you up . . . I think the sense of tawdry comes not from a lack but, like a sense of luxury, from excess: perhaps tawdriness and luxury are twin brothers . . . That same flat would look quite different not by adding but by removing things: throwing out the dark-red wallpaper, the print of Pi i Margall in his Phrygian cap, half the chairs, the umbrella stand and in particular that ugly light, that gaslight which has been adapted to electricity and hangs from the ceiling above the dining-room table threatening to singe all who eat there.

Father wasn't home. Mother said he rarely was nowadays – in order to avoid arguments with Llibert. It turns out that Llibert wants to move them to a first floor flat on the passeig de Gràcia, which has, of course, been confiscated from its owner: when he heard him, father was so incensed he hit the roof: "I'd die of shame," was his response; mother says that they quarrelled violently. Obviously, this is now the best of all possible worlds for Llibert ever since he'd got his first taste. Father threw at him everything that's been happening over recent months: the murders, the burned churches, the many harmless citizens who've been hunted down like rabid dogs. Llibert listened with a condescending smile: "There will always be rejects unable to adapt to the new circumstances," was his single comment, "eternal rejects or resentful failures." Father was beside himself and told him to leave and never set foot in the house again. Mother had to struggle to pacify them, at least on the surface, establishing truces that could only last as balancing acts, avoiding the issues that might lead to the next flare-up.

She and I were in the back gallery that looks over the inner courtyard. You've never seen this part of my parents' flat because they don't want strangers to go there; it's where my grandmother lives. My paternal grandmother, Trini, after whom I'm named. She says when I was born they couldn't decide between Vida or Alegría; Vida would have been horrific, don't you think? But Alegría wouldn't have been as bad, although, poor me, it wouldn't have been very apt . . . As they couldn't make their minds up, Father finally opted for his mother's name, Trini, in her honour.

Grandmother is stuck in her invalid chair, from where she can see the courtyard, which is deep and narrow – just imagine, six floors! – shared by four buildings as down-at-heel as ours. The air gets stale and, apart from the summer months, is dark, heavy and damp as river water; it always reeks of enclosed spaces, a bedroom that's never aired; and you can always hear the neighbours shouting and arguing from one window to another. The gallery opposite had several potted plants with large leaves that were a dismal dark green and between the plants were a parrot on its perch and a monkey on a chain. For so many years this has been my grandmother's universe. A parrot and a monkey that quarrel; the monkey plays a thousand and one tricks on the parrot, who squawks in response.

For how long? I don't know. I don't remember ever seeing her different. She hardly speaks; she expresses herself with inarticulate sounds. Some days she doesn't recognise a soul, not even my father, her son. We talk in front of her as if she were a newborn babe.

My mother and I spoke a lot that day. Most conversations in Barcelona centre on the problems of rationing. It's a topic that makes me despair, since talking about it resolves nothing and it seems absurd to prolong our obsession with hunger this way. It would be better to distract ourselves by speaking of other things. I told her about our baptism.

She shut up and looked at me as if I'd gone mad. After a lengthy pause she came out with this gem: "How sinister and how stupid!"

"Why 'stupid'?" I asked. "Why on earth 'sinister'?"

"Dogma . . ." she replied, pulling a face.

And I recalled how she'd pulled exactly the same face and said "dogma . . ." the day I told her about the poor village priest on the waste ground behind our house. I told her how I'd found the corpse and the old man was wearing such a worn, patched soutane, how he seemed so old, and said I was sick of the way the authorities were doing nothing. Then she grimaced and said: "Bah, dogma!" That was her only comment on the murder of the old priest.

"So you've joined the bigots, have you?" she added after a sarcastic lull. "Does it make you happy to be with the blue-bloods? I suppose you did it to spite me: you know only too well that few things upset me as much. In my family we've no memories of anyone yielding to the yoke; my grandfather joined the uprising in 1835, my father the one in 1875 – at the time of the First Republic – I was in the middle of the *Setmana Tràgica*."

"And following the hallowed tradition Llibert was part of last year's turmoil," I replied. "Mother, I'm not a traditionalist like you and Llibert."

"A traditionalist? The Carlists are traditionalists!" she shouted angrily. "They are the traditionalists, the holy water birds, the sacristy rats who chew hosts by the handful!"

And all too predictably she came out with that nonsense about the nuns buried alive "with their fists chained". I can't think how often I've heard her rehearse that nonsense and how often Father told her not to tell it again because it was completely untrue. When convents were burning in the *Setmana Tràgica*, the arsonists happily disinterred monks and nuns, as they did last summer. In one ancient convent they found vertical niches; evidently that convent buried its nuns standing up. This led to the idea that they were buried alive; generally, their arms were folded over their chests and there was a small chain in their fists. According to my father, a doctor went to look and after a careful examination deduced that those little chains were the last traces of their rosary beads; as the beads were wooden, they'd disintegrated over the centuries and only the chains remained. But neither my father nor all the doctors in the world could dispel my mother's conviction that monks and nuns perpetrate frightful crimes inside enclosed orders.

I have the impression that when you and Lluís revolted against bourgeois prejudices you had no idea of the extent of the proletarian variety. She's not only shocked by our baptisms, she's also shocked by the *secrétaire* I bought the other day, and even more so by great-grandfather with the side whiskers and beret. That's why she lambasted the "traditionalists". She could have alleged it was dangerous to have Carlist grandparents, but that wasn't what was driving her: she found the Isabel II *secrétaire* and the grandfather with a red beret "terribly old-fashioned". Rather than the *secrétaire* she would prefer me to have an umbrella stand like hers, one of those with a mirror and brass hooks for hanging hats on and a glazed pot where you leave umbrellas. I can't tell you how alien I felt, and not just because of the umbrella stand, naturally. Or even her rude comments on our baptisms; she was at the end of her tether and at that point we don't know what we're saying. She said some really insulting things I'd rather not transcribe, but that's not the point either. My feeling of alienation from her dates back much further, to my childhood. It's sad when one doesn't love one's mother, but however far back I go I don't think I ever have . . .

You ask me, as if you're shocked, why I didn't mention even in passing the events of last week, whether we in Pedralbes hadn't noticed what happened. I said nothing because I didn't want to depress you; I didn't mention it to Lluís either. It's much better if you at the front don't find out about the shameful things happening at home. And because I was also loath to write about unpleasant things nobody will ever understand – really horrible things! Maybe it's selfish of me but I simply didn't want to know. There were moments when I just wanted to shut myself inside my house and think only of Ramonet and Lluís – and you as well, of course – and only of my own life and detach myself from the lunatic world around us. And we can do nothing to change the situation . . . It was another bloody battle like the one last July; they say five hundred were killed. Yes, we spent a few nasty days crammed in caves in Vallvidrera with other families that fled from Pedralbes. In Pedralbes we could hear the din of distant gun and cannon fire in the city centre and didn't know what was going on; then shells started to fall on our neighbourhood and we hadn't a clue who was dropping them. Some neighbours – the ones who always know everything – said a fascist warship was aiming at us to make the situation in Barcelona even more frightful; then we discovered it wasn't true, it was the anarchists. They'd got hold of a big mortar and were firing it without knowing how to aim. Other neighbours said they had acquaintances who owned a mansion in Vallvidrera and who, at the beginning of the war, had had caves dug out of the side of the mountain in their garden so they could take refuge during bombing raids: if we wanted to go, there'd be room and we'd be very welcome. I was reluctant to leave our house to go and live in a cave but at that very moment one of those big mortar shells dropped on the waste ground behind our house, at the spot where we'd found the old murdered priest. It was such a big explosion it shattered all our windows and that made my mind up for me. All three of us went off to Vallvidrera, the maid, the boy and myself.

We lived four or five days in those caves. I didn't know what to do to feed Ramonet and the maid; Barcelona was hell once again. I had moments when I was furious with the maid – the poor girl, an extra mouth to feed when Ramonet was problem enough. Why do you need a maid, I asked myself, when you're reduced to leading the life of a caveman? But I couldn't get rid of her: she comes from a village in Galicia and her whole family lived in fascist territory; I couldn't possibly tell her to go home! The nights were cold and damp in the caves and it was hard sleeping on the ground. I told myself that Lluís must always sleep like that, on the ground and under the open sky. Poor Lluís, I sometimes wonder if I wasn't to blame, if I'd not been understanding enough, and not just once. We crave to be understood in order to be forgiven . . . But why am I telling you this? You too must be sleeping any way you can, without even a cave to protect you from the cold of night. What a long war this is! Now that it has calmed down in Barcelona, it's difficult to grasp what happened. It was all the fault of anarchists: it's always the anarchists. Everyone is fed up with the anarchists, and what if I told you that no-one is more disgruntled than my father?

15 MAY

After those days in the Vallvidrera caves I sometimes awake in the morning with the feeling that it's wonderful to be home in this soft, warm bed, in this spacious, cheerful house. It's like when I woke up full of wonder at being a Christian . . .

Yes, I would wake up full of wonder at being a Christian, and that was before we'd been baptised. I felt I was a Christian, I felt it with all my soul when I awoke, yet what did being a Christian mean? Will I still feel like one when the Church leaves the catacombs? Will I recognise Jesus under all the disguises they will inevitably give Him? It was so easy to recognise Him in those July and August days, when they carried Him in rags, with His crown of thorns and His face covered in blood and spittle, on the way to the Camp de la Bóta or the Rabassada roadway to finish Him off with a pistol shot. How can one not feel full of compassion for Him when He's been bearing the cross of all our suffering down every road in the world? We would prefer to flee Him and take the most out-of-the-way track, the one that will lead us furthest from Him, but we will always find traces of His footsteps!

Lluís is incapable of suspecting that I am a Christian but you noticed straightaway! Yes, you soon realised I could no longer stand the emptiness: I *needed* to believe. "There is a kind of optimism that is simply the unawareness of vegetables," you once told me in a comment on the incredible self-confidence of some atheists.

We were talking about total atheists, who are very rare; I've hardly known any, except for Llibert – and even then I wouldn't put my hand in the fire: who knows what he's hiding within himself? What do we really know about other people if we hardly know ourselves? Why does my mother, who thinks she is such a complete atheist, get so uptight talking about religion? How could we hate something if we didn't believe in it, if we didn't believe in some way, however peculiarly?

That was before I got to know Lluís, meaning before December 1930.

You and I went on endless walks along the Rambla and the streets and back alleys of old Barcelona; we used to buy two wholemeal rolls in a vegetarian shop at the bottom of the Rambla and two chunks of Mahon cheese in another. Window upon window of things to eat to suit every taste! We would walk up the Rambla eating wholemeal rolls that we'd finish before we reached Canaletes where we drank cider at the kiosk. I remember that mixture of flavours, wholemeal bread and cheese and cool, sharp cider, the taste of our strolls together. I remember that as if I could taste it now, as if I'd just eaten one of those rolls and slices of Mahon cheese and had drunk one of those large glasses of cider they sold at the kiosk on Canaletes. Will these good things ever return? By this time I'd joined the Ladies' Sports Club and some mornings, when I had a free hour between classes, I'd escape for a swim in the Sant Sebastià pool. Why didn't you like me doing that? I never understood why you didn't, and I still can't. What was wrong with that? Besides, what business of yours was it? Every December they'd hold that competition they called the cross-harbour race. I participated for the first time in 1930, very soon after which there was that big commotion in the university when I met Lluís. At the time, I hadn't yet met him.

It makes me feel so strange when I now write "I hadn't yet met him" in relation to Lluís! As if it was absurd, rather than impossible, that I'd not known him for ever.

While swimming I didn't feel the cold because we greased our bodies before venturing across the harbour, then we removed the grease with a boiling hot shower. After the race we still had time to get to our last class. I bumped into you arguing with a group of students in front of the entrance to the university. You were holding forth on the rumours that had been circulating for days of a military insurrection to proclaim a republic and other heady developments so exciting that I didn't go to my class. I stayed and argued with you. I was standing quietly in the middle of the street and you noticed I was shivering; then I told you I'd just swum across the harbour.

"Are you crazy?" you said. "You crossed the harbour? In mid December?"

I burst out laughing and told you the race was really terrific and talked to you enthusiastically about the lad who'd won the race in the morning, "a big, broad-shouldered lad who with every stroke surged . . ." You wouldn't let me finish! "Is that what you admire? Brute strength?" No, I didn't admire brute strength, and never have, but I've always loved the spectacle of a powerful swimmer cutting through the water like a dolphin. The more I tried to explain myself, the more irritated you became. Why did you find it so annoying that I liked swimming and admired those who swam better than me?

You are very intelligent, Juli: I've always said so and don't regret saying it again. But you've always been rather peculiar in ways that – how can I put it? – I find disconcerting. On that occasion you left me completely dumbfounded over why you were so bothered by my participation in the cross-harbour race and my enthusiasm for the style of that champion swimmer. Some time later, when I'd forgotten the episode, you told me your aunt didn't let you swim in the sea even though you spent your summers on her estate by the coast, and that was why you didn't know how to swim. At the time I thought you'd been troubled by the fact that I admired a talent in someone else which you didn't possess: isn't yours a rather childish attitude? Can we all be good at everything? You have the most prized talent – intelligence: how could you envy someone else for a talent so puny next to yours?

You are very intelligent, Juli, the most intelligent person I've ever known. It would be stupid to compare you to that swimming champion: you are so superior to him. That champion who was wonderful in the water when they pulled him out was simply a poor boy who couldn't string a sentence together. Wasn't that another reason to admire him when he was swimming, as it was the only grace he possessed? Juli, you are very intelligent, but sometimes, I'm sorry to say, you act as if you're not.

Quite the opposite of Lluís' uncle, who isn't brainy but sometimes acts as if he were! A few hours after we met he'd guessed I was a Christian – when Lluís still suspected nothing! I can now tell you about all that and not worry I might be compromising him; I'd refrained from doing so until now for fear my letters might fall into the wrong hands. I've finally been notified via the International Red Cross that he is in Italy and out of danger after a long odyssey through the woods in the Guilleries, where he lived in hiding with others. Now I can tell you that I finally met this famous uncle whom Lluís always referred to so sarcastically. I can do so, knowing what

I know, because he hid in our house for weeks: he is a lovely person.

Lluís has this very curious tendency to take a dislike to those who only wish him well: like me, for example. Because his uncle does love him and much more than he realises.

It was the end of October and three months since you and Lluís had left Barcelona: he'd gone to the Madrid front and you to Aragon. One Saturday morning the maid came to tell me that a militiaman from a patrol wanted to talk to me. I went to the front door: in effect, a short, round-faced stranger stood there with a worker's cap pulled down over his eyes and a red and black scarf partially covering his face. He was wearing rope sandals and threadbare clothes.

"Forgive me for turning up like this, senyora! I'm the uncle of your . . . husband."

He hesitated before he said "husband", just like the priest who baptised us. I took him into our drawing room and sat him down. He apologised for having a "long and complicated" story to tell: at the beginning of the revolt, he said, everything had continued as before in the factory thanks to a committee comprising the accountant, the main overseer, long-serving employees and some of his most skilled workers. The first decision taken by this "factory committee" had been to vote to designate a "responsible companion" and there was unanimous agreement – not just a majority – to appoint him, Uncle Eusebi told me proudly, as they thought him the best man for the job. This way, as a "responsible companion" and backed by the factory committee, he had continued to be at the helm of management as if nothing had happened, the only headaches being those that stemmed from the situation in the country: the shortage of raw materials, breakdowns in the transport system and the loss of markets in central, western and southern Spain. But a couple of weeks previously some anarchist agitators had stirred up the labourers and a large number of unskilled workers had replaced the skilled ones on the factory committee. The person in charge now was a warehouse porter – "a sort of gorilla," said Uncle, who couldn't write or sign his name, but signed with a thumbprint, "and into the bargain hailed from Medellín".

"Like Hernán Cortés?" I exclaimed.

"Exactly like Hernán Cortés," Uncle replied. "Did Hernán Cortés also sign with a thumbprint? A time comes when anything seems possible. The fact is that this soup-pasta Hernán Cortés is a vicious fellow and his first ukase was to sack me. He shouted at me never to set foot in the factory again because they didn't need me. So I was living at home, resigned to being as bored as a comatose crocodile, when the accountant rang this morning – a man I trust wholeheartedly – to tell me to go into hiding, that the anarchist strongman had just come to the office in the filthiest of tempers and let it be known that the business was going so badly since I left because I was sabotaging it from the outside and as a result it was necessary to 'do me in' like all the bourgeois of Catalonia . . . 'Until we've got rid of every single one,' he raved, 'this country's industry won't get back on its feet.'"

Uncle Eusebi has a round, sweet-tempered face, but now and then a nervous tic make his bright little eyes go on the blink and that happens when he comes out with one of his shafts of wit, which is what he likes to do, and when he does he always stammers the first few words: "An . . . and it's obvious he and his lot know much about managing industry! If Hernán Cortés had earned a fortune in Medellín, why the hell would he have decided to go and try his luck in Paraguay?"

"So then, Uncle, what made you decide to come and hide in our house?"

"You know, my dear, I didn't know where I could go that would be safe; you are the only agitators I know. Besides, I was dying to meet you. I'm a nosey parker, you know, and that's hardly a crime, is it?"

By now the maid had dressed Ramonet as it was the time he got up, and she brought him in washed and combed. He'd just had his third birthday: much to my surprise, for he is generally prickly with strangers, he ran right over to Uncle and stood there scrutinising him: "Who is this gentleman?" "It's Uncle Eusebi.""Yes, my lovely little boy, I'm your uncle," replied Uncle, picking him up and sitting him on his knees. "How could I have such a darling little nephew and not know him! How can that be right, Trini? Am I such a monster for Lluís to treat me in this way? Just think how the boy came running the moment he saw me and how happy he is to sit on my knee. The voice of innocence! What did you say his name was? Ramonet? I can tell you that when Lluís was very young, no more than six or seven months old, I tried to take him in my arms and he played up like a little demon. How he bawled! He wasn't six or seven months and already he couldn't stand the sight of me. He's obviously from noble stock and I'm a mere pleb, you know, a common or garden Ruscalleda . . ."

I burst out laughing.

"You must be joking, Uncle. How do you expect a six-month-old baby to . . . ?"

"Joking? Well, not entirely, Trini! I've seen such peculiar things in my lifetime: you end up suspecting that these old manias never die in these people, that they're born to them . . . They possess them even when they've forgotten they ever existed and are totally unaware of them! I could tell you of so many unexpected actions and reactions . . ."

"If that were the case, Lluís would loathe me more than he does – I'm a sight more pleb."

He stared at me in astonishment and his little eyes went back on the blink: "Do you say so because you and your people are anarchists? Well, even if you've thrown lots of bombs on streets, bomb-throwing doesn't detract from anyone's nobility, you know – quite the contrary! Conversely, manufacturing noodles and macaroni is obviously beyond the pale. My crimes find no redemption in the eyes of a genealogist: I don't just manufacture noodles and macaroni but cannelloni, vermicelli, spaghetti and semolina. Semolina! Did you ever hear of Godfrey of Bouillon setting up a semolina factory in the Holy Land, however much it went with his name? My dear, when I change my clothes too drastically, when I put a dinner jacket on, everyone inevitably mistakes me for a waiter . . . these are the crimes they won't ever forgive me!"

After giving it a lot of thought we decided he would use the maid's bedroom that's at the top of the house under the roof terrace and slightly separate from the rest of the house; the maid would sleep with Ramonet. We told the boy that the senyor had only paid us a visit and gone back to his own house; so Uncle hid in our house for five or six weeks without the boy finding out – moreover, a few days later Ramonet started to go to the kindergarten. We took his meals up to his room and, as the boy often had an afternoon nap or was already in bed, I'd often lunch and dine with him and keep him company. He was really grateful because he was bored to death being shut away like that. He talked a lot about Lluís, and always affectionately, if wryly: "Lluís is exasperated by what he calls my self-importance as the owner of a soup-pasta factory, but my dear, if I didn't boost my own self-esteem, who would?" He often came out with these funny remarks that made me laugh and would have won over anyone except for Lluís: "Lluís? What can I say? I know by heart all the business of his starting to live with you without getting married, in order to put his family's nose out of joint! He likes to play the proletarian rebel, but I'd spend thirteen or fourteen hours a day in the office running the factory and he would pop in once a year, when it was dividend payout time." Uncle told me lots of things I didn't know: "As his guardian, I could have prevented Lluís from living with you because he had a year to go before he came of age: he was still only twenty. I did think of using this weapon, not to prevent him from living with you – you were pregnant and I'd have thought that a crime – but to force him to marry you. I'd already taken it on board that neither of you wanted a church wedding, but you could have at least had a civil ceremony . . . Whatever Father Gallifa says, I think a couple who've had a civil marriage are more respectable than a couple that hasn't married at all. Father Gallifa knocked that out of my head: 'A civil marriage is meaningless,' he said. 'It's not worth fighting battles over.' At the end of the day, I thought, if Lluís comes of age in a year's time, he can do whatever he wants, so we'll let him get on with it now and not get in his way. Father Gallifa praised my decision."

Father Gallifa is a Jesuit Lluís mentioned to me once or twice. I think he taught in his school and, from what I gathered, he was much loved by the family and someone Uncle asked for advice in difficult situations like this. Now I think about it, if this Father Gallifa taught at the Jesuit school then you too must have known him – so how come you never mentioned him? You and Lluís went to the same Jesuit school in Sarrià. Perhaps I've got it wrong and Father Gallifa wasn't a teacher at the school but the director of the Portuguese congregation, and that's why Lluís knew him, but you didn't because Lluís was a member of the congregation and you weren't. While Lluís' uncle was telling me all this the telephone rang. I ran to pick it up. It was the accountant from the factory; after checking that I was Trini, he asked to speak to Uncle. It must have been after ten; he was phoning from home, not from the office. When he'd finished speaking and was putting the receiver down, Uncle burst out laughing: "Do you know what he just told me? That the 'companion in charge', that gorilla from Medellín, wants me to go back to the factory because he doesn't know how he's going to pay the week's wages tomorrow, Saturday. Did you know there was a recent advert in *La Publicitat* that said: 'Collectivised enterprise needs capitalist partner'? I saw it with my own eyes as I'm a lifelong subscriber to *La Publicitat*. It's quite true! They must have faced the same problem: they're finding that paying out the weekly wages isn't as easy as they thought."

Poor Uncle, one day he was in the mood for telling secrets and revealed a real shocker. It was late night again after supper and I'd stayed on as usual to keep him company. I would take my knitting with me; I'd started on two thick jerseys, one for you and one for Lluís, as we were well into autumn and the end of the war wasn't in sight. Do you remember how at the beginning we never imagined it could last more than a few weeks or at worst a few months? And week after week, month after month had gone by and we were now in November; winter was upon us and the war looked like it was in for the long haul. I was knitting in the bedroom under the terrace and enjoying long conversations with Uncle Eusebi. We flitted from one thing to another when, unexpectedly, he started to talk about his daughter Julieta and how he'd had high hopes she would marry Lluís. What they say about mutual sympathy must be right: I'd liked him from the moment I first saw him and realised he felt the same about me, and that our instinctive empathy was the reason why he could so surprise me with a family story without offending me a bit.

"I'd have liked Lluís to marry Julieta, my daughter. They're first cousins – so what? That's why Rome gives dispensations; pay the piper, and the Holy See will sing! You know, a lot of shares for Ruscalleda's Son have gone to the Order of St John of God to pay for Ramon's schemes: at least those belonging to Lluís stayed in the family! I know I can pin no hopes on my son Josep Maria; I don't know whether Lluís ever mentioned him . . ."

Yes, he had, but not very warmly: his cousin apparently suffers from a serious congenital glandular deficiency and became grotesquely obese from a very early age. Uncle told me they tried all kinds of treatment, consulted every sort of doctor, visited all varieties of spa, but it was all futile. This poor Josep Maria has the mind of an eighteen-month-old baby though he's older than Lluís and almost Ramon's age.

"And he's a good boy, Trini, a good boy! But nothing we can do to help him . . . So Lluís was my only hope to succeed me at the helm of the business. Why do you pull such a face? Do you find it odd that I'd hoped Lluís would follow in my footsteps as director of the firm? You are very young, Trini, and I'm a wise old owl; I've seen such changes in my lifetime . . . such astonishing changes! It wouldn't surprise me if one fine day Lluís settled down, began working like a maniac and turned into one of the most important noodle manufacturers in Europe. I think he's capable of doing that if he decides he wants to and gives up his mad whims."

You can imagine how such a wild prophecy made me split my sides! "No, don't laugh. Greener fruit has been known to ripen. You must understand how appalled my wife and I were – especially my wife – when he got mixed up with you, but there was nothing we could do about that either. Except be very patient. Now I know you, I feel slightly more resigned."

And as the resigned expression on his face was so comical and so unflattering towards me, I burst out laughing again.

"Don't laugh, just listen. The moment I saw you, I realised you weren't at all what my wife and I had imagined, and as I've got to know you I've seen you are a girl with a lot of good sense. Believe me, my dear, I've always had my feet firmly on the ground. We've stormy weather now, but it will clear up sooner or later, because nothing is so wearying as being perpetually on the boil. As soon as it eases up, try to rectify your situation. A woman who lives with a man she's not married to will never gain respect. Why let yourself be insulted by women who don't reach the top of your shoes? Because it will always be women calling you names; we men are more broad-minded. You know, we all crave respect: it is as necessary as bread. And you must lead Lluís down the right path; you might find it hard, but you can do it if you decide you want to. Yes, it will be hard, no need to tell me: these Brocàs aren't ordinary people, I mean, like you or me. You must remember that his father was an army lieutenant and that there was real drama at home when my sister, may she rest in peace, pledged herself to him. We Ruscalledes have always been busy little bees. My grandfather made semolina in Agramunt – we Ruscalledes come from Agramunt – and the truth is our family has never stopped working or taken its nose out of its account books. Then all of a sudden our young girl marries an infantry lieutenant who hasn't a cèntim to his name, however many portraits in oils of grandfathers in full military dress hang on their walls or however many handles their names have! My sister Sofia was older than me but after all these years I can still say it was frightening how madly she fell in love with her lieutenant! I think if our father had forbidden her from seeing him she'd have thrown herself off our balcony, and we lived on the sixth floor at the time . . . There was no way her mind would be changed; they married, they had Ramon – who is now a brother in the Order of St John of God – then Lluís, and when Lluís was only a few months old my brother-in-law died in Africa leading his company, for in the meantime he'd been promoted to captain. They promoted him to the rank of Commander posthumously and honoured him with the medal of San Fernando. Sofia died soon after of a broken heart: she couldn't live without her man. All these Brocàs are bred to drive women crazy! They're all handsome, valiant and one-track-minded, with the gift of the gab but not a bit of common sense! From what I've seen of you, you have much more common sense than I'd have ever imagined; so when these stormy waters become still, it'll be up to you to lead him gradually back to the right road without him knowing. And it is obvious you *can* lead him by the nose whichever way you want."

"Uncle," I replied, "do you want me to make a bourgeois out of him?"

"Well, if you want to put it that way . . . If marrying properly and acting like anyone with an ounce of sense is what you mean by bourgeois . . . Tell me, what do you get out of free love and all this nonsense? Just a bad reputation? A woman needs to be respected, she needs that more than a man. You'll soon see for yourself. Now I know you, I'm sure you will want to be as respectable a lady as the most high-falutin' and that you'll take an interest in the factory, which is a quarter yours – I mean though it's Lluís' today – and a quarter of the factory is a lot. I'll go further, now that I know you, and say that if Lluís continues to be horrified by the idea of manufacturing noodles, if he won't relinquish his aversion to soup pasta, who knows whether in the end you might not come to shareholders' meetings instead of him – he never sets foot in them, as you know. Perhaps you'll become more and more interested in the factory, and I think you might when you see more of what it does. If Lluís turns his back on the place decisively, perhaps you could be the active partner, the one to give the good advice I've so often needed? Because, I can tell you, running a factory as big as ours is starting to be is no easy matter, and the partner Ramon might have been had he not joined the Order of St John of God . . ."

At the end of this astonishing speech he exclaimed, even more amazingly: "Is it a crime to manufacture noodles?"

No, it's not a crime. Uncle is right. Don't we all eat noodles? You bet we do! Or rather we did . . . And they were delicious! If only I could find a packet of those our grocer used to stock, I can see them now in my mind's eye . . . I don't know whether it was Lluís or you who was more unfair when it came to noodles. I remember how in one of our meetings of the *La barrinada* group you both mocked noodle manufacturers so cruelly that my father had to call you to order; after the revolution, said my father, there will still be noodle manufacturers, though they'll be organised in a combined workers' production co-operative and not a capitalist enterprise; apart from that, nothing will be any different: the more noodles the better, it's an excellent proletarian dish. You interrupted him: "If there are still noodle factories after anarchy has been proclaimed, we might as well give up now!"

I think you were having a good laugh at the expense of my poor father's naïveté.

Ever since Ramonet started going to kindergarten in the mornings, Uncle Eusebi hasn't had to spend so many hours imprisoned in his bedroom; he's been able to walk around the house. It was November and we could shut the windows without attracting attention. I am so lucky I can trust our maid; she's been with us ever since Lluís and I moved into this mansion and this girl from Galicia shows us a lot of affection: she dotes on our little one in particular.

Well, the first day the boy spent the morning out of the house, Uncle wanted a complete tour. "I'm dying to see how you've organised the place," he said. "The mansion," he added, though I was only too well aware of the fact, "belonged to my sister Sofia, may she rest in peace."

"It's the first time I've set foot in a mansion where the mistress is an anarchist," he said, still laughing.

He was transfixed when he saw the big ivory crucifix in the bedroom and said something that really stuck: "You know, I'm not a heroic kind of Christian. I burned all the prints and images we had, because the militia patrols could come at any moment and were vicious. I burned everything except for the Sacred Heart – *that* I didn't dare burn; I buried the Sacred Heart deep at the bottom of the garden. You see, my dear, my skin was at stake. I'm not the stuff martyrs are made of – I'm the sort that prefers to make noodles!"

He'd seen the drawing room the day he came, which was where I'd welcomed him, but he was so agitated he'd not noticed the detail. Now he was bowled over: "My dear, you've much better taste than my wife, though that's not saying very much: poor Carmeta has lots of fine qualities but no taste whatsoever. As a girl she learned to play the piano and paint tapestries, so our walls are covered in home-made tapestries. The most astonishing ones are in our drawing room: one is a representation of the Holy Shepherdess surrounded by her sheep, another has the Prodigal Son looking after pigs and a third – that's the real killer – represents camels trying to pass through that famous eye of the needle, since, according to the Jesuit fathers, Jesus wasn't referring to any eye of any needle but to one of the gates of Jerusalem which bore that name. Have you heard of anyone else using that parable as the subject for a painting? Carmeta dared to when she was very young: she painted the camels before we were married. I imagine it was her father's idea, I mean my father-in-law's; he was rich and very worried by the idea of camels and the eye of the needle. She has the same approach to tapestries as to playing the piano, and Carmeta can play the "Waltz of the Waves" and "The Tightrope Walker". She does everything with disarming goodwill; she's the sweet and innocent kind they don't make anymore! Just think, she once came to my office, a rare occurrence, and its forlorn state made her warm to the task. 'I'll put this right for you,' she said. 'I'll brighten the place up.' And to do that she gave me a leather three-piece suite, and to make it even livelier she placed a bust of Dante on top of my filing cabinet."

"What's the connection between Dante and soup pastas?"

"Maybe it was Italian . . . I'd have preferred an equestrian statue of General Prim, the one that was in the Ciutadella Park before the anarchists destroyed it – I mean a plaster reproduction. Not because General Prim is better connected to soup pastas than Dante, but at least he came from our neck of the woods. General Prim was from Reus! You know, I've always had a weak spot for General Prim, he was so brave and such a liberal . . . If only he was around now!"

As the weeks sped by, we'd forgotten the danger he was in. We thought he'd be able to live at home for as long as the war lasted, especially as we then thought the war wouldn't last long, till February at most: I don't know why we'd decided the fighting would end in February. Out of the blue a militia patrol appeared at our garden gate just before Christmas.

While I tried to engage them in conversation on the ground floor, our maid ran upstairs to warn Uncle. It all turned out fine. Luckily, I hadn't yet hung the portrait in oils of Colonel Brocà on the wall, so that the only visible object that could have annoyed them was the crucifix in the bedroom. There was a difference of opinion: some of the patrol wanted to unhook it and "chuck it in the rubbish bin" while others upheld the view that "Christ was an anarchist the bourgeoisie strung up". While they conducted this fascinating debate in front of the crucifix, Uncle had time to hide inside the maid's wardrobe and she had time to remove everything that would betray a man's presence in the bedroom: ashtrays, socks, pyjamas and shoes. When the patrol reached the top after searching the rest of the house, the bedroom seemed so convincingly a maid's that they only took a peremptory glance inside.

But it was a terrible scare. We decided it was rash for him to remain in hiding in Barcelona. We must have said our farewells on 19 or 20 December, 1936. Poor Uncle was almost in tears and he's not a man who cries easily: "I'm so happy to have met you, Trini. I'll tell you yet again: my wife and I never suspected you might be such a lovely person. I am so happy, my dear, and thank you for looking after me."

I heard nothing for months. I only knew that he was hiding in the woods of the Garrotxa or the Guilleries with other people in the same state of limbo. It had been relatively easy to go abroad during the first weeks of the war, but then it became increasingly difficult; the frontier posts were constantly watched by patrols. I was very anxious on his behalf and can tell you quite sincerely that I'd grown to love him. I hadn't ever imagined *him* "as such a lovely person" either: how could I have after the hateful way in which Lluís had caricatured him? Obviously, Uncle Eusebi says fanciful things now and then, but since when was that a crime? It's not, no more than manufacturing noodles is. When he guessed I was going to mass, he exclaimed: "Clandestine masses? They must be like cell meetings." And another day: "Your Lluís has always called me a Pharisee, but who doesn't sin on that side, apart from the saints?" He is crazy about the novels of Father Coloma and told me he'd bought them all in one volume: "The *Complete Works*, you know? Father Coloma's *Complete Works*; no-one is like Father Coloma." "But he's a very slight author . . ." "Father Coloma's slight? He cost me two hundred pesetas!" He once told me some entirely unexpected things about Lluís, or perhaps I've already written to you about that? I get into a tangle over these letters . . . "You won't believe me, Trini," he said, "I place more hope in Lluís than Josep Maria. Lluís will change over time but Josep Maria will always be as he is, and, believe me, I regret having to say that because he is my son. Lluís is still flexing his muscles, and I'm sure he will give you lots of heartache, poor Trini, because he's not yet been broken in. But he'll get there, it's only a matter of time, and when he does get over it he may find that noodle manufacturing has its attractions." When I said it seemed to me unthinkable that Lluís would ever take an interest in the factory, Uncle persisted: "Greener ones have ripened. I've seen such astonishing changes over my lifetime!" And then he made a most unlikely prophecy: "I wouldn't be surprised if he didn't emerge as one of the leading manufacturers of noodles in the whole of Europe."

His letter from Italy reached me two months late after taking the strangest of routes through the international port of Tangiers and the principality of Monaco and I think I can still see him with that contrite look on his boyish, mischievous face: "I'm not a heroic Christian, my dear. I'm not made to be a martyr, I'm made to manufacture noodles, end of story!" Didn't Saint Peter deny Jesus three times? Isn't it impressive how Jesus forgives cowardice so quickly when we young people can't? I blanch at the thought of that priest's ebullient expression . . . he was so full of himself, so convinced, so ebullient . . . really repulsive. He was so ready to become a martyr that I'm afraid . . . My God, don't let today's martyrs turn into tomorrow's executioners! Some people make you think they tolerated torture under one regime simply to make others suffer under the next; that's why when I recall the priest's face and Uncle Eusebi's, I much prefer Uncle's!

16 MAY

Now that the boy is also spending afternoons at the kindergarten, the days seem so long! He started going in the mornings, when Uncle was hiding with us, and it's amazing how hard he tried to wriggle out of going – he's only three. I'd bought him a brand-new shiny satchel because he didn't like the kindergarten idea one bit: "Look, this is a big boy's satchel. You're too young to own a satchel like this, but when you go to the kindergarten, you'll be a big boy and can have it." He was very struck by this. Every now and then he'd ask me to show him the satchel and would look at it in awe and enquire: "This is for when I go to kindergarten, isn't it?" And he asked again: "Do big boys have to have a satchel to go to kindergarten?" And he kept on in the same vein: "Can little kids go to kindergarten if they don't have a satchel? Are they too little if they don't have one?" I knew I'd hit the right note and replied: "No, they can't, they're too small, but you'll soon be a big boy and that means you can go and you can have this satchel."

The day came . . . and his satchel had disappeared. While I was looking for it, his gleeful face gave him away: he'd hidden it, convinced he couldn't go without one. When I told him he would go with or without one, he flew into his biggest tantrum ever: "I don't want kindergarten! I don't want kindergarten!" The maid had to drag him there. She pulled him by his arm along the garden path and he kept turning round to look at me with such imploring eyes they broke my heart, but I'd made my mind up to be implacable that day. Hours later I found the satchel in the hatching box in the chicken coop we hadn't used since Lluís' mother died – the Sofia who was Uncle Eusebi's sister. The satchel was in there, hidden under the fallen leaves on top of the hatching box; it was the size of the pile of leaves that had alerted me.

At midday I asked him if he'd liked it, if it was a nice kindergarten: "Quite nice," he allowed. "Is your teacher nice?" "Quite nice." "What about the other kids?" "Quite nice." "So you liked it after all?" "Not much," he replied. "But you will go back tomorrow, won't you?" Then he came out with one of those unexpected responses we find so upsetting: he sighed and said in a resigned tone, "I don't have much choice."

Then he grew to like it and his teacher suggested he should stay on in the afternoons as well. It's a very cheerful place, with a cage of budgerigars in the garden that's as big as a small house and a huge bowl of red and gold fish in the classroom. The children always play under the watchful eye of their teacher, who is very young, lively and fond of children. It's not really Ramonet I'm worried about; he's delighted to be there the whole day. I've suddenly realised that if he's not at home I've got next to nothing to do. The empty hours seem endless . . . Apart from ration days – hours queuing for a kilo of lentils or three ounces of sugar, when there is any to be had – I don't know what to with myself. I sit in my armchair by the French windows and write to you; if only you knew how much you keep me company as I write, hour after hour! Otherwise, I sink into thoughts that have no rhyme or reason and interminable reminiscences, reviewing things from the past as I look out of the window, stirring the dregs of oblivion as if they were at the bottom of a well from where amazing things surface which you thought had been lost for ever.

This inclination to scrape the linings of memory must be an illness that might be cured if I had more to do: what does the lady of the house do when she has an only child who spends the whole day at school? In times past they spun, they wove, they mended, they kneaded dough and baked bread; they washed clothes and made their own soap and lye. All this fulfilled them and gave meaning to each hour, each day, each year: to their lives. Sometimes the void is so deadening I start to feel nostalgic for the way of life of my great-great grandmothers on the farm in Forques de Mont-ral. Did I ever tell you about the Forques de Mont-ral farm?

It was Lluís' idea to go: all I knew was that my grandfather was born there. He came to Barcelona at the age of twelve to find work and never went back: he thought he'd been the victim of an injustice because the estate hadn't been divided up equally between the thirteen offspring – he being the youngest – and there was yet another reason not to go: the family on the farm were Carlists.

It was at the beginning of our relationship, those first months that now seem like a dream. We went out on long excursions by ourselves; I didn't have to give any explanations at home – some good must come from having anarchist parents. He was the one who had to invent convoluted excuses, study trips with fellow students and the Economics professor or similar stories, to pull the wool over his parents' eyes. We'd sometimes spend three days wandering in the wilds; when night fell, we'd sleep in the barn of the first farmhouse we came across if they didn't have a bed for us. We acted as husband and wife and always met the same outcry: "You're so young!" He was eighteen and I fifteen: we'd add four or five years in response to questions.

That spring of 1931 was so exciting! Will there ever be another spring like it? Lluís and I and you and all of us student revolutionaries had assembled outside the palace of the Generalitat on that unforgettable afternoon of 14 April when Colonel Macià proclaimed a Catalan Republic. That old conspirator of a colonel was so white-haired and had such a poet's eyes that welled up with tears whenever he appeared on the balcony to greet the crowd gathered in plaça de Sant Jaume! We were all brothers in those days: there were only Catalans. A white-haired old colonel and a brightly coloured flag that had united us over centuries had made the miracle possible. How it flapped in the blustery spring wind! What joy was in our eyes! How that luminous piece of cloth made us feel like the children of one big family! What a glorious 14 April!

The whole country was perfumed by blossoming thyme, a land emerging from long hibernation, and we were so young and so free and felt we'd come into this world to change it! Who could have held us back! Everything smelled of thyme, of Easter! It was the glory of an April day we didn't anticipate would be so uncertain: who'd have thought that explosion of joy would end five years later in the most absurd butchery . . . You were the only one who had any idea, but at the time we took very little notice of you!

Summer came and for the first time Lluís refused to go and spend it in Caldetes with his cousins and aunt; his excuse was research he had to carry out in Barcelona, near libraries, research in Economics, naturally, since you both always used your Economics professor as a cover, a man you couldn't stand the sight of. We roamed the Guilleries, the valleys of Andorra, the Cadí mountains, Alta Ribagorça, and elsewhere! I'd never been out of Barcelona before I met Lluís and was delighted to discover peaks covered in eternal snow, forests of fir and beech, and herds of mares in the meadows of the Pyrenees. It was a new universe for me: one long surprise from the cuckoo singing in the depths of the forests to the narcissi carpeting the wetlands of the Montseny. I was discovering the universe and it was wonderful to do so arm in arm with Lluís.

One day he suggested we go to the Prades mountain range to see the Forques farmhouse. It was his bright idea: I'd never have thought of it. All I knew was that my grandfather came from there, because that was all my family had ever told me. My father never felt intrigued enough to go and see the farmhouse where his own father was born. In fact he never showed the slightest interest in anything beyond Les Planes. My own grandfather had come to Barcelona at the age of twelve and had never left the city since; he came to work on the trams when they were still horse-drawn and when they were electrified he worked as a driver until the day he died. They never had holidays, though if they'd had any I don't think he would have headed to the farmhouse.

He had always hated it.

It was Lluís' bright idea. We lost ourselves in ravines covered in pine and yew, following streams that crashed furiously from crag to crag. There were no cart tracks and few well-trodden mule trails. Once, when we were completely lost, we stayed in a farmhouse where the year before someone had died who'd never seen a wheel. Sensing that he was dying, he'd asked them to go to Reus to buy him a bar of chocolate: he didn't want to depart the earth before he'd tasted chocolate! It was late September and they were busy harvesting hazelnuts; men and women, old people and children, all those living in the nearby farmhouses were harvesting and sacking the nuts. A ninety-year-old woman whom we asked if the harvest was good replied: "Better than we've ever seen. We must have filled six sacks. The mule will take them to Reus later." She stopped, as if worried by a riddle she couldn't solve: "Who on earth eats so many hazelnuts?"

We found the Forques farmhouse on a plateau between two sierras and from its threshing floor had a view of the Tarragona lowlands and the distant sea. It was a very humble little peasants' house, as was to be expected, but it was so lovely – like a Nativity Scene made of higgledy-piggledy stones, with a sagging roof that had turned green and yellow and was covered in black patches of moss and lichen of every kind. You'd think it was the work of nature, not man-made: golden, velvety black stone melding into the hues of the surrounding rocky outcrops. Lluís was entranced: "If they ever decide to sell," he said, "I'll buy it. What a place to spend the summer!" To be frank, I didn't find it so remarkable: the idea that it was my "ancestral seat", as Lluís kept insisting, was a novel idea I found unconvincing: the farmhouse was picturesque but very much the worse for wear . . . We went in. Everyone was out gathering hazelnuts. Only an old man sat there warming himself by a fire of vine branches.

He wore breeches and a *gorra musca*, a kind of purple beret I'd never seen on anyone except for Barcelona street porters, who wore bright red ones. He got up from the low chair where he'd been stooped over the fire warming his hands and cut an impressively tall, burly figure. His eyes had a kind of film over them and we learned later that he suffered from cataracts. He was eighty-nine, so he told us, and no longer went to work in the fields because of his eyes, not his age. He was the owner of the farm, my father's first cousin. My grandfather was more than twenty years younger than the oldest of his brothers and that's why there was such a gap between my father – not yet sixty – and this cousin of his. While Lluís told him I was the grand-daughter of the son of the farmhouse who hadn't inherited land, and that he was my husband, the man swayed his head trying to make sense of it all: "So your wife," he replied immediately, switching to a more familiar tone, "must be the grand-daughter of an uncle of mine, let's see: was it Uncle Pere? There were twelve all told and my father made it thirteen: thirteen boys, not a single girl," he told me. "Many went to find their fortunes upcountry, we never heard of some ever again . . ." I wondered how on earth my grandfather could have complained about them not dividing it up equally if there'd been thirteen and the farm as poor and small as it obviously was. In the meantime Lluís told him, among other things, that he too was descended from Carlists and that his great-grandfather was Colonel Brocà from the First Carlist War . . . If he had uttered a magic spell, the reaction couldn't have been more immediate! When he heard the name Brocà, the old man gaped open-mouthed and raising his cloudy eyes to the heavens roared ferociously: "That blasted whore Cristina!"

The old man recalled his grandfather's days when Colonel Brocà had evidently waged campaigns in those fastnesses of Prades and Montsant. He became more and more impassioned, lost his thread, hugged Lluís, hugged me, and repeated quietly that shocking oath which, on his lips, in that tone of voice and the way he raised his eyes to the heavens, seemed distinctly blasphemous.

He insisted we stay for dinner and sleep over. The bedroom was big, with a bare untiled floor, like all the farmhouse's floors, and the walls had never seen paint. The bed consisted of planks on a timber frame with a straw bolster beneath three woollen mattresses. A cheap old print of Saint Michael overwhelming Lucifer was pinned above the bed. Lluís was spellbound, but I was less thrilled. He thought the old man was "a real character" – "You can see the Milmanys are from good stock." I thought love made him say that, a love that transfigured everything connected to me. After listening to Uncle Eusebi I could imagine how in Lluís' eyes that dilapidated farmhouse, containing an old Carlist who insulted the doubtful virtue of a bygone liberal queen with his every breath, was in effect much more honourable than a soup-pasta factory.

The next morning they invited us to have lunch with them in the woods, two hours' walk from the farm. Lluís left at dawn with a dozen men and boys, all armed with hunting guns – they were people from the Forques farm and four or five other nearby farms. Our presence was obviously a real event in that remote fastness where, as they told us, years went by without them seeing strangers. I set out much later with the old man and his daughter-in-law. We walked slowly to the spring where we'd prepare lunch, carrying a basket with the wherewithal for the meal. I was surprised when I saw the daughter-in-law put in only a large loaf of bread, a small barrel of wine, a cruet of olive oil, some heads of garlic and a cornet of salt. "Where's the main course?" She burst out laughing: "They'll find plenty in the woods."

When we reached the spring they'd already killed two dozen rabbits.

Tucked away in a ravine of slate amid huge clumps of fern, the spring gushed. The daughter-in-law lit a wood fire and when it had taken she put some slabs of slate on top – what they called *llicorella* – after sprinkling them copiously with oil. Once they were red hot the skinned and gutted rabbits, dusted with lashings of salt, were slapped onto them. I watched all this as if it were preparations for a Palaeolithic lunch – the genuine Stone Age item! I don't remember eating anything as tasty in all my life as those rabbits with the aioli the old man made with a big stone mortar while they were roasting. If only you knew how fresh my memories are of that smell of roast rabbit and aioli! And the wonderful wine to wash it down with! Now things are going from bad to worse in Barcelona . . . Some people say we've seen nothing yet: my neighbours, the ones who know everything, say the rebel aeroplanes will soon start bombing us from bases that the Italians have established in Majorca; until now warships out at sea have bombed us, but very rarely aeroplanes – "we'll soon see what real bombing is like," say my neighbours. And they reckon this war will last for years, with bombing raids from land and sea and more and more people starving: the worst is yet to come. If things really get that bad, if they're going to be bombing us all the time and it's so hard to find food for Ramonet . . . I'll up and off with him to the Forques farm. I could help them in the fields, I'm sure they would give me a warm welcome and I'd be a good worker and no burden.

But are *they* still alive? My God, they have massacred so many Carlists; those dreadful massacres in Fatarella and Solivella where they say not a soul is left alive . . . The whole country is shocked – when we thought nothing could shock us again after everything we'd seen. Why is there such hatred of Carlists who only want to live peacefully in their farmhouses with their faded memories of heroic deeds and forgotten wars? Whenever I think of Carlism, that huge eighty-nine-year-old comes to mind, raising his misty eyes to the heavens and roaring "That blasted whore Cristina!" And the smell of roast rabbit with aioli with that delicious red wine we drank from the barrel, with its refreshing tang, and the water gushing from the spring and the chattering brook that ran over a bed of slate between the ferns . . . Those memories are so vivid and I'd so like to flee the bombs and the hunger and head back there right now!

How mysterious that so many people cannot see mystery anywhere: I mean the incredulity of people whose starting point is the belief that nobody can believe. We should really pity them like those plain witless children one ought to love but can't . . .

Luckily, that's not by any means true of my father. He believes: he perhaps never grasps what, but he does believe. Else how do you explain his life? *La barrinada* . . . do you remember how we distributed it on the streets? We never sold a single copy.

That hapless weekly still appears every Thursday, now with articles against the "cannibals disguised as anarchists", the "hyenas who dishonour the most humane of social philosophies". Hyenas are one of his obsessions, though I don't think he has the faintest idea what a hyena looks like. I don't believe he could tell an owl from a magpie, and apart from pine trees – which anyone can identify – I suspect he couldn't name any species of tree. My poor dad, who was born and has lived in the heart of Barcelona and whose only excursions have been occasional Sunday trips to Les Planes with its ocean of greasy paper and empty sardine tins.

He must be thinking of Les Planes when he writes his articles on Nature in *La barrinada*: wondrous Nature would cure the world's ills if she were only allowed to work unfettered. His beloved paper would reduce the whole of medicine to lemon, garlic and onion: he's almost a vegetarian, and if he doesn't agree with nudists it's because, in spite of everything, he still clings to vestiges of a sense of the ridiculous.

How can a person as harmless as my father arouse so much hatred in other anarchists? I don't know if you heard about it – some dailies covered the story but I'm not sure they reach the front – but supporters of *La Soli* attacked the editorial offices of *La barrinada*, that is, our flat on carrer de l'Hospital, a few weeks ago, long before the events earlier this month, and threw off the balcony a pile of back copies – unsold issues – that we kept in the lumber room.* Luckily the police arrived before they could do worse damage. The government even advised my father and his friends to arm

* *La Soli: Solidaridad Obrera*, the newspaper of the Confederación Nacional del Trabajo, C.N.T., the main anarcho-syndicalist union.

themselves, avoid being caught off guard, and be ready to repel fresh attacks. "The only arms I need are ideas" was all he would say.

A few weeks after you and Lluís went to the front a taxi brought him home one day with his face covered in blood. It gave me a fright but fortunately it wasn't serious. That great lifelong friend of his, Cosme, had brought him in the taxi – you may remember that short plump fellow with a pock-marked face, a turner by trade, who often came to our clandestine meetings. Cosme in fact supports the C.N.T. but is a close friend of my father's and he told me what happened while I washed Father's face with hydrogen peroxide: "Just imagine, Trini," Cosme said. "A train of anarchist volunteers was leaving the estació de França for Madrid and my grandson was one of them – that's why I was in the station. The place was packed, what with people leaving and those who'd come to bid them farewell. All of a sudden we heard this bawling: 'What are you doing, you wretches? Where are you going? You want to impose your ideas with guns? Have you let them militarise you? What happened to our principles that you always supported?' They weren't far off lynching him as an agent provocateur! Lucky I spotted him! It was your father, old Milmany – who else could it be? It was one hell of a struggle to drag him away: he was refusing to come. I imagine he didn't recognise me, he was so overexcited. As I dragged him out of the station by the arm he was still bellowing: 'You're off to defend Madrid? That octopus sucking our blood?'"

Father said nothing as I washed the cuts on his face. Luckily they were only scratches inflicted by a handful of women who'd grabbed him. Cosme talked and talked: "I love your father, Trini. How can I not love him when we've always been friends? I love him more than he knows but it's sometimes very hard to keep faith with him. If volunteers don't go to the front, if we don't wage war with machine guns and cannons, the fascists will win and we'll be done for." Yes," I said, "it's hard to see how any ideas can ever triumph if they reject any kind of organised strength." I immediately regretted saying that: my father looked at me so sadly; he'd not said a word till then. "Trini, everybody is a pacifist in peacetime." He kept looking at me. "Cosme was too, and now . . . you've heard him. The point is to be one always, in times of peace and times of war, whatever the situation. If not, it would mean nothing; there'd be no point in calling oneself a pacifist."

Father stayed with me a few hours, during which I discovered that Llibert was climbing the greasy pole. "He's got an office like a minister's," he told me, "with twenty typists and countless employees jumping to obey his orders. He has a cream limousine with a uniformed chauffeur who opens the door for him, standing to attention and saluting. It's a requisitioned vehicle, naturally; it must have been the Marquis de Marianao's, and I expect they requisitioned car and chauffeur alongside everything else."

"Has Llibert no shame?" I asked.

"One day he wanted to show off and drive me home and I was the one who died of shame when I saw how our neighbours on carrer de l'Hospital who know me well were looking at me: they were amazed to see me in a vast vehicle that was so silent, creamy and shiny! And when his repulsive flunkey opened the door, stood to attention and saluted us militarily . . . I wanted the earth to open and swallow me up! If Llibert hasn't gone to the front like your man," he added, "don't think it's because he's keeping faith with the pacifist principles I inculcated in you from childhood – not at all! Later I'll tell you about his wall posters. If he hasn't gone to the front it's because he thinks he's more useful in the rearguard: to believe him, he is absolutely indispensable in Barcelona, he is irreplaceable because thanks to him, as he readily tells you, we are winning the war. We are winning the war, he says, thanks to the propaganda battle . . ."

In effect, they had made my brother something like the executive director of War Propaganda. It turns out that he was the one who plastered – and still does – the city walls with those justly famous posters: "Make tanks, make tanks, make tanks, it's the vehicle of victory!" or else "Barbers, break those chains!"* And so many others, half in Catalan and half in Castilian, respecting the two joint official languages, which would make us split our sides if Barcelona were in the mood.

One of these posters makes me want to vomit whenever I see it: it shows a wounded soldier dragging himself along the ground and making one last mighty effort to lift his head and point a finger: "And what did

---

* The barbers – and bakers – of Barcelona were organised in anarchist unions. The reference to chains also harks back to the early nineteenth-century cry of "Vivan las cadenas!" of the clerical-led anti-liberal crowds who wanted to keep their chains.

you do for victory?" This is the offering from my brother and the other people safely ensconced in the Propaganda department offices! Posters encouraging others to go to the front are his speciality. There's also the enigmatic variety, abstract posters where you can only see blotches of colour, and amid the crazy chiaroscuro mess of light and shade it says: "Liberatories of prostitution". I've never met anyone who understands what that one's all about. At the other extreme there's a very specific one: a hen on a balcony accompanied by a slogan: "The battle for eggs". Apparently the idea is to suggest that if each citizen of Barcelona were to keep a hen on the balcony, nobody would go hungry. As if hens don't need grain to lay eggs! As if poor hens live on fresh air!

It seems all this is the work of Llibert, or at least so says his father. He's not only involved in poster production. His hyper-activity encompasses broad and complex fields: the man is a walking encyclopaedia! He is behind various newspapers in Catalan and Castilian, all encouraging people to go to the front; he gives talks on the radio in a quivering tone that gives me the shivers, all to the same end; he contracts foreign lecturers to give similar talks – world famous celebrities nobody has heard of – and organises performances of "theatre for the masses" . . .

This "theatre for the masses" deserves special mention. According to Llibert, proletarian theatre must be performed by the masses. From what I've heard – I've never set foot inside – the masses fill the stage while the theatre remains empty, since nobody ever goes. This is the reverse of what used to happen when there were few actors – hardly any – and the theatre was packed from the stalls to the gods. Apparently that was *bourgeois* theatre.

Llibert's stirring dynamism and boldness aren't at all challenged by the difficulties of organising an equally proletarian opera season. He has requisitioned the Liceu and all they put on is proletarian opera. I don't know where my beloved brother found the libretti and music for the operas he stages, because I've not set foot there either, but a friend of mine from the science faculty, Maria Engràcia Bosch, was intrigued enough to go. She's a person I meet up with now and then and she tells me about what's happening in Barcelona: if it weren't for her, I'd never have found out. We met at the faculty years ago and although she's quite a bit older than me and was in her final year when I was only beginning, we felt close because we're from the same neighbourhood: she lives off carrer de Sant Pau.

I bumped into her not long ago on the Rambla and she invited me to a cup of malt in a café: "I've things to tell you," said Maria Engràcia Bosch. And she told me that as she often walked past the Liceu, that's on the corner of Sant Pau and very close to her house, she was intrigued by the proletarian opera they were advertising and one evening couldn't resist the temptation to go – I should add that the price of tickets to the Liceu is now within anyone's reach. She was one of the six who made up the audience that evening, and to compensate maybe two hundred people were on stage: "Opera for the masses, right! Where on earth did your brother get the score and libretto? An unbelievably awful tearjerker about a people's uprising! The exploited masses come and go on stage, exit to the right, walk back on from the left, singing incantations to the future with their fists held high. From the rather nebulous plot you gathered that one of the exploited proletarians, the youngest in fact and a tenor, was practising free love and caught a bad dose of gonorrhoea – one for the history books! He separates out from the masses and staggers to the front of the stage. There is a deafening drumroll and the masses sink into a highly tragic silence whilst the tenor threatens the six members of the audience with a grand flourish of his arm and blasts out the first line of an aria full of pathos: 'Accursed bourgeoisie, you shall atone for your crimes!'"

I couldn't believe it but Maria Engràcia Bosch had seen it with her own eyes and heard it with her own ears.

After this proletarian opera, what could one say of my darling brother Llibert that wouldn't pale in comparison? People who have been to his office tell me he gives all and sundry a big welcoming hug, calls everyone "companion" and is ultra friendly, that his every pore breathes out success, victory, dynamism, smarminess and efficiency; he is organisation, efficiency and audacity personified; he is the provident hand for all those seeking a "helping hand" or a "voucher".

He brings one of Uncle Eusebi's sayings to mind: "By dint of revolving around others, we end up believing that others revolve around ourselves." My brother had always wanted the entire world to revolve around him. When we were kids we crossed the courtyard of the Hospital of the Holy

Cross four times a day going to and from our street to carrer del Carme, and the lay school where Mother and Father taught. He'd sometimes stop in front of the "little pen" which is what we called the morgue; it looked out onto a side street that crossed Carme and a grille was all that separated it from passers-by. I had to hang on to the bars and stand on tiptoe to see the corpses. As they were laid out facing the grille, feet were what we saw best – yellow, filthy feet. Those feet were so sad! "Here's the end that awaits us all," was Llibert's invariable comment, "if we don't look after number one!" I must have been six or seven and he eleven or twelve. In my eyes he was already a "grown-up" who knew everything, the secrets of life and death, and I'd listen to him like an oracle. So a way existed to avoid ending up displaying one's filthy feet to the people walking from carrer de l'Hospital to carrer del Carme. I thought when I was Llibert's age I'd see it as clearly as he did.

One morning we found the traffic had ground to a halt: a funeral cortège, the like of which I've not seen since, was coming from Bethlehem parish church; six huge horses caparisoned in black velvet were pulling a black and gold open carriage that contained a coffin resembling a chest made of silver and gold; men on foot, in breeches and wearing white wigs and black dalmatics escorted the carriage; behind came fifty or sixty priests intoning dirges for the dead and in their wake a band of gentlemen in frock coats and top hats. "Here's a fellow who looked after number one," said Llibert. "Who?" I asked. "The men in wigs?" "No, love, they're only the flunkeys."

They've yet to give him a state funeral, but it will happen! Don't you find it incredible that people can envy a corpse? Anyway, he's already got a uniformed chauffeur opening the door to his cream limousine.

Perhaps you think I'm grousing too much, given that he's my own brother, but I was really incensed by one barbed comment of his. I'd muttered something about his cream car and uniformed chauffeur and he roared back at me in a rage: "Yes, of course, you've got it all sewn up: a young guy from a rich family and an orphan to boot. I must look out for myself – it's every man for himself, you know – I can't go dowry hunting!"

I'd never thought anyone anywhere could interpret my relationship with Lluís in such a tawdry way.

Luckily, I've got a good supply of potatoes in the pantry and don't need to ask him for vouchers, which I've had to do occasionally, because I can't let Ramonet go without his ration of bread and potatoes. I feel so angry with Llibert. I could ask him for another voucher but I've taken a firm decision not to ask him for anything at all unless it's vital – I mean vital for the boy. I'll get by on my own as long as I can. I found a tenant farmer in Castellví de Rosanes by the name of Bepo who had potatoes to sell: he played hard to get and only wanted banknotes "with serial numbers". I can't tell the difference: those in the know hoard them, so none are in circulation. I'd not thought to bring silverware or anything similar, which was what Bepo wanted in place of banknotes "with serial numbers". We finally did a deal: almost the whole of Lluís' monthly pay for a sack of potatoes!

The worst was to come: I had to transport it. Bepo refused to organise that or even carry it from his farm to the station; he didn't want any complications, didn't want to be caught as a black marketeer since the punishment is now so draconian. The maid had stayed at home with the boy; perhaps I should have brought them with me so she could help carry the sack, but then Ramonet would have been a constant nuisance ... Finally another fistful of notes helped decide Bepo to carry it to the railway station on his donkey: not all the way to the station – that was under police watch – but nearby. From then on I was on my own.

It was so heavy! That sack of potatoes landed me in bed for four days.

There is a heavy police presence in the Barcelona stations so you have to throw whatever you have out of the compartment window before reaching Sants station, and when the train begins to slow you jump out after your sacks. I confess that the trains reduce speed so much to help our feats that the acrobatics aren't especially remarkable: the train drivers themselves are into wholesale black marketeering. The spectacle of so many people jumping out of a moving train might even be a pretty sight if it weren't all so painful.

Once in Sants, the last act in the drama began: how to get the sack home. If you are really lucky you find a taxi, but it's more likely you'll have to carry it yourself – on your back and dragging it. There's always the danger the Supplies police will confiscate it or people hungrier than you will steal it. And, my God, there's no shortage of the latter. You can always see skeletal old men and women on wasteland searching through the rubbish accumulating there because it's hardly ever removed nowadays . . . I was exhausted when I got home and my aching back made me see every star in the sky and more besides. At least such episodes have the virtue of showing that people do sometimes help each other out of the benign understanding that comes from being in the same wretched boat. When I still had two kilometres to walk and couldn't take another step, two soldiers, who told me they were on leave in Barcelona, offered to carry the sack; they did it so disinterestedly that they didn't even want to tell me their names. All I know is that they came from Mollerussa. Would you believe it? Before their providential appearance, while I was walking with the sack on my back my thoughts were of Jesus walking along the Street of Bitterness with the Cross! It's always a consolation to think of someone who's had an even worse time: what you call a strange form of consolation.

Thanks to God, we got home and now have potatoes in the pantry once again. I'm back here and looking at the lime tree humbly doing its duty, which can't be as easy as we who aren't trees think it is. How comforting to have a house, a bolthole where one can curl up in the middle of the hostile, incomprehensible world that surrounds us! How happy the three of us – Lluís, Ramonet and I – could have been before the war if it hadn't been for Lluís' bad moods . . . He hasn't a clue about one obvious fact: we were happy, or could have been if he'd wanted. For him, having this large house and collecting the dividends from the factory was as natural as breathing: it never occurred to him that the majority of people have nothing apart from the clothes they stand in. I sometimes think Lluís would love me more if he were poor; I mean then he would at least be aware of his love for me. Because he *does* love me: the problem is he doesn't realise he does. If he were really, really poor, he would discover what a boon it is to have a quiet corner in the world with a table, two beds and three chairs – and a wife and son. In the end, we need so little to be happy: a little love is the secret, that's all there is to it. A little love for what you already have, and it's as if you have everything you could ever want! I am sure I could be poor and happy if Lluís loved me. I'm not at all like my brother Llibert . . . And that's where I find selfish consolation, the only silver lining in this never-ending war: the hope that with all these deprivations Lluís will come to appreciate his home and his family. We were once caught in a storm on an excursion of ours. There was a woodcutters' cabin nearby. We went in and lit a fire. It was lovely! Even Lluís said so: "It's so pleasant to listen to the rain when you're in the dry, even if it's only a cabin." We could be so happy in a cabin if we loved each other, so happy listening to the rain in the humblest of shelters! But he never stayed home, except on the evenings when you visited; you'd have thought the chairs were pricking his behind. He always seemed restless and unsatisfied: he expects more from life than it, poor thing, can ever give. He'll feel miserable until he realises that the best thing in life is that cup of herbal tea by the fireside drunk in the company of his loved one while out in the garden the wind is scattering the dead leaves. Uncle Eusebi used to say: "Lluís is always looking but he never sees a thing." When it comes to me, I think he's forever oblivious!

8 JUNE

You came so quickly, the minute you received my letter! If I'd known how you'd react, I'd never have mentioned the wretched sack of potatoes . . . It's the third time you've appeared unexpectedly with food for the boy. I worried when I thought of the sacrifice the new crates of tinned milk and all the other things you unloaded from the lorry must represent and I was thinking how time slipped by so quickly listening to you that evening and night! If my father knew you had reappeared . . . Days after your second visit I told him you'd been in Barcelona for the few hours that you spent at my house, "from ten at night to four in the morning". He shook his head in disapproval, saying he was shocked by my solitary night-time conversations with a man who wasn't my "companion". According to him, free love, precisely because it is free, must be allied to the purest, most austere acts to avoid the shadow of suspicion of anything unseemly. I burst out laughing: the suspicion of anything unseemly with you! People have such ridiculous notions . . . If he knew that my "solitary night-time conversations" had this time lasted from eight in the evening to six in the morning . . .

Time passed so fast, more than fast, it was as if time had been abolished. When you said: "Dawn is breaking over the port; we're now into the longest days of the year . . ." I couldn't believe it was half past four on the clock. You'd underlined those words the way you sometimes do, which can be annoying because it shows you couldn't care less about the feelings of the person you're talking to. You then added even more emphatically: "I detest these long days, give me the winter solstice with its never-ending nights! And polar nights, even better: let me sleep peacefully for six months on the trot so I can dream of endless nonsense."

I never dream and don't like nonsense, but it's strange how those words stuck in my mind from everything you said. We'd spent ten hours chatting and I recalled that cocaine addict you introduced me to long ago. It was before I'd met Lluís, and you and I used to distribute *La barrinada* on street corners by ourselves. As we never sold a copy, what we did was wander.

It was drizzling that evening and we'd sheltered under the awning of a big clothes shop on the Rambla, close to carrer de Sant Pau; the Rambla was glistening beautifully in that autumn shower, and we talked about this and that and about drugs and addicts. This was something new as far as I was concerned and I couldn't believe such people existed. You said: "Come with me and I'll introduce you to one," and you took me to a small chemist's on carrer de Sant Pau, a small, shabby place that you'd have thought was a little herb shop. "They've one person behind the counter – a student of Pharmaceutics," you said as you introduced me. I thought he looked rather old for a student, he seemed well past thirty, perhaps thirty-five. He had a dull, unnerving expression and you asked him what he felt when he took cocaine. All I remember him saying is: "I take a pinch of powder at ten in the evening and suddenly the sun is rising." The abolition of time – such an unusual pleasure!

P.S. Mother just telephoned to say that grandmother is dead.

13 JUNE

You write to me about your grandmother on the occasion of the death of mine and describe her in a way that reminds me, don't take offence, of the "old lady in the castle" in the English romantic novelettes I secretly read at the age of twelve because my parents had banned them from the house. On the other hand, I remember perfectly well that you always told us you'd never known your parents or grandparents. Why do you so like to lie and to mystify? Either you lied then or you're lying now. And if you are lying now, why do you feel the need to invent this "grandmother who made one think of the first violets of the year, the most shrinking of all"? For your information, I can't stand violets.

Whatever the truth of the matter, I'm grateful for the kind words you write on the occasion of the death of mine. She wasn't how you imagine; she didn't bring to mind shrinking violets. The poor woman dirtied herself unawares . . .

They say she was a very active woman before she had the stroke; they say she doted on me – I was three when she was paralysed. She was in service before she married my grandfather, who was a tram driver. They went without lots of things to enable my father to study to become a teacher. Father must have done everything to ensure she had a peaceful old age but she was aware of nothing. Her mind was blank for seventeen years. I'd prefer to imagine she was like a vegetable, but one could tell she wasn't completely unaware because of the expression in her eyes. She sometimes cried when she dirtied herself.

Her death hasn't saddened me, quite the contrary. Why should I lie to you? It moved me and that was all. Now that she's not sitting in her corner of our back gallery I feel the world has changed a little, but very little.

Then suddenly there's the mysterious grandmother out of a romantic novelette you felt the need to conjure up, I'm not sure to what end. She and all the "old ladies" who figure in girlish fiction perhaps spring from our unconscious desire to find innocence at the end of life, given we find precious little along the way. As if life were but a protracted battle to gain innocence – let's find it at the end as we didn't at the beginning. That's the only interesting slant I can find on this issue, and I beg you to spare me further mystifications, especially the edifying kind.

Your eternal mystifications, Juli . . . can't you live without mystifying? People lose track, don't know when you're telling the truth or mystifying. You once took me into the cloister of the cathedral; you often did. We both liked walking around chattering endlessly, particularly on rainy afternoons.

We were by ourselves that day. By the curate's office there used to be a table strewn with heaps of small pamphlets under a notice that said: *Please take one.* Naturally they were the kind of religious tracts churches gave out for free. You and I were carrying our respective packets of unsold copies of *La barrinada* under our arms: every time we took a stroll around the cloister we walked past that table and you'd stop and look at it silently. I couldn't imagine what you were hatching.

"We'll make your father really happy," you said the fourth time we passed the table. "Today when the issue has an important article by him, we'll make him think we sold out. He'll be so happy! Perhaps it will be the happiest moment of his life!"

You didn't give me time to reply. You'd already taken one of the piles of pamphlets and put in their place our joint offerings of *La barrinada.*

A few days afterwards, when we were on the corner of carrer del Bisbe, you said: "Why don't we take a look and see if they are still there?"

In effect, they were still there. Among novenas, Triduums and Sacred Heart bulletins, there, next to the notice that said: *Please take one.* The pile seemed untouched; probably nobody had taken one.

"It's turned out better than I expected," you said. "Nobody noticed. We could try out another idea."

"Another idea? What idea?"

"Another. I have lots of bright ideas."

You were already tacking a printed sheet – I later learned a printer friend of yours produced it for you – to the cork board on a wall where they used to pin notices of religious functions and the times for mass. That day too the cloister was empty: "Do you see? I've wanted to do this for ages. Now and then I get this mad desire to do something I just have to do, however wild it may seem. It's more powerful than I am."

The leaflet said in big black print

HUGE PROGRESS IN THE MANUFACTURE OF HOSTS

and then in smaller letters: "A Chicago industrialist has discovered a new technique that makes it possible to produce a million per second", followed by a string of gross idiotic things I've forgotten. How was I supposed to understand you? When were you mystifying: in the cathedral cloister or in Santa Maria del Mar? I was irritated by a joke I found stupid rather than irreverent as I was irritated the other day when I saw traces of tears on your face.

We were atheists at home. Father had inculcated in me a complete indifference to religion. Making fun of Catholicism made as little sense to me as making fun of Buddhism or spiritualism, so at times like that I thought you were a complete fool. I asked you why you'd had it printed in Spanish rather than Catalan: "Because it's funnier," came your reply.

I'd not found it at all funny. "It's funnier in Spanish," you insisted, annoyed because I hadn't laughed. "When Saint Philomena appears to my aunt, she always speaks to her in Spanish. It's always Spanish. She tells her: '*No temas, yo te salvaré*... Don't be afraid, I'll save you...'" You'd told me the story of the strange visions your aunt had so often I knew it by heart but I didn't feel like laughing. I refused to go back to the cloister with you for weeks after that. I thought your "bright ideas" had no substance.

Then there were those shenanigans at the university. It was December, 1930.

We students had started to meet in the basement of a delicatessen on the Rambla, past the Arc del Teatre. I think it was called *La extremeña*. It was a large dark basement with lots of hams and cold sausages hanging from the ceiling that gave it the air of a grotto with stalactites that smelt of mountain ham and draught brown beer. The owner of the shop was a survivor of the First Republic who still retained his Phrygian cap and sword from those days. You'd discovered this octogenarian supporter of Castelar and had dubbed him "the diplodocus" as we all felt he was some kind of antediluvian beast. You encouraged him to reminisce about deeds and anecdotes from the "Glorious" Revolution that were occasionally curious but more often than not dismally hackneyed. We were soon calling the basement "the diplodocus' den" and were delighted to be able to rely on that refuge where we could meet and plot. Once when we were twenty-five to thirty students all told, the *extremeño* brought down his two relics and put them on in front of us. Wearing his Phrygian cap, his sword girt on his waist, he told us with misty eyes: "I don't want to die before returning to the street like this."

We were lukewarm. We preferred to think that the republic of our dreams had nothing in common with that man's, the carnival of the poor that the first must have been, but it worried us and one day you told me as we were leaving: "At times I think we too will seem like old fools when we're eighty, just like this diplodocus who can't mention Castelar or Lerroux without tears streaming from his bleary eyes."

"What do you mean?"

"If only we could own a popular delicatessen like him . . . that would be some consolation. Perhaps we won't manage even that. I expect Lerroux purchased this establishment for him with money from the Town Hall."

You'd sometimes have lunch there by yourself. You liked that den, or so you said, because it was dark and cavernous. You'd pretend to your aunt that the Economics professor had invited you to his house for lunch. While he served you lunch the old *extremeño* recounted his interminable memories of the First Republic and the *Setmana Tràgica*. That was when he came to live in Barcelona and "was the last time I went into the street with my cap and sword". You had him recite whole chunks of speeches by Lerroux or Castelar that he knew by heart, the stuff about "the chariot of State is capsizing in stormy seas" and "let's lift the veils of the novices and make mothers of them". You thought it was a hoot, but I felt it was just trite, sad and depressing. Quite often when we other students arrived at around three we'd find you chatting to that poor fellow at a table where you'd already had lunch: he would rehearse your menu of snails *à la vinai-grette*, two slices of ham and Roncal cheese. We drank coffee together and launched into endless ideological arguments as if he didn't exist: there were representatives of the most irreconcilable tendencies, anarchists, republicans of the centre and left, social democrats, separatists and communists. There were many varieties and shades of the latter – Stalinists, Trotskyists, Catalan Proletarians and even some who, so they said, condemned the splintering of Marxism into squabbling sects and had founded another party that campaigned for "dialectical unification". They were always talking about Hegel's dialectics, the thesis and antithesis of which they aspired to be the synthesis. Perhaps the strangest of the communist groups that joined our gatherings was the one set up by that very thin, tall, fair lad by the name of Orfila, and by that other young fellow who was very fat, short and swarthy by the name of Bracons. Orfila and Bracons didn't agree with any of the other groups, not even the "dialectical unification" group. They promoted the "syncretic fusion" of Marxism and Freudianism, since, according to them, Marx's economic materialism should be complemented by Freud's sexual materialism. You once said: "If we complement Marx with Freud, we'll be combining a couple of giant Jews and I'm afraid the new road you think you've found will lead us straight to the synagogue; off you go if that's what you fancy, but count me out. On the other hand, your fusion is so new and bold the classics already have a name for it: *de cibus et veneris*." Another issue that gave rise to endless polemics was a guerrilla fighter operating at the time in the jungles of Nicaragua and Guatemala, Sandino if I remember rightly. We all thought this Sandino was a hero – of the struggle of the Latin American proletariat against Yankee imperialism. What can have become of Sandino? We've not heard a word about him for ages. It's curious how we got so worked up by those debates that were so interminable and stupid. We spent our lives in that dive convinced we were forging the future of the world, certain that the universe was trembling at the thought of what we might decide. We were complete idiots. Perhaps it was the *extremeño* who, in his way, made most sense as he listened in amazement to arguments he found completely incomprehensible and at the end he muttered: "You'd all do much better if you joined the Radical Party."

However, I met Lluís there. So even if the future of the universe wasn't decided in that diplodocus' den, the basement of *La extremeña*, mine was. For better or for worse, God alone knows.

He was arguing with the other students – I got to the meeting late that day. I immediately sensed that in my eyes this young man was different from you or any of the others. Right then the talk was about pistols – an issue that often cropped up in our conversations. Lluís was examining some that one of the conspirators had brought, saying he didn't think they were much use. "A Parabellum is what we need," was his verdict. "A Parabellum?" you said. "You might as well ask for the world!"

Rumours of a possible military insurrection against the king were gathering pace across the Peninsula and kept us in a constant state of nervous tension. One day it wasn't simply a rumour: it was the headlines in all the newspapers – a captain in the Foreign Legion had started an insurrection in Jaca.

Two days later the morning newspapers reported a summary court martial and the execution of that captain and another who'd supported him. We met in permanent session in the diplodocus' den: we had to raise the stakes, take the university and proclaim the republic. There were heated arguments over which flag to hoist. Each group wanted its own and it was amazing how each group and *groupuscule* had its flag, whether it was black, red, black and red, red and green, or whatever. I remember at one point you banged your fist on the table and proposed the flag of Baluchistan: "As nobody is familiar with it," you said, "it will upset nobody. On the other hand," you added, "given our idiosyncratic ways, if we were in Baluchistan we'd obviously hoist the Catalan flag, but as we are actually in Catalonia that would clearly show deplorably bad taste."

In the end the majority voted for the federal flag, because nobody there was specifically a federalist. Then we faced another problem: what was the federal flag exactly? We consulted the diplodocus, the owner of *La extremeña*, but he didn't know; he wasn't a federalist even in those days but a supporter of the unitarians, Castelar and Lerroux. It's worth saying that very few of us knew what a unitarian republic was either; the diplodocus had only a vague memory and assured us that he'd seen his idol, Don Alejandro, on one occasion with a little Spanish flag in the band of his panama. Finally it was my father who got us out of the impasse: he made a big effort and remembered the flag my grandfather, a lifelong federalist, had kept for ages at the back of a drawer among other faded souvenirs of his youth.

You gave me the task of sewing that famous federal flag we would hoist over the university. We wanted a large one so it would be seen easily from the university square, and it was a lot of work. I had to use different coloured materials – red, yellow and purple – with a sea blue triangle in one corner. I had to put white stars on this sea blue background to symbolise the federated states. Fresh interminable arguments: how many federated states should there be and thus how many stars? My father didn't know: he couldn't remember his father ever speaking to him with any precision on this aspect of federalism – the federalists of his day clearly felt that was a secondary issue. They weren't bothered about who should be in the federation; the object was to federate, though they probably didn't know what that meant either. We had to go back yet again to our diplodocus. The owner of *La extremeña* shrugged his shoulders: it was the first time he'd ever heard any talk of federated states and he barely understood when we tried to explain the concept to him.

How many stars should we put on the flag – four, seven or fifteen?

"Better have too many than miss any out," you said. "Put a good couple of dozen and everything will be fine: keep everybody happy."

The stars also had to be big so passers-by could see them from carrer Pelayo and Ronda Sant Antoni and you and Lluís came to my place to lend a hand: we cut them out from sugar paper, a whole sheet for each star, and glued them on with thick floury paste. When we laid it out on the floor for the glue to dry it took up the whole dining room and a section even made it into the passageway.

The morning came when we'd decided to make our mark on history; you wrapped the flag round your waist and put an overcoat on top. You looked a rare sight! So as not to attract attention we went to the university in a big gang, hiding you in our midst but making fun of you. Our companions were already there, mounting a barricade with paving stones from the square. The passers-by took no notice; it was the traditional time of year for students to erect barricades and demand longer Christmas holidays. There were only two or three pairs of police from that era, the so-called Security Police, men of a venerable age armed only with swords who merely stood and watched the students erecting their barricade with pavement stones. Now, when I remember the Security Police under the monarchy with their anachronistic swords and large grey moustaches, looking as if they'd all fathered large families, when I recall their blue uniforms and helmets, so like firemen, so good-humoured, gentle and henpecked and think of the horrors we've seen since . . .

When we walked through the groups erecting the barricade, they knew what we were planning and applauded and shouted: "*Visca la república!*" It was at that point that a respectable gentleman who happened to be walking by stopped and asked: "Hey, lads, are you by any chance proclaiming the republic? I thought you were asking for longer holidays as per usual for this time of year."

"Yes, sir," someone replied, "we *are* proclaiming the republic, but ours will be an orderly republic."

"Of that I have no doubt," retorted the fellow sarcastically. "You students and the Foreign Legion will give us a sensible republic of the sort that's rarely been seen before."

Without wasting any time, we crossed the lobby between the huge plaster statues of Ramon Llull and I don't know who else and on to the law courtyard with you still in our midst. We climbed the stairs and entered the library. We were supposed to be meeting some of our people there who were pretending to read enormous reference books: in the meantime while the librarian was yawning, which was most of the time, their task was to find out which of the small doors concealed in the library led to the winding staircase up to the roof with the flagpole. None of us had ever been on the roof: all we knew or thought we knew was that the door in question was one of the ones hidden among the shelves of the university library.

The university library . . . how little we went there! When I remember it now, the first thing that springs to mind is how it reeked of damp, of mouldy, worm-eaten paper and stale air. The rare occasions we set foot inside were to look up the odd word in the *Espasa Encyclopaedia* since its tomes were the few that were easily accessible. If you ever wanted anything that wasn't the *Espasa Encyclopaedia* or Cèsar Cantú's *Universal History*, you had to go into the office of the librarian who would give you an astonished, withering look. We called him "little old man" because that was what he was; he spent hours in his cramped, shabby office, that was more like a cave, reading scabrous works from the eighteenth century. He hated being disturbed when carrying out his exhaustive, erudite research into erotic literature in the Age of the Enlightenment, as his reading of Mirabeau, the Marquis de Sade, Diderot, Cholderlos de Laclos and other fathers of the French Revolution filled file after file that he kept in old cardboard shoe boxes; with the patience of a Benedictine monk he was preparing a monumental monograph on a subject that was as risqué as it was dog-eared. He took no interest in anything else: it was usually a waste of time to ask him for a book because he would never have found it – only a minute section of books was catalogued.

I understand the library was mainly set up with books from monasteries that were suppressed in 1835. They were salvaged from arson attacks of the time or were those that well-meaning citizens picked up in the middle of the street while the monasteries were going up in flames and then brought to the university. They included so many tomes of theology and the lives of saints, so many books written by friars in the seventeenth and eighteenth centuries that nobody reads and nobody is interested in nowadays. Tens of thousands of dead, fossilised books filling shelf after shelf and quietly turning into dust thanks to ravenous woodworm and an indifferent sex-obsessed librarian.

There are so many of these books – collected in huge quantities from monasteries in the era of Mendizábal – that they don't fit in the university and are beginning to invade bookshelves in the secondary school. There they fill a big inner yard covered by a huge skylight, a three-storey well the sides of which are lined by books of parchment that give off an intense stench of damp wood, fungi and mildew. I rarely dream, but in one that I had years ago I dreamed I was in freefall down a bottomless "well of books" . . . You and Lluís went to Jesuit secondary school and never saw the inside of that place. I should also tell you that the ground floor of that inner yard, where the dust and stale air are at their rankest, is where we students at the school had our gym lessons; it was there we did our breathing exercises. What made the place even gloomier was the skeleton they'd placed on the left as you went in, the genuine item articulated with wire so it stood up: the class was about giving us notions of anatomy as well as gym and breathing exercises.

Why am I telling you all this? Why did I get sidetracked into recalling the university library and the gym class at secondary school? I'm always reminiscing about the old days and flitting from one thing to another, as if I were adrift. I sit still in my armchair, staring blankly into space, unable to concentrate on anything, as if my memories were dancing a sarabande before my eyes – trivial memories of no interest, with no logic to them, of dead things from long ago that are meaningless except to me, and that's if I'm lucky!

I was telling you about the day we hoisted the flag and were in the library searching for the concealed door that leads to the winding staircase. Our companions whose task it was to find it got it wrong: they pointed us to one that wasn't the one we wanted. By the time we'd realised it was too late to turn back, we were already on the roof. That little door led us to interminably winding stairs that didn't go straight to the flagpole but to another side of the huge roof. From where we came out we could see the flagpole behind an expanse of tiles that looked like a mountain peak we now had to crawl towards.

Lluís went first, then me, with you in the rear. We crawled cat-like in single file, and the tiles creaked under our hands and knees. It might have been dangerous but I insisted on accompanying you: it seemed too exciting and too glorious an adventure for me to miss. You didn't want me to. I'd quarrelled violently with Lluís in the library – whispering! I'd stubbornly followed you despite your protests and now, with the three of us on the roof, was no time to argue. Lluís told me to hold on to his foot, you supported me with your free hand and we made our way over the roof.

"Anyone flying across the sky would think we were two tomcats after a she-cat in January," you quipped.

That roof was never-ending and suddenly we started hearing pistol shots in the square. We later learned it was our people firing those two pistols, the only ones they had – that Lluís had inspected in the basement and were next to useless. The Security Police didn't return fire because they only carried swords, but we later discovered they'd been replaced by the civil guard, because the students were firing pistols. That happened as we were crawling over the roof, making the tiles shift, and couldn't see anything; the burst of gunfire took us by surprise since we'd agreed there'd be no shooting. When Lluís heard the reports, he turned round and told me to go home, that my place wasn't there; he was furious but I refused, I wanted to follow you and do whatever you did! I was so excited and thought it all so wonderful and the gunfire made it even more so. Lluís got increasingly exasperated in that dangerous situation, crawling along and stretching a foot out for me to cling to, he turned round to speak to me, to insult me, calling me a crybaby and a bore, and chucking in a few really nasty obscenities. While he and I argued, you'd gone on ahead, unravelled the flag from round your waist, climbed on to the small metal platform at the foot of the huge flagpole and were fiddling with the rope. Poor Juli, you couldn't work it out, you're clumsy, hopeless with your hands; and soon you were in a fine pickle with the double rope on the flagpole. Lluís came to help and as the rope had got entangled near the pulley he was forced to stand on the platform railing and hang on to the pole to disentangle it. You in turn climbed up to help him. You draped the flag over some tiles and I sat on top to ensure a gust of wind didn't blow it away.

Sitting on the flag I poked my head over the stone battlements. You were so engrossed in trying to fathom how the rope and pulley worked you didn't give me a glance. My head hovered over the void and the square looked strange from up there: the centre was empty, without trams or cars; the barricade erected by our companions was on one side and the civil guards on the opposite, by the Ronda Sant Antoni.

I had no doubt it was the civil guard; I had a perfect view of their three-cornered patent-leather hats. "Clear off!" shouted Lluís. "Give us the flag and scram!" But I was fascinated by the contingent of civil guards. Our people, from behind the barricade, kept shooting their two pistols sporadically and the civil guards stood to attention on the pavement of the Ronda and didn't react. An officer had spotted us: he was looking through his binoculars while gesturing with his free hand to another next to him, as if pointing out what you were doing. You finally managed to slip the flag on the rope and hoist it. It billowed like a sail in the wind and gallantly flapped its paper stars. You were still standing on the rail, clinging to different sides of the pole; the civil guard sharpshooters could have easily picked you two off, but they still stood to attention with their hands clasped over the ends of their rifles, the butts resting on the ground, while their officer observed us through his binoculars and gesticulated to his colleague.

We retraced our steps over tiles that clattered even more as we descended. When we were crossing the library – the invisible librarian must have been in his lair reading the Marquis de Sade – we met some companions who were waiting impatiently for us.

"Did everything go O.K.?"

"The flag is flapping in the wind," you replied. "Such a wonderful flag! Everybody will think it's the flag of the United States."

"We've got a can of oil," they replied, "but don't know what to do with it. We ought to start a fire somewhere."

"As we're in the library," you suggested, "why don't we start it right here? We couldn't find a better place. It will burn like dry tinder."

You were already on your way to the shelves with the *Espasa Encyclopaedia* when Lluís, beside himself, swore at you, called you an irresponsible savage and other coarse names, grabbed the can and gave you a shove. You shrugged: "If all that had gone up in flames," you retorted, pointing at the shelves with the *Espasa Encyclopaedia* and César Cantú's history book, "do you think it would have been a great loss?"

"Let's go to the rector's wing," said one student.

"To the great hall," suggested another. "There's that large oil painting of the king wearing the habits of the Order of Calatrava."

"We could light a bonfire on the square under the noses of the civil guards," rasped Lluís. "We could throw on the king and whatever other junk we find in the great hall and the rector's wing."

The stairs to the great hall were already packed with people. They were carrying a big beam they'd found God knows where that they were now using as a battering ram to smash open the doors. Ten or twelve were holding it and to build up momentum they chanted: "One, two, three, go!"

The robust double doors creaked, shook and shuddered at each attack and the hinges and bolt began to give. One door collapsed quite unexpectedly and the ramming was at such a rate that soon they all crashed to the ground. The great hall was ours! At the back, above the directorate's dais, Alfonso XIII was smiling at us mischievously, impeccable in his snow-white garb.

"Let's put him on trial!" went up the shout.

The hall filled in a flash as people flooded in. A court area was set up and the magistrates donned their disguise of robes and birettas someone had found in a wardrobe in the secretariat.

"Let Soleràs be the prosecutor!" went up another shout.

And you stood to the right of that grotesque court, slipping on black robes that were too short for you, while others bawled: "Silence! Soleràs will accuse the king!"

"Comrades, listen to the prosecutor!"

The robes looked tiny on you and strangely made you seem taller and thinner, more like a rake than ever. It was useless calling for silence. You read out the accusation but your voice was lost in the clamour. Only those of us who were next to you could hear what you were saying: "We accuse you of being a king, of calling yourself a Bourbon, and being an unlucky number," you declaimed in a monotonous litany, while wagging a finger at the oil painting. "We accuse you because others are simply Jaume Puig or Anton Rafeques, but you are Alfonso the Thirteenth and that makes lots of people split their sides. Some people call you Mr Thirteen and think they are so funny, they laugh themselves silly and slather over their chops. We accuse you, Mr Thirteen . . ."

Those who of us who'd begun to work out what you were saying exchanged puzzled glances: what the hell were you building up to? You carried on unperturbed, still wagging an accusing finger at that king painted in oils: "We accuse you of being a short body on long legs, that's earned you the popular nickname of Ambrose and the equally popular Long-legs; we accuse you, Ambrose Long-legs, of not letting the lovely lads of the Legion rise up whenever they feel like it and enjoying an insurrection when they fancy . . ."

Now the few of us who could hear you were more bewildered than ever; you continued, averting your gaze: "We accuse you of having your portrait painted in this robe that looks like a winding sheet; we accuse you because your mother, the Holy Archduchess of Austria, never caused a scandal, and a virtuous queen is so boring and dashes the hard-working, honest people's legitimate hopes of excuses to gossip . . . we accuse you above all, Mr Alfonso Thirteen, above all we accuse you of committing the most heinous of crimes, the crime a university cannot forgive in the era that is now beginning, of being neither a Hegelian nor a Nietzschean, neither a proletarian nor a superman! Quite intolerable! You're still a Krausist – if that. Perhaps deep down you never even got as far as Krause. You thus deserve to be burned!"

The multitude that vaguely heard the words you were mumbling interrupted you every other second with ovations and while these resounded you shut up and modestly lowered your eyes in the manner of all great orators. The only ones not to applaud were those who could actually hear what you were saying.

When you indicated you had finished your accusation, the walls shook with the massive applause. Some students, who'd brought a ladder, were already taking down the painting; it looked huge un-hung, and we now headed en masse towards the rector's offices, painting in tow. As the offices had those tall windows overlooking the square, we decided to pour oil on it, set it alight and hurl it out of a window. It fell on the barricade but had already come apart from its frame as it burst into flame. We poured more oil out of the window while other students defenestrated other portraits, of dead rectors or who knows what dry, boring, be-robed and be-medalled characters together with any papers we extracted from the cupboards and everything else we could lay our hands on to make a big and visible bonfire.

We flung the windows wide open and after defenestrating everything inflammable and easy to throw down we organised tables and chairs into a barricade behind the balustrades. From our vantage point we could see the civil guards still standing to attention on the Ronda Sant Antoni pavement, on the opposite side of the square. They stood straight-backed and stiff, their hands over the ends of their rifles. Only the two officers stirred, walking quietly up and down past the line of guards who remained rooted to the spot like statues.

"A pity my pistol jammed," said one of the students who'd been firing from the barricade down in the square.

"I've run out of ammunition," said the other.

"We could give them a roasting from up here . . ."

While our frustrated sharpshooters bemoaned the divine pleasures they were missing out on, a lad ran up from the street looking very excited: "I've got a Parabellum!"

The word "Parabellum" triggered a religious silence and everyone stepped respectfully aside to let him walk through. "He's got a Parabellum," we repeated, glancing admiringly at the newcomer: "a Parabellum ..." "A Parabellum ..." the whisper went round the crowd. They craned their necks to try to see the prodigious student with a Parabellum.

Then you staged one of your really eccentric tricks: one of those strange occurrences that shock people and nobody can ever fathom until long after the event. It's taken me until today to grasp what you did then.

You bear-hugged the lad with the Parabellum and took it from him.

"Give me that Parabellum! I'm a first-rate marksman!"

"A first-rate marksman? First I've heard of it!"

But you had already made it yours, were holding it tight and you'd knelt down at the back of the barricade of tables and chairs behind the windows and positioned yourself to take aim at the civil guards. The pistol – I can see it now – was a lustrous black with a long, polished glinting barrel and you shot non-stop. As you emptied out the spent cartridges, the lad who'd brought it knelt by your side and handed you fresh ammunition. The empty brass cartridges clattered and bounced. The rest of us looked at you breathless, full of wonder; perhaps some were deadly envious.

Meanwhile, at an order from the officer with the binoculars, a civil guard had raised his rifle; the others kept their hands over the ends of theirs. I saw that very clearly, because I put my head above the balustrade: only one civil guard was returning your fire and he always had an officer next to him who seemed to be calling the shots. These were spasmodic and the bullets embedded themselves in the ceiling of the great hall – not right at the back, as would have happened if he'd aimed at our balustrade, but near the window, as if he were aiming the top of it. The bullets thudded softly into the plaster ceiling while you kept on firing.

A thought suddenly struck me: Juli can't possibly see the guards from this distance – he's much too short-sighted!

On our strolls down the side streets of old Barcelona I'd had plenty of opportunities to register how short-sighted you were. I knew you couldn't tell a man from a tree more than thirty metres away and saw next to nothing forty or fifty metres away. I'd soon worked that out though you tried to pretend you had normal sight. You'd fly into a rage at any reference to your short-sightedness, at any hint that you should visit an optician and get some proper glasses. Once, when Lluís was being adamant, you bit his head off in a furious temper: "I see much better than you! Why don't you just fuck off?" I suddenly realised the buildings on the Ronda Sant Antoni could only be a blur. So why had you grabbed the Parabellum? How could you shoot at civil guards you couldn't see?

Some days later we had a meeting on carrer de l'Hospital. You were our hero, the student who'd shot a Parabellum as long as his ammunition held out. Even the tough old anarchists, veterans of the struggles between the single union and the free union, regarded you with respect.

People wanted to see and hear you. Our dining room, passageway, lobby, bedrooms, small sitting room and kitchen were crammed.

When you began to speak, a sudden hush descended the like of which I'd never heard before; such a dense silence it was audible. You began modestly and that won more people over: "Everything we do, everything we can ever do, poor Kierkegaardians that we are, quite unbeknown to ourselves . . ." I don't think anyone present had ever heard of Kierkegaard, but that didn't matter: they gaped in awe. You continued: "All we can ever do is zilch compared to what the Hegelians are doing, let alone what the Nietzscheans are *about* to do." None present understood this nonsense and they began to exchange perplexed glances: silence metamorphosed into stunned amazement.

"To sum up, companions or comrades, or whatever you will, every-thing we are doing now, these heroic shenanigans, this glorious rumpus, this historic hubbub, should have been done in 1923. I could put forward a good excuse for not doing it then, that is, seven years ago, by saying I was only eleven, a very tender age. No matter: that's when we should have done it. Doing it now, however bitter it may be to acknowledge, however much it dents our self-esteem, is rather . . . chicken. No, companions or comrades, I'm quite happy to define myself as an extremely 'umble chicken from Kierkegaard's coop; if anyone here thinks he is a Hegelian or Nietzschean eagle, let him cast the first egg. Even though our flight may be a modest chicken effort, we should be helping the king, who is trying to re-establish a civilian constitution and not a captain in the Legion who thinks he has a right to proclaim a republic off his own bat because he fancies one. Remember, companions or comrades: bayonets are capricious. If we let them proclaim one thing today, don't let's complain if tomorrow they proclaim something else."

People finally got your message. They understood you were attacking the military uprising in Jaca and perplexity quickly gave way to indignation and uproar. You waved your arms and shouted like a man shipwrecked amid crashing waves in heavy seas: "I've been to Russia and Germany! I know what it's all about! I know what a show the Hegelians and Nietzscheans are putting on!" Your voice was lost in the tumult: people were roaring in our dining room, in our hallway and in our bedrooms. The flat seemed on the point of collapse under the torrent of screams, the stamp-ing on the floor, the whistles and the obscenities. If I could hear you and understand what you were saying, it was because I was sitting between you and my father.

My father gave me the biggest surprise of all. He stood up, intrepidly – I ought to add that he'd had long practice at speaking to hostile, vociferous crowds; he'd so often given an angry crowd the opposite of what it wanted to hear! With a broad sweep of his arm he calmed the waters: "Old Milmany will now speak," people whispered from our dining room to our hallway, from our kitchen to our bedrooms. Silence fell and Father proceeded to speak softly and deliberately, as if he were weighing up his words before dropping them into a sea about to seethe at any moment.

"It wouldn't be right, companions – and I would beg companion Soleràs never to call us 'comrades', a word with military connotations that we find repugnant – it wouldn't be right if we, who call ourselves libertarians, interrupted someone who is expressing his ideas. All ideas, whatever they may be, have a right to be freely expressed; if we don't respect the freedom of others, how on earth can we demand they respect ours? Companions, I agree with you, I hardly have to tell you that. I agree with you that some of the things companion Soleràs has just expressed, making use of his freedom, seem a little . . . surprising, especially when expressed here, in this bulwark of co-operative anarcho-syndicalism that is the editorial office of *La barrinada*. I know companion Soleràs well and I know he likes to shock people with his pranks and his paradoxes. However, once that's been said and once we've made allowances for the eccentric and shocking things he has said, I will be frank and confess to you – and among friends and companions, frankness is an indication of loyalty – that I am more in agreement with him than you might imagine. I don't believe, I have never believed, in the right of might, in the rule of pistols and even less so of bayonets, and so as far as that goes I agree with companion Soleràs. Between a civilian monarchy and a military republic —"

"What, have you turned monarchist too? That's all we need!" interjected Cosme, his dear lifelong friend who was sitting with us on the dais. That was the detonator and once again turmoil rocked our flat.

"I'm neither monarchist nor republican. I am an anarchist!" shouted my father, though hardly anyone heard. They were all gesticulating and yelling the coarsest of curses and grossest of obscenities. One fellow was so small he climbed up on to the sideboard so people could see and hear him. He was wailing and ranting, red in the face as if on the verge of an attack of apoplexy: "Fuck the king!"

While everyone argued heatedly and threw insults going down the endless stairs, Lluís tugged my right arm and stopped me on the fifth-floor landing. You'll remember how the landings in our house still have those wooden corner seats they put in buildings during the last century so people climbing up can sit down and catch their breath: our eight are big enough to take two people. Lluís sat me down beside him and those coming down rushed past us like a roaring torrent. We heard only the odd snatch: "Better Mussa the Moor* than the King!" Cosme shouted. The flood had already reached the bottom steps and for a moment we heard your voice echoing up the stairwell: "I'd like to hear from you in a few years – a republic ushered in by a military insurrection . . ." and Cosme's thunderous voice riposting: "Student revolts, daddy's boys playing up!"

But I wasn't listening and heard nothing: I was alone with Lluís on that corner seat and he was crushing me with all his strength. The torrent of bodies rushed past, arguing and insulting, but none of that existed as far as I was concerned: nothing existed apart from Lluís. The years have passed, seven this December, and my God, disappointments have come

---

* Mussa the Moor (640–716) was the Yemeni general who led the Ummayyad invasion of the Iberian Peninsula in 711, rapidly conquering cities from Sevilla to Lleida.

thick and fast, but the memory of that first kiss still turns me head over heels as it did then. What couldn't I forgive him for that moment, the most glorious I'd ever experienced?

I sometimes tell myself that if the old Jesuit from the attic near the Arc del Teatre had baptised me, I might have felt an equally strong surge of emotion, but I've never felt anything so powerful and I know I never will again.

A few weeks later the police arrested Lluís and others who met up in the basement of *La extremeña*, including Orfila and Bracons. As they couldn't pin anything on them, the police simply held them in the Prefecture dungeons for a few days. After their release they told us they thought they must have been seeing visions during the interrogations: the police were familiar with precise details from conversations in the basement that only someone who'd been there could have told them. The police knew, for example, about the whole debate over the federal flag; they even knew somebody had uttered the incomprehensible phrase *de cibus et veneris* at some point, which they interpreted as highly important and a code standing for some dastardly mysterious revolutionary slogan. This made our heads spin – was there a traitor, a police informer in our midst? Who could it be? Today, years later, I think I can tell you that Orfila and Bracons suspected you. I should say that Lluís and I defended you: they alleged you were an eccentric young man, that your reactions were unpredictable, your ideas incoherent, and that you acted strangely. "It must have been one of us and he's the only one who fits the bill, whatever you say."

It took us a long time to find out who it was and we did so quite by chance, though I don't remember how: the informer was the old supporter of Lerroux from Extremadura, the diplodocus. It transpired that they'd done a deal some time ago by virtue of which he let his basement be used for all kinds and colour of clandestine meetings; the police never intervened – that would have cut off their source of information – but he had to report on all he heard. The man made a living from what he got selling ham and from the handouts he earned from the filth. He wasn't a fake republican or a counterfeit Lerroux supporter, which is what we poor innocents concluded when we found out he was the informer. It's obvious that he didn't think the two things were at all incompatible: he was sincere when he whimpered and showed us his Phrygian cap and sword that he'd flourished during the *Setmana Tràgica*, sincere when he tremulously recited those harangues of Castelar or Lerroux, and sincere when he betrayed us to the filth – he was always sincere! We didn't understand him at the time: it's not that we understand him now, since there are things you can't fathom by their very nature, but we have seen much stranger happenings recently! Things that really make your head spin! What if I told you that there are days when I even suspect my brother Llibert is basically a species of diplodocus . . . We young people are quick to value sincerity above all else and never grasp that some people are sincere in whatever role they play; their duplicity, rather than lack of sincerity, is a Janus-faced sincerity – they are doubly sincere! And Llibert is unnerving: all his gushing spontaneity, his sincerity, his quivering voice are unnerving . . . This is only a very vague presentiment, a hunch that's probably mistaken: he is possibly a much subtler, more elegant and complex diplodocus than the man from Extremadura.

One mystery remains: how come the police didn't arrest you or anyone else – like me, for example? Why had the owner of *La extremeña* told the police some names and not others? He must have been swayed by personal likes and dislikes – that's the only explanation. He'd clearly taken a shine to you and didn't want you to suffer: riddles of diplodocus psychology we shall never solve. On the other hand he obviously couldn't stand Lluís and hated that inseparable duo Orfila and Bracons and their syncretic fusion of Marxism and Freudianism even more.

You then went on to publish that long article in the *Mirador*, "The Rebellion of the Youth," that we all read and argued passionately over. The whole universe seemed to revolve around us at the time.

They paid you twenty-five pesetas, you told us, sounding cock-a-hoop: "The first money I have ever earned." A few days later you told us: "Those twenty-five pesetas weren't only the first I ever earned but I suspect they will be the last: the *Mirador* has turned down my second article in the series. They say one is enough."

You didn't seem at all downcast, but in fact rather euphoric. And you added, "You wouldn't believe who's in charge at the *Mirador*. You walk into their offices and find them packed with important-looking people, celebrities, top writers and politicians, and you'd think any one of them could be the boss. Those privileged intellects and amazing talents dressed by the best tailors in Barcelona. All so ironic, so sceptical, sporting real Italian silk ties that cost a fortune and smoking Havana cigars! The glories of Catalan literature! In one out-of-the-way corner you see a skinny little man who looks as if he's just survived a shipwreck. I won't describe his tie because I've never liked talking about smut. This species of shipwrecked voyager is in charge and you feel like giving him alms, when in fact he's the boss. And he's really intelligent; it's hard to keep up with him! A kind of down-at-heel Talleyrand. In those battered shoes that produce mildew when it rains and even sprout fungi, he's the man who gives the orders in his frayed shirt, looking like someone who needs a hot meal and his frightful pockets bursting with books! He sits in a corner and listens to the others; he rarely says anything. From the little he does say you soon gather he's one of the sharpest minds in the country, a man who has read everything, who knows and understands everything. He told me: 'Don't build up your hopes, young man. We only publish one article a year on The Rebellion of the Youth. Our readers wouldn't tolerate more than one article on the subject per year. It's an article – how can I put this? – like the one entitled The First Roast Chestnut Sellers Are Here. I could perhaps tell you to come back next year, when there are more shenanigans at the university and students are back in the news, but it's not like the chestnut sellers: each year we must have a new person to write The Rebellion of the Youth, unlike the chestnut-seller article that can be written by the same journalist year in year out. When the subject is the rebellion of the young, we need a fresh youngster; last year's man has ceased to be young and not even his bloody mother recognises him.' He said that to my face, 'his bloody mother' ... As I said, he's a highly intelligent man!"

Why do these pitiful memories keep coming back to me? Things you did and said in times that now seem so distant ... How wan and faded they seem after everything that's happened and is still happening! After all we've seen and lived through, those times we thought so unruly now seem bathed in an aura of peace. You took the Parabellum from that young man for the same reason the civil guards – fantastic marksmen – only hit the ceiling. Will such times ever return?

Now we shall never see such times again, Juli; something has happened in this land to poison it for ever . . . Just so you know: your hopeful, encouraging letter arrived shortly after I heard that Cosme had been murdered. It will soon be a year since this tedious butchery began: could we ever suspect that Cain's seed has been scattered so widely across this land and is ready to germinate? How often in the past eleven months have we blindly believed the government would put an end to it or had already done so, that the arsonists and murderers would be rendered powerless, that if the war were to continue – that's bad enough in itself – at least it would be a clean war! Or has there ever been such a thing as a *clean* war? Are the sacrifices made by the soldiers at the front – on both sides – always condemned to be soiled by crimes in the rearguard? Must we not only crucify Jesus but do so between two thieves? Just so you know: you speak to me of happy times that are approaching, that are perhaps "already palpable", and of a "beautiful peace" the like of which has never been seen before; you say your heart tells you that you are about to "touch heaven with both hands", are about to take a decisive step in your life, attain what you always wanted, what you most dreamed of, what you wanted with "all your senses and your soul". Just so you know: I don't understand what you mean or what you are referring to, but if you are referring to a time of peace or at least of a clean war – and who knows if a clean war, even a tragic one, might not be more beautiful than peace with all its joy – if this is what your heart is telling you, Juli, then you are mistaken. The Cains are running amok in this world as they always have: last month's events that were a disaster so raised our hopes but only to dash them.

The crimes continue despite last month's events. Sometimes I would like to ignore them and lead a secret, marginal life far from this cruel, incoherent world, but that would be monstrously selfish, wouldn't it? And even if I did decide to bury myself in my selfishness and indifference, how could I prevent the news reaching me from a world that's falling apart? The stench of decomposition would penetrate every crack, would pursue me to my bed when I was trying to sleep the sleep of a lethargic animal about to hibernate and be stirred by nobody!

It must have been a fortnight ago that I was walking along Pelayo. If only you could see those bright, gleaming shop windows that were once full of goods and are now empty and drab, and the usual thronging crowd that now seems sad and tired and drags its feet . . . And I was dragging mine through the crowd, pulling a whining Ramonet by the hand, because I wanted to buy him new shoes he really needed, though he wanted me to buy an accordion, not new shoes. I could have said I'd buy both and thus deal with his tantrum but I'd decided not to give in to his whims anymore because if I do he'll become a spoilt brat and I will be to blame. Speaking of shoes, if you only knew how difficult it is to find decent shoes. The ones we get are made from a leathery cardboard that soon wears out and if you want real leather they cost a fortune – and Ramonet gets through them so quickly . . . So I was walking along the pavement on Pelayo dragging a Ramonet who wouldn't stop whining, feeling miserable and demoralised in that miserable, demoralised crowd, when, lo and behold, a complete stranger stopped me. He was a shortish skinny man I'd have taken for a poorly dressed labourer who'd not eaten for days, but he had the eyes of a defenceless, resigned, generous child – the eyes, my God, of a little old man who's been abused and only keeps going because of hope that belongs to another world.

"Aren't you Trini Milmany?"

"Yes, if I can be of help?" I replied, not realising who he was.

"Don't you remember me? I'm your godfather . . ."

I couldn't resist the impulse to kiss him on both cheeks – my godfather, the marquis I'd completely forgotten! He lifted the boy up to give him a kiss and he stopped whining, intrigued by that unknown little old man – he didn't remember him either – who was showing him such affection in the middle of carrer Pelayo. The poor marquis seemed so upset; his eyes had misted over, the passing crowd never stopped, kept pushing and shoving us while we talked; it was like being hit by pebbles swirling in a stream.

"Sooner or later the waters will settle," he told us and his eyes seemed to look far into the distance like the eyes of a blind man, "then you must often come to my house and bring Ramonet, because I'm his godfather too. If I don't tell you to do that now, if I'm not insisting, it's because a visit to a house like mine could bring you problems. But one day the victors, whoever they are, will realise that we are perfectly harmless and will allow us to become gradually extinct in the natural way of things . . ."

Then he vanished again, a poor anonymous old man amid that grey, starving, exhausted crowd flowing down carrer Pelayo as if it were the bed of a stream. Soon after the anarchist's wife, the one who lives on carrer de l'Arc del Teatre, came to see me in Pedralbes: the marquis had disappeared from his house, his daughter-in-law couldn't think who to ask when trying to find some trace of him and I was the only "red" who'd come to mind. She'd thought I – poor me! – might be able to help. All I could say was that I'd recently seen him still alive on carrer Pelayo.

That I might be able to help . . . and in the meantime poor Cosme has been murdered!

Perhaps I've not told you that Cosme had made a drastic break with the people in the union as a result of last month's events. He said it was playing into the fascists' hands to rise up against the autonomous government in the present circumstances: something that is blindingly obvious.

Apparently emboldened by the defeat of the anarchists, an examining magistrate decided to search part of the woods in Penitents, at the foot of Tibidabo, near the Rabassada roadway. Cosme, it seems, wasn't aware of the crimes his companions had been perpetrating wholesale over the last few months: however strange it may seem, he's one of many who still know nothing and believe blindly that the sinister times we've been suffering are a glorious people's revolution with not a single shadow to darken its dazzling light. A glorious people's revolution . . . if I were to tell you, Juli, that if this were true, if all this had really been a revolution by the people, there'd be good reason to hate the people with all our hearts! So much innocent blood, my God . . .

Pure chance put Cosme in touch with that splendid magistrate and – who'd have thought it! – the labourers had barely begun to dig in the woods when they found a secret grave with two hundred and thirty-six corpses. As they exhumed the bodies, the forensic doctor kept noting that almost all showed signs of having met a violent death, usually a shot in the back of the neck. All Barcelona knew that in those months the anarchists had taken thousands of people for "a ride" to those woods; they took them by car and, once there, killed them from behind even before they could alight. All Barcelona knew of this, except for Cosme and thousands of dreamers like him; this was nothing new, but now a magistrate had appeared and begun an investigation and a printed newssheet was keeping the general public informed about their findings. The majority of the corpses dated back to the first months of the war and it was impossible to identify them unless some form of documentation survived in the pockets of clothes that had half disintegrated, though some bodies were more recent. And my poor marquis was one.

Cosme kept publishing his reports in *La barrinada* and for the first time in its life the hapless weekly was selling thousands of copies. Cosme's articles didn't contain strings of sonorous adjectives like Father's, but stark, chilling figures, with exact details, dates and locations. All Barcelona was riveted to the series, and if there'd been elections at the time a wave of popularity would have carried my father, the magistrate, the forensic doctor and Cosme to the highest offices of Catalonia.

And then Cosme's body appeared as well a few days ago, on the Rabassada, with a bullet in the head. The magistrate and doctor have crossed the frontier but my father refuses to leave the country: "Better to die in Catalonia than live in a foreign land" – there's no way he can be made to leave. It's what the old marquis said, except he said it more gently and simply: "At my age I'd rather live at home than live among strangers . . ." At least I was able to persuade him to come and live in our house. I had to struggle to get him to grasp that he should go underground and suspend publication of *La barrinada* at least for a few weeks. It was a real struggle to convince him to lie low in my house where his enemies won't look for him because they don't know of its existence.

So there you are, I've got Father home, though it won't be for long because he's fretting to get back to carrer de l'Hospital and resume publishing *La barrinada*. He feels he is being a real coward by hiding and not bringing it out.

Poor Father, he's barely sixty and already seems as old as the marquis. I'm not at all surprised people call him "old Milmany". His moustache droops like a limp flag of defeat and his eyes communicate disillusion and fatigue. He now tells me at length in a sad, rather than sarcastic tone about the most recent family upsets: "I told your brother never to set foot in my house again. I would rather not see him. Let him get on with his life and I'll get on with mine: he's my son and I'm his father but the best thing would be for neither to know what the other is doing. I'm not sure if you know that he went off to live in a posh first-floor flat on passeig de Gràcia, where he's been housing a little friend for some time. You may not have heard of her but she's that Llopis woman who's a big star on the Paral·lel: Llibert calls her an artiste, an actress, one of the glories of Catalan theatre. Poor old Catalan theatre . . ."

"So what about his proletarian theatre? Has he given up on that?"

"Not likely, don't you know our Llibert? Because the government pays out, we've more proletarian theatre than ever: more and more proletarian performances without a single spectator. His Llopis, on the other hand, packs out the Espanyol. He says the queue outside the ticket office goes right round the block. As for the proletariat . . . if I could only tell you, Trini, how disillusioned I am! If I told you everything . . . For appearances' sake, so nobody can say Llopis isn't a genuine proletarian, Llibert composes ditties for her to mix into her usual repertoire, songs full of proletarians and bourgeois, hated fascists and libertarian dawns – it's all there! Together with that risqué number about the flea and other racy routines as old as the hills. And they pack out the Espanyol like sardines in a tin and the place shakes to the standing ovations! The proletariat, Trini . . . Hmm . . . When all's said and done, at least the show in the Espanyol doesn't cost the taxpayer a cèntim: they make a fortune. The cultural department doesn't have to subsidise them as it does proletarian opera or theatre for the masses; on the contrary, they rake in taxes galore. From that point of view, no complaints, whatever you may think . . . Some people queue for three hours before the performance starts and they say that on a Saturday night the queue reaches way past carrer de Sant Pau. Of all the little ditties my beloved son has written for Llopis to sing, this must the most moronic:

> Carai, Carai,
> how brave, how brave,

carai, carai,
how brave is the F.A.I.*

"Llopis actually sings those words?"

"While lifting the loveliest of legs! And winking at the audience! She's livewire and saucy with it! And I don't just say this to put her down, Trini: she is really clever. The history of this revolution will credit her with one of the most famous and apt of comments. One day in August she arrived at the theatre and was met by a committee of usherettes and scene changers, backed by the cleaning ladies and sweet sellers who'd decided to collectivise the place. From then on, they informed Llopis it would be governed by a libertarian communist system and everyone would earn the same from the star actress to the lowliest usherette. "Oh, you don't say?" she retorted. "So let an usherette bare her bum!"

Poor Father, he didn't laugh when he told me that; on the contrary, you could see he was desperately sad. It's only too obvious that he feels this liaison between Llibert and Llopis is a *mésalliance* that brings us dishonour: "I know that he and Llopis went through the charade of a civil marriage a few days ago. The fools, what's a civil marriage got over a religious one? I wasn't invited; I wouldn't have gone anyway. It's the dignity of the partner we choose that honours the union of a man and a woman, not any religious or civil hocus-pocus. Your mother and I may have spent our lives quarrelling and falling out, but she is an honourable woman. Now, by the way, we quarrel more than ever . . . and she did go to the municipal court to see how the lad married!"

Poor Father, the first day he visited the whole house – he'd not done that yet – he shook his head at the crucifix in our bedroom. "At any rate, I'm glad you're displaying it when others have been cowardly and hidden theirs away."

He looked at it silently, as if he'd had an idea that he finally came out with – as if he were talking to himself. "I've always worried about . . . this Jesus of Nazareth . . . Some say he was a kind of anarchist and I believed

* F.A.I., the Federación Anarquista Ibérica, the far left of the Spanish anarchist movement, in favour of collectivisation and revolutionary general strikes; membership went from individual pacifists to the pistoleros who killed many clergy and bourgeois.

that once, though it's not true. It's not so simple. Jesus of Nazareth . . . The Big Loser . . . the man who carried the cross for all our iniquities and wretchedness, who took on board all our failures . . . He wasn't simply an anarchist, he was something else I can't pin down, that I can't work out."

He even reacted benevolently to Lluís' great-grandfather: "What incredible side whiskers! Those cussed Carlists so liked to exaggerate."

He sat in my armchair by the window overlooking the garden: "Your house is really nice; I feel really at home, my love! If you only knew how lonely I have felt in our flat on carrer de l'Hospital in recent months . . . it was a real blow to me when you went all reactionary, you being the only one in the family on my wavelength. I've felt so disillusioned, Trini . . . And I don't just mean your mother and your brother – I mean the lot, this sinister revolutionary carnival we've witnessed over the past year. Such a sinister carnival! I could never have predicted this. I've finally come to the conclusion that any idea, however good it may be, turns rotten when it becomes too popular."

He said this on another day: "Trini, there are moments when I feel so tired, so exhausted, so squeezed dry: I so want to leave this world where it seems you can't fight one injustice without committing a worse one. I really feel as if I want to say goodbye to you all, to say: I'm leaving, if you want to stay on here . . . You'll do your best . . . At other times I feel this huge nostalgia for the old days, and not because I want to be young again, not because I miss being in my thirties or forties, no, I couldn't care less about my youth. It's water under the bridge! I don't want to go back there one little bit: I only want you and Llibert to be children once more and our ideals to regain their lost innocence. Our ideals were so beautiful: so beautiful, when nobody had tried to put them into practice! It's so beautiful to believe in something, to believe wholeheartedly, to believe you'll never be as happy as when you're dedicating your life to that faith! And you, when you were children . . . When he was three, Llibert was such fun . . . being able to believe in an ideal, to believe in your children . . . When Llibert was three, he was so lovable: he was such a cheery chappie and said such comic things. When you were little I would take you to Les Planes every Sunday. You know, that was my mass, my way to celebrate Sundays: taking you into the countryside, to the woods in Les Planes. We had such a good time, while your mother stayed in carrer de l'Hospital preparing a good rice dinner! What lovely times we had surrounded by nature in Les Planes! You asked me to tell you stories and fairy tales: I always tried to make sure the tales I told were educational, with some geography or natural history in them, and you two listened so intently! A father is a god in the eyes of his children. Now . . . Llibert . . . Now, how can I still believe in anarchism after all we've seen this past year?"

"Why don't you believe in Jesus, Father? He's never disappointed anyone who believed in Him wholeheartedly."

"I'm too old, my love. Snakes change their skins, men don't. It turns leathery when you're my age . . ."

He's been telling me such a lot over these last few days and some of it strange stuff that was news to me. It turns out that he really likes our little mansion; unlike Mother, who finds it "so very sad" that we live in Pedralbes, "so far from the centre", "in an isolated house with no neighbours". Apparently Father has always preached that every working-class family should have a little house of its own with a small backyard and with that in mind has always argued for building co-operatives and proper credit-granting bodies, and he even tried to organise one of these co-operatives many years ago that unfortunately went bankrupt. I knew nothing of all this. I'm now finding out – to my amazement – that I knew next to nothing about my own father's ideas, and what's even more amazing is that some aren't so crazy, like this one, for example: "Your house is obviously very bourgeois: it's a rich man's abode. The vast majority can never aspire to anything similar though the ideal would be for everyone who wanted one to have a little mansion with a garden like yours. Who knows? If progress were to go in this direction rather than the manufacture of increasingly deadly weapons . . . if everything the world wastes on arms and excesses – and I'm including those of the poor, the miserable excesses of poverty – and if all the effort expended on such dire things were spent to provide decent, comfortable housing . . . You know, your mother and I have never agreed on this issue, as on so many others: our arguments go back a long way. You were very small and won't remember, but one Christmas we had a bit of luck on the lottery. It wasn't *that* much, I'd only spent a peseta, but it was enough to buy a small detached house in Sant Andreu or the Poble Nou with a small yard to plant a couple of pine trees in. Lots of workers owned that kind of place at the time and it wasn't in any way incompatible with proper anarchist ideas, in fact, quite the contrary."

"What I've never understood, Father," I told him one day, "are your pacifist ideas. If we must always be pacifist, in whatever situation, if we can never defend ourselves, come what may . . ."

"My love, if we don't intend to be pacifists all the time, we might as well never be. In peacetime we should prepare ourselves for war: war is something you don't do, or you do properly. What was the point of all the years of pacifist, anti-military propaganda if at the moment of truth we've allowed ourselves to be dragged into fighting a war? The only point in fact was to ensure that our poor soldiers at the front would fight in inferior conditions: everything has had to be improvised, even the idea of an army that so many years of anti-army misinformation had erased from Catalan consciousness. If we aren't pacifist to the bitter end, accepting all the consequences, it is a crime to be pacifist: all we ever prepared was the bloody disasters that our fighters, whom nobody trained for war, are experiencing now – so don't have too many high hopes! For years we'd been saying there'd never be another war . . ."

"So what are you saying? You'd have preferred there to be no resistance?"

"You'll think it very odd, but that's what I would have preferred. So the militarists and the Falange would have won straightaway? So what? It would have made more sense to let them win without offering resistance, and as they're going to win anyway – let's not fool ourselves – at least we'd have been spared the bloodshed, arson and looting that only bring dishonour upon us. Then the responsibility would have been entirely theirs. We should not have gone to war – we'd been preparing the people not to for years! Some folk realise they have backtracked and spin these slogans about 'making war on war', 'defending pacifism with gunfire' . . . pathetic sophisms that fix nothing. To make war on war, to defend pacifism with gunfire, we should have given ourselves time to prepare for the war. Since we weren't prepared – quite the contrary – it would have been better not to fight . . . But let's drop this discussion that could go on and on and get back to what I was telling you. The fact is your mother always disliked those little proletarian houses with a couple of pine trees in the backyard. She wanted us to throw all our money from the jackpot on a trip that, according to her, would be both fun and uplifting. 'Travel broadens the mind,' she insisted. To be frank, I didn't understand what the hell you could see in Paris or Rome or Marseille that you couldn't find without leaving Barcelona: for 'Know your own town and see the whole world'. She went on and on about the education and culture that travel brings, and you know if people talk to me about education and culture I immediately give in, as it's not for nothing that I am a schoolteacher. So we went to Rome and Paris. You and Llibert were still very little – you must have been one and a half or two at the time – and stayed with your grandmother, may the poor thing rest in peace. It was before my mother had the stroke that later confined her to a wheelchair. We went to Rome and Paris: it's the one and only time I have left Barcelona. Our money melted like snow because your mother insisted we stay in the best hotels: 'I want a bit of the bourgeois life,' she said, 'now we have the chance.' So this was our educational travel – staying in lots of luxury hotels I found stifling! And once we'd spent our money, back to carrer de l'Hospital! Your mother is just like Llibert: if they hate the bourgeoisie, it's because they long to do as they do. Which means spending like them, but not worrying like them about expanding factories and businesses: they don't want to know about that side of our bourgeoisie and never will. Your mother and I have never really agreed about anything although we've both called ourselves anarchists, but then has anyone ever managed to understand me, besides poor Cosme – may he rest in peace – and even then not on every issue? If only a little of what I've written and preached over more than forty years had been understood, disseminated and put into practice, we wouldn't have seen this suicidal way in which the collectivisation of industry has been carried out. They are killing the goose that lays the golden eggs! They think capital is something magical, that you only have to take possession of it for it to blossom miraculously! They haven't a clue! They are killing off Catalan industry, the product of a hundred years of good common sense, hard graft and saving, Catalan industry that provided for us all . . . You can't change a social set-up overnight. First the working class has to acquire a culture that will give it the necessary skills, then organise itself, and both these tasks take time.

First it has to be organised in consumer co-operatives and these must learn to structure and manage themselves: only after years of practice can the workers make these consumer co-operatives they create – and the odd mixed enterprise – completely autonomous, like the house building one I described. Only then can the attempt be made to create producer co-operatives: up to now, we should never forget, they have always failed. When these co-operatives prosper rather than go under, we can think seriously about transforming all of industry, or at least the biggest concerns, into so many workers' co-operatives. Anarchism is not something that can be improvised in a day or a year! Precisely because it is the most grandiose undertaking in the whole of mankind's history, it requires many, many years, perhaps even centuries; it involves moving with feet of clay so as not to take a wrong step . . . Labour of this nature can never be a labour of hatred but a labour of love; love never rejects, it invites collaboration wherever it comes from, to help this world become a more beautiful, just, and comfortable place. What, my love, would a workers' production co-operative do if it had a proper sense of responsibility and sincerely wanted its members – the workers – to be prosperous? Well, in most cases it would appoint the same manager who's been managing for years, who is very often the owner, because who – with very few exceptions – can take charge of an industry better than the person who has already handled it efficiently for years and years? These morons only decided to murder the lot . . ."

I then told him about Uncle Eusebi who months ago had lived in the same bedroom where Father is now. I hadn't mentioned him before but Father's last comments made Uncle seem very relevant to our conversation. He listened to me attentively, shaking his head: "From what you say, my love, he's a fine person. You can be sure that the moment they got rid of him, the noodles from that factory started to stick . . . that's if they made any. And by now this good bourgeois must be as horrified by the barbarians on his side as I am by those on ours."

"His side? No, you're wrong, Father. He's not one of theirs at all. In his letter he told me in fact that he's decided to go straight from Genoa to Santiago de Chile, he's not in the mood to go over to the other side – 'that is no more attractive than your lot,' he writes, 'they're basically all the same.' Then he adds: 'Whoever comes out the winner, I will have lost.' It's something I've heard so many different people say – the poor marquis, for example. On 19 July Lluís' uncle and the marquis – I know this because they told me – were more supportive of the autonomous government than the military insurgents, like everyone else in Barcelona, but how could they feel enthused the day after, when anarchist patrols began to roam the country spreading blood and fire? Uncle had always voted for Acció Catalana and was a subscriber to *La Publicitat*, as the marquis voted for the Lliga and read *La Veu de Catalunya*; what could they do or how could they react, caught between the military insurgents on the one hand and the rabid anarchists on the other? 'Neither one side nor the other,' said Uncle Eusebi; 'neither the red nor the black,' said the marquis. 'Whoever wins in the end, I have lost,' added both. Something has gone terribly wrong in this country, Father, everything we have lived through since 19 July 1936 is as chaotic as any nightmare; the day will come when nobody understands anyone. My God, in what way were Uncle Eusebi or the marquis fascists? But how could Lluís' uncle, the owner of Ruscalleda's Son, stay in Barcelona now they were searching for him just to kill him? He would have met the same end as the marquis. He will go from Genoa to South America, he writes, feeling deeply sad: life far from Catalonia makes no sense to him, is absurd. And he already thinks it is a huge admission of failure, but what can he do except leave his country? He will start life afresh in Santiago de Chile – from zero."

Father continued to listen attentively, shaking his head: "People," he said, "should be united by our feelings rather than our ideas. When I think how they are murdering half of Catalonia to defend the abolition of the death penalty . . . Did I have to wait to be sixty to see that ideas are bloody worthless?"

29 JUNE

Dear Juli, I received a letter from Lluís the day before yesterday after weeks without one. I was so pleased to hear you are both in the same brigade. I hadn't heard from him for so long! The only news I had was the monthly postal order he sent me without fail.

I was really depressed; that's why I've not written to you for so long after sending you those long epistles. I wasn't in the mood to write and was reluctant to harp on at you about my personal hardships.

His is a very affectionate letter, and I put that down to you. You have such a big influence on him.

Next month it will be a year since he left home: a whole year since I've seen him . . .

Father has gone back to carrer de l'Hospital. They say the danger is over, that the government has finally reined in the gangs of murderers, but didn't they say that before the May events? In any case, the irreparable damage has been done: it's too late to put all that right. You at the front are lucky not to have experienced the hell Barcelona has been through over these past months.

I find it hard to believe that the murderers have truly been rendered powerless and I really suffer on Father's behalf. He has resumed publication of *La barrinada* and rails even more violently against "the cannibals of the F.A.I." – he now puts in the three letters – with more hyenas and panthers than ever and long articles framed in black to the memory of "true anarchist martyrs like Cosme Puigbò, immolated by executioners who have usurped the name of anarchism". In his last editorial he risks saying that in the end one suspects this sect is driven not by an ideal that's at all proletarian or acratic but by "the criminal desire to destroy the land that has so generously welcomed them and that doesn't distinguish – and never has – between its own offspring and newcomers." I've copied that word for word: I have the most recent issue on my table. Poor *La barrinada* and poor Father . . . he's probably more clear-sighted than most, but so what, if nobody listens to him?

This war is setting in for an eternity and I'm a real coward. Yesterday the evening newspapers carried dramatic headlines: Big Battle on the River Parral! I can't tell you how upset I was! Why did a big battle have to start there the second Lluís arrived? I was imagining the worst, him seriously wounded if not abandoned and bleeding to death in no man's land . . . The happiness I felt when I knew he was in the same brigade as you quickly turned to despair! Why hadn't he stayed where he was? It's quiet there now after so many battles.

Today's newspapers have published a correction: the battle isn't on the Parral, but the Parval, a river a long way from yours. I'm ashamed to feel so happy! As if the dead and wounded don't bother me as long as Lluís isn't among them. Or you, naturally.

As for my beloved brother Llibert Milmany, will you believe me if I tell you that he has found a way to strengthen his position despite the loss of influence suffered by the anarchist extremists? He's doing better than ever! If I make cutting remarks about the good life he's leading, he retorts: "You know, sister, I don't want my family to go without while we're waiting for equality and anarchy to show up." For the moment, his "family" is simply Llopis; and he says that with a wink, as if implying that he intends to sit comfortably while he waits for equality and anarchy.

25 AUGUST

Dear Juli, I've received another letter from Lluís, a letter that's so bullet point it's left me feeling quite depressed. I'm lucky I've got you to let off steam to; if not, I'd feel so alone. I've got my boy, of course, but how can you let off steam to one so young? He's been in bed the last few days with indigestion. Children's temperatures shoot up to thirty-nine for next to nothing. As he's had his tonsils removed, he won't be getting any more tonsillitis and that's a relief. And I have food for him, which is another relief. What if told you that the doctor's diagnosis of indigestion is a source of pride as far as I'm concerned? We've still not finished the first crate of El Pagès tinned milk and that leaves four to be opened. How beautiful they look stacked in the pantry! How I think of you when I see them!

As for Lluís, on the other hand . . . can you believe that in his letter he only writes about a former beadle in the science faculty whom he says he's found in your brigade? Did he really have nothing more interesting to tell me?

It's strange that you've never told me about the existence of this former beadle. In fact, I think I remember him, a beadle by the name of Picó, one of those handy men the physics or chemistry professors have recourse to when they are in the middle of an experiment and a piece of electrical apparatus breaks down or when water doesn't flow from the tap. That Picó was a man who could fix anything: he could even stuff the rare animals that the natural sciences professor sometimes bought from hunters.

What a coincidence that this fellow should end up as captain of the machine gunners in your brigade, but Lluís could write about other things as well . . .

You keep asking me to write more about what's happening in my life now – as if I didn't go on far too much about it in the interminable letters I write to you! I'm really worried about my parents who stubbornly refuse to move from carrer de l'Hospital: he would rather "be shot" than live with Llibert and she'd rather "be strung up" than live with me. We should separate them, Father with me and Mother with Llibert, but who could ever split them up? They need each other though they only row and fall out; besides, they are so used to their flat where everything has kept them company for so many years: they'd feel at a loss without their Pi i Margall in his Phrygian cap, their dining-room lamp and rows of chairs – elsewhere they'd wither away. But someday a bomb will blow them to smithereens along with all the neighbours on their landing. The fascist pilots obviously can't get their aim right so when they bomb the port and train tracks they also scatter bombs over the old city. With each new raid, I suffer on their behalf; they are so used to it that when I mention a raid they look at me in astonishment as if to say: The things you come out with!

"You've always been funny about our flat," Mother told me one day. "I think you're ashamed you were born on carrer de l'Hospital. You've always thought our flat was seedy. Well, you know, my love, we're proletarians and proud of it."

As if that was what was at issue! The first sortie had a big impact on them, the second hardly at all, and by the third they felt completely indifferent: now they listen to bombs as if to the rain. They never go to the shelter.

Maria Engràcia Bosch, that friend of mine in the science faculty I mentioned, comes from a family that's as "proletarian" – as Mother says – or more so than ours; just imagine, she lives with her mother, who is a widow, on one of those streets that go from carrer de Sant Pau to Barbarà.

Carrer de l'Hospital seems quite "posh" in comparison, given that everything is relative in these matters. Well, you know, a few weeks ago they decided to go and live in a rural hamlet as they've had enough of bombs and sirens. I've just received a letter from her in which she tells me about the last bombing raid in her neighbourhood, and I'll copy it here since you keep asking me about life in Barcelona. "The air-raid sirens woke me up," Maria Engràcia Bosch writes, "and Mother, realising I was awake, opened the door between my bedroom and hers.

"'It's a bombing raid,' I said.

"'Yes, here we go again,' she replied. 'What a pain!'

"The electricity had gone. From the fuss they were making we gathered the neighbours were on their way down to the shelter. I opened the window shutters to take a look out: the bright moon lit up the whole bedroom. We could hear distant gunfire as if from out to sea and that made us think the navy was bombing us, not the usual aeroplanes. The boy was sleeping soundly."

Maria Engràcia was referring to her six-year-old brother.

"'Mother, why don't you take him to the shelter?' I asked.

"'Are you serious?'

"Recently we've stopped going: laziness, indifference, fatalism, whatever. Mother lay back on her bed and we listened to distant gunfire, a soothing rata-tat-tat compared to the din the bombs had been making. So we both went back to bed. I heard her mutter: 'I feel really relaxed. I think it's over.'

"It was then, when I was back in bed and asleep, that I suddenly found myself in the next-door flat. According to Mother and the neighbours a bomb had dropped; they'd heard it but I hadn't. If it weren't for them, I'd have thought I'd flown out of my bed through the door to the floor of the neighbouring flat by magic. Thanks to God we were both safe and sound.

"'It was like the end of the world,' they said. Out of the window we could see a thick haze over terraces and roofs down to the port. It was whitish, gradually turning black, and in the meantime we could hear the ambulance bells tinkling and the strident sirens of the fire brigade.

"It would soon be daybreak and I wanted to go out and see what had happened. I was already dressed and combing my hair in front of the bathroom mirror. Mother was saying: 'We'll have to find a workman to repair that wall.'

"I hadn't noticed the big hole. I was still making myself up in the bathroom when we heard the crackle of anti-aircraft artillery from Montjuïc. The puffs of smoke from the explosions were hardly visible over our heads in a sky that was beginning to clear. Suddenly, every now and then, ten or twelve little snow-white clouds blossomed among the few stars still twinkling and that made me think of the blue *fleur-de-lis* flag Jeanne d'Arc grasped in her fist in the French chapel where I went as a child. Those puffs of smoke that silently erupted – the buzz didn't reach us for some time after – made me feel safe, protected and almost happy: our anti-aircraft artillery was looking after us! I forgot that if they were shooting it was because enemy aircraft were back circling above us.

"The second time I did hear it. A massive explosion shook the whole house; I felt the floor rock under my feet as if I were travelling in a boat. I thought the ground was going to open and swallow us up. Strangely, the bathroom mirror was still up and I could see the stupidly calm expression on my face. A tremendous blast of air filled the whole flat with dust that made us cough; it was so thick in the street we could see nothing. There was a big brass coffee pot on my bed I recognised immediately: it was the one from the El Dàtil bar opposite our house. The smoke and dust didn't disperse. We could see nothing but heard screams and cries.

"Then we heard the tinkling bells and sirens again, now on our street. I was in the middle of the road among the many onlookers. I saw a man – or was it a woman? – get to his feet among the rubble from the two houses that had collapsed; he was completely white, as though his clothes, hands and face had been coated in lime or chalk. Others were struggling to stand, yet others tried to and couldn't, and more were completely still: they were all eerily coated in white. Blood on that white looked so shockingly red that a thought struck me: I'd never have believed blood could be such a deep scarlet.

"A military ambulance the size of a lorry drove up and army nurses began picking up the injured: one was a four- or five-year-old who was shouting: 'Mummy is there!' pointing to a pile of rubble. The firemen were working hard but it was obvious they'd take hours to extract the buried.

Half the body of an elderly man was pinned under a huge beam which had to be lifted. Four of the brawniest firemen could barely budge it. They got the local carpenter to saw through it. 'Give it your best!' shouted a neighbour to encourage him. They finally dragged the old man out; he'd lost a leg. In the meantime other firemen were putting out fires with water hoses. We could see several bodies among the flames, some still moving. It was impossible to advance towards them until the firemen had the fires under control. They pulled them out as they proceeded: some were dressed and others were stark naked, some were white with dust and others completely black. The latter, I soon realised, had been incinerated. Sometimes, when two soldiers tried to lift one, the body would come apart in their hands. In the midst of all this a gentleman, naked except for his hat, was shouting down from a sixth-floor balcony that had only preserved its façade. He'd been thrown there from the bar counter in El Dàtil, where he'd been drinking his breakfast cup of malt when the expansion wave from the bomb stripped him of everything except his hat. The soldiers told him to be patient, the firemen were busy for the moment.

"After that," concludes Maria Engràcia, "it didn't take us long to decide to go to this farm that belongs to one of Mother's cousins. May God reward their hospitality."

All this my friend describes. What can I add? That I feel genuine remorse because I live in a quiet district like Pedralbes where we only hear the distant thunder of bombing – apart from the very few occasions when the bombs drop much nearer?

It's surprising to think many people still live in those districts around the port as if nothing were amiss. One day, when I'd been to see my parents, I went for a walk around the streets and back alleys that had been so punished by the bombing: there were the usual shopkeepers, many of whom had been around when I was a child. I talked to some. They were flummoxed at my being surprised. Why should they leave their neighbourhood? Where would they go?

"And what about the soldiers?" one asked.

Another told me she ate her meals in a collective dining room. There are a lot of these now and this one is on passeig de Colom, right by the port. They serve a single course.

"If I'm lucky and there's a bombing raid at dinnertime, I eat mine and the dinners left by the people running to the shelter as well."

To return to that beadle in the science faculty who's now a captain in your brigade, I've just remembered that once, when the Physics professor was away at a congress in Koenigsberg, Maria Engràcia Bosch taught us a class – she was more advanced in her studies than me and preparing her doctoral thesis. This beadle would sit in on our classes whenever his duties allowed. He'd stand by the door, cap in hand, listening to the discussions and observing the experiments that seemed to enthral him.

On that occasion Maria Engràcia Bosch was talking specifically about freezing points and boiling points and lo and behold the beadle interrupted her very respectfully.

"With your permission, senyoreta teacher," he said, "I'd like to say something. You say that distilled water under normal pressure freezes at zero degrees, and if I understood you rightly you call zero degrees the temperature at which distilled water freezes under normal pressure. I would be very upset if whatever I say might be interpreted as showing a lack of respect for science and culture, but I would call this a vicious circle."

People burst out laughing and I laughed as much as anyone; Maria Engràcia laughed on her professorial podium as did the beadle in the doorway, very pleased to have triggered such good cheer. Yet why were we laughing? We were laughing because it was a beadle who had said this; we were laughing like the fools we were. Years later, when I found the same statement, almost word for word, in one of Einstein's youthful works, I was left feeling deeply perplexed; I certainly didn't want to burst out laughing.

30 AUGUST

You talk about childhood memories and ask me if my grandmother's death hasn't brought lots to the surface. Yes, but never relating to her – I only remember her stuck in her armchair – and never rose-tinted. I don't think any childhood has ever been rose-tinted; old age, possibly. I think I've already told you as much previously; innocence is really very difficult, and in any case we can reach that state only after a whole lifetime of struggle.

To succeed in attaining innocence! That may be our spirit's utmost aspiration . . .

But can childhood be innocent? My mother made me wear much shorter skirts than the other children: it formed part of her advanced ideas, which were more set in concrete than ever after "she'd been to Paris and Rome". The worst of it was the other girls making fun of me; that really depressed me. One day a new girl came wearing a skirt even shorter than mine! A circle immediately formed around her and everyone tried to find the cruellest, most hurtful barb and I was the one who found the most cutting remark. Pleased to be a victim no longer and to have been promoted to the rank of executioner!

As you've asked me, what childhood memories do I have? I'll tell you, those Sundays when Father took us to the woods in Les Planes. We would sit under a pine tree and eat chufa nuts and peanuts: each pine tree had its requisite proletarian or artisan father eating peanuts and chufa nuts surrounded by children like us. Ours told us stories and we listened, mouths agape; they were educational rather than entertaining although my father, like the good schoolmaster he was, tried to combine the two: he mixed in a lot of geography and notions of physics, botany and homespun medicine, lots of secular ethics and references to the progress of humanity and the emancipation of the proletarian classes. These were my fairy tales, the spiritual nourishment of my early childhood. It was all I had and I really loved them! I preferred them when they were only slightly educational, when Father emphasised his pedagogic role less and let himself be driven by his imagination. We so need imagination when we are children, when we are new to this world; we need to transform this world where we've ended up – we're not sure why or how – with touches of fantasy and mystery! That's not all: there is more to it than this intense need children feel for fantasy and mystery – children are afraid. All children are full of fears: of the dark, of strangers – whether animals or people – of being lost, of going astray, of the unknown. Like all unbelievers, my parents denied that this was something innate and attributed it, on the contrary, to the vice – as they put it – of telling children about things that provoke fear, like death and the devil, ghosts, wolves and witches. But nobody had told me of such things and I can remember my fears as if it were yesterday, terrible fears to which I woke in the middle of the night, shapeless, endless fears that floated threateningly in the darkness of my bedroom. One day, when I was older, I met a girl at school who told me that when she was afraid at night she prayed to her guardian angel. She said:

> Guardian angel,
> every day and night,
> be at my side
> to guide and light.

I learned these lines without saying a word to my parents and from then on, whenever I awoke, I'd recite them aloud. Mother heard me once and scolded me severely; on the other hand, when Father found out, he simply shrugged his shoulders and looked at me as if intrigued, in fact rather tenderly.

I believe that if we so need poetry and faith to spare us from feeling unhappy about the fact of our existence, it is because poetry and faith *are* existence and life: without them this whole world would collapse into nothingness like an empty, hollow phantasmagoria. If you could only see Ramonet's big eyes when he is listening to stories; I mean, you know what he's like, you've told him so many. And how he likes to know that the guardian angel, the Infant Jesus and the Virgin Mary are watching over him – he finds that comforting! We would feel so forsaken in this world if there wasn't another invisible one sustaining us. What does it matter if our sustaining fantasies are childish? The fact is we *are* poor forsaken children – can we ever aspire to being anything else? Is there so much difference between what we understand at the age of three and what we understand in our twenties? How can we ever imagine the Deity in a way that isn't childish?

One Sunday, in Les Planes, it suddenly started to rain cats and dogs. Father sheltered Llibert and me under the skirts of his raincoat, a very loose raincoat that I can see even now, extremely worn and shabby, a proper schoolmaster's raincoat! And I still have warm memories of the feeling of protection and security that spread through me the moment I buried my head under that raincoat like a little chick under the wings of a mother hen. It's one of my earliest memories; I must have been three at the time. Another very distant recollection, perhaps from the same era, was one Sunday morning when we went to the port rather than to Les Planes. We did that sometimes: we went on a pleasure boat round the port and it was so exciting. But it's not the boat that has stuck in my memory, it's the legs of passers-by on the Rambla. We walked from our street to the port and that stretch of the Rambla, between carrer de l'Hospital and Porta de la Pau, was always packed with people on a Sunday morning. As I was so little, I could only see legs and more legs, a forest of legs on the move: those men's and women's legs used to make me so sad! Why do I bother telling you? Well, you asked for some of my childhood memories and there you have one . . . though that's enough: I find them depressing! That gloomy forest of legs was only interrupted by a side street I had to cross. In those days there was a red-capped street porter by each gas-light waiting for his next customer and a woman selling balloons – we called them "bombs". On the corner of each side street the bright red of the porter's cap and the lurid colours of the "bombs" made me so happy, though it was short-lived: after crossing the street I was plunged back into that ocean of legs and more legs . . .

How odd now to think we called those coloured balloons bombs when we were children . . . and what if I said those waxen faces come back to me now when I tell you about all this nonsense from my childhood that is hardly riveting. Some nights when I wake up and try to get back to sleep I see them in the dark with their open, unseeing eyes – can God ever forgive us? My brother has turned them into huge posters with incomprehensible faces you find stuck on walls everywhere in Barcelona – the faces of children who have never thought bombs were coloured balloons. Yes, the brilliant Llibert has turned our balloons into propaganda – it's sick-making! I know the things our side is keeping quiet about and I know because a middle-aged man told me – he happened to be in Melilla on business when the colonial troops rebelled. His wife and children were in Barcelona so he wanted to get back right away, however difficult it was to escape from the Spanish protectorate. He managed to travel in secret to Casablanca and then embark on a steamer en route to Marseille. I met him in our local air-raid shelter, where I always go with Ramonet and the maid when the bombs start raining, though he only goes when it's fiercer than normal. So thanks to this gentleman, whom I hardly know, I discovered our people were the ones who started that kind of thing. He says that a week after the insurrection of the Foreign Legion and the Moorish troops the warship *Jaime I* bombed Melilla; it was three o'clock on Sunday afternoon and the Europeans were napping. As it was so hot they'd undressed for the purpose, so that men, women and children were fleeing half naked from their bombed houses. The shells from the *Jaime I* fell over the whole city, but mostly in the European quarter. When they exploded on a block of flats, the top ones flew into the air "as if made of paper", says this gentleman who saw it all. The buildings disappeared in smoke and when it lifted only piles of rubble were visible. It was 26 July, the war had begun the previous week and the Europeans, unlike the Moors, were almost all republicans! If it hadn't been for this trader from Melilla, who is quite old – he must be over forty – I'd never have known about this: the Lliberts of this world have been careful to conceal such actions and made us think that only fascists bomb cities. The details he explains are very similar to those in Maria Engràcia's letter that I copied to you the other day: both sides are equally savage, however saddening it may be to acknowledge this. And don't think that our conversations in the shelter always centre on the same topics; a great variety of people go there and you'd be amazed how frivolous and superficial most are, especially the ladies. One is made up like a parrot and carries a Pomeranian in her arms: you'd say her head was full of wind. She's always laughing and speaking silly nonsense; and, strangest of all, if the other people's conversation takes a political turn, she comments sententiously: "It's what I always say: it's all down to bad management." By the way, before I met this gentleman from Melilla, I felt relaxed on nights when it was the navy and not aircraft bombing us, but now I realise that shells from the sea can be as big, or almost, as bombs from the air – and are better aimed: he says they blew up whole buildings in the European quarter of Melilla. And don't imagine that this gentleman isn't republican – he is as much as we are. I asked him how he could remain one after living through horrors like that and he replied with a sigh – "What choice do we have?"

And, you see, that's why I feel nauseous when I see those photos pinned on the walls of buildings, the faces of children that shrapnel has transformed into visages of the dead. They were children from Madrid who had come to Barcelona as refugees from the bombing there; I have no idea why, but we thought they'd never bomb Barcelona. They'd been housed in the monastery of the Oratory Order, next to the church of Sant Felip Neri; now the monastery has caved in and the entire stone façade is pockmarked as if it had had smallpox. I sometimes walk by and stand and stare at it in the square for a moment.

I take one look at what's left of that monastery and think of the Holy Innocents, not the ones in the Gospel but all the innocents who've been sacrificed in atrocities committed by adults since the world has existed.

Why do you want us to find escape in childhood memories, Juli? Wouldn't that be selfish and frivolous given that as children we saw none of the delights which we – and I mean all of us – offer children today? I went to look for the first time soon after the bombing raid and the dailies were full of photos of children who'd been blown to bits. I then walked to the cathedral just round the corner and sat down on one of those big stone benches on either side of the monument to the martyrs of the wars against the French, in front of the entrance to the cathedral, where I'd not sat since the November evening when we were there together. Of course, you don't remember but I can never forget that night. It was when we went on those endless walks in the old city with the unsellable *La barrinada* under our arms. We were tired and sat on those benches.

And you talked to me about your childhood, quite unawares, obsessively. You told me about your aunt for the first time; I didn't know who you lived with, if indeed you lived with anyone. Then I discovered you were an orphan, had never known your mother or father, that you'd always been with a maiden aunt, your father's sister who, with you, was the only surviving member of the whole Soleràs family. That evening you spoke so animatedly of your aunt, so enthusiastically and so unexpectedly! You've never spoken to me as you did that day. It was a damp November evening and we could see the pious old ladies entering the cathedral to take candles to the Holy Christ of Lepanto and others who were leaving after they'd finished their prayers. You spoke to me passionately – yes, there was real passion in your voice – of your maiden aunt, about whom you've only spoken since sarcastically or ironically, another great devotee of that Christ who even at the time had a blood-curdling impact on me.

It makes me think – since to this day I've still not met this aunt of yours – that you were bewitched by her as a child; it's the only word that comes to mind when I remember you talking that evening. You said that as a child you lived for the never-ending fantastic stories she invented; that you were never so happy in those distant days as when you had the flu because each bout meant she would tell you stories for hours, keeping you company. Even today, you said, the word "happiness" conjured up a state of flu without much of a temperature and time spent blissfully in bed: "I've never met," you said, "anybody with so much imagination: her imagination had expanded in all directions like a monster at the expense of other aptitudes as if it had flattened them. I only needed a slight temperature and I knew what joy awaited me: the abolition of reality! Yes, reality was abolished with the whiff of the first mallow root infusion she forced me to drink; the medicine came with the most incredible stories she made up non-stop. Later, as an adult, when I heard about opium and its effects for the first time, I could only imagine the stuff in the form of icing sugar, since my aunt sweetened her ineffable infusions with icing sugar."

While you talked about your aunt, the pile of *La barrinada* that we'd put on the stone bench next to us got wetter and wetter in the drizzle. You were telling me how throughout your childhood you felt you'd lived all there was to live via your aunt's stories, from caveman to martyr in the catacombs, from Knight Templar to hero of La Vendée: "Naturally," you explained, "my aunt was on the side of La Vendée." And then you added: "What a pity we are anarchists! We could have revived La Vendée or even the Templars. I've often suspected that all the evil in the world comes from the suppression of the Knights Templar. In any case we'd have had much more fun pretending to be clandestine Templars rather than anarchists. The fact is that reactionaries have incomparably greater imaginations, and besides the past is their preserve. On the other hand, as the future is pure non-existence, they leave it to people with no imaginations. Yes, Trini, you need lots of imagination to be a reactionary and that's why there are so few of them: my aunt is the only person I've known who can really claim to be one."

At the time I was always left dumbfounded by your *boutades*. It was the first time I'd ever heard anyone speak positively about reactionaries; I mean, the first time I'd heard them spoken about as real living people – how could they have ever existed if they were like the horrors I'd been told about?

"Godfrey de Bouillon," you went on, "could be mistaken for a Jacobin in comparison. Just so you know: he is almost as familiar to me as she is – my aunt tells you about Godfrey de Bouillon as if he were the only man in her life."

You and I talked about our childhoods ironically and complaisantly as if they were far behind us: you were seventeen and I fourteen. We seemed so blasé when you said that evening: "One day we will be so ashamed to have been seventeen." "Why?" I asked, taken aback. "Because it's a foolish age. Just imagine, we are the people of the future! Pure non-existence! We are nothing, yet we've betrayed ourselves a thousand times." "How exactly did we do that?" "Once, when we were chatting after lunch, my aunt said it was a pity I'd grown up, since we were both so happy when I was five – and we will never be again, my aunt assured me. At the time I was annoyed by her outburst: how on earth could she want me not to grow up? Well, Trini, I've thought about it often since and the idea doesn't seem so horrendous: my aunt was right. Like Jesus Christ."

"Like Jesus Christ?"

"Yes, Jesus Christ. Jesus Christ and my aunt. Wasn't it Jesus Christ who said: 'Do as these children do and you will enter the kingdom of heaven'? You know, Trini, I've often thought about that strange remark my aunt made that day after lunch and the more I do the clearer it becomes. And I'm telling you now because I'm in the right mood. I probably won't mention it again, not because it's not on my mind but because I won't feel like it. I'll never tell my aunt, for example, though it would make her happy and take no effort on my part. On the other hand, what's the point in my seeing things so clearly if there's nothing we can do about them? Where's the brave man who can take the spirit of childhood on board if those of us who see it so clearly can't, don't know how to and don't want to? Perhaps the saints could, but not even all of them . . . Now we're always swearing that we'll never betray or deny our youth, that we will always remain faithful to it, but what if we've already betrayed and denied our childhood? So why won't we betray and deny our youth when the time comes? The great betrayal is already a fact of life; the cock has still to crow and we've already denied Him three times."

But for now, Juli, I implore you: don't stir up any more memories of childhood! It's a subject that fills me with grief, though I couldn't tell you why. Perhaps because of what I just wrote, because I see children these days and feel saddened that our childhood was so peaceful by comparison; or perhaps because of what you said the other evening, that we've already betrayed and denied it at the age of seventeen, so from then on we are the loathsome thing known as a grown-up. I simply have to tell you that I've never met anyone so able to be at one with a child, to act like a child when with one: you find it so easy to keep Ramonet amused, to put yourself on his level and enter the mysterious, illogical world of children ruled by laws so different from ours. He listens to you all agog when you spin him one story after another and then he tells me I don't know how, and it's true mine aren't much fun. Will you believe me if I say I have bought myself an *Art of Storytelling*, written by a distinguished pedagogue, so they say, and that I've read every word intently? But isn't it pathetic when we have to learn rules in order to practise an art: art should be like love, if it's not instinctive, nobody can teach you. "Do as these children do . . ." In a nutshell, that's the art of storytelling, I'm sure, but it's so difficult!

10 SEPTEMBER

Your letter arrived so opportunely that it now seems providential.

This morning the postman left me a letter from Lluís, franked in Sierra Calva. The most loving letter he has ever written me and he ends it by asking me to marry him.

I felt happy, like someone who's just won a battle her life depended on. I'm such a dupe!

The postman returned at midday. Your letter stunned me.

I had to close the bedroom door so my little boy couldn't see me. I stretched out on my bed, hid my face in a pillow and tried to cry. Impossible. I felt horribly dry.

Now I feel empty, but at least I'm calm. Dry and empty, but calm. Your letter came to my rescue in time and I am so grateful. What would it be like now if we'd married? And yet you still ask if you did the right thing by telling me.

I'm so lucky not to be tied to Lluís for ever! Could I love him more than I did? What a dreadful man not to repay love with love! Could I have needed him more than I did, or given him more than I did? Poor Juli, you've spared me such a cross – one of those crosses that crush you under the weight of your own absurdity.

From now on I will simply see him as my son's father; that aside, he will be a stranger as far as I'm concerned. Once a month I'll send him a short, polite letter with news of his son, who by chance also happens to be mine. By chance, that's all! And Ramonet will always be a "natural son" at the end of the day, like his mother, and that's no tragedy. It's never been one for me, so why should it be for him?

I couldn't find the words to express the affection I feel for you right now. If it weren't for you I would feel so alone in this world, so terribly alone, that I might end up in a lunatic asylum; loneliness scares me, I can't handle it. If anyone saw me now, they'd think: "What a desiccated, spinsterish face . . . that's a woman who doesn't know what love is!" I know what my face looks like: I've spent a long time gazing at myself in the mirror.

12 SEPTEMBER

The arguments you deploy to demonstrate that I am free to marry anyone I like seemed odd on the page. Of course I am free! Why are you telling me this? Do you think I don't know? It's my only consolation. Clearly, I'm single. Why remind me?

I'm single, completely free; nothing ties me to him. That's my stroke of luck in the midst of unhappiness, and thanks to it I don't feel crushed by the absurdity of the situation I find myself in. But think of marrying someone else? Such an idea is eccentric at the very least, I would say. Marry whom? I'm not interested in Lluís, and even less interested in other men: who might that be? Such a stupid idea never crossed my mind. Why would I want to give Ramonet a stepfather?

I've lived for years ingenuously with the expectation that someday Lluís and I will sort out our relationship and become husband and wife in the eyes of God and men; now I couldn't care less. Nothing in this life is worth worrying about. Do I have a right to lament the absurdities in my own life after the horrors we have lived through, are still living through, and may live through for months if not years? A country that has burned and bled, so many families destroyed, so many innocents sacrificed on both sides? Am I going to create a drama because Lluís is having an affair? God may punish me but I can tell you sincerely, Juli, that I'm more grateful to you than ever for helping me open my eyes to another life in which the frightful nonsense of this one can never get in. I'll always keep on my desk the Gospels you gave me as a present years before the war: the bookmark is still where you left it. I only need open it at that page to find the words you underlined in red. "If I don't follow You, whom will I follow?" I followed Lluís and you can see where that led me, can't you, poor Juli!

If Lluís had died at the front, do you think I'd have wanted to marry someone else? You know me well enough to anticipate the answer is no. At any rate I beg you by all that's most holy not to tell him any of what I write to you; don't tell him how upset I am. Don't try to repair what's beyond repair. I don't want him to know I feel so unhappy; a woman who's been deceived is doubly ridiculous if she is unhappy. And I don't want to be that in his eyes! I don't want to have to put up with more of his shit! Yes, shit – why not call it by its proper name? I'm no Daughter of Maria! I'm the natural daughter of anarchists who practise free love! I won't stand for any more of his shit, but marry somebody else? The very idea is . . . appalling.

15 SEPTEMBER

Your letter, just received, made me cry and I couldn't tell you if the tears were sad or happy, or something else. "A serene, trusting love, a brother and sister's love". Is such a thing possible? I think it's absolutely necessary to have you at my side as always, my only friend and true brother, to have you there as usual and, if you'd like, even more often. I think this is natural and imperative. But, poor Juli, if we were to take it a step further, wouldn't that be . . . incestuous?

I'm sorry, I have always thought of you as a brother!

If you could also imagine the bad taste the thing they call love has left in me: a murky storm where faces become blurred and cease to be human to atone for the crime of becoming too intimate . . .

I've made various plans over the last four or five days: I will resume the studies I interrupted – my beloved geology – and will ask for a teaching job. I've already put out feelers; the science faculty is offering me the post that Maria Engràcia Bosch held, of assistant to the chair in crystallography: you can imagine how her decision to go and live on that farm has helped me. They'll turn a blind eye to the fact that I've not yet passed my final degree examinations and that crystallography isn't exactly a specialism of mine. They can't be choosy in times of war when there is such a shortage of teachers! I'd written to Maria Engràcia – I didn't want to fill her position without her express agreement – and must start at the beginning of next month when the new academic year begins, that is, in twenty or so days. And your letter caught me in the throes of re-adapting, leafing through thick tomes I'd almost forgotten existed, learned treatises gathering dust on a library shelf from where they'd never budged since Lluís and I started living together in this Pedralbes mansion.

At one stage in my life I came to hate them, when I suddenly thought this chasm in time was senseless. Now, on the contrary, I find them a consoling sedative: our petty domestic disputes, our absurdly ridiculous *chagrins de ménage* are so petty on this scale. If our poor bones by some extraordinary stroke of luck managed to fossilise instead of turning into minute specks of dust blowing in the wind, they would be so puny resting under layers of sediment four or five kilometres thick . . .

If a teacher of geology like me discovers a few petrified bones in a hundred million years – the last traces of me and Lluís – how will she guess, or what the hell will it matter to her, whether we were unhappy or blissful, exemplary in our faithfulness or ghastly in our adultery? In a hundred million years how will that geology teacher imagine my life with Lluís – or what will it matter to her?

Such thoughts are hardly consoling, you will say: they are certainly not cheerful, but what can we do about it? Sorry if I'm boring you with my geology – I know it's never interested you – but I'm up to my neck in it at the moment.

I would like to be completely independent from Lluís, to have my own means and manage to be a single mother, with all the consequences – and satisfaction – that brings. A single mother who doesn't need to depend on her son's father and can walk head held high through this world, and you can only hold your head high if you are independent. I will be.

My only hesitation concerns this house. He made it over to Ramonet and me as a gift before a notary: should I now renounce his gift, return his mansion to him and spit in his face: I want nothing from you? But that way won't I hurt Ramonet – who is not to blame in any way. Wouldn't I be acting blinded by a pride that is never good counsel? Isn't it just and right I keep it as compensation for all the wrong he's done me over the years? I'd like you with your law degree to give me advice: could I, for example, in my turn give my share to my son – who is his only son and the only grandson of his deceased mother, from whom we inherited this property. That would quieten my conscience. Perhaps I could – you must tell me – hold my share in reserve as usufruct: I'm due some right to shelter. I would really appreciate your advice: I will certainly do whatever you tell me; you see, with respect to the house in Pedralbes, whatever you decide is the right and just thing to do.

As for the other . . . about you and me marrying . . . your other suggestion . . . my God, where would that land us? I'm afraid we would both lose out; we would ruin our friendship, that's now long-lived – I was fourteen when I met you and I'm now almost twenty-two. This friendship that has sustained me and still does, and that ensures I don't feel alone without a helping hand in this world. Alone without a helping hand! Obviously, I have Ramonet, but as I've told you before, what companionship can a child give? Children can't keep us company; they only crave it from us.

I try to imagine our friendship as transformed into something else . . . and fail. I'm sorry, Juli; perhaps you are offended by my saying this, but I feel your suggestion is absurd because of the very things I admire in you. You are too intelligent and love is a jungle. A couple of wild animals howling on the edge of a precipice.

The thought horrifies me.

When I think of the hand you flourish so expressively in debate or conversation but which can't hold on to anything – it is too white and too contorted – and then of that hand holding mine, I want to run from it, as if from something unnatural and monstrous. I owe it to you to be frank. I would like to love you with all my soul, but only with my soul. Yet I think loving you with my soul and nothing else wouldn't amount to love, and there'd be no merit in such a love because it would have come too easily. And then I think I do love you more than this, and lose sight of myself.

Or who knows if I'm not woman enough, am too childish and too old like fruit that doesn't ripen, green in the morning and rotten in the evening! I am afraid that the hurt Lluís has done may have marked me for life. He did so from the first day, from the time he hugged and kissed me on the corner seat on that fifth-floor landing. That first kiss was a brutal revelation, however much my happiness made me lose my senses. Yes, a brutal revelation: he hurt me from that first day and has kept on ever since! His scandalous affair with the feudal lady in Olivel, "the most beautiful, romantic woman in Aragon", as you said in your letter, really amounted to very little: it was an explosion of light that suddenly made me see all this. In its merciless brilliance I saw and suddenly grasped that he'd never loved me or I him, that what I loved in him was his youth, his strength, his dash and his sensuality – everything I now find repugnant.

I want to tell you something I've never told you. To lower my opinion of you, when he was talking about you Lluís often came out with details . . . things you'd said or done that at the very least were very peculiar. Even now, in one of the few letters he's written to me since he joined your brigade, he has told me other odd things . . . I recall him mentioning a cave where he says you read some book or other about Charlemagne or maybe Roland . . . and other really weird and wonderful things I couldn't fathom. I never bothered to try and discover the extent to which the things Lluís wrote were true, since they involved you . . . and involved him! When he's not making mischief, it's only on account of inertia.

I do know for sure that you have always behaved well towards me and that you always will: I know you won't hurt me. I'm horrified by the thought I might be left all alone in this life – a stray with nobody to keep me company. I need you and I trust you; that sums up my feelings towards you and I'll entrust myself to them. You decide: I will do whatever you tell me.

On the other hand you love Ramonet so dearly . . . I'm certain you will never be a stepfather. Yesterday we started on the last crate of El Pagès tinned milk. Would you believe that I've kept all the empty ones as souvenirs? I'd thought of keeping them forever in memory of these difficult times; the poor things get in the way . . . Someday they will have to go into the fire, but I'd like to wait for a day when you are here. Then I'll burn them all at once – these poor crates that are always around to remind me of your kindness. The way things are going, who knows if, by the time they are crackling cheerfully in the flames, who knows if we might not both be sitting in these armchairs by the fireside – you and I, husband and wife?

Who knows . . . ?

I can tell you one heartfelt thing: I'm moved to discover all of a sudden that you are so much more sensitive and kind than I'd ever imagined. Your silence over all these years . . .

PART THREE

His uncle, who was a bishop, was
surprised that he wasted his time
on astronomy.

VITA COPERNICI

I

Personally I realised, when it was too late, that God had decided to teach me a stern lesson. People like me are never careful enough; when we think we have covered our fault lines, the subtlest still remains: self-love. We risk mistaking our innermost frailties for virtuous impulses; we assume every summons comes from Holy Grace and think we are acting like angels sent by Providence when in truth we are flying straight to perdition.

When, oh when, will we ever grasp this truth: that we should hope for no company other than God's in the wilderness of this world? Solitude is our daily bread, and it comes freshly baked.

In the seminary Dr Gallifa once said we don't face our worst temptation while young, as most people imagine, but when we cross the frontier of our fifties. That is when we plumb the depths of solitude; when our hearts begin to harden and we long for a tenderness we have never known; dearth of love is the most painful burden we must bear in that exile. Nothing weighs as heavily upon us as that emptiness.

A cup of lemon verbena by the fireside when the November wind scatters the dead leaves and a scent of damp earth wafts in from the garden, a cup of lemon verbena by the fireside, exchanged glances of silent understanding ... My God, release me from my guilty longings!

Monsenyor Pinell de Bray lived in Paris, but he would come and stay in Barcelona, in my aunt's mansion. He was a bishop *in partibus*, I think for Samarkand; I remember him as if it were yesterday, slinking between the Louis XV furniture in the drawing room with the elegant indolence of an angora cat. Tall and thin, his snow-white hair underlined youthful tanned features, where his eyes smouldered like embers beneath the ash. At the time he adopted the condescending tone used to address a boy who has finally reached the age of reason; I was twelve – when my aunt had given me that telescope to celebrate my top marks – and some of his veiled, velvety sentences, full of vague references to things I didn't understand, made me think of passages from the Apocalypse that I'd just read for the first time. My aunt listened to him as if he were an oracle.

In effect, Monsenyor Pinell de Bray *was* the family oracle; my aunt, a first cousin of his, always presented him as an example to follow. I felt proud to belong to a family Heaven had endowed with such an illustrious man.

It's as if I could see him now in that gloomy, hushed drawing room where gilded furniture glinted, flanked by tawdry red-velvet curtains; as if I could see him now, so slim and ascetic, with that humble, restrained smile, hear his voice deep and silken like the bass notes of a muted grand piano. It was 1931. I am now reminded of some of his expressions: the prior catastrophe, the re-establishment of the Kingdom of God . . . He made veiled allusions to the mysterious visitors he welcomed in his elegant apartment on the Champs Elysées, though I never grasped what lay behind those riddles. I was too young; my aunt, who had good reason to grasp much more, sometimes took fright: "But you're exposing yourself to real danger . . ." He'd smile gently, as self-deprecatingly as always: "It is only right that we should risk our life for a good cause." He sometimes referred to our cardinal primate in unctuously pitiless terms: "A moron, a spineless character . . ." and occasionally spoke openly of the need to restrict his activities. But I was naïve and continued to be so for quite some time.

I now know that the atrocities committed in His name are infinitely worse than the atrocities committed against His name.

When I'd finished my studies I went to live in an industrial slum overlooked by the grey mass of the Rexy Mura factory. At night its four hundred windows, a hundred per façade, seemed like so many eyes scrutinising every centimetre of the wretched slum where hovels sprawled. The fortune of Sr Creus – which he insisted must be pronounced Kroitz – was an offspring of the catastrophe. The remarkable change in the way his name was pronounced wasn't an isolated case in that era; I should add that he didn't renounce Kroitz and return to Creus until the end of 1945. According to him, another genealogist – genealogists struck it rich in those years – had carried out fresh, more penetrating research into that business and just as the 1939 specimen had plumped – with precipitate hindsight – for German forebears, the new genealogist in the last weeks of 1945 was rather drawn to the hypothesis that Creus might mean something like Cruces in Castilian, and that it wasn't impossible, but in fact highly probable – declared the genealogist – that Sr Creus was descended from Godfrey de Bouillon in person.

He'd owned a factory pre-war, but it was little more than an engineering workshop with fifty or so workers, like hundreds of others in Barcelona. Without the turmoil he could never have scaled his present heights – not even in his dreams. In 1936 he was forced to flee abroad like so many: he hasn't forgotten and will never forget that for almost three years his factory, adapted to the needs of war, worked for the reds, as he likes to put it. It wasn't collectivised by the anarchists, and the autonomous government ensured it continued to function during the maelstrom. When he returned from abroad, Sr Creus or Kroitz – he would maintain the latter pronunciation until the end of 1945, I'll remind you – discovered it was fitted with the latest Skoda machinery and that four building extensions had been made; he had no scruples appropriating such unexpected improvements. No sooner was he back in the managing director's chair than he took his first decision – to offer substantial shares in Rexy Mura to three or four individuals whose sense of strategy and tactics had enabled them to straddle the crossroads between official and black-market prices. In the wake of the catastrophe, what better reward than to be able to buy at rock-bottom official prices and sell on at your asking price? It was wonderfully simple, as all miracles are; Sr Creus had no need to over-exercise his brain to lead his firm, now much enhanced by Czechoslovakian equipment, on to ever dizzier heights.

Not forgetting the stunning publicity: advertisements for Rexy Mura sprang up everywhere as if by magic. Immense, amazing, fantastic, multi-coloured billboards: the great, indispensable Llibert Milmany had waded in. He was the one to suggest that the business could be expanded via the manufacture of chemical products for the embellishment of ladies; later he recognised that the new era also made it possible to make a profit by prettifying gentlemen. Brilliant comrade Llibert Milmany – more of a comrade than ever in those new times – was quick to adapt all the tricks he'd learned organising war propaganda to the fresh set of circumstances. Barcelona had never forgotten those "Make tanks, tanks, tanks" posters and so many others worthy of being remembered for ever. A brilliant comrade! The Rexy Mura advertisements re-created their brio but were bigger, flashier and more categorical: "No more bald pates!" "Axe excess fluff!" "Look after your armpits!"

To show his gratitude to Divine Providence, Sr Creus decided to dedicate his factory to the Sacred Heart. What's more, he decided to make the Sacred Heart a shareholder. As such a unique beneficiary couldn't attend meetings or accept bank dividend payouts, it was agreed that Monsenyor Pinell de Bray should act as its representative. My relative blessed the factory and showered the Czechoslovakian machinery with holy water. From then on there was a stream of soirées and receptions in the Creus family castle, because – I should add – they now lived in a Gothic castle that had been sumptuously renovated. This family, whose roots were so deeply Catalan, now went by the name of Kroitz and spoke only Castilian. Sr Kroitz staged the most dazzling of parties on the occasion of his entry into the Order of the Holy Sepulchre: ennoblement was all the rage.

Glossy magazines published photographs of a party that became the talk of the town; I've kept some I look at from time to time to remind myself that it wasn't simply a dream. Sr and Sra Creus appear in one surrounded by their guests, all wearing grotesque paper cornets and blowing fairground trumpets, splitting their sides evidently under the influence of copious intakes of alcohol. Nothing was prized as much as frivolous excess in that period of emaciation and poverty for the majority, and the saddest side of such events, given that they were held to honour the Holy Sepulchre, was the occasional attendance of a cardinal from Rome at the ceremony to present a sword to a new knight or a sash to a new lady. No cardinal from Rome attended the party for the Kroitzes; they had to be content with Monsenyor Pinell de Bray, but the frivolous behaviour was blatant; they say that in the course of the soirée a young or middle-aged couple would discreetly disappear and then only resurface in the drawing room after a lengthy absence. All I know is that subsequent to this famous soirée, each time Sra Creus hosted a party she locked all the bedroom doors in the castle by way of precaution: in spite of everything, the poor lady still clung to some of her pre-war principles. I should also say that the Creus couple had a daughter who was about fifteen at the time. When it was her birthday at the beginning of summer, they threw an open-air party in the castle grounds. The climax of the party was undoubtedly the "mock joust" when guests bombarded one another with cream or custard éclairs rather than confetti and streamers. The idea, so the gossip went, was the brainchild of publicity ace Llibert Milmany; apparently he wanted to use the furore to get Rexy Mura into the headlines because he was sure the credit ratings of Sr Creus and his company would soar, boosted by a cream pastry bacchanalia that in the circumstances beggared belief. The whole of Barcelona wanted to know what had gone on; it monopolised the news for several days and even *La Soli* felt duty-bound to denounce it.[10]

I had rarely seen the Creuses' daughter because the family didn't usually go to mass in the church near the shanty town. I'd only conversed with her once and been shocked, almost dumbfounded, by her absolute ignorance of what had happened in the country over the previous years. She'd no idea what life was like in Catalonia before the war; and when I tried to explain she'd look at me as if I were telling her a story about some lunatic asylum. Once, when I tried to explain to her that everyone used to eat bread, and that anyone could buy it at any bakery without needing a ration card or to queue, she looked at me, shook her head in astonishment, and exclaimed – in Castilian as always – "How frightfully disorderly!"

Twenty years on it may seem that I've invented this; not at all, it is her reaction *verbatim*. I don't think she was an idiot; she thought it very chic to be blasé about everything that wasn't her own self, and believed that to be so was the last word in femininity: "Agh, politics!" she'd groan and grimace: as far as she was concerned, "politics" meant everything that wasn't fun. Her group of friends acted likewise and they weren't at all feminine, as soon became clear. The life this young girl led was as hollow as it was frenzied, always with the same group of friends who drove her to all manner of stupid entertainment at lunatic speeds.

One afternoon she turned up at the rectory most unexpectedly. She seemed in a state of shock.

She looked at me and said nothing. "Well?" I said. Two tears rolled down from her motionless eyes; she didn't blink and her face was blank.

10 *La Solidaridad Nacional*, the newspaper of the Falange, the single party allowed under Franco.

"Mummy wants to take me to a doctor she can trust . . . I've run away from home!"

After that outburst, her eyes became horribly dry again and silence fell.

"I don't understand," I whispered, "You're attractive, enormously wealthy. I don't see why he wouldn't want to . . ."

"There are seven," and she laughed nervously as she stared at me hard. "Seven."

She laughed mechanically; her hands shook and kept shaking; her horribly dry eyes kept staring at me and that nervous laugh made her wriggle as if someone was tickling the soles of her feet.

I promised to see Sra Creus and dissuade her from taking such a criminal path. But an hour later they had gone abroad in her mother's huge Cadillac, accompanied by the doctor.

A few months after, the extravagant parties resumed in the castle. The news that she'd married Llibert Milmany completely stunned me. He had had his previous civil marriage to an artiste from the Paral·lel annulled without difficulty. In those years, civil marriages were thought not to have happened in any real sense and many who weren't bachelors remarried on the excuse that a merely civil tie had no legal standing. This scandalous situation lasted a long time. The great Llibert Milmany made the most of it to rid himself of the embarrassing burlesque singer and dancer who was an obstacle in his climb to the top.

I now live in a mountain village with fewer than two hundred inhabitants.

I fled the shanty towns. I'm a coward. Monsenyor Pinell de Bray was very clear about that: "He'll get over his infatuation with slums soon enough." Even so, I owe my victory over my aunt to the Monsenyor. Auntie . . . when did I begin to be repelled by her? I have only hazy memories of my mother; I was four when I went to live with Auntie – and I can detect instinctive repulsion even in my earliest memories. When I was nine or ten they started to be tinged with admiration. It was a complex, morbid feeling, like those aroused by a mummified saint. She was always engaged in pious works: at the time she'd concentrated her efforts on Help for Ecclesiastical Vocations, usually known by its acronym H.E.V. After lunch she'd explain to her illustrious cousin the workings of this institution, of which she was the factotum. "How admirable," exclaimed the bishop *in partibus* as he held his tiny coffee cup under his nose so he might inhale the intense aroma: Auntie was apt to serve strong coffee which we drank from cups that were more like thimbles. Monsenyor sipped slowly, holding the handle between his index finger and thumb while ostentatiously lifting his little finger. After a meal he would hiccup and with each hiccup he lifted a handkerchief of the finest cambric to his mouth. He did everything with exquisite elegance, with refined manners that belonged to another age: he'd say "pardon" after each hiccup and the conversation would resume:

"How admirable ... The H.E.V. is a most holy work, if ever there was one."

After Auntie had given me that portable telescope – I'd managed three outstanding passes in my second year at secondary school and the instrument was my reward – I'd spend a couple of hours every night on her mansion's terrace watching the moon and the planets. When Monsenyor found out, he cracked a little joke: "Luckily the boy will get over it," he said. "Nobody has made a career out of staring at the moon." And leaving this childish tomfoolery of mine, he would return to H.E.V. and the "holy work" being undertaken by Auntie; she had started it, she was quick to emphasise, not out of any love for children but out of love for her Creator. "I know that some seminarists we give grants to will be unworthy, but that doesn't matter; I do it for the sake of God." Which God, which God, oh my God, if not the one she'd forged in her own imagination, one to her liking, one that was simply an unconscious idealisation of herself? "This *is* holy work," our illustrious relative insisted. Auntie lowered her eyes and blushed. She produced figures and yet more figures: statistics of parishes without priests, slums without priests. She knew the yearly percentages of ecclesiastical vocations in every bishopric in Catalonia, percentages that kept going down by the year – this she attributed to the dastardly influence of the republic, however much earlier the continuous decline may have begun.

"Nobody's coming forward," the Monsenyor reiterated, ecstatically inhaling the aroma from his thimble of a cup. "Vocations are indeed on the wane."

H.E.V. had small posters put up throughout the city reminding people of the lack of vocations and asking for gifts to create scholarships to help poor seminarists. To this end Auntie organised so many collecting tables, so many charity tombolas! One of her favourite strategies consisted in dressing plainly and knocking on the doors of the grandest mansions in Sarrià; if the maid didn't recognise her, the trick worked: "Tell your mistress that a poor woman is asking for alms, but would like to see her in person." The mistress would appear, immediately recognise her, and the outcome was moving and edifying.

After my twelfth birthday she granted me the honour of helping in her "works". I typed up hundreds and thousands of addresses. Auntie sent out an incredible number of letters, circulars and prospectuses, forever driven by her obsession with the dearth of curates and priests. It distressed her greatly and she communicated her anxiety to me. At times I would feel so miserable thinking about the souls that weren't being saved because of this shortage of priests and curates; I couldn't imagine how the damnation of a soul could be someone else's fault – a knotty problem. In any case, Auntie's mistake wasn't to pose it as such, the problem being real enough, but to imagine that she'd found such an easy and straightforward solution. As far as she was concerned, a soul was lost because of the absence of a *mossèn* to look after it in the same way that we might miss a train because nobody was in the ticket office to sell us a ticket. Auntie would have judged it unthinkable to slip on to a train without a ticket, on the sly. But how many must have beguiled their way through – starting with Dismas, the first to successfully jump the gate!

As she found it unthinkable for anyone to get on the train in such a "vulgar" manner, it was all about buying a ticket in time, so she needed lots of employees to sell them. She understood that there were first-, second- and third-class tickets, and as one who underlined her patronising attitude towards the poor with a saccharine smile and a wealth of diminutives she would even have gone so far as to create a fourth class of passenger: "We must provide facilities," she'd often say, to buy tickets for the train that did the Earth-to-Heaven run. When every kind of facility was available, when every slum had its priest and every village its curate, it was the devil's work that accounted for people missing the train.

The admiration I then felt for her pioneering activities had finally erased the instinctive repulsion she'd aroused in me as a young child.

Among her many properties, Auntie owned a house divided into flats on carrer Balmes near the Diagonal. We thought the concierge there was exemplary; she was pious and deferential, and often came to visit us in Sarrià. She had a son not much older than me and brought him along one day to tell us that he was entering the seminary: in fact with a H.E.V. scholarship. Deeply moved, Auntie wrapped her arms around him: "You have chosen the most worthy path, even the angels will envy you . . ." I witnessed that tender scene; Auntie even wept as she embraced the concierge's son.

I couldn't sleep that night: her tears, the concierge's excitement and the boy's blissful expression kept going round in my head. The idea came to me all of a sudden, naturally – I felt extremely ashamed I'd not thought of it before – that I'd not been worthy of such an aunt! I couldn't get to sleep and impatiently waited for day to break. My aunt has always been an early riser.

She looked at me taken aback: "What's got into you?" She hadn't had time to comb her hair; I was hoping she'd take me in her arms like the concierge's son and that her tears would meld into mine.

"But . . ." she looked disconcerted, "we must talk about this later. I don't think you're seeing things at all in the proper light."

Soon after Monsenyor Pinell de Bray came from Paris and stayed with us a while.

"Our boy wants to become a priest," Auntie told him, "a priest in the slums . . ."

She gave her voice that indulgent tone she often liked to adopt, the same saccharine sweet inflection she used when speaking to the poor while feigning an interest in their little household and children. O Eternal God, you could so bring us to account for our cloying diminutives and condescension!

Monsenyor Pinell de Bray looked at me as though he found the idea amusing, if perplexing.

"We need to talk this through," Auntie said, "and, of course, not in his presence."

I felt irritated. I wasn't crazy; why had she told the bishop *in partibus* of my decision in that ironic, pitying tone? I stood behind the door; I wanted to listen to their conversation. It was the Monsenyor's velvety, sinuous voice: "Some down-and-out priests do well; I know one, the son of the Duke of Albi's sharecroppers, who is now a canon in Tarragona. He'll get over his infatuation with slums in time, like the telescope. It's adolescent nonsense. He has plenty of time for second thoughts before he finishes at school. His idea isn't as peculiar as you think; most of our serving bishops come from the lay clergy and not religious orders . . ."

At that time a bishop *in partibus* was more distinguished than one in a real post, because most of the latter had in effect risen from the ranks of "down-and-out priests" as Monsenyor said. However, I didn't feel at all inclined to "do well"; the very expression appalled me. I kept listening behind the door: "I've said it once and I'll say it again: the boy's idea isn't as peculiar as you imagine. A secular priest can retain his wealth since he doesn't have to pledge himself to poverty; on the other hand, if he becomes a Jesuit, as you'd prefer —"

"Some things are more important than wealth," Auntie interrupted. "Look at me: I'm giving everything to the poor."

*

And, as you see, God steeped me in solitude. I had no friends until war broke out; until I met Soleràs. I had lots of companions but I was desperate to have a friend, not friends but *a* friend. Not really knowing why or how, I found myself enlisted in the army of Catalonia before I was twenty. I'd gone to a hospital to give blood in those terrible July days in 1936; I was a nurse, then an auxiliary, and one fine day I was allotted to a brigade in the 30th Division as a medical adjutant. Once at the front I felt happy, and why not? It was a regular brigade, militarised from the start, and the ideas and feelings around were in essence similar to mine – those people were congenial, why shouldn't I have liked them? Weren't they my brothers? Later I was often asked if I hadn't been aware that, while we were at the front, in the rearguard they were burning churches and beating priests to death. Of course we knew, it was impossible not to; at the time we didn't know the incredible extent of the killings during that summer, but we did know they were going on. We were only too aware of it, but reasoned that if there'd been a plague epidemic we wouldn't have abandoned our country. We were trapped between two lines of fire and knew that was the reality.

When I've been asked so often since what I was doing with the "reds", when I've asked myself the very same question – yes, I have sometimes wondered why, and even did so during the war – I've always come out with the same reply: I had no choice. Beyond all the ridiculous ideological excuses, there was a geographical divide; for the vast majority – of which I was one – who knew nothing about politics, there was that and perhaps little else. We were republicans because the zone where we happened to be, where we were born, was republican; if we'd been born in the other zone, we'd have belonged to the opposite camp. There were certainly people who went from one to the other and vice versa; I myself – as I'll explain – almost did so, like Soleràs and so many others, but by and large everyone simply followed the flags of the geographical area where they happened to be living. That was so for the bulk of the population and that's probably how it is in all wars; anyway, I can say that if anyone was ashamed of the arson, killing, and absolute disorder in the republican rearguard, we were more ashamed than most. Strictly speaking I can say this only for our brigade, the only one I knew in any depth. And I should add that, on occasion, especially at the beginning, there was talk of organising a march on Barcelona with the other regular brigades in order to crush the anarchist gangs ravaging the country. Someday someone will elucidate the murky and mysterious ways of anarchism: all we know right now is that they did exactly what was necessary for the war to be lost.

At the beginning, just after I'd joined up, I remember officers and brigadiers talking openly about a coup that the odd general and various colonels were apparently planning in order to sweep the streets of Barcelona clean of arsonists, thieves and murderers. The names of distinguished soldiers, Guarner, Farràs, Escofet, filtered down even to us subordinate officers and everyone else who might have been in favour of such a thing. But that couldn't have happened without endangering the front.

I remember a meeting of officers in our brigade almost at the very beginning of the war in which Soleràs spoke. Some raised a serious objection against the supporters of the "march on Barcelona": the fascists would walk through the gaping hole we would open up. With his razor-sharp mind, which made him so many enemies because people found it irritating, he prophesied that if we allowed the rearguard "to fuck up" we would lose the war: they cut him off in full flow and warned him that an officer could not speak in such defeatist terms, that defeatism in an officer warranted the death penalty. Exasperated by this interruption he strode out, slamming the door behind him and shouting: "You can all go to fucking hell!"

He was a strange, brusque young man at once repellent and attractive. I felt a kinship with him from this time when he spoke so lucidly and courageously, and because he displayed a combination of courage and eccentricity. The oddest stories were told about him and a legend was thus forged around him within the brigade. He liked to wallow in contradiction and disconcert people: just as he'd been the most strident supporter of military action against the anarchists – "An army which doesn't feel defended by its rearguard cannot possible win," he'd said – he also came out with the most amazing apologies for anarchism, "the only serious attempt to transform the world into that huge creel of crabs we all crave". Depending on the phase of the moon, he could defend the most contrary ideas; many people thought he was incoherent when in fact he was the most intelligent person I've ever known.

He took no notice of me. He wasn't avoiding me, it was worse: it seemed he wasn't even aware I existed. One day, I talked to him about that meeting of officers in order to express my support for what he'd said; I told him I suspected that devious provocateurs were at work among the leaders of the murderous gangs terrorising Barcelona. This was no vague conjecture on my part since I'd met Lamoneda: I'll say more about him one day. Soleràs cut me off: "That's all so obvious. One shouldn't waste one's breath on things that are self-evident."

My attempts to speak to him in a more personal fashion also failed, for yet again he stopped me in my tracks: "We've all got aunties desperate for us to go over to the other side."

He once threw this remark in my face that he was to repeat several times: "Every nephew has the aunt he deserves."

Our aunts, his and mine, had nothing or almost nothing in common. He felt genuine affection towards his, however much he concealed it behind his sarcasm, whereas I have always felt repelled by mine. Despite his barbs I retained my feelings of sympathy towards Soleràs; his cynicism didn't win out. I guessed he was a loner consumed by secret anguish: was he a Catholic? At most, a cynical Catholic; religious truths assumed the most surprising shapes on his lips, often the most exasperating ones.

When he was stripped of his rank of machine-gun lieutenant because of odd behaviour in the course of a battle – I won't go into that now – I went to see him and express my unflinching friendship.

I did so with all my naïveté at the time; I thought he might need me, now that he'd been demoted – Lluís hadn't yet joined our brigade. I imagined that a few soothing drops of balsam on the wound his demotion had inflicted might be welcome; now, many years later, I find it strange that we could at the time think of the loss of a second lieutenant's stripes as so important – he was a second lieutenant though his post was a full lieutenant's – stripes that were replaced by an adjutant's, the immediately inferior rank. But the fact was that after a few months at war we'd so assimilated the military spirit that a drop in rank seemed unbearably humiliating. After he lost rank, some people turned their backs on him whenever they saw him.

I found him one day in the brigade's supplies store, sitting on a sack between crates of tinned milk and sacks of rice and chickpeas, engrossed in a tome that he was reading.

"Sit down," he said curtly. "I was just thinking about you, as you are our medical adjutant. You ought to be able to describe to me the exact symptoms of gonorrhoea."

His eternal nonsense . . . but it was totally unexpected and I almost burst into tears, because I am so meek . . .

"Don't take it like that, for heaven's sake. I'm not referring to myself. I have Casanova in mind. You may have heard of him? Casanova de Seingalt: a professional Venetian. His memoirs have got me really worried. To believe him, he was cured of the clap as easily as he caught it. Now, is that possible?"

"In the eighteenth century, that would have been nothing short of a miracle."

"A miracle! It would be fantastic to be cured of the clap like that, but

Casanova was an adept of Voltaire, so we should discount the miracle hypothesis."

"I didn't come here to talk to you about Casanova."

"Perhaps you came to bore me to tears with politics?"

At the time people were still always talking politics in the brigade; there was so much political talk everyone quickly became sick to death of it – this was just before Lluís arrived. We finally settled down to fight a war, "since we'd joined the dance", without giving ourselves any more political headaches. Soleràs was the first to weary of political harangues; he often poured scorn on the speeches the radio was constantly spewing or that reached the front via the newspapers.

"Here you see," he pointed to the sack of chickpeas, "how I am hero-ically waging war on the fascists, I mean, the baddies. We scream: 'Death to the fascists!' They scream: 'Death to the reds!' We are both saying the same thing: 'Death to the baddies!' Everybody is against the baddies; everybody everywhere is rooting for the goodies. My God, it's so boring! Does nobody on the planet have the slightest imagination? But the worst side to wars is the fact they're turned into novels; at the end of this war – and I assure you it's a war that's as shitty as any – novels will be written that are especially stupid, as sentimental and risqué as they come: they'll have wonderfully courageous young heroes and wonderfully buxom little angels. I don't mean you, Cruells; you'll not be stricken by one of these tomes. But foreigners . . . It's a pity you don't believe in my gifts as a prophet; I could tell you, for example, that foreigners will turn this huge mess into stirring stories of bullfighters and gypsies."

"Bullfighters? I've never heard mention of any, so far as I know . . ."

"Right, poor Cruells: a bullfighter has never been sighted in the army, let alone a gypsy, but foreigners have a good nose for business. Business is business, as all foreigners say, and time is money; if a novel with a Spanish theme is going to succeed, the hero just has to be a bullfighter and the hero-ine a gypsy and by the third chapter they must be fornicating in a tropical jungle full of wild bulls; anything else is a waste of time and time is money. Foreigners are idiots; I know what I'm talking about because I've travelled. The world would be a better place if there weren't so many foreigners."

"What have you got against foreigners?"

He looked at me as if my question astonished him: "What I find most annoying," his bass voice droned on, "is the thought that I too am a foreigner. That's the first thing you learn when you travel. The first time that a government official addressed me as a foreigner – I was in the former kingdom of Saxony – I was on the point of punching him as if he'd insulted me. 'Me, a foreigner?' I squealed. 'Not likely! You're the foreigner here!' And the fact is that we all like to think foreigners are the others. We're *all* foreigners, and that's a real pain! We like to live under the illusion that only the others are, when yours truly is the most out-and-out foreigner of the lot."

"Poor Soleràs," I said, "you are so fundamentally right. The most out-and-out foreigner . . . But what do you gain by always seeking out fundamentals?"

"I simply gain a load of shit," he rasped. "If only I could be as stupid as everyone else! Take a look at this newspaper that's spread out over these sacks of chickpeas; look at this huge headline on the front page: 'On your feet, proletarians!' It's from a harangue that emanated from our brilliant comrade Llibert Milmany, Director General of War Propaganda. I apologise, I see you don't know who I'm talking about."

In truth, at that time, I'd hardly heard a word about Lluís' brother-in-law – I'd not met Lluís yet – even though he'd been enormously active in the propaganda department from a few weeks into the war. I'd joined the front in the very first days when Llibert Milmany was still an unknown quantity and nobody at the front talked about him, just as nobody talked about any of the new people who came and went on the political stage in a rearguard charade we found incomprehensible. On the other hand, Soleràs *was* very well acquainted with him: "A brilliant comrade! He's our age and as fit as a fighting bull, but he is *indispensable* in the rear, it's plain to see: 'On your feet, proletarians!' rolls off the tongue so easily when you're sitting in your office in Barcelona. When you walked in, my conscience was wracked by doubt; you must have noticed how I was sitting on a sack of chickpeas reading the memoirs of Casanova, yet the newspaper headline clearly insists: 'On your feet, proletarians!' Should I continue to sit on the sack of chickpeas? Should I be 'on my feet' as our brilliant comrade instructs me? Apparently this 'on your feet' means 'stand up straight', but do I qualify as a proletarian? What a dreadful worry! In fact I only aspire to be a notary; a letter should be written to our illustrious Llibert – anonymously because he knows me only too well – suggesting he vary his speeches a little. In the next one, for example, he could say: 'On your feet, notaries! On your feet, apothecaries!' My dear sir, a little variety . . ."

After this encounter we didn't see each other for several weeks; he travelled in the Transport Corps van searching for food in the rearguard and as a result he often didn't appear around the brigade for days. One evening he turned up unexpectedly at the battalion's first-aid post where I was working. He'd come to that village a long way from Supplies, so he said, expressly to see me for a long chat. After dinner I took him to the basement where my bed was; I carried down another straw mattress for him.

"If I were to tell you that from my earliest childhood I've always . . ." – he uttered the opening words of a monologue that was to last for hours the moment we'd stretched out on our respective mattresses – ". . . I've always thought of the universe as if it were a female ocean . . . oh if only you could dive into her lukewarm, spellbinding waters! But one is a Tantalus nailed to the beach. The ocean is very near, but it's impossible to dive in! The females won't let one. *You* can delude yourself that you don't plunge in headfirst because you are virtuous; I can't. I'm not allowed any more delusions: I've tried everything; *they* don't want it to happen! On the other hand, my situation is really complex, because I am fiercely pro-Church. Some people believe in nothing, not even the black mass; naturally, they are quick to tell you that, but they know not what they say. Very, very important people, you know, managing directors of big limited companies, professors of Economics, amazing pedants. They never once suspect that they are worshipping the Anti-eternal Father in person."

"The Anti-eternal Father?"

"Yes: the Anti-eternal Father. That's what I call him and if you give it a little thought, you'll see how it's the name that best fits. I am sincerely convinced that it is his real name and that if he's not known by this name it's because he prefers to go incognito. He likes to assume the most anodyne shapes in his reincarnations, which are much more frequent than you think; he likes to mingle with the drabbest crowd in the street and be adored unbeknown to his adorers. He likes equivocation, ambiguity and mystification; he likes luxury, though he likes it to be shabby rather than sumptuous – the kind that hits you in dens of vice within the reach of all purses: yes, he ensures there are hells available for all, because he too remembers the poor. He doesn't forget the modest clerks who must make the most of the five-day week to let their hair down. Barcelona enjoys long summers; the nights are short, if hot and oppressive, the unforgettable nights of Barcelona's dog days! I would escape from Godella, where I spent the summer on my aunt's estate, on the pretext that the professor of Economics wanted to see me, so I could immerse myself in that world I found so tempting and that I knew so well; I knew it particularly in the winter, but it's at the height of summer that it opens up like a large fruit which bursts in the heat and reveals its succulently ripe, if not overripe, insides. And there you see them roaming the backstreets, tortured by heat and lack of sleep, like so many butterflies flitting from flower to flower until they find one that seems mysteriously attractive; oh, much more than any other, though they couldn't tell you why. She looks like the others, standing in her doorway or on her street corner like a sentinel rigorously doing her duty; she has nothing special, nothing the others don't, but one falls irresistibly on one's knees at her feet. The fool doesn't realise this – how many unknowing idolaters there are! – but he is driven by a fascination for the Anti-eternal that the ancients knew so well: '*fascinatio fugacitatis*', the irresistible fascination for what is fleeting, for what will only last a short midsummer's night! Idolatry of idolatries! Adoration of what is fleeting! Falling on one's knees at the feet of what will be ravaged by sickness, old age and death; kiss and adore it! Reject Eternity and rush to be enslaved by Time! At least I'm not the director of any limited company, I never pontificate from any chair in Economics, and afterwards – inevitably afterwards! – I would go, as dawn glimmered over the port, to prostrate myself in a dark, forgotten, deserted church, and fix my eyes on the illumination emanating from the most Holy Son and allow myself to be swept away by sweet repentance. Yes, it's sweet to be able to say to that crucified, forgotten God: 'Lord, *You* taught us this ploy, this fantastic ploy, the prayer of the publican.'"

His cantor's voice vibrated in the dark like the bass notes of an organ; he kept varying his emphasis and it was difficult to separate out emotion from mockery.

"Woman is the Ocean, man the Sahara. These two vast, hostile expanses, water and thirst, are side by side and never mingle. If they were to mingle, the most glorious of continents would come into being, but that's impossible. In the depths of the Sahara, where the dunes are most scorched by the sun, a species of cactus grows to a great height; from afar the very occasional caravan of Touaregs has glimpsed the only example of the species, a species of which there is only one specimen. Its vertical silhouette projects a shadow over the sand that extends to the horizon; Touaregs have glimpsed the shadow, not the cactus. Now, as well as being the single living specimen of the species, this cactus has another unique feature: it lives a thousand years only to flower for a second and die. You see, the Sahara is remarkable from more than one point of view."

"I've never heard of this cactus."

"Haven't you? That's astonishing. Finally, the moment to flower comes: 'Bah, what *would* be the point?' it asks and prefers to expire without ever experiencing its moment of glory, that moment it has been preparing for, for a thousand years. 'Flower? What's the point?' it asks when the time comes. Yes, when the time comes it says 'Bah' and expires without deigning to flower. Have you really never heard of it? That's astonishing. Uncultured folk, as Captain Picó says. It is a renowned cactus, the *Cactus solerassus*. Are you really unfamiliar with it? What about the insects? Haven't you heard about the insects either?"

"Which ones?"

"Which? All of them! All insects! Insects, no matter which. It's strange how insects, quite unlike ourselves, begin life in a state of decrepitude; which of the two systems works best? Some drag themselves painfully around for years in order to enjoy a youthful instant, a nuptial flight: at root it's the story of the *Cactus Solerassus* retold; everything meets the same end, as if everything was made specially for the nuptial flight, for that moment of glory, though we are only allowed to taste a single drop, a single moment! And for this single drop, for this single moment, for this glimmer of uncertain glory . . . Bah, one wanders astray in a labyrinth of absurdity.

For example: when animal life had barely moved beyond the insect stage – given that we're talking about insects – vegetable life had already experienced the most splendid flowering; the most monstrous, terrifying orchids had already blossomed in the heart of the densest, hottest jungles when our granddaddy, the eyeless earthworm, was slithering along. Then you might have thought that vegetables were destined to the highest glory; we now know that was not to be. God wanted descent from the earthworm, not the orchid: please confess that trying to understand a scrap of all this is driving you crazy."

It was futile to attempt to interrupt his soliloquy; his rhetoric was driving him on, his cantor's voice became increasingly resonant. I knew he was gesticulating too, because the luminous tip of his cigarette traced strange arabesques in the pitch dark of that basement. He jumped from one topic to another and I think even came to forget I was there: "The least we can say is that everything is unfathomable – apart from nothingness. It's amazing that people don't realise this, via an infallible algebraic equation, non-belief in nothingness = belief in nothingness; if nothing existed, there'd be no problem, everything would be as clear as water. Nothingness is the only logical, rational thing that is free of mystery, perfectly simple and understandable; but nothingness is the only thing that doesn't exist – by definition – and all existence is a mystery. Which all goes to show that thinking is a waste of time, since one can never reach a conclusion: either there is nothing or, if something is out there, it is an unfathomable mystery. On the other hand, we were talking about something else; let's return to our thread. I was telling you that *they* – not I – are the ones who don't want to let you, because I assure you that the lily of chastity is hardly my strong point. As you are a priest, or are going to be, you are duty-bound to listen to my confession on this subject, which makes up ninety-nine per cent of the content of all confessions, I imagine. So here's the essential point: *they* won't let you – naturally, with honourable exceptions, but who has ever been interested in exceptions? The exceptions, those that do let you . . . if I were to reveal that from the moment they let you . . . if I were to reveal that from the moment they let you I lose all interest . . . One must admit there is a mystery here: a mystery everywhere! We only feel a real need with those who won't let us; perhaps atheists, damned atheists, could explain this mystery to us. But no, they can't explain any mystery or anything that's worth its salt; they can only talk about progress. They stun you with their progress! They go to America and start selling newspapers on street corners; they make huge fortunes and come back to tell us how they did it, as if this was of any interest. Progress is to blame, because in other eras those who went to America never returned to bore the pants off us. As you see me now, I too have sold newspapers on street corners, unsellable papers, *La barrinada*, can you believe it? Though not in America, where one would undoubtedly have made a fortune, but on the Ramblas of Barcelona. It's amazing how these fellows who come back from America aren't ashamed of the fortunes they've made: they keep telling you about it and never blush, unable to grasp the profundity of a phrase my aunt came out with. She had been introduced to a very suave tycoon: 'A very polite fellow,' she said later; 'they say he'd made a fortune by himself, a self-made man, but I think that must be a slander.' Perhaps this big tycoon started off selling newspapers on street corners in New York; it's highly regarded there, it's *the* thing to do, the first thing all millionaires have ever done. They'd be ashamed to have sold papers on the streets of Barcelona, but in New York it's the cat's whiskers. And you see that's another mystery, the business of shame, and I'd like our wonderful atheists to explain *that* to us: of all the things I have done what I'm most ashamed of is replying to an advertisement in *La Vanguardia* that promised a 'confidential prospectus' on how to get an athlete's muscles in a couple of weeks. For fifteen pesetas: a peseta per day. So yours truly was able to spend fifteen pesetas in exchange for the secret key to athletic muscularity. And while I'm in confessional mode, why don't I reveal all to you? I even went so far as to attend a 'private consultancy' given by Madame Zoraida, 'an expert in the psychology of amorous conquests'. Of course, I never made any conquests; not even of that Zoraida who was, nonetheless, the most shameless of gypsies. You don't believe me? What if I were to tell you that I even bought a tube of Barbyl, not the small two-peseta tube but the super-giant effort that cost forty; when I shave, I'd so like the blade to rasp . . . I managed one extra hair; only one, but it was a hell of a long one."

He sighed as if suddenly burdened by a painful memory and immediately launched back into his monologue, now switching to geology. At the time I couldn't see why he'd brought geology into his soliloquy: "I've even sunk so low as to cram on geology; I've swallowed volume after volume not understanding one jot. Because *they* adore geology, did you know? All to no end! The only chink of light I extracted was the knowledge that we only make it to fossilisation if we're extremely lucky; you see, we're not even granted that consolation. Because in another era I did find minimal consolation in the idea that one day I might be a fossilised skeleton in a museum display cabinet labelled *Homo solerasssus antiquus*, scaring children from primary and secondary schools. Farewell, beautiful dreams of lost innocence! I had to swallow a frightful tome to rid myself of any illusion on that front; I will never be a fossil unless it is an extraordinary case of serendipity. I now declare that it was all a waste of time and effort: the Barbyl was as big a failure as Madame Zoraida's course in psychology and those sessions cramming geology, as was everything else I had a shot at. By the way, what *does* make our hair grow? We do, of course; we do, but not our conscious will – that would be too easy – it's a quite different will, one we are completely unaware of, buried deep within us, another will we don't even suspect exists which makes our hair or nails grow, that shapes our body and face; everybody has the face he wants, but hush! Nobody is aware of this other will. Hush, hush! Do not stir the murky waters at the bottom of our well. I could say so much on this . . . because I've thought long and hard about these issues. My whole lifetime! And that leads me to tell you about my childhood and my aunt who is so different from yours. Your aunt thinks life is as logical as a current account in the bank: how many good works have you paid in? How much have you withdrawn from your account? What's the remaining balance? That's how yours lives. But mine thinks everything is mystery, pitch black and strange; she floats quite naturally adrift in the supernatural."

"Saint Philomena . . ." I ventured.

"Let Saint Philomena rest in peace," he interrupted tetchily; "many or not so many celestial visions hold no surprises in the end. I have much better things to tell you, because I want to tell you all tonight – when will we ever have a better opportunity? This is why I came to see you. I'm sure you won't let on to the others in the brigade, because you're a priest and must keep confessions secret; remember I've told nobody that you are a priest. They are such beasts in this brigade, bright sparks ready to do their worst . . ."

"I'm not a priest."

"No matter, you will be; you look the part. One has only to glance at you and feel driven to confess – confess everything, even the saddest, nastiest, most hurtful secrets. As if one's shame were rising from one's gut to one's gullet and turning thick and sweet like honey. Yes, Cruells, tonight you shall listen to my nonsense because tonight I don't feel sleepy and am in the mood to talk till daybreak, as you will soon see. It's all stuff and nonsense, of course, but it marks you out for life. I breathed rarefied air from my innocent childhood to the outbreak of war. For many a long year, for endless years, but even so I'd not change my aunt for yours on any account. Justice, according to Papinianus, is about giving each person what is his; so let each man stick with his own aunt. *Suum cuique tribuere*."

"The quotation is from Ulpianius, not Papinianus."

"Please let's not argue over trifles. There are so many phenomena that are beyond us . . ."

I could feel the hesitation and unease in his voice that he tried to hide behind his wisecracks until the moment came when he fell into a long silence; that was after he'd made the remark about "so many phenomena", which I found disappointing because it was really banal. His cigarette had gone out and he was so still I thought he must have nodded off.

"There are so many phenomena that are beyond us," his booming voice repeated after the silence. "Do you think when it started Christianity was any more respectable than a band of spiritualists? I mean in the eyes of the profane – please don't lose your temper – in the eyes of the eternal jokers, that are and will forever be the most numerous of sects. I beg you to hear me out before you hit the roof; you are in fact one of the few people who might understand since, as you once told me, you've had several attacks of sleepwalking in your past. Every man must put up with his own aunt, and as far as mine is concerned . . ."

When I was twelve, shortly after Aunt Llúcia gave me that telescope to reward my outstanding grades, I did in effect suffer an attack of sleepwalking and Soleràs was the only one in the brigade I'd told. They found me walking round the side of the terrace of the mansion where we lived in

Sarrià, as if I was looking through the telescope while walking, but with my eyes shut. If my aunt hadn't said anything, I'd never have known, for when you wake up you don't remember a thing. At the time I had this conversation with Soleràs there'd been no repeat performances, so that early attack was put down as an isolated case; soon after Lluís joined the brigade I had my second: some soldiers on night patrol found me sleep-walking on the streets of Olivel de la Virgen, again as if looking through my telescope, but this is all beside the point now.

This conversation took place towards the end of November and the rain began to beat furiously down on a skylight that wouldn't shut properly; gusts of cold wind blew in tiny drops of rain. He re-lit his cigarette and I saw his face for a moment: like an apparition. It seemed skinnier than ever and he looked as if he was suffering an attack of migraine. With a cigarette between his lips and a match between his fingers he wiped his left hand over his forehead and stared at me myopically, seemingly to communicate a shameful kind of suffering one would prefer to keep secret. Then he disappeared back into the darkness and resumed his soliloquy: "In her case, without electricity, far from fresh air and daylight, like a pharaoh deep in his pyramid, my aunt – who has pots of money, Cruells – has created a secret world for her own private use. This is the only enviable advantage the wealthy enjoy – the ability to create such a haven, to do what they want and ignore what others might think. Some nights I'd hear the scraping which I've always heard and recalled in my most distant memories. It wasn't very loud but sounded eerie, as if it came from within the wooden furniture. My bedroom is at the other end of the flat, a long way from hers, and looks over a convent school. Auntie had chosen the smallest, innermost bedroom for herself; as it is a nineteenth-century building – she always refused to move – it still has inner bedrooms without natural light and hers is one, the only opening being the door that leads straight into the hallway. One night, when I was almost thirteen, I heard scraping that sounded louder than usual; it came from the sitting room next to my bedroom, as if someone was sawing through the mahogany console or sliding their fingers along it. The strange noises grew louder and louder and now sounded like a horse galloping in the distance or a rubber ball being bounced rapidly up and down. I was intrigued and jumped out of bed; a moonbeam filtered through a crack in the shutter to the back of the sitting room and was reflected from the blurred console mirror onto my grandfather's portrait in oils. A breeze blew in from the nuns' garden heavily scented with orange blossom: it was a night in June. I walked barefoot; the noise stopped the second I entered the sitting room. Shortly after I heard it again, fainter, and not in the sitting room but in the hallway. I headed in the same direction; the noise receded as if it were running away from me. I chased after it and found myself quite unintentionally in Auntie's bedroom . . . Are you still there?"

"I'm listening," I answered.

"I simply must tell you all this, Cruells; I must! The bedroom smelt stale, since Auntie slept with the door closed. Normally my footsteps, even if I was barefoot, would have woken her, since she has very good hearing, not to mention the fact that I'd opened the door. Normally it would have been pitch black inside yet I caught a vague glimmer, something bluish and hazy coming from somewhere or other, and enough for me to be able to make out her features. Her eyes were open and she was smiling. Spittle trickled from the corners of her lips onto the pillow; she was motionless and smiling and couldn't see me; she was asleep, though her eyes were open wide. Her small mahogany bedside table seemed to hang in the air; only one of its three legs was touching the ground, and it swayed gently as if dancing to the first movement of the slowest of waltzes. All this, so long in the telling, lasted a second; as soon as I walked in the table quickly put its feet back on the floor, the bluish glimmer faded and the noise stopped. Are you still there?"

"Yes, I'm listening."

"The next morning I tried to talk to her about it, though I didn't say I'd gone into her bedroom. I only mentioned the strange noises and the vague glimmer; she grimaced scornfully, incredulously, and touched her forehead with her finger: 'This is stupid nonsense,' she replied, 'spiritualist rubbish. You'd fare better reading the complete works of Bossuet.'"

"Does it have to be Bossuet?"

"It was obvious that Auntie had heard nothing; that much *was* obvious, although she had very good hearing. I knew that only too well because I had to work miracles to make my night-time sorties; by the age of thirteen

I'd started my night-time forays. We were the only people in the flat after ten at night, when her maid – an old woman who'd worked in a nunnery for years before joining us – went to sleep in the attic, where her bedroom was much bigger and more comfortable than Auntie's. I should add that the building is one of the many she owns, and definitely the oldest; we live in the smallest flat, but the attic is huge. So, from ten o'clock only Auntie and I were in the flat, and the rattling – for that was what it was, don't laugh – always took place between midnight and four a.m. I'd worked out that when the rattling started, Auntie slept more soundly than usual. I took advantage of this discovery for my sorties. I could walk along the passage and open and shut the front door next to her bedroom without her noticing. She was in a trance."

"You really expect me to believe —"

"Yes. Yes, I expect you to believe that, because it's the only possible explanation. You've had attacks of sleepwalking and you know from your own experience that one remembers nothing subsequently. Some nights my aunt falls into a trance when she is asleep and does so totally unawares. Let's say, to put it plainly, that she is a medium but doesn't know it; you wouldn't know you were a sleepwalker if nobody told you. Might it be relevant at this point to remind you that others have written prose without realising they have? We do so much without knowing! On the other hand, my aunt's isn't as rare a case as you might imagine; many like her have been studied. They are the rule rather than the exception: the majority of mediums operate quite unawares. If my aunt who is so devout and so fond of the Oratory Brothers suspected any of this, she'd want to throw up. Once, when we were chatting after a meal, I skilfully guided our conversation in the direction of certain metapsychic experiments that were in the news at the time and had counted on the presence in person of Einstein and Marie Curie. She interrupted me: 'Don't ever talk to me about such things, I beg you; they make me so queasy I want to throw up.' All I can add is that after this whenever I heard the name 'Einstein' my stomach gave a turn. Well, you know, these strikingly queasy feelings give us a clue: doesn't her unease at the mention of para-psychological phenomena derive from the fact that she too is deeply infected but doesn't know she is? We find nothing more upsetting than what is so deeply hidden within us. Now, Cruells, you can perhaps understand who I am: I'm genetically infected and have lived for twenty or more years up to my neck in an atmosphere as dank as stagnant pond water. I'm merely the hysterical nephew of a semi-epileptic aunt, the only surviving male of a family with a screw loose; the only surviving male, credit this, brought up and spoilt by a millionaire spinster aunt who saw visions. Cruells, I horrify myself; sometimes, at night, when I'm alone at the back of that huge supplies store – that's where I sleep – I feel cold shivers as if somebody were blowing on my face in the dark. The hair along my spine bristles like that of a dog howling opposite . . . opposite what? Dogs know, we don't. I suppose there's no point my telling you that spiritualists are generally the nicest of people with no imaginations, who are happy to enjoy the innocent illusion that they are chatting a while to their dearly beloved deceased aunts? But there's nothing there; the poor defunct dears don't involve themselves in any of that. If they did, it would be so simple; but they don't. Beings who are much disturbed do so: our own selves. It's our 'other will', that 'alter ego' we carry within us quite unawares. It's that 'alter ego' which operates from the moment we are conceived; it organises matter into hands, eyes, feet, at puberty it makes hair sprout suddenly, taking us so by surprise. And there's a good reason to be surprised! We are surprised by spiritualist phenomena with mediums to the point of refusing to believe in them and yet we're not at all surprised when our nails and beard grow, as if the one wasn't as inexplicable as the other. That spittle I saw trickling from my aunt's lips was probably ectoplasm; that's right, but in the last analysis that's what beards and nails are too. Everything is ectoplasm! On the other hand, there *is* one metapsychic phenomenon within everyone's grasp, namely dreams; in our dreams we see things, we see faces, we hear noises, we hear voices: we manufacture all that ourselves, not with our conscious will, but with another will. How often have we wanted to dream at will! Not possible. We'd like to dream of wonderful things, if we could choose them! We could, for example, dream of wonderful, beautifully proportioned dames, their eyes full of the most steaming, tempting complicity. Yet, you know, I dream of frightful women; what if I told you how often I've dreamed of that Madame Zoraida, who was horrible! If we could exercise our 'other will' as we do our conscious will, we could even do better than dream at will; we could have a face like a god, a thick, luxuriant beard, muscles like a stevedore, a chest like a horse. Not possible! Not possible! We can't influence our 'other will'; it is blind and gropes its way. It can take bizarrely wrong paths in the same way as it organises matter during gestation – into a hand or a foot, a liver or a spleen, or else a monstrous cancer."

"You've lost me," I muttered.

"I'm lost too," he replied. "Yes, I've lost myself too. All this is beyond me. Everyone has the face he wants: it simply depends on the other will; and that's the worst of it, since everyone has the face he deserves, the one he creates for himself. Yes, that's the worst of it, because my face . . . better not to mention it, I beg you; I'd die at the thought! My face is beyond me. And the robot that rules us, this unconscious will, this double abyss where it has flung us . . . I say 'this double abyss' because it all takes place between two mysteries, our origin and our end, the obscene and the macabre, a couple of bottomless pits. Everything, and I mean everything, comes down to this: ectoplasm phenomena as much as dreams. It's not for nothing that spiritualists have thought they have discerned messages from the dead there; their funereal air often makes you believe it. Though they've never succeeded in telling us the other side of the story, they are always left feeling disconcerted, and often when their beloved, disembodied aunts send messages from the beyond, they come out with ludicrous rubbish."

"Always the same old story," I muttered nonplussed. I couldn't follow the thread of what he was saying and at the same time I was dead tired and the rainy gusts from the skylight kept hitting me in the face.

"Yes, always the same old story," said Soleràs, trying to light his cigarette – the wet blasts kept putting his matches out. "Conversely, the Freudians, the fucking Freudians see only the obscene side; they are like the carnival giants who see the world through their flies. They miss out the macabre. Each sees only one side, but there are two! It's a double abyss! And we're sunk up to our eyes in the mud in this double abyss, though even so, our eyes still get a peep, enough to see the other abyss, the one up above . . ."

He was still trying unsuccessfully to light his cigarette; the wet breeze kept putting his matches out; his voice grew gruffer and gruffer in the dark: "Around that time I'd begun systematically to start enjoying a real man's night on the tiles. I'd wait for the rattling to start and slip out of the flat barefoot. Between midnight and four o'clock I lived my other life in dives that stank of rum and piss, in the heart of the *barri xino*; people drank litres of rum and then did what came easiest, pissed it out in the corner of the room. Later the rumour spread that these dens of vice had been set up by the town hall for the benefit of tourists – a wily ploy, but it's a slander; I swear that in my time I saw no sign of any tourists. I came home at dawn dead drunk. One Monday I slumped into bed more pissed than usual; my bed rocked like a boat and made me feel sick. The grandfather clock in the sitting room was striking four when a bluish-green phosphorescent glow, the size of an apple, appeared in the dark, level with the ceiling: it jiggled along, not losing height before coming to a halt. It assumed a viscous consistency or was perhaps more like sticky dough, and an eye formed within it that stared down at me. I lay on my back, looking at the ceiling, trying to tame the waves of drunken retching and that single eye stared down at me from the ceiling; the other eye didn't open, I could make out its shapeless outline in the whitish, phosphorescent dough. The features of a face began to emerge as well, first a big blur, then it became easier to recognise: it was mine. Yes, it was a face that strangely resembled mine; I heard its voice, a husky voice like the voices from those old phonographs with a horn from our childhood or perhaps more like the voice of a war-wounded man who'd lost his vocal cords and was making a supreme effort to speak. The voice said: '*Eppur si muove.*'"

By now I was half asleep and couldn't stop myself from laughing because it was all so unexpected.

"Don't laugh," said Soleràs. "It said: '*Eppur si muove.*' As surely as I'm speaking to you here! And while the face with a single eye began to disappear like melting wax I heard that voice again, huskier than ever: 'Millions and millions and millions . . .'"

"Millions of what?"

"I don't dare repeat that in your presence, poor Cruells, but no matter. You can imagine the scene. Right then my guts won out and I puked up all the gutrot I'd drunk in the dive run by la Tanguet – that was her name, or what they called her, one of the most hardened madames on carrer de l'Arc del Teatre, you know, overripe like those figs nobody's bothered to pick that in late autumn drop by their own weight from trees and burst open. I went there precisely because I was fascinated by the stench of autumnal mulch she gave off; that was why I went to her dive – which I think I've described to you on other occasions. Because, indeed, as in my case, you dream of the most virginal girls, the ones that look so aggressively innocent, the scent of thyme from the world's first dawn in their hair, and elusive as wild rabbits . . . but, Cruells, when your head is full of impossible dreams, of unfulfilled longings, one finds exquisite peace in a dive run by an overripe, sleazy, worn-out whore."

He sighed, hurled his empty matchbox at the skylight and continued after a pause: "You now see me embroiled in keeping an account of the chickpeas you stuff down, but I was born for better things. Who on their deathbed can't say like Maine de Biran: '*J'étais né pour quelque chose de mieux*'? But what can we do? We were all born to conquer the universe, and we conquer bugger-all! The universe is beautiful but it resists, like the virginal girls with bright aggressive eyes who are so wild and elusive. It always boils down to the same old story. One has tried everything: taming angels who like to kick, cramming geology, straddling the slimy abyss of the paranormal and Freudianism and the redemption of the enslaved. And wouldn't it be glorious to redeem them! But they resist too. The proletariat resists, probably for the same obscure, hence powerful, reasons that the universe, ectoplasm, angelic shepherdesses and geology resist. It's our voracious impotence before the feminine ocean, nailed as we are to the beach like so many Tantaluses – before the entire universe that is so beautiful it is scary! Take a look in the autumnal twilight and see for yourself. Why is it so beautiful if we can't possess it? Why aren't this immense hunger and this immense universe made for each other? No wonder man tells himself: damned hunger, what more could you want than the universe? Yet the whole universe wouldn't satisfy you – it's God you should devour!"

I was stunned when I thought I'd heard a terrible blasphemy; the cantor's voice had taken tremulous flight, not up but down, becoming gruffer and gruffer like a black bird spiralling downwards. You'd have said the cellar walls were shaking as his voice echoed round and I went into a cold sweat at what I believed to be hateful blasphemy.

"Hey, a time comes when man tells himself: it's God I want to eat up! And God lets him."

I suddenly understood him, curled up in my bed, and started to sob quietly because I couldn't take any more; because I'd understood him and couldn't stop the tears streaming down.

"Don't take it like that, don't be such a fool," he reacted. "If God didn't let us eat Him, humanity would have starved to death a long time ago! But perhaps it's time to sleep. We've turned over enough nonsense."

II

I hardly recognised Barcelona in December 1937.

I'd not been back since going to the front eighteen months earlier; the city had none of the initial excitement of that July crisscrossed by vociferous crowds brandishing guns amid the smoke from burning buildings. On the contrary, it was the deathly silence of Barcelona that struck me now.

The air tasted pestilent in a silence that was still, sad and icy. Gone from the streets were the women with cropped hair, dressed like men and carrying weapons, that were part of my last vision of Barcelona. Now you saw almost nothing but women in the street, though they didn't remind you of the "militiawomen" of those early months. What stood out now were tresses of brightly coloured hair, the strawberry and platinum blondes and redheads who left a whiff of cheap and nasty perfume in their wake. There were so many they sent you into a spin; the excess of freedom, fruit of a year and a half of revolution, hovered like a fraught, nervous shadow over those blue, green, brown and grey eyes. Here you see, I reflected, how war has separated out the Ocean and the Sahara that Soleràs talks about; men at the front and women in the rear – and all of a sudden I had been plunged into that Ocean.

What on earth was I doing in Barcelona in December 1937? It's difficult to say. For the moment, I was roaming the streets and feeling a total stranger in a city that was nevertheless mine. I felt much more of a stranger in it than in July 1936: the heady excitement had gone, to be replaced by something I felt repugnant because it seemed both hypocritical and incomprehensible, and more than a touch sardonic, weary and disillusioned. After being intoxicated by "strange cries", Barcelona was now crestfallen, resigned and cynical.

Its walls had disappeared under an astonishing number of posters. The passion of 1936, now dead and forgotten, tried to live on in those posters that nobody looked at apart from me. They were a novelty; when I'd left the city a year and a half earlier those stirring posters hadn't yet flourished and spread. Ordinary people, disenchantment writ large upon their faces, dragged themselves along like a sluggish muddy river beneath those huge multicoloured posters exalting the revolution, the proletariat and the "war on fascism"; they dragged themselves along and didn't even notice them. One displayed a foot shod in a Catalan espadrille stamping on a swastika; others, would-be republican soldiers I'd never have recognised, struck arrogant poses in spotless uniforms; there was the infamous poster we'd heard so much about, that exhorted – who? Women in the rearguard? – "Make tanks, tanks, tanks." I knew that array of hortatory, garish, bewildering posters was the work of a Llibert Milmany I'd never met. I'd learned of him from all the letters I'd read surreptitiously, but in Barcelona where everyone spoke of "comrade Llibert" as an influential person and the biggest of the wheeler-dealers, I'd have come to know anyway. The very moment I got away to Barcelona, the great Llibert Milmany had jumped ship from the *Soli* – it was beginning to go down – to scramble aboard another vessel chugging full steam ahead, or so it seemed. I didn't meet him till the following spring; while his reputation hit me from every side and he was on the lips of everyone I spoke to, he was signing off those enormous posters that were plastering the city walls: "Every single one is his work."

And recently I'd been feeling as weary and disillusioned as that grey, surly crowd. The disappearance of Soleràs, soon to be followed by Lluís' had made me feel so alone, so alone in the brigade without them – my God, how lonely I felt!

Soleràs had disappeared all of a sudden towards the end of October. One fine day we heard no more news of him, as if the earth had swallowed him up. From then on, Lluís was a changed man and always in a vile mood that we put down to the disappearance of his lifelong close friend. And then in the course of the last bloody skirmishes he too disappeared. Some assumed he was dead, others that he'd been taken prisoner. As for Soleràs, we assumed he'd gone over to our rivals, the flatfooted brigade, but we'd just learned that the flat feet had no news of his whereabouts either.

Without Lluís and Soleràs, I felt the brigade had no meaning. We were now aware, with chapter and verse and no room for doubt, of the many horrors that had been perpetrated in the rear while we were at the front; the church burning and priest murdering had stopped months ago, but they'd left bad memories that could only be erased by the re-establishment of public worship. The months slipped by and the hope began to fade that had kept us going in our worst moments of anarchist madness: a hope that the lack of order was transitory, that the autonomous government would reassert its authority and give the war the only meaning that could make it worthwhile in our eyes: the defence of what united us, of what could have united us against all the odds – the threat to our land. The months slipped by and the "strange cries" from the beginning of the war were replaced by other strange cries. We were at a loss, understood nothing, exhausted and disillusioned. What was the point of so much toil, sacrifice and spilt blood? What were we defending? Why hadn't the freedom to worship our Catholic religion – the religion of the majority of Catalans? – been re-established? There were times when one felt remorse or at least doubts about belonging to the republican side; I'd felt this keenly from the moment I was so alone, without Lluís or Soleràs.

Without them I'd sunk into depression and nothing could lighten my mood. Worse, the war was going downhill for us as one debacle followed another. Our grenadiers and infantry had to launch attacks on enemy trenches without any protection from tanks or the air as they edged forwards, and were lucky to receive occasional support from our artillery. They'd find barbed wire intact and had to cut it with pruning shears under crossfire from enemy machine guns. Some were shot to shreds and left hanging on the thorns of the wire to dry out in the sun and icy winds of the Aragonese steppes.

Even so there was a lull I particularly remember because of certain cabins I'll describe in a moment: a lull that was short-lived. We believed the front had stabilised after so much coming and going and that we would spend the winter in the lines we had finally occupied.

Autumn was advancing apace and brought one downpour after another. The parched landscape we had experienced for months now turned into a quagmire in which men and mules found it more and more difficult to get purchase. The mules sank to their girths in the low gullies along the floors of ravines where streams flowed full to their banks. If the downpours continued – and everything pointed in that direction as the clouds gathered thicker and darker – the mud would make it impossible to carry out operations in the area: orders went out to the battalions to camp down as best they could and prepare to winter there.

The soldiers in the brigade's four companies began to organise cabin-building competitions. Now the challenge was not to improvise shacks, as in the summer or when we thought we'd only need them for a few days, but shelter to protect us from the great rainstorms that had begun and from the snow and ice that might catch us in the future. The votes went to two cabins that were as different as the regions in our country. Six soldiers in the 1st Company, all from the Segarra, built a dry-stone vaulted hut so skilfully, given we had no mortar, that you'd have thought it was a stone vault – the last trace of a medieval building – had it not been for its modest proportions. They'd used clay to fashion the arch into exactly the right shape and fit; once the vault was closed, they removed the clay and used it as thick rain-proof covering for the outside. They erected more dry-stone walls at the end of each opening in what was a kind of tunnel, leaving a gap in one to serve as door, window and chimney. We were astonished by how quickly they'd erected such a solid refuge which looked like it could withstand rain, snow and ice, and even mortar shells and shrapnel bombs if it ever came to that.

This construction won votes because it was so solid, while the other attracted votes because it was so ingeniously light. It was put up by seven soldiers from the 3rd Company, who were from the Cerdanya, in the style of shelters erected by charcoal burners in the Pyrenees when they had to spend weeks in the woods keeping an eye on their stacks of green holm oak. They dug twelve trunks in deep; these supported each other like flying buttresses, six against six, after they had cut holes in one set where the others could slot. They put a mass of tangled branches over this frame, on top of which in turn was placed layer after layer of leafy pine branches with cones that were linked like roof tiles; the leaves sloped downwards to drain away water, even in torrential downpours.

Captain Picó's self-esteem was challenged and he wanted to build one too: "It would be quite wrong if the captain weren't as handy as his troops." Impartiality forces me to confess that if the construction he imagined and built was much grander and more comfortable than the others, it was all down to tricks of the trade; it had none of the elegant simplicity that we admired in the creations of the men from the Segarra and the Cerdanya.

First he used a spade to dig out the ground floor of his building, which he had conceived as circular in shape. Helped by a soldier and a machine gunner he dug a metre-deep hollow. He used a chisel and string attached to a stake in the ground to ensure the floor was completely circular; once they finished digging he looked for the dead centre, "because," he added, "things have to be done properly: that's why we are irrational beings." My secondary-school geometry was still fresh in my mind so I gave him a helping hand, a display of culture that enhanced me in his eyes. He planted a trunk in that mathematical centre; as I've no reason to hide the fact after all these years, I must add that this trunk wasn't cut in the woods. Whether it was to save time, or because he wanted them to match, all the trunks he used were posts from the telephone line to the nearby village, which was empty after the recent offensives and counteroffensives, so the line to it was out of order. He planted ten around the circumference and embedded an equal number of rafters between the trunks, with one in the middle, like so many spokes in a wheel; they were in fact rafters taken from ruined village houses. He put a layer of reed matting over the rafters he'd also stolen from those houses. Finally, he covered it all with a proper tiled roof. As he said, "I get the tiles for free."

I used to visit on occasion and have to confess that the soldiers' cabins blended into the landscape, whereas Picó's peculiar construction simply jarred and, to tell the truth, even made you feel sick. It was far too high even though the posts were fixed in a hollow: he made walls by nailing old doors, beams and other wood scavenged from the ruins in between the posts. Perhaps the machine-gun captain's outstanding qualities didn't include aesthetic taste, though I never said as much to his face. He furnished the inside using all his wiles; old ammunition boxes supplied material for a table and even a bed he stuffed with straw – people strongly suspected the mattresses in the village were lice-infested as they'd apparently been used by enemy infantry before we seized it. The central post, bristling with hooks, acted as a clothes hanger and between it and the surrounding posts he placed a ring of stones on the floor where he lit his wood fire. That was the reason he'd wanted it to be so high: the smoke collected in the ceiling and slowly made its way out through a hole between the tiles. Even so, it was best to sit, or rather lie down, if you wanted to breathe tolerably unsmoky air; the moment you stood up, you got one hell of a cough. Picó was worried by this drawback and didn't rest until he'd found the solution in a sufficiently long, centimetres-wide pipe among the rubble, probably from some system of water pipes. He used wire to suspend the pipe from the ceiling, with one end over the hearth and the other poking out of a hole in the wooden wall. He didn't set it vertically, as any of us might have thought necessary, but almost horizontally; we were filled with admiration when we saw the pipe draw the smoke and puff it out in big clouds like the chimney of a steam train.

He'd offer me breakfast if I got there at the right time. We were beginning to run very short of powdered milk; our breakfasts were usually black coffee that Supplies still managed to provide, though it was disgusting. He'd put a pan with a little egg on the embers and fry breadcrumbs, which he'd put on his tin plate and pour boiling coffee over. His red-hot soup of coffee and egg-fried breadcrumbs was very tasty, I will vouch for that: it had been his usual breakfast in his heyday as a foreign legionary in Africa, or so he said.

All these cabins had been built close to the trenches in muddy, rainy weather because it was thought best to avoid long walks between guard duty and relief. I can't remember if I ever said that our machine-gun captain had huge corns, which meant he struggled to walk when it was wet, and he reckoned his corns could forecast the weather better than any barometer. I finally managed to tackle them at the beginning of that exceptionally wet autumn; until then all my suggestions had foundered on his stubborn decision to hang on to them. One day it was agreed that I'd bring the necessary tools the following morning; I would be the one to remove them. "If Dr Puig tries to touch me," he'd threatened, "I'll turn the company's machine guns on him."

When I appeared that morning, they told me he was in the trench. Unusually, the sun was shining and I found him chattering excitedly to two machine-gunners, not right inside the quagmire of the trench but sitting on the parapet sandbags. It was lovely sunbathing in that mellow autumnal light; with binoculars you could see the enemy trench three kilometres away. It was a good long way and the front was perfectly calm at the time. We decided to proceed to the operation there and then, and not in the muddy trench. I sat Picó down on an ammunitions box; the parapet broadened out at that point because it was where the machine-gun nest was positioned. He jokingly asked the two soldiers to stand up behind him and grip his shoulders tightly, "this is the first fucking operation I've ever had and I'm not sure how my reflexes will react." I knelt down in front of him and very carefully began to eradicate the hardest of his extraordinary calluses. I heard him say: "Don't be upset if I chuck you as far as the enemy trenches; it will only be a reflex action, nothing personal." And then something happened that none of us were expecting.

A tremendous explosion blew up Picó's cabin – it was, as I said, close to the trenches, like the others – and sent telephone posts, doors, planks and tiles flying. Shrapnel bombs devastated the other cabins, which were similarly blown to smithereens, and began to explode on the parapets, destroying them and bursting the sacks of earth. The expansion wave from one of these shrapnel bombs blasted the four of us into the bottom of the trench.

Picó and I struggled to our feet, bruised and battered by our violent fall; the two soldiers were dead. Bombs occasionally fell on the surrounding rocks and, as they couldn't sink into soft clay like the others, lumps of dry shrapnel hurtled into the distance, whistling over our heads. Some whizzed into the trench and scored the wall like a blunt knife blade. This flying shrapnel had hit the two soldiers in the face because they were standing up, while Picó and I had survived because we were closer to the ground. The shelling continued and we knew it was only a warm-up by their artillery. An infantry attack would inevitable follow, as it was unlikely the enemy would otherwise waste so much powder on salvoes.

For the first time in the entire war the lust for blood went to my head, as it did to the others' – to everyone.

Rather than try to join Dr Puig and the stretcher bearers, I stayed in the trench with Picó, and through a gap in the sandbags we saw small contingents of the enemy crawling towards us through the brush as if they'd suddenly dropped down near our barbed-wire fences. I was fascinated by the expressions of amazement rather than hate on their faces.

Our machine gunners mowed them down as they tried to cut the barbed wire and pull themselves through between the wooden stakes. Their tanks and aeroplanes must have been engaged at a more crucial spot on the front, so that was probably just a "diversion" as they say in military jargon; at the time it was unheard of to attack entrenched positions without the support of tanks. Two of the soldiers had managed to slip through the barbed wire and were now on their feet shouting: "Don't shoot! We're coming over to you! Long live Russia!"

That cry ought to have seemed highly suspect, as odd and ridiculous as it did to us, but one of our lieutenant fusiliers from the 1st Company, a veteran who should have known better, put his head above the parapet and greeted them with a message of peace. One of the two climbed up on the sandbags as if to embrace him. His colleague stayed between the parapet and fence, aimed his Mauser and shot the lieutenant, who fell flat on his face in the muddy depths of the trench, a dead man. The first soldier, still standing on the parapet, now threw hand grenades at us; he pulled them out of a big bag by his side, scattering them as if he were sowing a field, while he urged his side to climb up and make the most of our disarray.

I have only hazy memories of what happened next. Picó had sat down behind the machine gun and was firing serenely but he soon emptied its chamber, though we had replacement guns, excellent Mausers, and a large box of hand grenades. Only six of us were left in that corner of the trench; Picó and I had each taken a Mauser and when the barrels were red hot from so much firing we switched them to allow them to cool; now and then we threw grenades at the enemy: "This'll make your day," shouted a strangely content Picó with every one he chucked. Those I threw didn't explode; he had to show me how to release the safety catch a few moments before hurling them. I didn't have a clue. I don't know how I managed to shoot the Mauser as I'd never shot one before. All I do know is that I felt an excitement you can't compare to anything else in this world.

We repelled that attack, though not the others which followed later from tanks, aeroplanes and much larger numbers of infantry. The line of trenches where we thought we were going to spend the autumn, if not the winter, was obliterated. The rout came next.

This may now seem difficult to understand – and it is – but I tried to go over to the enemy immediately after these exploits. When I think back now I see how incongruous that was. Perhaps war and peace are like sleep and wakefulness; when we're awake we can't recognise the man who was asleep a few moments earlier. The man in peacetime doesn't understand the man at war: all these years later I'm as ashamed that I shot at them as I am that I tried to go over to their side so soon after.

Ours was part of the biggest debacle of that autumn. Entire brigades and divisions had fallen apart and all manner of soldiers were mixed up in a motley gang of fugitives from the front. It was total panic, a nightmare. I was one more stray among groups of panic-stricken fugitives. I saw only strange faces. I heard talk of divisions that were news to me: the Durruti, the Líster, and God knows which others. Nobody could tell me where our division was – it was equally unfamiliar to them – let alone our battalion or brigade. I spent days trying to find my bearings and my colleagues. In that chaos it was like looking for a needle in a haystack.

And then one evening a medical captain "reclaimed" me and attached me to his company. I don't really remember what division it belonged to, only that they were anarchists. This doctor-captain was tiny, a dry stick sporting a pencil-thin moustache that gave him a Don Juanish air, a Don Juan from a shanty town. He blinked all the time and told an endless stream of racy stories, usually starring a priest.

Why on earth would I have wanted to continue in that division, where I felt a total misfit? I couldn't stand the diet of scabrous jokes – it never varied – a minute longer. One night, when the Don Juan anarchist of a medic was snoring, I slipped silently out of bed and left the shack. I was carrying my haversack with the portable telescope I hadn't yet lost: that happened in the last weeks of the war.

I started walking in the opposite direction to the troops in flight, all alone. There was mayhem in the area, so anything was possible. I walked throughout the night and nobody asked me where I was going.

The first light of dawn caught me in a juniper wood. I spent the day curled up in some kind of animal lair. The silence was intense and threatening and the solitude so oppressive I found the occasional stray bullet that whistled by strangely comforting company. At the time several kilometres separated the two armies and I was almost in the middle. I had four crusts of bread and four cans of condensed milk I'd snaffled from the anarchist battalion before scarpering on the quiet – enough to keep me going for four days.

What I was attempting wasn't at all easy as I didn't know the exact position of the front lines. Nor was I sure what I really wanted to achieve: either go over to the other side or reach the frontier with France by walking at night and hiding by day; perhaps I'd reach the Pyrenees over four days' hard slog. The truth was that I was lost and had surrendered myself to chance or Providence; all I knew for certain was that a never-ending sadness had taken possession of me and was gradually eating me alive. Soleràs had left the brigade and Lluís was probably dead. Who could assure me that Picó, the commander and Dr Puig weren't dead as well? Who could assure me that anything was left of our battalion, our brigade, our whole division? If not, why wasn't there a trace of them to be found?

When night finally fell I started walking again, guided by the constellations. Above all, I wanted to know where the others were and get some idea of the situation in general. All I knew was that the others were to my west. So I walked towards Sagittarius which, at that time of year, appeared on the horizon above the spot where the sun had just gone down. When Sagittarius set in turn, the Milky Way served to guide me, and how it sparkled in the heart of that steppe, in that dry, transparent air, in that pitch-black sky! It's the most vivid memory I have of those strange nights: it was like a whirlwind of diamond specks and I would stop to look at it through my telescope; at other times I'd suddenly feel my solitude was a claw strangling me. How I would have cried, crybaby that I am, how I would have cried like a lost child without those stars for company! And the bitter scent of thyme, with the spindly juniper, the only vegetation on those deserted wastes – a bitter scent of thyme the icy wind swirled into my face . . . ! I walked so instinctively, training my eyes on the Milky Way, that I sometimes suspected I must be suffering a fresh attack of sleepwalking: today, all these years later, I wish I had been, that my conscious, responsible will had played no part; now I feel I was deserting, something I never felt then, but I wasn't sleepwalking. Such attacks leave no memories: I'd never have known I'd had any if other people hadn't told me.

I should be under no illusion: I was fully aware that I was trying to desert.

The following night I heard voices in the distance, the first I'd heard in three days. And once more I hesitated and couldn't decide; I realised it would be almost impossible to reach the Pyrenees. Go back? Why should I if Lluís and Soleràs were no longer in the brigade and perhaps Picó, the commander and the doctor dead or taken prisoner? I was about to take one of the most serious steps in my life: I was about to choose my enemy. Up to that point I'd found myself on one side not through any choice of my own, it was the situation that chose me – not because I'd ever taken a decision that way, and I'd never thought the others were my enemies: they were simply the others. I'd never thought of them as my enemies! Not even when I'd fired bullets or hurled grenades at them: that had been a bout of bloodlust that left me feeling deeply ashamed when it faded. Instinct had taken hold of me and made me act not like myself, but like someone else: the same thing would have happened if I'd been on the other side, that seemed self-evident. I hadn't shot at them in that surge of madness because they were enemies, but for reasons I couldn't explain. And it had been like this from the moment I hadn't chosen my side; I'd simply stayed where the war had taken me by surprise. That was how it had been so far. Now I was going to decide; from now on, as a result of a choice made by my own free will, my friends would become my enemies and *vice versa*.

The voices were right there, in the end, some thirty metres away.

My mind was such a haze I never registered that I couldn't understand a word they were saying. It was a long time before I took any real notice: their strange gabble contained not a single intelligible word.

They're Moors, I thought, and curled up silently between two junipers, the branches of which were shaped into a kind of grotto. The guttural, nasal noises became clearer as they drew near; I cowered and shrank like a cornered animal. Moors had never remotely entered my head until I heard those shrill nasal sounds, but when I listened carefully they didn't in fact seem at all shrill or nasal, simply incomprehensible. Could they be Basques?

I knew that the last remnants of the Basque army, survivors of a desperate struggle, had reached the coast of Gascony to join up with

Catalan troops via France. Blessed Providence has taken me by the hand, I thought suddenly. Better to go over to the Basques than the Moors.

Their voices came and went, as if they belonged to a patrol searching those woods. Despite the cold, I was sweating; I could feel beads of sweat on my lips, and one slipped down my spine like quicksilver.

That very second I glimpsed a campfire through the junipers a hundred metres from my den. They'd just lit the dry gorse and the flames spat like firecrackers. I crossed myself before crawling out: I just had to find out who they were. I'd stopped sweating and felt unusually lucid; a branch of thorns scratched my cheek like a paw with nails of steel. I managed to draw close to their fire without alerting them, close enough to see their faces lit up in the darkness by the flickering flames as in a chiaroscuro.

What horrific faces! My God! Their faces were so horrific!

I straightened my back ready to run for it. It was an idiotic thing to do.

Bullets buzzed round me like a swarm of hungry mosquitoes. I had one wish: to fly. And I flew. Not through the air, but downwards. Until my flight came to a sudden halt and I felt stunned, like a bird felled by a bullet.

I tried to move my legs but they wouldn't respond, as if they belonged to someone else; they felt alien to me whenever I touched them. I could make out the penetrating voices of the Moors as they came and went: then the noise gave way to a strange silence.

Why couldn't I see any stars up above? It had been a peaceful night, at least until I fell. But where had I fallen? It was so silent, so cold, so pitch black, and I couldn't move my legs . . . If only day would break! Though they'd find me with the first light of day . . . In that stillness the damp cold penetrated to the marrow of my bones; then the voices came closer . . . My God, may night be eternal!

It was a miracle: I could hear them now and understood everything the Moors were saying! I relaxed, my legs responded again; I saw the starry sky, the Milky Way with its trail of diamond dust, and started sobbing.

The tears streamed down and I could do nothing to stop them: they were speaking Catalan. I'd have liked to cry out for help, but I lost consciousness.

"What a fucking mess" were the first words I heard when I came round. And when I opened my eyes I saw a face I wasn't expecting to see at all, the cross-eyed look of Commander Rosich's aide-de-camp. "What a fucking mess. What the hell are you doing at the bottom of this millpond? Lucky it's empty!"

And still on a high from the latest battle, Cross-eyes started to tell me about recent encounters: we'd fought off the Moors, those shit-bags; there are piles of corpses everywhere, piles of wounded, fucking awful, but the rout's over, we've stopped running like rabbits."

"So where's the commander?"

"He's very near here. The Moors almost ambushed us. Did you know we finally found Lluís? He was discovered by chance in a field hospital a long way from here; he's very badly wounded. A nasty wound! He was picked up by stretcher bearers from an anarchist division – they took him to Almirete and never bothered to inform us. Each brigade and division looks after itself, do you know? Do you also know that an anarchist division opened fire on a communist division? What a fucking mess . . ."

*

However, it was futile trying to convince Auntie that not all battalions and brigades were the same, that the air on our side was fresh and healthy and not like the rotten stench in the rearguard. In her eyes it was all very simple: there were two fields, one wheat, the other wild oats, separated by barbed wire fences. I'd have preferred not to set foot in her place to avoid all these annoying arguments – she was still living in her mansion in Sarrià – but I was forced to by a ridiculous piece of bad luck.

I took a tram as soon as I got off the train, because there were hardly any taxis. People piled in at each stop: we were bunched together on the platform like grapes waiting to be pressed. Then I suddenly felt a warm, sinuous body lean hard into mine so I could feel its heart beating; tresses of red hair were tickling me around the mouth and her scent was making me feel dizzy. All at once two yellow eyes stared shamelessly into mine; could eyes possibly be that yellow? It was a quiet, cynical stare the like of which I'd never seen before, and I felt her shifting, as if she were trying to stand on tiptoe to press even harder into me, perhaps so her mouth could reach mine. I did my best to elbow my way through the crowd to jump off the moving tram. My God, I thought, that's because I'm wearing a military uniform; a surplice earned the respect of the most vulgar women.

I put my hand instinctively into the hellhole of my pocket: my wallet had walked.

What could I do now? That panther, I thought, prompted by her yellow eyes, that underwater panther must have got off at the next stop and disappeared among the thousands of anonymous faces; it would be like looking for a needle in a haystack. Strange to say, I felt a degree of warmth towards the woman and could only admire the skill with which she'd relieved me of my wallet. That panther, I kept repeating to myself, that underwater panther . . . Why underwater? An underwater panther floating in the warm waters of the feminine Ocean: Soleràs' peculiar outpourings had come to mind.

I put my hand on my chest – where the absence of my wallet created a depressing emptiness – and tried like a fool to remember if I'd ever seen a girl with yellow eyes before the war, and this worried me more than my missing wallet. Then I realised I couldn't have lunch and would have to sleep on a street bench, unless I went to Military Headquarters, but how could I do that now the papers justifying my presence in Barcelona had vanished with my wallet? They'd clap me straight into a cell as a deserter until they could investigate my case!

I had no choice but to head up to Sarrià and ask Auntie for a handout.

After the inevitable emotional outpourings – after all, we remain nephew and aunt – the conversation became as absurd as I'd anticipated: "Why do you side with those ragamuffins?"

"But, Auntie, if you could only see the others! They're more ragamuffin than we are, I assure you; think for a minute how the whole of the textile industry is in republican territory."

"Have you forgotten that your people have murdered relatives of ours?"

"So what do you expect me to do, Auntie? Go over to the other side? Every day somebody or other changes trench; you have to understand that it's a two-way flow. And people desert from each side for the same reason: they're all disgusted by the horrors being perpetrated by their respective rearguards. Soleràs – someone who has disappeared 'without leaving a forwarding address' as postmen say – often said the most outlandish things, but he was right. He once told me that if the war lasted long enough we'd find that all the republican soldiers had gone over to the fascists and vice versa."

Auntie wouldn't listen to reason; in her eyes the others were knights of the Holy Grail, tall, slim, fair, clean-shaven and clad in spotless ironed uniforms – grasping a sword, a noble sword, a sword like a lily, like an Easter candle . . .

But let's get back to why I was in Barcelona in December 1937. It was all down to those letters that I'd read surreptitiously; for as long as I can remember I've suffered from this shameful weakness: I'd stand behind the door and listen to the long half-whispered conversations between Auntie and Monsenyor, or would read, when she wasn't looking, a letter that happened to linger on her table, or even glance at a letter being read by an unknown woman who'd happened to sit beside me in a tram. I'm not the sensual kind, but I am a nosey parker. It's as if the attraction others feel for those of their own flesh, I feel for their own lives – something that's equally shameful, if not more so.

It was all down to those letters that Lluís kept well hidden in his haversack.

Once the front had been re-established after a series of routs, it was decided that our brigade should be sent to a "dead front" to re-form. A deserted valley lay between our positions and the enemy's, within which lay five or six hamlets that had been abandoned by the local country people because they'd been shelled so often. Seven or eight kilometres as the crow flies lay between our trenches and the enemy: we were out of range of their infantry fire and supporting weaponry. Moreover, there'd been heavy snowfall and so long as three feet of snow covered the mountains, new operations would be impossible on that front: all was quiet! That's why we'd been sent there. We'd suffered heavy casualties in recent battles, a lot of dead, a lot of badly wounded men and, above all, lots of men who'd disappeared, as was usual after a rout. The brigade had to recover, look after its wounded and, if possible, trace those who'd disappeared. We needed time to receive new supplies of arms to replace those lost or destroyed, and new recruits to fill the gaping holes.

Our battalion occupied two villages on that dead front, Santa Espina del Purroy and Villar del Purroy. The Purroy is a river that flows between the two: the road, a mere cart track, follows the course of the river. It was ten kilometres from Villar to Santa Espina.

Both villages were uninhabited at the time and were falling into ruin. They'd been taken, evacuated and retaken at the beginning of the year, burned by anarchists and fascists and finally bombed out during recent battles. The battalion headquarters and medical section were in Villar, closer to the rearguard, and the company of machine gunners in Santa Espina, closer to the trenches. The four artillery companies, or more precisely the little that was left of them, occupied trenches along the ridge, facing the deserted valley, quite a way from either village.

Local game had multiplied magnificently in those mountains and woods that had been more or less completely abandoned by their inhabitants for eighteen months; our men hunted rabbit, hare and partridge, more than we could ever eat as it was child's play following their tracks in the snow. We found olive oil and wine, almonds, walnuts and coal in the cellars of the ruined houses, everything the unfortunate country people had been forced to abandon in their rush to escape. Then there were villages in the valley where the most unexpected things were to be found: for example, a hurdy-gurdy the machine gunners hoisted triumphantly on the back of one of their mules and brought back. Our men sometimes met up with soldiers from the opposite lines and like good brothers shared out whatever they found. Why should they have felt like killing each other in this lull between operations?

I lived in Villar with my superior, medical lieutenant Dr Puig, and often went to Santa Espina to see my machine gunner friends. Captain Picó had established himself in the only house still standing that had belonged to the biggest landowner, Don Andalecio, murdered by the anarchists in the first days of the war. They'd also set fire to his house, but the enormously thick walls had resisted. There were good size sitting rooms and bedrooms, because it was a huge house even though the walls and ceilings had been blackened by smoke from the blaze and there was no furniture at all. The dining room occupied a large part of the ground floor; the chimney hood was ample enough to accommodate three large, high-backed benches that

Picó had requisitioned from another house: he'd put one on each side and one across, so the three made a kind of small, cosy compartment around the fire. I remember them well because we spent our evenings on those three seats over the nights I spent in Santa Espina, those endless autumnal and winter evenings, before and after the ladies came.

Picó had big fires lit using whole beams retrieved from the house rubble. On rainy nights we'd hear the sound of walls collapsing here and there in the village: a dismal rumble of stones toppling that made you feel sad when you thought of the humble family that wasn't going to find hearth and home when they returned to their birthplace after the war.

When Lluís left the field hospital in Almirete he was sent to join the machine gunners because nothing remained of his old artillery company; initially he'd been sent to the Weapons Support section, but their 0.70 cannons and 0.85 mortars only existed in the imagination or on paper. The hospital in Almirete was clearly a waste of time, though luckily Lluís wasn't there long, just the time it took to extract the Mauser bullet from his left forearm and for the wound to heal. The first rumours had grossly exaggerated his wound – soldiers often magnified injuries – but Lluís *was* behaving strangely. We assumed he was in a bad temper because Soleràs had disappeared; they were close friends and had been inseparable from secondary school.

We celebrated Lluís' return with a dinner in Santa Espina given by the machine gunners' captain. The commander, Dr Puig and I drove from Villar in the usual Ford, the survivor of so many battles and routs. "More loyal to the army of Catalonia," the commander would say, "than many political commissars." At the time we were bereft of political commissars, and that was how we and the commander wanted it; the commander, who couldn't stand the sight of them, said "they've all made a run for it" in the recent battles, which wasn't true – or at least not in every case – though it was true enough that we didn't miss them.

"Now," said Commander Rosich, "we've supplied our soldiers with hurdy-gurdies rather than commissars; they may not be as educational, but they're a sight more entertaining."

In the course of that dinner in Lluís' honour Picó announced his latest find in no man's land, that is, the deserted valley: he claimed it was a gilded silver cup "undoubtedly from the time of the Moors". He had his cook fill it with mellow wine to drink to our health.

"Captain!" I shouted.

"What's wrong?"

"Where did you find that cup? It's a chalice!"

The commander gave a start: "Picó, did you find it in a church? Have you never heard of the blood of God?"

"The blood of God!" said Picó, dropping the chalice and sending wine all over the flagstones. While I picked it up and put it in a safe place, he mumbled: "Cruells, if you think I don't know what a chalice is . . . I also studied in a seminary."

"Obviously," commented Dr Puig.

Lluís was very surly; he said hardly a word during the meal. All the same he insisted I stay overnight with them in Santa Espina and Dr Puig raised no objection. At the time, we had almost no work in the battalion's medical section.

That was the first time I had spent the night with Picó and Lluís; subsequently I'd often go to Santa Espina from Villar at the end of the day in the brougham the captain sent me so I could dine and sleep with them. In a ruined stable he'd found a brougham with huge wheels that could really speed along. One of its springs was broken but Picó soldered it one morning; he was quite a handyman. My first outings were a success and pulled by one of the machine gunners' mules it covered the distance between the two villages, nearly all downhill, in three quarters of an hour.

The brougham also proved excellent for expeditions to the deserted valley, to no man's land. Shortly after that first dinner in Santa Espina, an order came from the brigadier forbidding soldiers to visit the villages in that valley; only Picó and Lluís had permission to make forays there. The commander issued this order because he was shocked by our soldiers organising games of football with the enemy in the threshing areas of the villages. The hierarchy wanted to put a stop to such friendly get-togethers.

Picó, Lluís and I slept together in the same top-floor room, practically the attic, in Santa Espina. Picó had chosen it because the room had escaped fire damage and the first night Lluís and I spent there, Picó warned us: "It's forbidden to do a 1902 out of the window."

It was true that the window looked over the village high street, but the street was only a pile of rubble and rubbish.

"This village is one big heap of manure," grunted Lluís. "You don't mean we must go down to the yard in our pyjamas if we have an emergency?"

"Doing a 1902" was an expression we used in the brigade; in the course of the war each brigade created its own slang. The commander of the flat feet was a Josep, "something which in itself," said Commander Rosich, "isn't at all reprehensible." For his saint's day our commander had sent him a bottle of Sauternes, "Genuine Sauternes, vintage 1902", with a card: "I'm sending you this gift, to which all the heads of battalion in my brigade have contributed." I hardly need tell you what the collaboration consisted of. "We want you to see this as proof," he added to the congratulations card of which he circulated numerous copies, "of the true spirit of fraternity that exists between our republican brigades. May this bottle bring to your mouth the best possible memories of us all!"

So Picó didn't want us to do a 1902 out of the window and onto the high street; he felt he was the feudal lord of the Santa Espina manor and took his responsibilities seriously: "This isn't like Villar," he said. "I'm the one in charge here. I want hygiene and culture."

After that he showed us "a hoard of cultural treasures" he'd been assembling: a huge suitcase full of books. They were slim, soft-covered volumes in bad condition and piled together without rhyme or reason. We didn't need to dip into them to get a fairly exact idea of the literary genre.

"It's my campaign against pornography," he told us. "Our soldiers are too young and too uncultured to read works as fully fledged as these. I confiscate them. By ensuring that they don't read anything unhealthy, I've found a way to dedicate my own evenings to literature, thus killing two birds with one stone! I'd not get any shut-eye without a touch of Romanticism."

One rainy night the candles had been snuffed out for some time, but I couldn't get to sleep. Picó was snoring: powerful, resonant, even snores that nurtured a feeling of peace and security. I slipped stealthily off my mattress – we each slept on our own on the floor; the straw mattress rustled with every movement I made. I was intending to do what Picó had forbidden: I felt an urgent need. Once I was out of bed, the cold made my teeth chatter and that reminded me of Picó's: I remembered he'd left them on the only chair, in a glass of water. Careful you don't bump into the chair! The small, low glassless window beckoned from the back of the bedroom; I tiptoed over, striving not to disturb the other obstacle, the suitcase of fully fledged works. I was soon level with the window: in the meantime the rain had turned to snow and thick flurries of flakes were falling softly and silently. The only light in the world was the hazy gleam from the snow; the sky seemed darker than the earth. Some flakes strayed into the bedrooms. Picó hadn't heard me and was still snoring; Lluís was also asleep, I could hear his regular breathing. I was now groping my way back; I was following the wall round when, surprise! surprise! my hand came upon Lluís' haversack on a hook. His haversack, Lluís' haversack. My hand slipped inside quite spontaneously and emerged with the bundle of letters.

I'd been so intrigued by that bundle of letters! I'd often seen Lluís read and re-read them as if obsessed. Once I even asked him who they were from and he replied drily, with hatred in his eyes: "From my wife." That was all I knew.

It had been too much for me: I'd taken the letters from the haversack and was now going downstairs. A cold wind from the North Pole was blowing up the stairs and my teeth were chattering: I sneezed loudly on the landing. I stood still for a few seconds. Silence. They hadn't heard me.

With the tongs I stirred a mountain of embers in the hearth and the cinders suddenly sparkled, so welcoming on a night like that! I lit the oil lamp, sat on one of the fireside benches and started to read.

I now feel horribly ashamed; reading those letters is one of the most shameful acts I have ever committed. What small, delicate handwriting, what comforting embers; I read eagerly, became more and more passionately drawn into that secret life I was discovering, increasingly alarmed from letter to letter, anticipating an unhappy ending – unhappy for Lluís . . . I felt so relieved! Nothing was beyond repair, nothing was broken forever; it could be soldered. It only needed a third party with goodwill to take on the task, and I would be that third providential person.

I felt a wave of tenderness course through me: life was so lovely! There were good works to do, wounds to anoint with balsam, unhappy friends to restore to their lost bliss; at the time I thought the irresistible impulse to read those letters must have come from on high. Yes, that much was obvious: a voice had summoned me! I could do so much good now that I knew where the problem lay!

It was late, very late; I'd spent five hours reading letters and yet more letters. I had to go back to the bedroom before they woke up and return the letters to their rightful place.

Life is so lovely, I told myself as I crawled back to bed; if only I could consult Dr Gallifa . . . but where might he be? What if it were him? That most ordinary of apostles . . . I curled up under the four cotton blankets, shuddering delightfully like a cat; Picó was still snoring; Lluís had heard nothing; the snow was still falling. The snow! My mind felt suddenly inspired. That was a dead front; now with that snowfall . . . Just a few days earlier we'd found out that the officers of the flatfooted brigade – also stationed on the dead front like us – had smuggled their wives to the front with the idea of spending Christmas with them. Lluís couldn't go to the rearguard to see her; no leave was being given, and the Ministry for War was being very strict about it. But she could come to Santa Espina. She had to come; it was vital for them to make peace with each other.

My bed had grown warmer and I curled up feeling tender and confident. Life was so lovely! Other people's lives, I thought all of a sudden; then I wanted to cry. I was dead tired and full of self-pity, but the pity and sleepiness were also tender and lovely. It is so comforting to go to sleep feeling good, generous and better than everyone else; so comforting to curl up in a warm, dry bed while outside snowflakes fall endlessly. . .

*

So that was how I came to be in Barcelona in December 1937.

But now my wallet, which contained my papers, had been stolen – the precious "official paperwork" we'd concocted between us: the report from medical lieutenant Puig to battalion commander Rosich informing him of the "urgent necessity to send medical adjutant Cruells to the rearguard to procure various indispensable medicines for the courageous soldiers engaged in the fight against fascism", followed by the permission from the battalion commander to the brigadier – who'd promised to turn a blind eye and let us get on with it – and finally the latter's order to medical adjutant Cruells to go immediately to Barcelona "using his own means to carry out urgent tasks on behalf of his unit"; all this red tape duly stamped at every control point, the inevitable controls at every crossroads. If only that underwater panther had left my documents alone! As soon as I had some money, thanks to Auntie, I sent an extremely urgent telegram to the battalion asking for another set of "official paperwork". In the meantime if the military police in Barcelona asked me for my papers, how would I ever justify my presence in the city?

I first paid a visit to Dr Puig's wife. She lived in a luridly luxurious flat, with a surfeit of mirrors, gilded frames and imitation crystal-glass chandeliers. A uniformed maid ushered me into the drawing room. I felt guilty at leaving footprints from my mud-spattered military boots on the waxed and polished parquet, marks that were as visible as those the rabbits left on the snow on our dead front. Sra Puig kept me waiting for half an hour; I'd foolishly arrived early and I expect she was still making herself presentable. Her toilette, as I later discovered, was a complex, arduous business. Finally she appeared, wrinkling her nose slightly as she looked down on me from a great height. She was most elegant, a tall, statuesque platinum blonde with deep aquamarine blue eyes – a lady fully conscious of her own splendour. Personally, I feel inhibited by this kind of woman; I tried to say my piece as naturally as I could, despite feeling so awkward. She listened intently but seemed taken aback, if not sarcastic, and looked at me askance, a touch suspiciously. She'd received a letter from her husband and knew the essentials; she agreed to travel "since my husband wants me to" and she had to obey him. I finished what I had to say, apologised, and dithered over superfluous detail, feeling as gauche as ever: "It's a unique opportunity, perhaps there'll never be another in this whole war, and God knows how long it will last. And as it's a dead front, with such deep snow . . ."

"Why doesn't he come to Barcelona? That would be much easier . . ."

"That's impossible. They're not granting leave. We're lucky they've given the whole brigade leave, to be spent on a dead front. You can't ask for more at the moment. It's a completely dead front; we're out of range of the firepower supporting the enemy infantry, just imagine . . . the 0.70 cannon, for example . . . the range of a cannon is usually a kilometre for every centimetre of calibre and we are more than seven kilometres from the enemy's advanced positions."

I'd wandered off into unnecessary explanations and she was looking at me as if to say "What the hell do I care?"

"I'm telling you all this because I can see that in Barcelona you don't realise that a dead front is an oasis of peace. Women and children can spend the Christmas holidays there in holy peace and be much better fed than in Barcelona. We're not short of anything!"

"You can forget the children," she interrupted drily with the aplomb this kind of woman assumes when talking about her children. "I'm sure they would only see behaviour that would set a bad example."

When she'd received the letters from her husband, she'd decided straightaway that the children would stay with her parents. I already knew from Dr Puig that his in-laws owned the biggest pork delicatessen in the Boqueria market and were filthy rich. Back in the street my mouth felt parched after so much talk; a new wallet now warmed my heart, stuffed with notes thanks to Auntie: a swollen wallet brings such peace of mind! There was a drone in the air and distant explosions; the streets were deserted as if the whole city was dead. Just then sirens began to wail and I realised what was happening; the explosions sounded much closer. I started walking; Picó's flat wasn't very far, perhaps half an hour away. On the way I went into a bar – the only one from which the bartender hadn't run off to a shelter – to slake my thirst and deal with my other need while I was about it. "You soldiers," said the bartender as I came out of the lavatories, "must think this bombing of Barcelona is child's play. Even *I* have got used to . . ."

Sra Picó opened the door. I was ushered into a small, cheerful flat with white-wood chairs brightly painted by the lady of the house herself – she told me that: pale red, almond green, canary yellow, their knobs splashed with glitter. She must have been between twenty-five and thirty and was slight, slim and olive-skinned, and a nervous chatterbox: "My husband also studied for the priesthood," she told me with a jolly laugh as if it were an idea that should amuse me. "You must imagine I have a weak spot for aspiring priests."

"How do you know I'm one?"

"He says so in his letter. He's written to me about everything. He writes incredibly well; his forte is his spelling. I know everything: who you are, why you have come to Barcelona, and I'm so happy! It's a year and a half since I last saw him . . . he must have said all kinds of things about me! I also know that this wonderful idea of a Christmas get-together was yours However . . ."

Her eyes opened wide as if she'd had a sudden surprise, and looked me up and down and back again: "Quick, go into the bedroom and take a look in the mirror. You must be very absent-minded!"

After she'd mercifully shut the door, I stood in front of the mirror and understood what the mystery was all about. I'd not buttoned up properly in the lavatories and a piece of shirt tail was sticking out.

She was waiting for me in the dining room with the aperitifs on the table; it must have been midday. I felt downcast.

"Don't worry, it could happen to anyone."

She laughed out loud. Just as well something so stupid happened here, I thought, and not at Sra Puig's! Sra Picó apologised: "You'll have to drink it without olives, anchovies or crisps. You can't find food these days! Though any amount of alcohol . . . !"

Afterwards she insisted on showing me various samples of her husband's talents. I'd noticed that she only referred to him by his surname: "Picó is such a handyman!" She particularly wanted me to see how the electricity worked in the dining room: it was very complicated, with different-coloured bulbs you could combine in a number of ways. You could have red, green, blue and yellow lights or a mixture. She wanted to show me other tricks invented by her husband, the ex-beadle: "They admitted him into the Science faculty because of his talents." I remembered the pedal fan that Picó had invented to frighten off flies during the good times we enjoyed in Olivel. He was in fact a tremendous "do-it-yourself man" and it was evident his wife worshipped him.

When I left there I headed off to see Commander Rosich's wife, who lived in a large, gloomy flat on carrer de Cervelló, one of those narrow side streets that look over the Boqueria market. The furniture was very *fin de siècle*, tawdry and handed down; you couldn't imagine anything more unfashionable and pretentious. Sra Rosich was small and dark like Sra

Picó, but gone to fat, already grey-haired and well past her forties. She was polite and friendly and summoned Marieta, who seemed very tall for a nine-year-old, skinny too, sallow, with huge dark eyes. Her mother told her to greet me properly, which she did with a small curtsey; then she suddenly shot this question at me that she was to repeat several times: "They won't kill my daddy, will they?"

"Of course they won't!" I exclaimed, taken aback. "Why would they want to kill such a lovely person?"

The commander's wife wanted to know how they would get through the army control points. The presence of women, except for locals, was strictly forbidden along the whole front; the Rosichs were professionals, unlike the rest of us, and she was the only one to ask such a question.

"We'll go by train," I explained, "as far as Puebla de Híjar, where the militarised zone, properly speaking, begins. Our Ford will be waiting for us outside the station; you will wear traditional rural dresses over your own and then it will be full steam ahead. The farmers' wives in the area often ask us to let them ride in army cars and trucks to travel from one village to another, so you won't attract any attention. We've found lots of traditional costumes in the villages in no man's land and in all sizes. Everything's been carefully thought through! Obviously once you're in Villar you can take off the local costumes and make yourself comfortable once again; the only military authority there is your husband's. We'll be 'in our own little fief,' as Picó likes to say; you won't have to worry about a thing."

My "official paperwork" had still not arrived; in my telegram to the commander I'd asked for it to be sent to his wife's address. The delay was beginning to irritate me: it could undermine a whole operation that had left nothing to chance. I told Sra Rosich I would be back that evening.

It was past two o'clock and I was starving. Walking in the labyrinth of side streets around the Boqueria I could feel that well-padded wallet pressing benevolently against my heart when the board in front of an inn caught my eye: *Rosted see bass*. Spelling must have been that innkeeper's forte, as it was Picó's, and this was remarkable on more than two levels, but the aroma of roast sea bass made my mouth water. I sat down at a round marble-topped table on the pavement; despite the time of year, I preferred to have lunch in the open air than venture into what looked a rather dubious dive. I felt the dampness rather than the cold from Barcelona's tenements seeping through the soles of my shoes and climbing my legs. From my small table I could see the great covered market, appallingly empty: hardly anything had sold there for months. A down-at-heel woman who'd just picked up some thing or other from a small pile of rubbish insulted me as she walked by: "Stuff yourself, you chancer, and scoff while my men rot at the front!"

I'd like to have told her it was my first day in Barcelona since the start of the war and that the roast sea bass was all I had eaten and would eat that day; but the old woman was quite far away now, although I could still hear her curses: "Yer all the same! A gang of scoundrels! Republicans or fascists, yer all sons of the same bitch!"

That one dish cost me a hundred and twenty-five pesetas: what a whole month's full board and lodging cost before the war. Auntie had refused to let me mingle with the other seminarists – "they could be sons of the concierge or heaven knows who" – and had placed me in a boarding house for seminarists from good families; I don't know why, but memories of the big dormitory in that boarding house came flooding back. Twenty boarders slept on as many iron beds; the air at night turned as thick as water and we were like twenty large static fish. We were twenty lethargic sturgeons, each on our narrow iron bedstead, and our dreams spurted like gas that stank higher than that air – the big white walls were the screens on which we projected absurd films from our subconscious, and our regular breathing was like a muffled concert . . . Why did all this rush back at the sight of the innkeeper's bill? The exorbitant sum made me immediately understand how loathsome I must have seemed in the eyes of that old woman. I knew, as we all did at the front, that people ate very little and very poorly in Barcelona; we knew, but could never have imagined how badly . . . At a stroke I understood the glimmer of excited anticipation that had surprised me in the eyes of so many girls, and how the scrofulous mouths and strangled waists were all about hunger. Poor underwater panther, I thought. And while I thought that and got up from the table, there she stood, right in front of me.

A high narrow doorway on the other side of the street opposite the inn caught my eye because several copies of the same poster were stuck on surrounding walls: "Liberatories of prostitution". I'd seen it lots of times on my comings and goings along the streets of Barcelona next to the one that said "Make tanks, tanks, tanks" and so many others that were justly renowned. This one really perplexed me because I couldn't work out what it was supposed to represent. A house? A woman sewing? Several women reading books? Or with a baby? Then, lo and behold! The high narrow door opened and I was astonished to see the girl from the tram in the dingy entrance. I walked over, quite bewitched. Her yellow eyes looked at me without a trace of shock: she clearly didn't recognise me.

"I was just off," she said. "Now's not a good time."

"When would you like me to come back?"

"After midnight."

She had a very strong foreign accent. Right then that old woman reappeared by a mound of rubbish at the bottom of the street; while she poked at it she glared at us, her look full of hatred and contempt. She started to sing so we could hear her:

Allons, enfant de la grand'pute,
le jour de merde est arrivé.

"She's got a screw loose," said the underwater panther, taking it lightly. "Don't take any notice. She knows I'm French and sings that to annoy me."

"Did you say I should come back after midnight?" I asked, amazed she'd offered me such a late appointment. "In any case, I don't want the pesetas back, just the documents. I'd even give you more money in exchange for the documents . . . five hundred, say."

She stared at me.

"Come upstairs."

The steps up those dirty narrow stairs were worn down. We walked through a small lounge furnished in terrible taste where other women were sitting who didn't even give us a glance. She ushered me into her room at the end of a corridor with numbered doors just like a hotel; in fact I thought we were in the lowest of low hotels. But her room could have been a monk's, it was so small and sparsely furnished, and there was even a plaster image of the grotto in Lourdes on the bedside table, in front of which a wick burned in a glass of oil.

The panther made as if to pull her blouse over her head.

"What are you doing?" I exclaimed in astonishment. She looked at me perplexed, perhaps wondering about my mental state. "I only want my papers! The military police . . . I need them! You can keep the pesetas but give me back those papers."

"What's this nonsense all about, kid?"

I could see she was angry and now I saw that her hair was black whereas the girl in the tram – I remembered it well – had very bright flaxen hair. I apologised. I'd put my foot in it and mumbled such pathetic excuses that all she gathered was that I'd mistaken her for a pickpocket. As I stumbled down the stairs, she stood on the landing in a furious temper and unleashed after me the most obscene insults I'd ever heard.

It was four o'clock when I turned up at the mansion in Pedralbes where Trini lived. She wasn't at home. The maid led me to the drawing room and said she'd soon be back. I was surprised by everything I saw.

Not that I'd imagined it would be any different from her letters; indeed I'd not really imagined the place at all. I only knew what Lluís had told me about her and what I'd been able to infer from the letters; at the time I never wondered what right I had to interfere in the private life of a woman I didn't even know. I felt so sure of the path I'd taken and so convinced it was my duty to help Lluís regain his wife's love and restore peace to their relationship. I didn't realise how slippery the path was; I could only see the good it would do Lluís and Trini – Trini, the converted anarchist, the daughter of a couple united by a free love she too had embraced, and now about to take another wrong step perhaps and go astray for ever . . .

I looked around me: nothing bohemian or disorderly. Surrounded by pine and cypress trees, the mansion was located in the top part of Pedralbes. A huge bougainvillea in full flower displayed its crown, despite it being December, across the drawing-room windows. From there I could see the whole city stretching down to the sea. There was little in the way of furniture: what there was gave the impression that it had been selected piecemeal by someone choosing friends for a lifetime. A Louis Philippe armchair stood by one window, high-backed with wings, upholstered in yellow and green striped satin, its arms and wings fringed with lace. From where it sat you could see the garden, with a tall bare lime tree in the foreground. I felt it was wonderful to be seeing that window, armchair and lime tree so close and real, just as I'd read in the letters. This is the lime tree, I told myself, this is the armchair and this is the table lamp. It was here that she was reading a geology book when she heard the pistol shots . . . I could see that mahogany *secrétaire* in a corner of the room, so ethereal, as if it wanted to pass unperceived, and above it, on the gleaming white wall, the oval portrait of the Carlist colonel. It was the only painting in the drawing room; the walls were so white and bare they brought to mind lovingly ironed linen napkins. The slanting light of that December evening, muted by the thick curtains, came to rest on the mahogany polished by age, on the yellow and green striped chair, on the large red beret worn by the romantic colonel with huge side whiskers; the light caressed him like a gentle loving hand, and when the sun was about to set, one last ray shone on the rock-crystal chandelier – a small chandelier, almost a toy – generating the glittering colours of a rainbow.

How long did I wait in that drawing room, taking in every detail and lost in my dreams? How lovely it was to be there! It was so well positioned – the three windows faced south – you almost didn't feel the December cold in a Barcelona without coal or firewood; the fire in the hearth was out and so was the stove but the sun had been warming the room the whole day and you simply forgot it was the threshold of winter. How different from my boarding-house dormitory, so icy and grey with its twenty iron bedsteads and endless walls . . .

Trini walked in at that very moment.

Now that I know how this woman was to mark me for life, I'm trying to re-create the impression she made when I saw her for the first time. But strange as it may seem, I can find nothing startling in the depths of my memory. The woman I saw in front of me didn't reflect any of the images prompted by my reading of her letters. At the time she was a young twenty-one- or twenty-two-year-old – I'd had my twentieth birthday a few months before – tall and slim, with a bright-eyed, determined expression I found unsettling. She already knew the reason for my visit from a letter Lluís had sent and didn't seem to be at all interested in talking about it. Right from the start I'd made the mistake, as I realised later, of suggesting to her that a husband and wife need to show understanding towards each other and avoid harsh judgements. I'd hoped that she'd see my comment as a general one and not as an allusion to her situation that I only knew about from the letters. I broached the matter so clumsily she immediately saw it as an attempt to interfere and make peace between her and Lluís. I tried to explain. She interjected to tell the maid to serve tea: "I must warn you that you'll have to drink it without sugar – we don't even remember what that is. On the other hand, you'll find as much tea as you want in Barcelona, because nobody drinks it. We got the habit from Soleràs, who'd lived abroad: he got us into the habit of drinking it and once you're hooked you can't do without it. What a pity one can't nourish oneself on tea alone; today I went after twenty kilos of dry, maggot-eaten marrowfat peas . . ."

I tried to swing the conversation back to the matter of our excursion that had to be organised in the next forty-eight hours; she kept interrupting.

"They were very expensive; fat, yellow marrowfat like horse's teeth. You could see the maggots snug at the bottom of their holes. Perhaps we're not as unlucky as we think we are in Barcelona; when you're really hungry, it should be cheering to find maggots in your marrowfat: protein!"

I persisted and tried to get her to tell me whether she and her son would be coming on the expedition; she interjected yet again: "I know, because Lluís mentions it in a letter, that you are studying for the priesthood and that I can talk to you in good faith, as if you were my confessor. On the other hand, I assume that you have taken it upon yourself to give me edifying advice; it's a pity I'm not in the mood to follow any. As far as I'm concerned, it's all over with Lluís. It would take too long to tell you why, but you should realise that *is* the case. So I'd ask you not to mention him."

I was upset by the lighthearted tone she adopted when saying this; I'd have preferred a tearful scene – even though other people's tears always inhibit me.

"You are a Christian," I said.

"How do you know?"

How? From the letters, of course. I shuddered: it was the first time I realised I couldn't justify having read them and I was so embarrassed. My cheeks and ears were burning. She gave me a curious look: "What's the matter? Lluís doesn't know, so he couldn't have told you."

I looked down.

"So why don't you tell me the truth for once?"

"The truth . . ." I stammered, staring at the floor.

"Yes, the truth: Soleràs told you. You've been talking to Soleràs."

She doesn't know Soleràs gave the bundle of letters to Lluís, I reflected, trying to gather my thoughts; if she did, she wouldn't say that Lluís doesn't know she is a Christian.

"Soleràs may have spoken to me about you," I said evasively. "Before disappearing from the brigade, he could have told me, for example, that you'd informed him of your conversion. He could even have told me that you'd been baptised; I could in fact have learned all this from Soleràs."

"My God, I'm so hungry!" she interrupted me, as if barely paying any attention to what I was labouring to tell her. "Do you fancy a glass of Chartreuse? You can drink as much as you like. A pity the peas take so long to cook – we could eat a soup-plate full while we chat. Wouldn't you like to know what I've been doing while you were waiting for me? I'd heard that an Algerian barge had managed to fool the fascist torpedoes and make it through to the quayside in Barcelona last night; they said it was carrying a cargo of kidney beans. Kidney beans! Do they still exist in this world? Well yes, they do, but only for whizz-kids, literally! By the time I reached there, there were no kidney beans left, only maggot-ridden peas – and think yourself lucky. I'm not complaining; there are plenty worse off, like the ones who got there and saw the peas run out. I brought twenty kilos of peas on my back, like a man with a sack; nowadays no-one bats an eyelid; we've lost all those hang-ups. Everyone is too busy trying to survive. At least war has this good side to it. The alarm went up, the sirens wailed; I had to go down to the metro and sit on some big steps among the crowd, holding the sack tight. What if it was stolen after all I'd done to get it! You know, when the alarm goes off they steal everything in these packed places. It wasn't too bad down there: a warm draught smelling of tar wafted up from inside the tunnel and in the end became a form of heating. Besides, I've always liked the smell of tar. And the feeling that you belong to the mass, that you're in the same boat with thousands of others as anonymous as you sharing the same dangers, the same hunger, the same cold, the same filth . . . it keeps you company. Your main worry in this world is to make sure you're not the only one who's unhappy."

"One is only unhappy to the extent that one wants to be," I replied rather sententiously, pouring myself another glass of Chartreuse. "It's better to speak frankly about such things."

"Fine, let me be equally frank: I don't think you have much of a grasp of the situation."

"You are making too much of an affair that's a damp squib. You are highly intelligent and should be a little more understanding."

"Lluís is more intelligent than I am or at least he thinks he is. I mean, if the situation was the reverse, should *I* be even more understanding? Let's imagine – it's only a hypothesis – that I'd taken advantage of the fact that he is so far away and seems to have forgotten me and had a little fling with some feudal grandee in the rearguard, or don't you think they exist? Bah, the place is crawling with them. What do you think my brother Llibert is? There are lots: using the excuse that they were emancipating the proletariat they've emancipated themselves – and just look at them! They are the freest of the free! Bah, if we start on this, we'll be here all night. But let's get back to what I was saying. Once they're broken, some things can never be soldered back together. Besides, I find it so hateful to talk about this!"

I admitted defeat.

"So then, senyora, I'm to understand we'll be making our trip without you. You will be the only one —"

"Not at all. You've quite misunderstood me. I'm not going to let slip such a fantastic opportunity to give my boy peace and quiet and good food! At the front, far from starvation and the bombs . . ." and she burst out laughing. "I tell you I find all this quite amazing! I'll soon be on holiday from the university; it's all coming together; the loose ends are all being connected. Your idea is wonderful!"

III

Don Andalecio's house looked very different from the moment Trini and Sra Picó arrived. Each of them put their ideas into practice and, incredibly, never argued. For example, now – and this was the work of the "*capitana*" as we called her – a washing line stretched from one dining-room wall to another, with all the white bed linen drying in the heat of the fire. The day after she'd arrived she'd tried to hang the washing out to dry in the fresh air, and at ten degrees below each item had immediately turned stiff in her fingers: "Like slices of salted cod," she said.

The smell of clean sheets drying became part of the atmosphere in the house. For her part Trini had discovered a bag of quicklime in one of the abandoned houses and with the help of Sra Picó, two assistants and the odd soldier she whitewashed the walls. Then she furnished the dining room with items she found in other houses, furniture she rubbed and rubbed until the antique walnut glowed. That room was no longer a burnt-out living space, unfurnished apart from the three fireside benches and the table we were so familiar with: all was now welcoming and comfortable. We spent the endless December nights around the fire in the light from four or five oil lamps positioned on the furniture; rows of copper chocolate pots – which we found in every house – glinted red along the shelf of the chimney hood. One of the gleaming white walls was now dominated by a huge baroque chiaroscuro portrait of an old hermit: "San Onofrio", according to the huge Roman script on the frame. He was the only surviving saint from the village church that had been razed to the ground.

Trini remembered the former beadle though he didn't remember her – natural enough since beadles are few and students many. He was delighted to learn she was now a teacher in the faculty and felt most honoured to entertain her as a guest in his "fief in Santa Espina", as he liked to call it. As soon as the ladies arrived he rushed to give her his latest find: an eighteenth-century agricultural treatise, in Catalan for good measure, that had turned up in a box in the corner of an attic in an abandoned village house.

As for Ramonet, his cheeks soon had good colour thanks to the cold dry air and plentiful healthy food; every morning his father took him for a ride in the brougham. They followed the cart track downstream halfway to Villar: Trini and I sometimes accompanied them. On the first few days, the boy looked wide-eyed at the frozen waterfalls; he'd just had his fourth birthday.

I divided my life between Villar and Santa Espina. In Villar, the commander's wife killed time knitting jerseys for her husband. I've never met anyone with so many jerseys as our commander, and all knitted by his wife. It was strange how the couple were so alike: the same sallow yellow, the same dark droopy eyes. Their daughter was surprisingly serious for an eight- or nine-year-old, overly so; she seemed marked by the horrors she'd heard about since the start of the war and was still hearing about – seventeen months, a long time for her: she hardly had any pre-war memories. Even so, she was a quiet, biddable girl, though she occasionally did peculiar things. One morning in Barcelona – her mother told me – she escaped from their flat on carrer de Cervelló and stood in one of the entrances to the Boqueria market asking passers-by for alms: "I'm an orphan," she told them. "The baddies have killed my mother and father and now my step-mother beats me." There was something else that made me suddenly feel affectionate towards her, and it was much to everybody's surprise, particularly her parents: soldiers on night duty found her between one and two o'clock in the middle of the street in her nightshirt; she was walking very stiffly, eyes half closed and apparently not feeling the cold. When they stopped and shook her, not realising what was wrong with her, she reacted as if she were in great pain. "An attack of sleepwalking," was Dr Puig's diagnosis. "That makes two of you in the brigade," he added. He prescribed ordinary vitamin pills and answered the commander and his wife's anxious queries: "Absolutely nothing to worry about; look at Cruells, he's as right as rain." The fact that she also suffered from similar odd attacks made me suddenly think of her as a little sister and at a stroke she was also more affectionate towards me; invariably, when I arrived back in Villar from Santa Espina, she'd run over and hug me, and she often asked me the same question she'd asked that had so taken me by surprise when I visited her house: "They won't kill my daddy, will they?"

The six of us would sit round the table at mealtimes in Villar – the commander and his wife, the doctor and his, and Marieta and I, as if we were one big family. Headquarters had been set up in the rectory; it had a large dining room. Before the war it had obviously been used as the parish office and the rector had had the following inscribed on the wall in large letters:

NO BLASPHEMING

The anarchists had scratched off letters and changed it to

DO BLASPHEME

The first time Captain Picó came to El Villar – I saw this with my own eyes – he asked the commander to reinstate the previous text in the name of culture, but however much he insisted, the commander and Dr Puig turned a deaf ear. The room was heated by a big iron stove and had the most beautiful tall grandfather clock I'd ever seen; naturally, Picó was the one to get it to work after an entire morning spent fiddling with screwdrivers and tweezers. It was a joy to hear it strike every hour, half and quarter with its chimes; I felt a slice of peacetime had been reintroduced. The commander's wife spent hours and hours next to the fire listening to the clock's tick-tock and knitting jerseys in a Viennese rocking chair that must once have been the head maid's.

Marieta invariably refused to eat what was on offer at lunch and she'd be given the omelette that was all she ever ate. The child's lack of appetite was a worry for her mother; imagine her astonishment one day when she discovered that Marieta had gone to the soldiers' kitchen when the bugle had signalled grub's up. "My parents are starving me," she announced, before knocking back three helpings of watery stew. After I'd brought her a drowsy frog that was as stiff as a board and showed her how it would liven up in the warmth from the stove and start jumping, Marieta often explored the river banks looking for frogs hiding under piles of rotten foliage. Once they'd been warmed and woken up, she treated them with a mother's loving care and played with them as if they were dolls; she spoke to them like babies, made soup and fed them with a baby's bottle, which, of course, they refused. Then she forgot them and the frogs lay overheated and abandoned in a corner of the house.

As for the commander and Dr Puig, they pledged abstinence after their wives arrived and went together to throw a bottle of rum, "a symbolic bottle", down a hole in the ice on the river – a solemn ritual performed in the presence of Picó and Lluís who had been "summoned as witnesses". From now on there'd only be table wine in Villar. It was kept in a cupboard in the parish office – we used the cupboard as a pantry – and the commander had all other barrels and hogsheads collected up from village cellars and kept under lock and key in the sacristy: he gave the key to his wife. It was total control; Dr Puig could rightly say that "one day posterity should know that they died of thirst like real men."

The battalion's medical store or first aid post occupied a semi-basement in the rectory where my superior and I went at fixed times each day to attend to soldiers who might appear. They rarely did, so most days we just chatted by the stove we'd installed there. We had very little work: the battalion had lost half its men, the dry cold and good food fortified the soldiery, and in those deserted villages they couldn't possibly catch the classic clap. The doctor began to confide in me, telling me "personal secrets", as he called them, that generally centred on his often stormy relationship with his wife. Initially, as long as he remained strictly faithful to his "solemn pledge", it would go like this: he'd let off steam by telling me about his father-in-law, a filthy-rich purveyor of pork delicatessen – number one in the Boqueria market – whose only daughter was Merceditas. I replied that there was nothing shameful in being the daughter of a pork butcher: "But don't you understand?" he exploded. "Don't you get it? The shame is on our side, we're a total waste of time!" From the very first day the soldiers had started to call her "Dr" rather than "Sra Puig" and he was well aware of that; he, too, often addressed her as "Dr".

But, oh dear, his fidelity to his "solemn pledge" was short-lived. One day, when I went down to the medical store, I caught him swigging a bottle. He'd not heard my footsteps. In the half dark he tried to hide it among the medicine, but I'd seen it was a bottle of Fundador, the famous Andalusian cognac, and it really caught my eye because the brand had vanished from the republican zone soon after war broke out.

"Yes, it's genuine Fundador," he crowed, slightly shamefacedly. "Cruells, I was literally dying of thirst! A few days ago, Lluís appeared in the rectory with a bottle of eau de cologne and you'll understand that *that* wasn't for me. So I asked Picó why, if Lluís could find eau de cologne in no man's land, he couldn't seek me out a drop of Fundador. It's an act of mercy to give drink to a thirsty man! So Picó brought me some from no man's land, a lovely lot! So what if it's fascist cognac? I couldn't care a damn! One's real friends remember you when you're having a bad time, don't they? Picó is one; he thought of me whereas Lluís thought only of my wife. Poor Lluís, if only you knew how he strives to keep her happy; misfortune tells you who your true friends are; when you're really down, a friend brings you a good cognac rather than trying to sweet-talk your wife."

He spoke more expansively than usual: he'd clearly been drinking for some time.

"So what if it's a fascist cognac? She is too! She'd like me to go over to the other side . . ."

"Just like my aunt?" I exclaimed frankly.

"Just like your aunt! All these aunts are the same . . . and Merceditas is one . . . One of those who walk down the street and the shameless students shout out: 'What a beauty!' A fascist like all the other beauties; the proper thing to do would be to execute her but that would upset Lluís."

He sighed: "Doesn't it rile you that Lluís and Picó find such strange things in no man's land? When I think how the innocent Lluís . . . hmm . . . when I think how half the human race . . . Can I be frank with you? In this brigade we've never had a good word for Soleràs yet he was the only one to hit the nail on the head. He was an idiot, I agree, but he hit the nail on the head. Ever since he vanished, this brigade's not been worth a monkey's fart. Soleràs would say: 'Everyone gets cuckolded as he deserves, with a few honourable exceptions.' Well, you know, I am an honourable exception – I've never been cuckolded as I deserve; Merceditas has never done such a thing to me, quite the contrary. She's quite the opposite of a cuckolder! To cuckold me, she'd have to make someone else happy, and she'd kick the bucket rather than do that."

From that day on he often drank surreptitiously in our underground medical store. When it was lunchtime, he'd keep himself steady so his wife never realised he'd had one too many. In any case she was inclined to look only at herself, and wasn't alone in that. When they are all pretence, as was the case with Sra Puig, their foolishness is stunningly obvious, like a millionaire who stands out because of his millions. That aside, she was a fine woman; she lived for herself and for a family that was an extension of herself. If she hadn't been such an attractive and shapely platinum blonde, we'd simply have said "a fine woman". Because that's what she was, basically. Her husband feared her even as he mocked her. He'd say things to send her into a fury. One day, when we'd had to go to Santa Espina to deal with a soldier with a dislocated foot and returned to Villar in time for lunch, he started to wax enthusiastic about Picó's wife: "She's niceness personified! She was a delight helping us to put that poor fellow's bones back in place; and no anaesthetic, you know" – he glanced at Merceditas – "because we didn't have any, we'd forgotten to take any. She kept encouraging the soldier; she could turn a tame heifer into a bull! And a dark-haired beauty into the bargain, yum!"

"And you, my dear," she retorted – she was always calling him "my dear" –"you are a donkey, and what's worse, most uncivil."

Back in the basement, he told me: "Cruells, you heard her – a donkey! Did one cram anatomy and pathology for that simple soul to call one a donkey to one's face? Oh, Cruells, if only you knew! Oh, Cruells! I adore that simple soul! Yes, I adore her. There lies the rub: I adore her. Oh Cruells, oh Cruells, if only you knew! You don't, but I'll tell you: I'll let you in on another 'private secret'."

He closed the basement door with a grand mysterious flourish and after a pause, as if pondering over the great confession he was about to make, he got it off his chest: "All men fall for Merceditas in the street. Especially adolescents – hmm, adolescents! The eyes of adolescents bulge out of their sockets, like somebody starving in front of a pastry shop window. And, you know, those fucking adolescents eye her up and down – in the middle of the street with no respect for my humble presence."

"That's hardly *her* fault," I suggested.

"Not her fault? Her father is the wealthiest delicatessen owner in the whole Boqueria market! The king of cold meat and sausages! Every year the guild of the purveyors of delicatessen used to give a ball: this was way before the war, before we students went crazy. A torrent of silk and diamonds! Dinner-jacketed men and ball-gowned women. They elected a committee to choose the 'guild princess' and I happened to be its secretary. The chair was Josep Maria de Sagarra, who never missed a single beauty contest: he chaired the lot! On this occasion there was no need go to a vote or a second round because the committee was unanimous from the start: we were captivated by Merceditas! To huge ovations, Sagarra proclaimed her Miss Barcelona Delicatessen, the Chorizo Princess!"

Once again I tried to come to the defence of Sra Puig.

"She has her qualities, you say? Of course, she does, who doesn't? *She* certainly does: the rump of a Renaissance popess," and he kept repeating "the rump of a popess", an expression I found rather shocking, while his hands described it with a broad circular gesture. "Is her popess' rump what you'd call a 'quality'? Yes, I won't deny she has undeniable qualities. She has, for example, if you could only see it, a beauty spot, that's as hot as pepper . . . oh! she has qualities . . . !"

I tried to halt this stream of "private secrets" that were too close to the bone, but he lost his temper: "Aren't you my subordinate in this army? Since when isn't one allowed to let off steam with one's subordinates in this damn awful brigade? Can't one talk about anything in this brigade?"

The first time I went to Santa Espina after this set-to I asked Picó not to give the doctor any more bottles of cognac. He eyed me sarcastically: "But he keeps asking for them," he said, "and I'm at his mercy. I can't refuse."

I was totally in the dark about the medical attention Picó was receiving from Dr Puig – didn't he swear time and again he'd turn his machine gun on the doctor before letting him touch him? I was utterly unaware and it came as a complete surprise; I kept quiet so as not to put my foot in it, because you never know . . . I vaguely remembered that when Picó talked of his years in the Foreign Legion in Africa, he'd mysteriously said that "every lass leaves you a lifelong souvenir". In any case, Dr Puig had never said a word. One afternoon, when I was alone in the medical store tidying our stocks, reorganising the contents of the big cupboard, I found a little bottle I'd never seen before: it was labelled Polierotikol. I showed it to the doctor the next morning.

"So you've finally found it," he said, "even though I'd hidden it as best I could. I have my bright ideas, you know, my very own! Like a Renaissance pope. Yes, Cruells, don't give me that po-faced Jesuit look; don't try to tell me there weren't any popes in the Renaissance."

"I don't really know what it's all about," I replied, "but I don't think you should have recourse to pep pills. They are bad for your health, or so they say. People say that medicines made from extract of Spanish fly" – I'd seen the ingredients on the label – "are extremely dangerous."

"I shouldn't? Well, I don't need it. My heart's still young. You know, it's for Picó, but don't tell anyone. A professional secret! He came across it in no man's land; you can find everything there, it's a wonderful place. When *you* had the bright idea of inviting the ladies, Picó was worried stiff: 'Doctor, please,' he said, 'I'm twenty years older than my wife and I've not done it for eighteen months, I'm out of training!' He was afraid he'd make a poor fist of it. You never know with men from the Foreign Legion, they all suffer from their prostates. They've all had '*maladies d'amour*' as Picó calls them: he wanted 'a little something to help me achieve an honourable outcome'. For a case like this, in which a man's honour is at stake, there's nothing like Polierotikol, a classic cure, tried and tested down the ages. The only problem being you can't find a drop in the republican zone. 'Don't you worry, doctor,' said Picó, 'I'm sure to find some in no man's land.' It's amazing what he and Lluís find there! But Picó would have been capable of downing it in one swig and he'd have exploded like a frog! That's why I keep it in the cupboard and give it to him in small 'dioceses', as he calls them. He's very pleased with it, and according to him, he feels as frisky as a fighting bull."

Soon after, Commander Rosich remembered that one of these days it would be Saint Llúcia's day – in fact 13 December had already come and gone – and that she was the patron saint of infantry. We tried to tell him that he was wrong on two counts. The patron saint of infantry, as we all knew, had always been the Immaculate Virgin, that is, 8 December and not 13, and, besides, it was already 16 December. All to no avail. He wanted us to have a "gala lunch" in Villar "in honour of our patron saint" and that was that. At least we all agreed on one point: whether Saint Llúcia was the patron of whatever, and whenever her day happened to fall, she was a most worthy excuse to let our hair down. Now, as these memories drift hazily back, I feel shocked by how grotesque it all was, when I think how all that happened during the most vicious war . . . the battle of Teruel was about to start or had perhaps already started in which thousands of soldiers died of gangrene because of the freezing cold. But we were on the dead front, and the theatre of war, as far as we were concerned that winter, was as remote as the other end of the world. I'm sure that all wars are similar: those who've lived through their horrors and know they will live to see them again give themselves up to the most ludicrous tomfoolery when there's a lull. We never talked about colleagues from the brigade who'd been killed in action, already in the hundreds since the war started; anything that might depress us was banned from conversation, as was that sublime genre of patriotic or revolutionary anthem now sung only by the two-timers in the rearguard – however much the political commissars strove to impose them at the front – where we thought they were unbearably trite.

Now when I recall that soon after the "gala lunch" we started to see squadrons of serried aeroplanes pass overhead on their way to or back from Teruel, now when we are aware of the icy horrors of that midwinter battle in Aragon . . . However, I must describe our "gala lunch" as it was and not as it ought to have been – as if it could really have been any different.

As well as the usual half dozen diners at the Villar rectory, Captain Picó and his wife, and Lluís and his together with Ramonet, were invited: eleven all told. The commander ordered a soldier attached to the general staff, a professional calligrapher, to prepare eleven menus in Gothic script that were placed opposite each table setting: "Partridges without cabbage, jugged hare, home-produced wine . . ." I should add that some time earlier the satirical magazine *L'esquella de la torratxa* had reached us from Barcelona with a joke about a gentleman in a bar. "Vermouth without olives," he ordered. "It will have to be without anchovies," retorted the waiter, "because we ain't got no olives." This joke was a huge success in Barcelona at the time when there was nothing at all to eat, but it was evident that the *capitana*, that is Sra Picó, wasn't familiar it, since she asked, in a surprised tone, why the menu made a point of saying that the partridges were being served "without cabbage".

"They will have to come without cabbage," the commander told her affably. "We'd rather have served them without truffles given the solemn nature of the occasion, but truffles . . ."

"We ain't got," Dr Puig rounded off his sentence in a deadpan tone.

"Home-produced wine" naturally meant retrieved from cellars in the village, the ones the commander had locked away in the sacristy. For this "gala lunch" they'd prepared a large table with linen napkins brought from no man's land and it was a handsome sight. We wanted to put Sra Puig in her place, to force her to recognise that our brigade had style, that nobody could be more refined or well mannered. Each of us tried to recall proper "form", pre-war "form", all with a view to making her recognise that we weren't like the flat feet, that our forte was our savoir faire.

To abide by these rules, couples weren't to sit together at table. The lunch got off to a flying start with animated conversation.

"In spite of everything, senyora," the commander told Sra Puig who was seated between him and Lluís, "we're not as uncivilised as the fascists say. Let's be frank: the fascists are right if they are only referring to the flat-footed brigade. Oh, Senyora Puig, if you were to have lunch some day in the headquarters of the flat feet, you'd be horrified!"

"Before the war," muttered Dr Puig, "I'd have my shoes polished every Saturday. Nowadays . . ."

He raised a leg and displayed the extremely grimy leather of his lieutenant's high boots. Even Sra Picó behaved most properly, though she did look out of the corner of her eye at the others eating their partridges without using their fingers. Picó was telling Sra Rosich a string of stories.

"Our brigade," the commander insisted, leaning over the doctor's wife, "has real style; it's not like the flatfooted brigade. Can you hear the tales the machine-gun captain is spinning my wife? Nothing to make a Daughter of Mary blush! In this brigade we are wonderfully well mannered."

Sra Puig admitted magnanimously that the banquet – and she said so in French – "*ne manquait pas de tenue*." As I said, Lluís was the other side of her and she was striving to engage him in conversation, but Lluís was rather taciturn. White wine was served after the partridge.

"As we don't have any fish," the commander apologised, addressing her as ever, "we must drink white wine post-partridge. You must forgive us, senyora, given the circumstances."

Trini hardly joined in the conversation. They'd sat her next to me and I felt her mind was elsewhere. Her absent air and Lluís' silence made me surmise they'd had a row before the "gala lunch". The commander thought that was a timely moment to give the first toast: "To the good health of our splendid brigade!"

The white wine looked light but it soon went to the head. Its effect on the doctor was palpable: he'd poured himself three large glasses and now stood up with his fourth to offer a toast like the commander: "To the very good health of my father-in-law! He can't sneeze without cash dropping from his pockets."

"My dear, I presume," his wife interrupted, "you're not trying to make us laugh at the expense of my papa."

"Her papa is my father-in-law, you understand," the doctor told the captain's wife as he sat down. "What I don't know, Senyora Picó, is whether you've ever heard about what Letamendi did in his student days, when the man he wanted to be his father-in-law sent him packing. Letamendi was expecting he would; he was the most starving of students, while that gentleman who was so reluctant to become his father-in-law was as filthy rich as mine. But Letamendi was a man never caught napping; such a man is worth two – and the great Letamendi wasn't one to curb his tongue!"

The cross-eyed aide-de-camp brought on the jugged hare at that point in the story; red wine was served after the hare and the commander made a second apology: "We ought to drink champagne after such wonderful hare, but I beg you, Senyora Puig, put your imagination to work. A little imagination and this red wine can taste like champagne. Which champagne do you prefer? Veuve Cliquot? Nothing can stop us imagining that we are drinking Veuve Cliquot."

He felt duty-bound, "as we've now reached the champagne", to propose another toast. "The only widow here is the Veuve Cliquot and may it remain that way for years to come!"

He became droopier-eyed with each toast and started to stare hard at Ramonet and Marieta. The two children pinged breadcrumbs at each other from opposite sides of the table. Naturally, Marieta refused to try the partridge or the hare, and Squint-eyes had to make her a plain omelette as usual. Her father stood up once again, with another glass of red wine: "To the new generation! Home-produced children! Blasted Cristina, they'll soon all be orphaned! For the new home-produced generation! May that never happen!"

It was one of his favourite expressions: "For many years may we fashion such works, home-produced children!" But Sra Puig acted as if she was hearing it for the first time and asked Lluís, "What does he mean, exactly?" He shrugged: "It's just his way of speaking, senyora; people say a lot of very odd things in this regiment." Picó, who was head of table, winked at him as if to say: "Lluís, this is beginning to get out of hand; the commander is as pissed as a newt." The doctor realised that too: "Citizens, calm down! Danger over; that was a false alarm. Here comes Squint-eyes, that most glorious hero of the army of Catalonia, with our coffee. No ersatz here, citizens – that was a false alarm! I swear to you it's the genuine item, no ersatz here!"

"A discovery from no man's land," the commander informed Sra Puig.

"One finds the richest veins of coffee in no man's land," added the doctor, "inexhaustible mines of coffee."

"Senyora," continued the commander, "you must excuse us yet again. It's not mocha; it's coffee from Guinea, you know, fascist coffee; it isn't by any means the coffee that you deserve . . ."

"It's excellent," she replied, "like the coffee we used to drink at the beginning of the war that you can't even dream of nowadays in Barcelona," and poured out a second cup.

"I'll have another too," her husband chipped in, raising another glass of red wine rather than a cup of coffee.

"My dear, I can't imagine you drinking red wine after coffee."

"As it's not mocha . . ." he rasped by way of excuse. And turning to Sra Picó he added: "The great Letamendi was so witty . . . Whatever they say, Letamendi was a real character. When he went to ask for the girl's hand —"

"My dear," Merceditas interrupted him, "we weren't talking about Letamendi."

"But," said Sra Picó rather bemused, "Senyora, if your husband would like to tell us an antidote . . ."

"I presume she means an anecdote," the doctor's wife corrected her indulgently, addressing Lluís.

"No, I meant antidotes, I really did: the great Letamendi's antidotes," and the doctor added emphatically, "Letamendi had some fiendish antidotes!"

"Anyone would think you were in your dotage, my dear."

He repeated even more emphatically: "Yes, they were truly fiendish!"

This devilish witticism was a hoot and everyone in the brigade started telling antidotes. Merceditas vaguely shrugged her shoulders and lit a cigarette; Lluís had offered her a packet of Camel, also from no-man's-land.

"Fucking no man's land," grunted the doctor. "They evidently grow forests of tobacco there . . . huge trees that make fantastic cigars . . . There's something rotten in that land. Yes, rotten is the word!" he repeated, staring straight at his wife as if he were defying her. "Can't people talk about anything else in this brigade? They should make *The Horns of Roland* compulsory reading in all convent schools and we'd soon see if that could reduce the number of starry-eyed sillies in this world! *The Horns of Roland* is such a great read! The hero is cuckolded by page three; it's my kind of book, you don't waste time wading through descriptions of landscape. And when you get to chapter six, entitled 'Terrible doubt', the plot gets so wickedly entangled that poor Roland exclaims to himself: 'Zounds, no doubt about it. I've cuckolded myself!' Because, for your information, Sra Picó, the woman he thought was someone else's wife was his own: family dramas it would take me too long to explain. The wretched Roland had married by proxy, you know, before he'd ever seen the young girl he was marrying; he didn't realise she was a real knock-out, the kind that floors you. I mean the novel doesn't describe landscapes but describes that girl . . . hmm . . . lovely descriptions . . . one chapter in particular, when the girl is getting dressed, that's what you call *good* literature, for Christ's sake! No detail left to the imagination! And plenty of drama too, chapter eleven, the one entitled 'Wolves against wolves . . . at each other's throats!' The two families had created such a fantastic farrago by cuckolding each other that the wretched Roland raised his hands and eyes to the heavens and thundered: 'Has anyone ever worn horns the size of mine?'"

"Perhaps you should shut up," his wife interrupted. "You haven't a clue what you're talking about."

"What? You reckon I haven't a clue what I'm on about? I know chapter and verse. Indeed, in chapter fifteen, 'Peace treaty in Cornwall', which is the final chapter, Roland appears to be more resigned and remarks in the banquet that brings everyone together to celebrate the treaty: 'Sooth, what a mess! I was turning into my own father-in-law, or at least into my own brother-in-law – not even a resurrected Sherlock Holmes could have untangled the threads in that yarn!'"

He followed this up by telling the captain's wife: "If you want to wind up Merceditas, you only have to say the words 'streaky bacon' to her face."

His wife was deep in conversation with Lluís and didn't hear him. The stove, stuffed with wedges of evergreen oak, glowed bright red; it was giving out a lot of heat.

"Papa," piped Ramonet, "why didn't they put me next to Marieta?"

"The child is quite right," nodded the commander's wife who was by his side. "And doesn't he speak up for himself like a proper little man!"

"Do you want another cup of mocha?" the commander asked Merceditas, who was already pouring out a third. "There's nothing like coffee from Mocha. You possibly don't where it is; it's a city in Arabia, just imagine!"

"I'm perfectly well aware . . . it's where they buried Napoleon."

When he heard his wife's remark, the doctor gave a start, looked taken aback and peered at the end of his nose, then continued his conversation with Sra Picó: "This story I wanted to tell you about Letamendi is a love story, you know, but here they won't let you say damn all. I ought to go and tell it to the flatfooted brigade where it would have the success it deserves."

"If it's a love story . . ." said the captain's wife, looking at the doctor with renewed interest, "but I thought doctors never talked about love."

"Whoever said such a thing? We do it all the time!"

"There's nothing to beat culture," Picó remarked sententiously to the doctor's wife. "I have a weak spot for Napoleon Bonaparte."

"We speak of love," continued the doctor, "and usually approach the topic from both angles: *Thëorie und Praxis*."

"I think we're getting our wires crossed," said the commander. "Napoleon Bonaparte? Hmmm . . . You mean that the corpse lying in Mocha isn't . . . hmmm, damned if I remember."

"Then whose is it?" interjected Picó, lighting his pipe and looking at him askance.

"Let them argue, Sra Picó," the doctor whispered to the captain's wife, "whether Napoleon and Bonaparte were or weren't one and the same; it's one of the knottiest riddles in history. What you can't deny is that Napoleon was cuckolded a couple of times, in a most extraordinary way on more than one count. In my student days we used to sing a couplet in French on the subject of Napoleon and Josephine; it's a pity I've forgotten it, because it was a very spicy couplet."

"Don't listen to that quack," the commander interrupted, leaning in turn towards Sra Picó on the other side of him. "All doctors are charlatans. He thinks he could go over to the flatfooted brigade any old day simply to let his hair down telling rude stories. I know that couplet he used to sing in the good old days and I can tell you it's not suitable for a lady's ears. You must have noticed the letters painted on the wall: DO BLASPHEME; I wanted to change that to NO BLASPHEMY but the doctor wouldn't let me. In the name of Freudianism, you know. He says we must fight relapses and I can tell you that he preaches by example at least in this area. He hasn't a clue about culture or education!"

Picó pricked up his ears at mention of the word "culture". He looked at his wife and the commander who'd got embroiled in a very lively conversation à deux and then asked the commander's wife in a tone worthy of Versailles: "What if we applied the law of retaliation?"

He was very proud of his knowledge of this expression, which he thought very cultured and which was the title of one of the novels in his suitcase. The commander's wife nodded; she most certainly didn't know what the "law of retaliation" was, but she always thought everything was a good idea and was forever in agreement with both sides and perennially drowsy at the end of a meal. She usually went upstairs for a quick snooze, but as that was a special "gala lunch" day she didn't dare leave and it was obvious she was struggling not to doze off. It was cognac time; Squint-eyes brought up genuine Fundador for us to fill our glasses. The commander and the doctor poured themselves several on the pretext that we were toasting the glorious patron of infantry, or so they claimed. The situation quickly deteriorated.

"In my day," Dr Puig began, "there was an undertaker's next to a house we students visited a lot. Because in my day there were proper funerals; it's not like now when we bury people like so many dogs. We had such a good time at that undertaker's! No, I got that wrong, it was next door . . . It was a finely appointed establishment, a place *comme il faut*; there was even a large photo of Guimerà in a gilt frame in one of the bedrooms. It was, as you can see, a highly respectable establishment and just round the corner from the Clinical Hospital. Well positioned and familiar to all students. You are perhaps aware that medical students sometimes thieve items of anatomy in order to play stupid jokes, and that once, showing no respect for Guimerà, I hid the leg of an unfortunate fellow who'd died of cancer between the sheets of the bed in that particular bedroom."

"Is that the *only* kind of love story doctors can tell?" asked the visibly disappointed captain's wife.

"Oh no, the love story is Letamendi's. He'd stolen . . . how should I put it? Hmmm, some of those items one can't mention in the presence of ladies."

"We are so incredibly well mannered in this brigade, it's such a pleasure," said the commander. "So what *did* Letamendi do?"

"Perhaps he made tanks," exclaimed Sra Picó, bursting into laughter. 'Make tanks, tanks, tanks', did you know they've stuck up thousands of posters with that slogan all over Barcelona? I wished I'd been a handyman like my husband and I'd have started straightaway."

"When I saw that poster," Sra Rosich chimed in blithely, "I started to knit that tight-fitting grey jersey for my husband."

"You were supposed to make tanks, not jerseys," said her husband reproachfully, before bellowing at the doctor: "Do you mind telling us whether Letamendi made tanks or jerseys?"

"Hmm . . . Letamendi . . ." And, pouring himself another glass of Fundador, Dr Puig then began: "Letamendi made jerseys and tanks that were —"

"Yes, we know, they were fiendish!" the commander interrupted him impatiently. "We'd like to know what happened to him and his father-in-law."

"When his father-in-law, who was filthy rich, refused him the hand of his daughter, he left him a well-wrapped parcel on the table, saying: 'Well, here you are, this won't be any use to me now . . .'"

The commander and Picó laughed so much, the tears came to their eyes. The conversation moved on from this joke that was as stupid as it was macabre to the topic of Soleràs. He'd disappeared from the brigade "without leaving an address", so the commander said; we imagined he'd joined another republican brigade and some were even inclined to think he'd joined an anarchist outfit, he was so eccentric. When the commander managed to rein in his laughter, he exclaimed: "Here we are celebrating the day of our patron saint and all we can talk about are corpses. At least might we reach agreement about the one in Mecca."

"In Mecca?" queried the doctor.

"Yes, Mecca, weren't we talking about Mecca?"

"I can assure you that Letamendi is not buried in Mecca."

"Agreed," Picó interrupted, "but we were referring to Bonaparte, not Letamendi."

"What a corpse!" rejoined the commander heartily. "He's as dead and buried as the renowned Åse."

"'The Death of Åse'," Picó explained to the commander's wife," is a score I can play on my trombone and that the battalion band plays too."

And to show off his musical talents, of which he was legitimately proud, he puffed out his cheeks and struck up "The Death of Åse" in imitation of the sound of his trombone.

"Agh!" protested the commander. "Enough of 'The Death of Åse'! That Åse always makes me think of Soleràs; not as an Åse but as a corpse. You won't deny that Soleràs has a cadaverous face . . ."

Trini looked up in surprise; she'd hardly spoken during the whole lunch. No-one, apart from me, noticed that a single glistening tear of astonishment had formed in her bright eyes. Her shocked expression remained forever engraved on my memory. Years later I can still see her eyes wide open and shimmering. The conversation grew spicier and spicier and it was impossible to stop the commander and the doctor on their final fling. Engrossed in her *tête-à-tête* with Lluís, Sra Puig puffed out clouds of cigarette smoke and stared at the ceiling with the resignation of a martyr: "Yes, he likes to pretend he is grosser than he really is simply to annoy me. Because he knows only too well that I'm sensitive to the point of infirmity."

"That's evident at a first glance," replied Lluís.

"Just imagine, Lluís, how sensitive I am: I can't look at the full moon without bursting into tears."

"How curious! The full moon indeed?" replied Lluís. "When I see it, I split my sides."

"I find that astonishing," said the doctor's wife. "I believe one can't be truly sensitive until one has seen a full moon. I would have so liked my husband to take me for a walk around the Gothic quarter of Barcelona on a night when the full moon was shining . . ."

At that precise moment, as her insensitive husband argued with the commander, his rant rose in a crescendo above the buzz of general conversation like a clap of thunder: "Agreed, Soleràs was a fool, but he *always* got it right."

"And I say, what about perfidious Albion?" shouted the commander. "It's been a long time since we heard from her."

"And who might that lady be?" the captain's wife asked the doctor.

"I'll tell you in song," he replied, and began singing in his deep baritone voice:

> Every month English lovers
> write letters to each other.

"Sra Picó, perhaps you may not be aware," remarked the commander, "that you can't stage bullfights in rainy weather, because bulls go tame if the sun doesn't shine. Well, it is always raining in England, just imagine! It's a disaster! At the beginning of the war, a Labour MP visited our trenches and criticised everything he saw. The guns weren't properly greased, the troops were undisciplined and the officers were unshaven . . . Soleràs caught him *en passant* with an 'Every people gets the climate it deserves . . .'"

The captain's wife loved this barb by Soleràs; short and olive skinned, she thought of herself as a "sultry southerner". She wanted to learn to sing the couplet and while she hummed "Every month English lovers" she snapped her fingers imitating castanets. The doctor shouted out loud so the head of table could hear: "Picó, you never told us you had such a racy wife, and so sultry, wow! She's got sex appeal, yum-yum . . ."

"Are you trying to wind me up?" asked Sra Picó, wriggling and laughing as the machine-gun captain smiled from the head of the table, flattered by the praise the doctor was showering on his wife. It was the last straw for Sra Puig, who whispered to Lluís: "It's pathetic. Did you hear that, Lluís? 'Trying to wind me up' indeed . . ."

"'Trying to wind me up!'" exclaimed the doctor. "I've just been reminded of another antidote. There once was a corpse in Mecca . . . Yes, Merceditas, don't look at me so disgusted, we were talking about Mecca, weren't we?"

The commander's wife had almost dropped off and had said nothing for some time. She followed the conversation from far away, as if from inside her dreams; now and then she gave a start and sat up, fought off her drowsiness and smiled vaguely in the direction of whoever happened to be speaking. Marieta and Ramonet were arguing.

"The man buried in Mecca is Mahomet," said Marieta.

Unfortunately, she said it so loudly everybody heard. And silence descended. A shocked silence. Aroused by that curious silence, Sra Rosich suddenly gave a start, under the impression that her daughter had said something out of place: "What do you know, child? You don't have *any* experience."

"Well, it's what it says in the book they're reading to us at school."

"And the one they're reading at mine," retorted Ramonet, "says quite the opposite."

"Quite the opposite, hmm . . . quite the opposite of what?" growled the commander.

"Quite the opposite of cuckolded," interjected the doctor. "We'd be in a fine pickle if all the books said quite the opposite!"

"And supposing Soleràs has gone to Mecca?" asked the commander.

"Soleràs in Mecca!" exclaimed Dr Puig. "That would cap the lot!"

"It's only a hypothesis," replied the commander, as if apologising for presenting it.

"Who is this Soleràs fellow they keep talking about?" Sra Puig asked Lluís.

"That's what I was wondering too," he replied. "At the end of the day, who *is* Soleràs? A hypothesis perhaps? An enigma? I'd give my right arm to find out."

"Solerás, senyora," interjected the commander, "is someone who disappears without trace; he's a phantom."

"Well, let's agree that Solerás is a mere phantom," granted the doctor, "but the eau de cologne some greasy young lieutenants find in no-man's-land is genuine enough. There is something rotten in the state of Denmark."

"In Denmark?" asked his wife, perplexed. "What's Denmark got to do with Mecca?"

"And what's a backside got to do with the Four Seasons?" he bawled back.

Merceditas' cheeks flushed with indignation but she restrained herself. Lluís rushed to offer her a third Camel. "Thanks," she replied, voice all a-quiver.

"Well, that's right, Denmark," retorted her husband, addressing the captain's wife. "Denmark is where one finds everything from bottles of Fundador and cologne to coffee beans and packets of Camel. Absolutely everything! One even finds big fat jars of Polierotikol; they obviously grow the lot in Denmark. Everything must be rotten in Denmark."

"Doctor Know-all, what they grow there," cut in Picó quietly and ever so cleverly, "is Sauternes 1902 for a doctor who can't keep a professional secret. I don't think you'll taste another drop of Fundador if you don't shut that gob of yours."

At that precise moment the commander unbuttoned his leather jacket and shirt as if boiling hot; he stood up, called for silence with a wave of his hand and solemnly proclaimed: "Officers, petty officers and rank-and-file: I'm as pissed as a newt!"

His wife ran over to him. He was beating himself on the chest.

"What's wrong? Don't you feel well?"

"As a newt!" and he burst into tears as he embraced her. "I'd pledged not to drink while you were here and look at me now, pissed as a newt!"

"Today's a special day," she said soothingly. "There's no shame in tippling on such a day! The patron saint of infantry!"

Husband and wife decided the best thing to do would be to go upstairs and sleep it off. Marieta and Ramonet had gone off to play away from the stove that was giving out too much heat. With all these desertions, the table began to lose heart.

"It's pathetic, my dear," muttered Merceditas, looking at her husband. "And you wanted me to bring the children . . . what bad examples you set!"

"You are quite right, senyora," Picó chipped in. "That such cultured men —"

"And what's it to you, Picó? What's it to you?" asked the doctor. "I wipe your culture on my —"

"My dear, you too ought to go and sleep it off."

"I don't want to! Culture . . . can't you read? It says it all there in capital letters: DO BLASPHEME. You are all witnesses. Sleep it off? Bah, an injection will cure that. An injection, ouch, and you're right as rain!"

"An injection of what, my love?"

"Of streaky bacon, my darlin'."

Merceditas blanched. She threw her cigarette away. She got up from the table. Her husband quietly poured himself another glass of Fundador. She was going to add something, but snarled and left the dining room slamming the door behind her.

"Now, at last!" he said, looking at the end of his nose, "I am free to speak. Poor Letamendi left with his tail between his legs! It's amazing that my father-in-law didn't sock it to me as well, given he's so loaded with money. Merceditas softened him up. You know, she'd just seen a film about a poor doctor who'd saved a city from cholera and she thought I was like the doctor in the film. But I had no cholera, no cash, and no clients . . . And to think I went to the war in search of peace!"

IV

And every life is a solitary path.
MÀRIUS TORRES

The brigade was at a standstill, waiting on the weapons and recruits it needed to re-form. As I had hardly any work in the medical store, I spent more and more time in Santa Espina where I often stayed overnight. If there was an emergency, Dr Puig could call me on the field telephone that linked the two villages. It was never necessary.

When I stayed, I slept in the room near the attic where there were still three mattresses, although I'd slept by myself ever since the ladies came. That's where I kept the chalice that Picó had found in no man's land, which I have mentioned previously; I knelt before it to say my evening prayers. I prayed in front of that chalice I'd set on a wobbly table that I'd managed to salvage; I prayed remembering what used to fill the chalice. At such moments I often thought of Dr Gallifa; not having any news of him, not even knowing whether he was dead or alive, I sometimes instinctively addressed him in my prayers. I wasn't addressing him as a saint; it was more as if I were conversing with him mentally, seeking his advice. Like a fool I then thought that he'd have approved of what I'd set out to do, and that I sorely needed his advice to avoid slipping on that slippery slope! Dr Gallifa was so remote from the everyday, but possessed a rare insight into decisive, fundamental matters. He would have intuited the guilty motives driving my apparently generous intentions, although I personally wasn't at all conscious of them. And Dr Gallifa was not one to dilly-dally over scruples; quite the contrary. Until the outbreak of war I had suffered from lots of nightmares and I'd often asked God to spare me my dreams; I tried to do as much with Dr Gallifa. "My son," he'd interrupt, "don't waste my time: there's a big queue." He was in fact a confessor who was much in demand, and the queue to his confessional often reached as far as the entrance to the church. So I was left with my dream as if it were a counterfeit coin nobody wanted; I couldn't get rid of it.

Dreams are quite something: one way or another we carry them within us from the moment we dream them. Each person's dreams become a part of that person, a peculiar, incoherent part, but a part nevertheless. Their meaning eludes us; the interpretations Freudians give barely scratch the surface; our dreams are much more varied and fantastic, sometimes even more criminal than anything they might say about them! Their meaning escapes us and yet they seem strangely clear when we dream them. It's only later that we don't understand them; awake, we can't follow the man who was asleep a few moments before. That's why a man who is awake feels vaguely ashamed of the man who was asleep a moment earlier, who was simultaneously himself yet somebody else: we're ashamed we can't control this other part of ourselves which is our dreams. "A dream is a no man's land between life and death," Soleràs once said, "between the obscene and the macabre."

What does being in love mean? I still don't know and a quarter of a century has gone by! Perhaps my heart has never dared to ask itself. Might it be our desire to share that mystery so we can gain release? The mystery of life and death, of the obscene and the macabre; the haziest of desires, however painfully we may think it pricks, the most obscure of impulses that perhaps only becomes clear deep within our dream but eludes us yet again when we awake. It's all as murky as the phenomena Soleràs described to me on a night I shall never forget; happy are they who can act like the birds in the sky, who live and die without ever worrying about life or death. But I've been troubled throughout life by nightmares, by attacks of sleepwalking and scruples of conscience . . . when I'd have liked to fly in the full light of day! So much darkness oppresses me, O my God: we would like to live with the utmost simplicity, in the full light of day, in air that's really free; we would like to live, as You Yourself said, like the smallest of children, happy with the world as it is, with things and people as they are, given that You created everything. Accept everything as it is, as it comes, humble in spirit, in all its simplicity, life in all its simplicity, but by her side.

When a man and a woman are in love, a wooden hut is a palace; that is an ancient secret. Don Juan knew it well enough, the man who knew only the most fleeting moments of love, because, O my God, our hardship derives from this, from our fleeting life. If we could only make this or that transitory moment eternal . . . the world would be such a wonderful place . . . Because one finds happiness not in things, but in love; the spirit of wealth is born in the void we try to fill with things in love's absence. The spirit of wealth is relative, is about possessing what others don't have, but love is absolute, only love can be love – even when it is fleeting, even when it is sin, even when it is criminal, because it *is* a crime "to covet one's neighbour's wife". However brief, however sinful or criminal, it *was* a moment that *was* absolute! Don Juan knew that well enough and so do all those who have loved for good or for evil, for a moment or for ever, saintly or criminally, but with all their soul.

That breath of the absolute is enough to transfigure life and death! That breath of love makes everything glorious. The hallowed house in Nazareth must have been a humble abode: little more than a wooden hut. And that's what we think of when we want to imagine a happy household – that represents the very idea of happiness! Those bright, cheerful days in Galilee, that humble, silent peace surrounding Jesus, Joseph and Mary . . . The Gospel of the Passion would not attain its full meaning without that other Gospel of Childhood: more than once we will have thought it but a string of childish tales barely credible in the eyes of critical reason, but can critical reason ever understand love? The horrors of the Crucifixion would be meaningless if it weren't about Jesus of Galilee, love and poetry. The Gospel teaches us to accept the Cross when its time comes, but doesn't it also say we should accept happiness? Isn't that the greatest crime of all, to reject love, happiness and poetry, and nail them all to the cross? Hallowed be happiness: it is the end the Almighty wants for man and it is terrible to reject that.

And yet we will all be crucified. Every life must inevitably end in death. We will all be sacrificed, but hush! Don't let the little children hear that. Let's rather tell them about humanity in the future – that will be wonderful. And why should humanity in the future be wonderful? Poor humanity, how could it ever *be* in the future? It will always be present, grimly present, torn between two summonses: happiness and crucifixion.

The summons of crucifixion . . . isn't that what war is all about? Naturally, people flourish pretexts: causes, noble words, but how hollow, incomprehensible and ridiculous that all seems in the eyes of another generation! Will we ever grasp why our great-grandfathers slaughtered themselves so willingly on behalf of the male line, as opposed to the female line, of the Bourbons? It makes us laugh now, but our great-grandfathers *did* slaughter each other over it. Our great-grandsons will laugh when they discover how we did the same as proletarians against bourgeois or Aryans against Semites: yet Stalin's and Hitler's concentration camps were created in the name of these empty derisory words. Derisory words, empty words that the multitudes followed . . . Point the hatred of the multitudes towards the villain and they will follow; what does it matter that villain is but a word? Aristocrat, bourgeois, priest, Semite, fascist, red, no matter! As he is the villain, he is to blame. To blame for what? For everything! Death to the bourgeois, to the priest, to the Jew, to the fascist, to the red! Long live death! Burn, kill and gorge on blood: *qu'un sang impur abreuve vos sillons.* Always the same old story. Butchery.

One day, when she and I were by ourselves in Santa Espina, I asked her why she thought such a motley crew had come to the front – Lluís, Picó, Solerás, the commander, the doctor: all of us and all the others, the "reds" and the "fascists". She replied, seemingly surprised by my question: "They must do it for the cause, I imagine." "The cause!" I exclaimed. "The cause would be different for everyone . . . And what could it be? No, it's not for any cause; they have come to crucify one another, on both sides. It's the same story in every war and that's why there will always, always, always be wars. Because man was created to sit by the fireside with his beloved, yet he feels the need to crucify. If you'd seen these coarse, simple-minded, frivolous fellows at the 'gala lunch', you can't imagine the pain they can suffer and inflict when the time is ripe! They advance and fall, one after another, yet continue to advance."

What drives them? Not the cause – nobody knows what that is – but glory, which is something everyone feels. But what glory, O my God, what kind of glory, if nobody will ever know the names of so many soldiers who have fallen in so many battles? Posterity? How foolish! If posterity had to remember all those who have died in one battle out of the many, all those whose names are written on sand . . . Even their closest comrades forget them after a while, sometimes after a few weeks. There are so many! They are searching for the glory man cannot give; what they want is to be crucified. War has no other meaning, but it is such a profound meaning!

Whoever wins, whoever loses, no sacrifice is in vain. Whatever happens, the crucified win and the executioner loses. "Pick up your cross and follow me," and they picked it up and followed Him, quite unawares, perhaps not even believing in Him, or believing that they don't believe, and some even blaspheming.

Like all mysteries of life and death they are resolved in Jesus on the Cross! What does it matter to be requited, what do not being understood and loneliness matter if one loves; who is the fool who spoke of love without hope? Where there is love there is hope, and where there is hope there is faith! How many who believe they don't believe will be saved by love, how many others by hope . . .? But Soleràs, who was so clear-sighted, was so badly wrong; perhaps without realising, he sometimes ended up with the illuminists, those most repellent of heretics, or in a pessimism that left hardly a trace of hope in the supernatural. He was so clear-sighted – but at other times! The winners are the ones most to be pitied, whoever they may be; "I pity with all my heart he who finds victory within his grasp," he would say. As for the defeated, vanquished through the centuries in the name of whatever cause, they are redeemed by their very defeat; they felt the thirst for glory – and that, and nothing else, is what drives men to crucify themselves – the thirst for great, heroic, absolute things; they wrote on sand and the wind of centuries erased their words; human memory seems to have forgotten them as if they'd never existed, but "every sin will be forgiven except for blasphemy against the Spirit" and doesn't every man crucified for a cause he thinks just proclaim the Spirit? Nobody risks his life if he doesn't believe in something worth dying for, and what could *that* be but the Spirit?

He wrote on sand and was crucified and you, in defeat, whoever you are, have only to raise your eyes to see Him as we saw Him in those last, incoherent days of our final routs, when whole armies pulverised by artillery, tanks and aeroplanes had to embark on endless marches, leaving behind a trail of corpses, the dying, the sick and exhausted stragglers. Often at sunset, above the ridge, among the bent silhouettes of soldiers the evil machine gunners were mowing down, I thought I could also see His silhouette etched on the twilight sky. Also bent under a weight – of the Cross – He marched before us, defeated among the defeated, pointing us towards the path of failure: in solidarity with all the pain, all the defeats, and all the shame. He was dragging along His bare, bleeding feet and I wasn't the only one to see Him in the course of those days: so many eyes opened and saw Him then! How could I ever forget that moment when we arrived at the ridge of the Pyrenees and looking back at the great plain and those villages and cities going up in smoke, and by way of goodbye to the crucified fatherland we were about to abandon, we sang the "Virolai".* We all did, even the anarchists! In the final days of the war we were all jumbled together in the indescribable havoc of the final defeat.

Yes, Soleràs was clear-sighted, but he lost sight of the fact that an ideal survives even in victory, however much of a caricature it may be. We could have been the victors and could now feel the shame experienced by so many miserable victors, but our ideals would survive as much as theirs. Our means are woeful; our violin strings are made from catgut, but Bach exists; love exists and is as immense as the Great Fugue, even though our means are so pitiful. And what of God Himself? Didn't He appear to us as a young victor resplendent in His glory? Gentlemen, please . . . That night it was Soleràs, of course, it was always Soleràs who spoke to me in depth about that: "We don't have an exact idea of what the crucifixion was like; our own crucified don't give us the slightest idea," he said, before adding: "The sight of God is as unbearable in His glory as it is in His shame.'"

Curled up on my mattress in the dark, I said nothing and listened. He was telling me about Constantine, who abolished crucifixions and replaced them with the gallows: "If he'd done so to save the condemned a drawn-out death agony, he'd deserve our eternal gratitude, but he did it so criminals didn't die like Him, like He who had precisely wanted to die like a criminal! Did you know, Cruells, that Christians avoided portraying Jesus on the Cross for four centuries? They knew only too well what *that* entailed. It wasn't until long after Constantine, when that was long forgotten, that the first crucifixes began to appear. They now gave no idea . . ."

* The anthem of the Abbey of Monserrat, composed by the poet of the Catalan late nine-teenth-century renaissance, Jacint Verdaguer.

I listened to him, mouth open wide, unable to stem his list of atrocities though they were too much for me to take: "Those condemned were stripped stark naked. Which moron imagined that executioners in those days jibbed on the job? And there was no wooden shelf to rest your feet on; feet were nailed into the wood and to that end they had to bend knees and separate thighs . . ."

"Shut up," I said; "I can't bear any more."

"Nor can I, one cannot bear to imagine the Cross! You see, poor Cruells, what we succeeded in doing with our Creator once we had him in our power?"

But Soleràs was gravely mistaken because he refused to accept humbly the wretchedness of our means. However great our wretchedness, life is immense! If it is cowardly to refuse crucifixion when God summons us, it is a crime to refuse happiness when God wants us to be happy. Soleràs proudly rejected that and fled. He stubbornly stared at the Obscene and the Macabre as if they had bewitched him; he, who knew better than most how God had assumed all our shame, for isn't that what Christianity is? The absurd lunacy of the Cross? Christianity is strange, is absurd – and strange and absurd as it is, it is *the* only answer. God assuming the immensity of our wretchedness and to that end stripping Himself of the immensity of His glory, offering Himself up crucified on the Cross in an obscene and macabre spectacle to redeem the Obscene and the Macabre . . . '*Eloi, eloi, lama sabachtani*', how can I complain I am alone and isolated in this world, when I know He was infinitely more so?

V

On the night of 21/22 December, when we'd all been sound asleep in Santa Espina for some time, the battalion band that had come unannounced from Villar woke us with the jolly blasts of a strident festive reveille. They'd marched ten kilometres along the cart track to wake us like that! I grumbled as I got out of bed, thinking it was yet one more of those ghastly jokes we played on each other: awful in that icy cold! Coming down from the attic I bumped into Picó, Lluís and their wives on the first landing, dead tired, freezing to death and cursing that "bloody crowd from Villar", "who didn't let us have a minute's peace". "The Villar crowd" was creating an unbelievable racket in the dining room: some were dancing on the big table, others sang or bawled slouching on the fireside benches; others were belting it out on their trombones and bugles. Some were cheekily drinking rum and cognac from the bottles we kept in the cupboard.

Commander Rosich, the doctor and their respective wives had arrived behind the band, albeit in the Ford; in fact, the doctor and he were in the group on the table dancing a zapateado that made the walls shake. Their flushed faces, bright eyes and frenetic gestures signalled that they'd been drunk out of their minds for a good while.

"*Gloria in excelsis Deo*," cried the commander when he saw us emerge from the staircase door, "and let's shit on the flatfooted brigade!"

Sra Puig was standing in a corner of the room, far from the fire and visibly apart from everyone else, looking deeply shocked. When I went over to say hello, she said: "They are worse than the people in Sodom and Simorra."

Certain highly incoherent expressions half suggested it wasn't simply another round of frivolity for the sake of it; that night there was something to justify the jubilation. It was very difficult to get to the bottom of it but finally we did establish that Villar had just heard on the telephone line linking them to brigade headquarters that the republicans had taken Teruel. When we realised what the good news was, we joined in the jamboree and sang and bawled and drank till the first light of day when they returned to Villar bugles blasting and trombones honking.

In the silence of that bright and icy dawn I then remembered another day, this time in June, exactly six months ago. I had gone to Parral del Río to try to see Soleràs; Lluís had joined the brigade the day before but I hadn't yet met him, and as for Soleràs, he wasn't in Parral. Captain Picó took me to an advanced position where he thought we might find him and from where one could see a line of poplars sinuously following the river and beyond that the brick belfry and houses of Vivel, a village in fascist hands. While we contemplated the view, the bells of Vivel began to chime frantically and we could hear a raucous din of gleeful shouts and cannon salvoes. Picó and I were quiet, trying to act as if we'd heard nothing, but the racket wouldn't go away; we were both thinking the same thought that we kept to ourselves: They are celebrating the conquest of Bilbao. Days later, in effect, the news reached us in the newspapers – late as always. And lo and behold! Six months later we were the ones celebrating the conquest of Teruel; we didn't know then, and found out only much later, how horrendous the battle had been. On the other hand, the worst wasn't taking the city but the enemy counteroffensive that lasted weeks and months.

We knew none of this then and our Christmas that year was happy and hopeful. On the morning of 24 December the snowfall was one of the heaviest that winter; it stopped only in the evening. The snowstorm caught me in Santa Espina. When I stayed in Don Andalecio's house we'd got into the habit of "seeing a movie" to keep Ramonet amused over the long evenings; that day nobody left the house because of the snowstorm and even the adults came to the showing as they couldn't think what to do to pass the time. We "saw movies" in Lluís and Trini's large bedroom comprising a sitting room and bedroom separated by an arch. I hid in the bedroom and used the brougham light to project a luminous circle on to a sheet that hung from the arch; I passed cardboard cutout characters in front of the light that appeared like magnified Chinese shadows on the sheet: the audience, usually just Ramonet and Trini, watched from the sitting room.

That night, after the show, a sumptuous supper awaited us by the fire. We should have gone to Villar, where the commander wanted to offer us a "gala supper" to celebrate Christmas Eve, but the snowstorm had cut us off. After dinner Lluís decided to take the boy – swaddled in a very thick woollen blanket, not an army cotton blanket but one he'd found in a village house – for a stroll along the streets to see what sort of impact the spectacular snowstorm had made.

The snow had stopped falling, the clouds had splintered into streaks that stretched across the sky and the Dog Star glinted between two of them. A row ensued: Trini thought it was "frankly idiotic" for Lluís to want to take the boy out on such a cold night. It was one of the few occasions when they argued in front of everyone else.

Lluís was adamant, so Trini decided to accompany them; the snow was very dry and spongy and their boots sank deep but didn't get wet and made that swishing sound which heavy silk makes when shaken. She wore over-size soldier's boots that the captain had given her: they were loose on her and she had to wear thick woollen socks over her stockings. She never adapted to those rough ugly shoes, though, strangely enough, they suited her. On the other hand, didn't anything she wore always suit her?

I stood in the doorway and watched them walk down the main street, leaving the houses inhabited by the troops to go towards the least devastated part of the village where the men were playing a hurdy-gurdy and singing Christmas carols. They'd lit a big bonfire in the middle of the street on snow that was melting under the spitting embers, and were creating a terrible racket. It was a silent, icy, moonless night.

When they disappeared round the end of the high street, I went out by myself and walked towards the lower part of the village which was all in ruins. The soldiers' carousing and the shrill notes of the hurdy-gurdy faded as I moved away.

The great bellows from the forge half covered by snow in the middle of the street looked like the corpse of a giant wrapped in a winding sheet. That wasn't the only thing I found flung far from its rightful place; I also spotted a wooden bench, a church bell, an olive press, a sprung mattress and other junk. I walked through that lumber, my boots sinking almost to my knees in the snow, as if I were wading through the remnants of a shipwreck. The shattered harmonium lay on the far corner of the church square, almost outside the village, as if they'd thrown it from the choir stalls through the rose window after they'd smashed the glass, and it had stayed there, numbed by its fall.

The church entrance gaped like an empty black mouth, a maw which blasted out a freezing draught that seemed to come from beyond the grave. I crossed myself before going in.

Only bare stone remained of the interior. I placed the chalice on the main altar, lit two tallow candles and prayed.

You'd have thought that bitterly cold silence was about to turn into ice. Waves of sound reached me through the almost crystallised silence. Bells! It was hard to tell whether I was hearing or dreaming them. I stopped praying and listened. Bells on Christmas Eve! Now and then they sounded clearer, however faraway they were. So faraway and pure, they too could have been made of ice or glass. I was astounded to hear them; were they bells from Heaven? How could they be of this earth if bells hadn't chimed since the start of the war – besides, hardly any had survived!

Suddenly, I understood: they were in enemy territory.

Enemy territory? What meaning did those words have on such a night?

I realised they must be singing midnight mass in a village in enemy territory, beyond no man's land; the extraordinary silence and density of that icy air was why I could hear them. That's what the mystery was. The bells were ringing merrily and reminded me of toads piping on a midsummer's night.

Entranced by the sound of distant bells, I left the church. I was back on the cart track, out of the village and on the frozen river bank. I could no longer hear carousing soldiers or the hurdy-gurdy; only the distant bells that were audible or not, depending on the breeze. The snow was so bright and white it was like being in the moonlight. I walked up into a pine grove and the dry snow crackled as my boots sank.

The branches of the pines bent under the weight of the snow; crystals of frost, studded on pine needles, sparkled iridescent in the dim starlight and made me think of the toy-like rock-crystal chandelier I'd seen in Trini's drawing room when I'd visited her. The stars also sparkled like crystals of frost. The Dog Star, the Dog Star yet again, scattering the brightest of sparks among ragged clouds; blue sparks at the heart of a universe solidified by cold.

I'd reached the top of that pine wood but could see nothing. I'd have liked to see the small lights, the bonfires of the soldiers that could point me to the village whence the sound of bells came. I still heard them from time to time but could see nothing.

I walked slowly back to Santa Espina. A light was flickering in the church. I thought that was strange. I went in.

It was the two candles I had forgotten on the main altar; they'd almost melted away. The gilded silver chalice gleamed dimly between them. I kneeled down to pray for a good long while.

I prayed to Dr Gallifa; it was the first time I'd really prayed to him, as if I'd been praying to a saint, yet I still didn't know whether he was dead or alive. I knew, or thought I knew, that *he* was the old Jesuit on carrer del Teatre, something that was becoming increasingly self-evident as far as I was concerned. I prayed to my old seminary teacher at length, asking him to help me and not leave me alone at that crossroads where I was beginning to feel I had gone astray.

*

The last time I'd seen him was in the house that belonged to a brother of his, a rich landowner from the Plana de Vic who lived in Barcelona for most of the year in a flat on the riera del Pi, a huge old flat with high ceilings. He'd received me in his room, its walls invisible behind four ceiling-high bookcases that left space only for the door and the window; the bed was hidden in a very small alcove. He was sitting with his back to the window, opposite a table strewn with books and papers. It was the only item of furniture apart from the rush-bottomed chairs where we sat and another set opposite by the other corner of the table. The air smelt of antique books and snuff; my teacher was one of the rare surviving takers of snuff. While he read and spent hours there every day, he kept taking pinches of tobacco dust from a small box that was open next to his book; a silver box that, I can see now, had tarnished. The smell of snuff was inseparable from his person, as if he were impregnated with it.

He could have returned to his monastery when they repealed the anti-Jesuit laws in 1934, but because he was so old and frail he preferred to stay in his brother's house. He lived with his family like a lay priest;

he went to the seminary every day and taught his moral theology classes. From the day he left the convent he took more snuff than ever; perhaps his chronic addiction to inhaling tobacco dust was the cause of the migraine and nausea attacks he suffered so often. He was around eighty at the time.

That smell of snuff and antique books was accompanied by the regular tick-tock of a very old grandfather clock that you couldn't see because it was by his bed in the alcove. He'd insisted on putting it by his bedside; he slept badly and said its tick-tock kept him company at night during the hours he couldn't sleep, hours that would have seemed endless, he'd say, lying in his bed in the pitch black, without the regular beat of the clock. He also liked to hear it strike on the quarter, half hour and hour so he didn't lose the sense of time. If I'm lingering on these trivial details it's because I want to give an idea of the atmosphere surrounding Dr Gallifa in the last months of his life, a life that belonged to another century. And it was relaxing to be in that spot where the riera del Pi sloped and where one could imagine oneself in the eighteenth century, only a short walk from the Rambla at the heart of a frenzied city. I'd spent ages talking to him there – before the war, when people still had time to talk.

That was two days before the war broke out, although we didn't have the slightest idea what was coming. Or rather he'd heard a rumour via a nephew of his by the name of Lamoneda, a relative he was worried about, and with good reason. He talked to me at great length about this nephew, with whom I'd been acquainted for some time. He was extremely worried on his behalf.

It's now also time for me to say something about Lamoneda, who over time would become something like my own personal ghost. Dr Gallifa's strange nephew was like his shadow and I knew him well by this time, though I never suspected he would become mine too. When I say he was his shadow and is now mine, I mean that he seemed like someone who followed us everywhere, as if he had emanated from our selves and yet was our negation, as people sometimes say the Devil is God's shadow. In my eyes – and I wasn't yet twenty – he was a confirmed bachelor; according to his uncle he was well past the forty mark, although he'd simply say evasively: "I'm thirty plus." He still lingered around the university, where he was vaguely enrolled in the faculty of pharmacy. How long had he been studying there? Dr Gallifa would declare, though everything about his nephew was a blur, that he had tried his hand in several faculties, Law, Philosophy, Medicine, and had wasted a few years in each. When I met him, he was working as assistant to an apothecary on carrer de Sant Pau that I'd visited several times; it was so small and humble you'd have thought it was a neighbourhood herb shop. That's where the police arrested him one night on suspicion of dealing in cocaine. Though they couldn't prove he'd sold any without prescription and in the end had to release him, the apothecary decided not to continue with his services. He always insisted he was innocent and had been the victim of a mis-understanding, and his uncle believed him or at least acted as though he did.

I, on the other hand, never thought the police had got it wrong. More-over, I'd suspected more than once that Lamoneda himself was an addict. Sometimes I'd seen him with a face looking so far gone it was quite painful to behold; with his gaping mouth and vacant eyes staring into the distance – quite different from an alcoholic's – I'd always thought he was suspect. He'd occasionally have pots of money and I could never work out where it came from. I suspected it was in those good times that he was a secret addict; generally he was rather broke, particularly after he'd been sacked by the chemist on carrer de Sant Pau.

Lamoneda's father, a widower, lived in the countryside the whole year; Dr Gallifa's sister, his nephew's mother, had married the heir to a landed family that was as rich as the Gallifas. She died soon after giving birth. Lamoneda lived by himself in Barcelona on money his father sent him, his only child – which also seemed to make his father resigned to letting him lead the life of an eternal student.

He was also what we'd call an eternal youth. In his forties, according to his uncle's calculations, he'd still speak of "us youngsters" in a distinctly obsessive manner. He was tall and skinny with a spotty, stubbly face; when he walked along the street he kept himself very straight-backed and tried to give himself what he thought was a military air by swinging his arms at a stiff, regular tempo. Moreover, he liked to shroud himself in mystery, as if he were involved in some top-secret business. He lived in a boarding house but rented an attic which he called his "bachelor pad", on carrer de Tallers. Here he sometimes invited me up to read me fragments from things he was writing. I remember how one afternoon he reeled off a string of enigmatic paragraphs about Baron de Koenig, a murky figure from the First World War years, about whom I had only the foggiest of notions, given that I was born at the end of the war. He'd clearly been the talk of Barcelona in his day, but who exactly was this baron? "A genius," Lamoneda assured me on that occasion, "a man well in advance of his times. Before anyone else he'd grasped how useful the anarchists were. In the name of anarchy and the proletarian struggle, the anarchists liquidated the Catalan industrialists who were supplying arms to the Allies; people today still haven't understood that there was a Kaiser behind the anarchist gunmen . . ." At the time I paid no attention to the strange things Lamoneda came out with, because I thought they were the product of his delirious imagination. It was only years later that I realised, to my amazement, that it was all mysteriously coherent.

Nevertheless I knew he had some incredible bedfellows; I knew, though his uncle didn't, that he was involved with anarchists; he even told me that they were gunmen though he didn't let on what they were up to. Neither his uncle nor I had ever shown the slightest interest in politics, least of all in the politics of clandestine terrorist groups. I now know – I didn't find this out until many years later – that Lamoneda was in secret contact with Llibert Milmany, but at the time it wasn't his political activities that worried me. His uncle thought he was an unreliable fellow who lived "with his head in the clouds" and that his enigmatic references to mysterious transcendental matters were simply motivated by a desire to appear important in our eyes. "A simple lad," he'd say, "that's all he is."

My teacher was unaware of a side to his nephew that would have changed this view. Lamoneda believed in nothing – although he pretended to be a Catholic, and a devout one at that when with his uncle – and was heavily engaged in erotic experiments. He thought he was a Stendhal and wrote a great deal; Dr Gallifa knew nothing about his literary aspiration. It was basically pornographic, however much he presented it as "minority literature". He read with the expression of a fool who thinks he is really clever; it was a real pain watching that sourpuss bachelor gone to seed who thought he was a Don Juan, and in an ambience that reeked of the most sordid, solitary pleasures!

Could he have been the Judas that betrayed his uncle? I went into a cold sweat each time that suspicion came to mind, because Lamoneda was in effect one of the very few people – two or three – who knew where he was hiding. I never discovered where. The last time I saw Dr Gallifa, he'd spoken to me at length about his nephew as if he'd been worrying him more than ever. He told me Lamoneda had been to see him the day before to inform him that he was in "grave danger" – that was imminent, or so he said. "I didn't really understand him," he told me. "I don't know what he's up to; he's involved with some sort of clandestine committee and other strange activities."

He continued to think, as ever, that this was just nonsense his nephew invented, things he dreamed up in order to lead an idle life: "He's living more than ever like a character in an adventure novel; I think he must be mentally disturbed . . ." That was what worried Dr Gallifa, and not the "grave danger" Lamoneda had warned about. "He tried to persuade me that I should go into hiding, because he says I am in serious danger, but who could ever want to harm me? I'm afraid the wayward life he leads has damaged his brain."

Less than a week later I recognised Lamoneda among arsonists setting fire to a church in the Sant Gervasi neighbourhood.

"Fascist!" they shouted at me, because I was trying to put out the fire. I'd recognised Lamoneda despite his disguise. A days' old beard darkened his face and made me think he hadn't shaved since he'd last spoken to his uncle. He was wearing a worker's overall and a large black and red kerchief that half hid his face. He came over as well and shouted "Fascist" at me.

"Lamoneda," I whispered, "aren't you ashamed of yourself?" "Fascist!" he cried, as he pulled my arm to get me to follow him. With me in tow he slipped through the thick of the crowd of arsonists. The smoke billowing inside the church made us splutter; the flames were beginning to take hold of the chairs they'd piled up in the middle of the nave. Their faces blackened by soot, the arsonists screamed as they ran out. He dragged me out of the church, which was starting to crackle and go up in flames.

"Aren't you ashamed of yourself?" I repeated.

"I did warn you," he replied, whispering, "Now fuck off or this lot will lynch you. Is it my fault if you never take any notice of anything I say to you?"

The arsonists began to throng around us, taking a strong interest in me. It wasn't as if I was wearing a soutane – of course I wasn't; I never wore one in the summer holidays. But I was the only one not dressed as a proletarian. I was wearing my summer suit, ironed white piqué: it stood out a mile! Some of those troglodytes were muttering: "If he's a fascist, why don't we do him in?" Lamoneda heard it and gestured to them to shut up, saying: "*Compañeros*, this man you see before you was a priest, but is one no longer. He has just told me he regrets ever being one and will now join us in shouting: 'Long live anarchy! Long live free love! Make way for the youth!'" I was really struck by the way he held sway over that ragtag mob; they listened to him open-mouthed as if he were some kind of oracle and furiously chorused each of his slogans. The final one stuck in my mind more than the others: "Make way for the youth!" How often and in what strange circumstances I was to hear that cry go up; how often . . . Finally, when I managed to extricate myself – and I can say that I owe my life to Lamoneda – I ran to the mansion in Sarrià where I was living with my aunt, dying to look at Barcelona through the telescope from her terrace roof. You could see a great expanse of the city and I watched all the churches going up in smoke: every single one at the same time.

That night we learned they weren't simply burning churches but also murdering priests. At dawn the next day I ran to the riera del Pi; Dr Gallifa's brother told me he was no longer living there and for safety reasons they didn't want to tell anyone outside their closest family where he'd gone into hiding.

Now I didn't belong to "closest family" but Lamoneda did; he knew where he was hiding. Barcelona was spitting smoke and fire beneath the stifling sky of the dog days of summer and those gangs of ragamuffins were coming in from elsewhere, faces blackened with soot, running all over the city in their search for priests to murder.

Their implacable round-up went on for months and months and Lamoneda, the leader of one of those gangs, knew where Dr Gallifa was hiding. I know for a fact that at the start he'd have tried to save him, as he'd saved me, but what might his crazed mind have decided later? Would he have sold his uncle in a moment of weakness?

And so, lo and behold! I prayed to him for the first time on that Christmas Eve though I didn't know for sure that he was dead. I prayed at length in the Santa Espina church that was as cold and bare as a tomb. I don't know how long I prayed to my former teacher, wherever he was, in this world or the next. When I left the church the bells were no longer chiming. I stopped for a moment in the entrance when I saw something that startled me: the footprints of two other pairs of boots beside mine in the snow. It was obvious that two people had come and gone while I was praying. I remembered that mine were the only footprints in the snow when I entered the church that second time. Two unknown people had entered the church while I was at prayer, and I hadn't heard them.

VI

Sra Puig and Sra Picó went back to Barcelona the day after Twelfth Night. The commander's wife and Trini had decided to stay on for several weeks as the fresh country air and food were doing the children a world of good. Barcelona was suffering ever more bombing raids from fleets of aircraft based in Majorca and hunger was striking ever more cruelly. We all felt it would be better for Ramonet and Marieta to continue with us as long as the snow covered our dead front: this was unanimously agreed. We didn't think the fact that the battle for Teruel had been fought despite the snow was an argument against, as the element of surprise played such a key role there. So Trini asked for two months' leave from her university and I recall how her dean, in his letter granting it, offered her tongue-in-cheek congratulations for "being able to live a tranquil and plentiful life at the front".

Ours wasn't the only dead front; many sectors were as becalmed as ours and the situation in which Trini and the commander's wife were placed wasn't as unusual as it might seem. We'd sunk into the endless calm of that winter as if it were a chronic disease that had become everyday and tolerable; in any case, and despite Teruel – that *did* seem so unusual and so remote – none of us thought battle could resume in any of the mountain sectors before the snows melted. As if to confirm us in our delusion, high command never got round to sending us the weapons or new recruits required to reconstitute so many battalions and brigades, devastated by the previous summer's campaigns and now living a kind of winter hibernation along the frozen sierras. If I dwell on this I do so to justify myself; my opinion weighed heavily in Trini's determination to stay on into the spring, a decision that was to have dramatic consequences.

I'd gone up to spend a day in Santa Espina soon after Twelfth Night. I sometimes went there without telephoning beforehand, and it was the case that day and I discovered that Picó and Lluís had left for an expedition to the abandoned valley, no man's land, where they now made frequent incursions. Trini was alone with her son in Don Andalecio's house.

She'd made a find the day before and wanted to show it off to me: a mahogany armchair, apparently from the Louis XVI period, that had appeared in an attic of the ruined rectory. She'd placed it in her bedroom, in front of the large window through which sunbeams now slanted; from there you could see the small cultivated terraces along the Purroy, now buried under two or three feet of snow. A big baroque brazier – another of her discoveries – was heating the room. We'd found a large number of sacks of pressed olive stones in the houses in the two villages, so it was easy enough to keep the braziers lit in every room of the house. When I went in, Ramonet was drawing in a notebook; being an only child he knew how to amuse himself and sometimes even talked aloud to himself, arguing and quarrelling as he might have done with a playmate.

I sat down in the armchair facing the window with Trini on a low chair opposite me so I saw her against the light. The rays of the sun – and the January sun in that intense cold could be really bright – made her hair gleam; that was the day I realised for the first time it was red, a very pale red only the full sunlight brought out, which was why I hadn't earlier noticed that particular sheen. Ramonet came over and asked me to make him a cardboard doll; his mother told him to leave us in peace. She wanted to talk to me.

I realised that she needed to, which made me happy; I felt at ease by her side in that room.

"I'm so happy," she said. "I'd never seen my boy with such colour in his cheeks. This dead front is working miracles for him."

"And for you as well," I added.

"Bah, as far as I . . ."

Silence descended and I was too inept to know how to proceed; I didn't understand where she was heading, why she was so interested in talking to me, all alone. I felt at ease by her side in that room. She must have found red ochre in one of the abandoned houses, because the tiles were a luminous red and the radiant red floor contrasted pleasantly with the resplendent whitewashed walls. How it's changed since she arrived, I thought; most astonishing of all was the difference in the appearance of the junk furniture, those survivors from previous centuries; the friars' chairs, sideboard, baroque table and trousseau chest. Trini had had them all brought up to her spacious bedroom – very spacious, as I said, with a sitting room and a bedroom. She had plugged the wormholes with wax, and by rubbing the antique walnut hard with a rough woollen cloth had teased out a warm glow that soothed the eyes. She had positioned the mortars, oil lamps, candlesticks, chocolate pots and other various copper items she'd collected around the different pieces of furniture, after rubbing and polishing them furiously to remove layers of mildew: they now shone like red gold. If a slanting ray of winter sun slipped almost horizontally through the window and landed on one, fiery sparks seemed to shoot everywhere. They weren't only for show; she was using the candlesticks and oil lamps. At nightfall, which came early, she would light them and dissipate the gloom of the long winter evenings. Lo and behold, I thought, this room has been touched by a magic wand; it's so nice and comfy here . . . In that bedroom you felt you were in a well-established patriarch's farmhouse: there was a strong scent of lavender from the small bunches she had spread around. A scent of woods and meadows, I thought, the scent of a fine house with a young mistress – it was the first time I'd realised this: quite unawares, Trini seemed born to be the mistress of an ancient mansion. I felt so at ease by her side in that room, even in that deep silence; you have to feel relaxed by someone's side to be unthreatened by silence . . .

"The fact is," she added after that lull, "I'm simply a failure."

"'A failure?'" I exclaimed, taken aback. "That depends on you."

"Do you think I said that because I've broken with Lluís? I beg you . . . life is absurd, but not to that extent. I couldn't care less about Lluís."

Her eyes flashed and glinted and I looked down at the floor. Then she suddenly fired another question I wasn't at all expecting: "Do you know my brother?"

"Llibert?" But I stopped myself in time; I knew almost nothing about Trini's brother in that period except for what I'd read in the letters.

"Lluís hates him and quite right too. I hate him as much as he does. That's at least one thing Lluís and I agree on."

"Lluís told me a bit about him," I lied, since Lluís had never – or barely – mentioned his brother-in-law. "Soleràs also . . . and please forgive me if I bring him in."

"Forgive you? I asked you up to my room precisely to talk about

Soleràs; I so much want to talk to you about him . . . And we will do so later; now we're on the subject of Llibert, who is quite the opposite of Soleràs. Llibert belongs to the race of people who only believe in success."

"I'm familiar with that race," I said. "But who knows whether Llibert . . . ?"

"I beg you to leave Christian charity out of this; it would be extremely tedious to talk about Llibert and not be uncharitable. As I said, Llibert is totally at home with the race of winners. As far as he's concerned, any faith, religious or not, is simply consolation for failures, 'opium for the immense mass of failures' were the words he used once. He likes to be emphatic and is the kind that listens to his own voice when he's talking."

"That race is all the same. They're infatuated by rhetoric."

"So then, I detest the race of winners as much as I love the race of failures. When I said 'I am a failure', I meant 'I belong to Soleràs' race.' You see I'm giving you a clue."

"But Lluís has nothing in common with Llibert; he's no 'winner', as you say. He's not fond of rhetoric and doesn't like to be emphatic."

"Lluís? You don't know him at all! You're quite wrong about Lluís, Cruells, as I was too, unfortunately. For the moment Lluís is more interested in women than in banknotes; his 'successes' are different in kind, but basically, aren't they all the same? Why should we only measure success in terms of money? It's a large, diverse world and there are many other equally selfish aims. And Lluís . . . one should bear in mind, has never had to go without, unlike Llibert. Why would he chase after money if he didn't need to? Lluís is still very young and for the time being he prefers to chase after women; give him a few years and maybe he will surprise you. Who knows if one day he won't become the most important noodle manufacturer in the whole of Europe . . . ?"

She said this in a vicious, sarcastic tone, simply repeating Uncle Eusebi's wild prophecy which I was only aware of from the letters I'd read. I tried to defend Lluís: "You hate him now . . . and hatred . . . hatred is a warped mirror that disfigures everything . . ."

"One day you'll be forced to admit I was right. Lluís is hiding a capacity for plunder that so far he's only revealed in relation to women. But let's forget him for the moment; I find conversations about Lluís particularly deadening. I didn't want to talk about Lluís or Llibert as individuals, but about their race in general, this race of winners that so disgusts me. Everything that isn't success is stuff and nonsense as far as they are concerned. They think the only worthwhile success is of this world and that it must come quickly, not be drawn out or bring on a sweat. Well then, as you know, I am a geologist, or, more modestly, a teacher of geology. In geology the centuries are but a breath of air, and millennia a dream; things only begin to possess substance for us after a million years. Don't worry: I don't intend boring you stiff with geology. All I'm wondering is what the success of these winners represents in terms of geology – less perhaps than that of a mosquito from the Carboniferous Age that manages to become a fossil in a drop of amber?"

I looked through the window and said nothing; I was trying to guess what I should be answering, how I would lead the conversation where I wanted it to go. I'll have to say something shocking, I thought, but what?

"A mosquito?" I replied. "A mosquito from the Carboniferous Age? I beg you, Lluís is no mosquito! Not even Llibert . . . I wouldn't want to deny – it's so clearly the case – that with our efforts we can never become more than dust scattered by the wind of centuries, much less than a mosquito in a drop of amber. I know that to be fossilised is an amazing stroke of luck. For a non-believer, then, death is complete failure. That's why non-believers are so obsessed with success. But we should be understanding and indulgent with these poor non-believers! They only have success – success in this world that they enjoy now, this very minute; it's all they have to give meaning to their lives. You dub them winners; you could also dub them the self-satisfied in life, since it's all pretence with them. They pretend to be satisfied by making us believe they have won; we should feel sorry for these people who go through life looking satisfied, all those who, if they even considered the possibility, would like to be fossilised for eternity wearing an expression of contentment! But are they really as satisfied as they pretend? Of course not: far from it. They are satisfied with themselves, not with other people or with things. You should never lose sight of this, Trini; if being self-satisfied is laughable, being satisfied with other people and things isn't simply being good, it's being saintly."

"That's not what I meant," she replied. "I wasn't talking about saints, but about Lluís and Llibert."

"I don't know your brother and wouldn't want to refer to him; it's always rash to judge individuals. I simply wanted to refer to a way of being without pinning it on anyone in particular. I was referring in general to people who live their lives obsessed with success and continually simulate successes that end in failure, since every moment draws them closer to the death that represents irrevocable failure in their eyes – because they are non-believers. Blessed is the man who feels he has failed! The feeling of failure is the first step on the road to the only possible achievement. Where is the success of those who feel satisfied – I mean those who are self-satisfied? They are the great failures and that's why they are so obsessed with success. I didn't intend any allusion to your brother Llibert: God spare us from making judgements on others. Only God knows the inner-most souls of individuals; only He can judge them. Invariably – you too must have experienced this – when a man or woman reveals their inner-most soul, they only arouse pity or compassion. We are all worthy of pity! People rarely bare their innermost soul because no-one likes being pitied."

"Yes, we'd prefer to explode than allow others to imagine that we are unhappy."

"So let's leave Llibert then. As for Lluís . . ."

Just then Ramonet interrupted us to show me the house he was draw-ing in his exercise book: "A wolves' house," he said, "and the wolves have got everything, peppers, hammers, scissors, and grandparents." I suggested he should add a cooking pot so the wolves could make soup. Talking to that child took a weight off my shoulders; I felt so inhibited by his mother. Trini was beginning to frighten me.

"The other day I was thinking about that 'gala lunch' in Villar," she said. "You'd told me about the unhappy wretches 'who barefacedly deny that they are'. There are lots, you said; people prefer to be seen as barefaced liars rather than as unhappy wretches. Most would rather be thought of as smart operators, or even skunks, than miserable good-for-nothings. Just think, you continued, of the way all the words that mean 'worthy of pity' sound or are beginning to sound pejorative: ranging from 'unhappy' to 'wretched', sorry, 'miserable' . . . we are as ashamed of wretchedness as we are of the most shocking ridiculousness. You said so among many others things at that 'gala lunch' and it all came back to me yesterday; you also told me about that teacher of yours in the seminary, whose name escapes me at the moment. I gathered you love him dearly. Didn't you say your seminary teacher was the Jesuit who'd been leader of the congregation when Lluís was there? Lluís mentioned him occasionally, a Father Garrofa or Pellissa, or whatever, but in terms very different from yours . . . !"

"That 'gala lunch' ended deplorably," I replied, "but now we're talking about something else. I basically agree with you, though we shouldn't exaggerate. There is such a thing as legitimate success; good Christians suffer failure with resignation, but to search it out on purpose would be akin to committing suicide. This was one of Soleràs' mistakes; he seemed intent on failing in everything and that isn't Christian because it isn't human. Blessed be failure when it comes in the form of poverty, sickness, incomprehension and aloofness, or in defeat or dissatisfaction with some deep longing we'd felt was our very reason to be alive. Blessed be failure when it comes, since it comes to improve us, though it's not right to seek it out deliberately. Blessed be death when it comes, but it isn't right to anticipate it! Soleràs was sorely wrong on this point as on so many others; he even told me once: 'If I've never got round to committing suicide, it's because I'd rather be a suicide that's failed – failure even in suicide!' Yes, he did really say this once, those very words; perhaps it was just one of his shafts of wit, but his wit often had real content. And please do forgive me for harping on about Soleràs."

"Forgive you? But I've already told you it's Soleràs I want to talk about. Or is it forbidden to talk about him?"

"I'd gathered at that 'gala lunch' that you didn't like people talking about him."

She went quiet and stared at me: "What do you imagine there is between him and me?"

"Oh, I'm certain there's nothing. I simply recognise the influence of his ideas on yours and that's not surprising, since he's swayed all of us. It's impossible to know a character like Soleràs and not feel his influence! Strange how three boys without a father or mother between them have ended up in this brigade – Lluís, Soleràs and me; three orphans raised by their aunts and uncles. Don't think that's funny; whoever's been an orphan as a child is one for ever. Childhood leaves a mark that never fades. Well then, Soleràs used to say you get the aunt you deserve; if you knew my aunt . . . Aunt Llúcia . . . if only you knew her! Did I ever tell you that all I ever wanted was to be a priest in a shanty town? Well, you know, for the past few weeks I don't feel so sure of myself; I don't really know what I want. If only you knew Auntie Llúcia! Quite the reverse of Soleràs' . . . and that's the only family warmth I've ever known, I only have the haziest memories of my mother; I was four years old when she died. And my aunt's place offered all the family spirit you could want, but as far as warmth goes . . . I'd come to hate the family and the family spirit, and it was her blinkered attitudes that made it seem hateful. I sometimes wonder whether it wasn't her family spirit that led her to be a spinster; she is horrified by any man who doesn't belong to our family. She's not aware of this, naturally, but her instincts would lead her to incest: never go outside your family! Even as a child I felt there was something dubious about this family spirit which suffocated me like the stale air in a bedroom that's never aired. My God, even the holiest things can become so perverted! Because the family is sacred; Jesus lived thirty years within a close-knit family. I now realise Auntie made me hate the idea; in recent weeks I've suddenly realised that I'm made to create a family."

I took a deep breath and silence descended.

"From everything you've just said," she replied, "I think I've gathered you no longer want to be a priest. Now, as someone who's not a Catholic, it makes no odds . . . whether you become a priest or not . . ."

"But you are a Catholic," I said, rather shocked.

"I wanted to be one. I did want to be one, but perhaps only because he is one. And of course I'm not talking about Lluís; that would be ridiculous . . . And where is he now? For without him . . . Catholic! What does the word 'Catholic' mean? Something like Buddhist, spiritualist, Muslim or Mormon? There are so many religions . . . why choose one in preference to any other? Catholic . . . what does that mean? Let's not say 'Catholic', let's say 'Christian', that's broader. Even so, what does 'Christian' mean? Nobody knows! On the other hand, lots of people do know where Soleràs is."

I knew nothing about his whereabouts at the time and the turn in Trini's conversation took me by surprise. What did she mean? How could she think someone knew where Soleràs was when we'd had no news of him at all? It's true I'd more than once wondered at the range of goodies Picó and Lluís found in no man's land – as did Dr Puig. I'd suspected, or rather was certain, they came from wheeling and dealing with the enemy – swaps – but I'd never thought they might be connected to Soleràs'disappearance.

"Please, don't make such a face," said Trini sarcastically. "They know only too well where Soleràs is, but they won't let on. You may remember that Lluís and I took the boy for a walk on Christmas night. Lluís was carrying him swaddled in his arms; we walked very slowly because the military boots the captain had given me sank almost to my knees in the snow. Then we heard bells trilling, almost imperceptibly, a long way away, and Lluís let slip: 'Perhaps Soleràs is listening to midnight mass.' 'Is Soleràs in fascist territory?' I exclaimed, angry that Lluís could suggest such a thing. 'Everything is possible where Soleràs is concerned; perhaps in essence he is simply a traitor.' That's what Lluís told me and then he refused to say another word, however much I badgered him. So much toing and froing in no man's land, so many unexpected finds there, so much reticence about the whole operation . . ."

"What are you implying?"

"Nothing in particular. I can't get to the bottom of it either. They said and still say that one fine day Soleràs disappeared from the brigade and they've had no news of him since; well, I repeat, I feel that you gentlemen know only too well where he is."

I didn't, and protested my innocence.

"Don't try to deceive me, Cruells. This is why I so wanted to talk to you today by yourself, taking advantage of the others' absence. I want you to tell me where Soleràs is; I don't want you all laughing behind my back, and I mean all of you!"

Strangely enough, while she was talking about Soleràs I thought about Lamoneda, but how was he connected to Soleràs or his disappearance, or indeed to Trini? I was thinking about Lamoneda and the disappearance of Dr Gallifa, about whom we had no news, as we had none of Soleràs.

"I don't know where he is," I replied, "or whether he is dead or alive."

"Soleràs is not dead!" she shouted.

"I didn't mean Soleràs, but Dr Gallifa. He may have been sold by a Judas; yes, he had a Judas by his side, like his shadow. His name was Lamoneda . . ."

"Now you're joking at my expense," she cut in bitterly. "What's the relevance of any of this?"

"What's the relevance?" I'd liked to have retorted, and to have added: "How the hell should I know? Everything is so confused . . . perhaps if I were to say that Lamoneda, in a way, is like a caricature of Soleràs. A monstrous caricature, I grant you! I expect they're not connected at all, but the fact remains I can't think of one without the other coming to mind." I'd have liked to react like that but I said nothing. The expression on her face was her way of suggesting she wouldn't follow me along this entangled path, where even I was losing my way.

"I'd like you to know," I muttered, "that this Lamoneda is the first person who enabled me to understand things you could hardly imagine . . . I don't know if you, from a family of anarchists, have ever heard of Baron de Koenig?"

"Now you're talking about Baron de Koenig!" she exclaimed and her expression became mocking, almost cruel. "What do I care about Baron de Koenig? Why don't you talk to me about Soleràs?"

"Soleràs is an enigma, like Lamoneda. As we all are! But Soleràs is more enigmatic than everyone else; you lose your way with him. There are much more disturbing riddles around Soleràs than the one that's worrying you, because, at the end of the day you could understand if he's gone over to the fascists. So many others have done so before him! I can tell you that even I did once . . . No, the Soleràs enigma is not that straightforward. I must be frank, Trini. I must tell you about one of the last conversations I had with him. I must be frank: if Soleràs has helped you so far, Trini, from now on he can only hurt you. Irremediably. Soleràs is an enigma and he'll lead you completely astray. He can only lead you to disaster."

Her green eyes glinted painfully, wanting more; she listened in awe, hanging on my every word.

"'What does "adoptive father" mean?' he asked me the last time I spoke to him at any length. I'd no idea what he was referring to. 'The other's ghost,' he went on, 'will always intervene . . .' I couldn't understand him; just imagine, he was recounting an *adoptionist* heresy! 'If Jesus had only been God's adoptive son,' he told me, 'the other would overshadow God and we'd all be fucked.' They were his words, literally. His usual sarcastic barbs, you know. But I'm now beginning to grasp what he was referring to, and it's my duty to tell you plainly that there are some extremely bizarre sides to Soleràs. Once – and this was ages ago – he told me about a long November evening between midnight and four a.m. in his aunt's house . . . well, about things that would shock anyone. Was he inventing them? I don't think so: he seemed ashamed of what he'd done! Things only make you feel ashamed when they are true. And even if he had invented them, because anything is possible and his imagination was boundless . . . he was eternally far-fetched . . . He grumbled sardonically: 'The other's ghost would always intervene. Don't we have enough on our hands dealing with our own? Do you still want to pin another's ghost on us?' Trini, stick with the good he's done you so far and beware of the evil he could do you in the future. Yes, Soleràs could hurt you a lot. And it will be irremediable."

A cloud full of rain seemed to float across her eyes: "More than evil, much better than any evil," she muttered contemptuously. "There are things you can't understand unless you've lived them. Why should evil worry me if it comes from him? One loves this kind of evil more than all the good in this world. You can't understand that – you've never been in love!"

"I've never been in love? And why not? Do you think those of us who aspire to the priesthood are a different species? We are men like any others, woe betide us . . ."

"*Have* you ever been in love?"

"Why not? To tell the truth, I . . . I'd never have dared speak to you about such things, but as you seem to be encouraging me . . . no doubt only to make fun of me. I'm shy, I know, and I suffer as a result. Shy people suffer most because we know we are shy and that awareness upsets us. Because we know we are shy, we can never decide what to say and what to keep to ourselves; we find it such an effort to say what we ought to say that we end up saying what we should keep to ourselves."

"Why don't you just come out with what you want to say? That's always best."

"What I *want* to say?"

"Of course! Just that and say it simply."

"One might want to say something the other person would rather not hear . . ." I replied, feeling extremely inhibited.

"Say it anyway."

"What I want to say . . . ? Well, fine, I will: I want to say that love is the only thing that makes life worthwhile; if it weren't for the love that transfigures us in the eyes of others, we men and women would amount to very little . . . But our dreams lead us so far away from love, plunge us into such pits of darkness . . ."

"What kind of dreams?" she asked.

"I've always suffered from nightmares and have even had attacks of somnambulism. I think I may have mentioned them to you earlier. What's strange about all this – and I'm not referring just to my sleepwalking but to my ordinary dreams as well – is that they belong to a family of phenomena Soleràs told me about one night, a very long night in November I mentioned. I know next to nothing about these things, apart from what Soleràs told me and what I found in the occasional book we read in the seminary. Apparently these phenomena everyone finds so disturbing are closely connected to sleepwalking and hypnosis. Almost everyone denies the reality of the former and accepts the reality of the latter, which is quite incongruous. Besides, without recourse to sleepwalking or hypnosis, aren't ordinary dreams, the ones almost everyone dreams, quite inexplicable? And yet who would deny that we dream them? We dream them, but who could ever say what inspired them?"

"I never dream," she said, "or almost never."

"You don't know how lucky you are; because it's a nasty burden and horrible to bear. We know nothing about ourselves and are full of things we haven't a clue about. That's why we appear to be so opaque, particularly to ourselves."

Trini appeared not to be following my thread.

"I'm sorry, but you did encourage me to talk about whatever I wanted – didn't you use those very words? Let's go back to the beginning: what does being in love mean? Nobody knows. One says one is Catholic, spiritualist, Mormon, fascist, republican, in love, but what do these words mean? What does any of this mean? Are these names any more precise than our dreams? What are our dreams? What are faith, ideals and love? Everything is so confused . . . We all carry a pit within us that we never plumb, that is, if there is a bottom . . . We occasionally descend that far, in our dreams, but once awake it's all a complete blank again. I'm sorry" – she still looked as if she wasn't following me – "but you did ask me to say what I wanted to say and as straightforwardly —"

"If that's what people call speaking straightforwardly," she retorted.

"Alright, I will say it as simply as I can: love is a tree, like faith; it spreads its leaves in the fresh air and full light of day, but its roots are mired in the mud. I can't say it more simply: we are burdened with a double standard that is both incomprehensible and intolerable. On the one hand fresh air and light beckon to us, and on the other muddy earth drags us down. You asked me if I knew what it was to be in love; I don't, but nor do you."

Silence fell; she seemed to be reflecting on what I'd just said.

"I'd never thought that," she said finally, "but you may be right, Cruells. Anyway, what do I care? If only you know how little I worry about being in love, whenever. It's there, and that's it."

"Dr Gallifa . . ."

"That Dr Gallifa again?"

"But . . ."

I felt sad and tired. He *was* Dr Gallifa! It had to be him with that expression without conviction but full of faith, the most ordinary of apostles, an eighty-year-old bent double by the afflictions of age, defeated yet invincible. It had to be him, it couldn't be anyone else, but how could I tell her? Would I ever be able to pluck up the courage to tell her I'd read her letters? You saw him, it *was* him, it couldn't have been anyone else, I'd have liked to scream, like you do in nightmares when your voice is strangled in your gullet. I stopped myself just in time. Say everything I wanted to say? Impossible! I was dying to talk about her letters to Soleràs but I couldn't; I felt the heat from my shame rise to my brow, the disgrace that came from reading them.

I made an effort, because I could see the mocking glint in her eyes when she saw I'd gone so red: "I don't know how far I have a right to speak sincerely, but as you were encouraging me to . . . With my hand on my heart I can tell you that over the past few weeks I've been thinking the ecclesiastical path is not my path to happiness. Don't interrupt. I'm in love. For the first time ever. So it's not surprising that I've not had any practice."

I shut my eyes and stayed like that for a while – not saying a word; then, with my eyes still shut – I was afraid to look her in the eye – I slowly said: "I'm free to marry: I just have to change my course of studies. But is she . . . free? Yes, she is. By the terms of canon law, she lives as a concubine. Excuse my use of that word; I don't like it either, but it is the precise legal term and in any case the right one if we are to understand each other. Either marriage is or isn't a sacrament; I mean the only thing that can make it indissoluble is its sacred character, which doesn't derive from any external ceremony as so many people think who don't know their canon law, but from the express wills of husband and wife. Could we say that such a will has ever been expressed in the case that concerns us? Well, no, we couldn't. I've thought it through a lot before reaching such a negative conclusion. If you, senyora, only knew how often we debated these subtle, entangled issues in Dr Gallifa's moral theology classes . . . But don't worry; I'll not involve Dr Gallifa, I won't mention him again. I'll sum up and simply say that after I'd given myself a headache wondering whether the person that interests me is free or not, I concluded that she is and always has been, not for the lack of any external ecclesiastical or civil ceremony, which, at the end of the day, is of scant importance, but because neither he nor she ever wanted their bond to be permanent."

At that precise moment Ramonet pulled on his mother's skirt: "Mummy, I'm hungry . . ."

"Go and play a bit longer. Can't you see I'm talking to this gentleman?"

The child was miffed because we weren't paying him any attention and went back to his drawing books near the brazier, but immediately came back and said: "He isn't a gentleman, he's Cruells."

"Don't disturb us now, Ramonet. Please continue. I'm interested in everything you've started to tell me; you were saying the person in question is living as a concubine according to canon law . . ."

"In fact that's no longer the case. Even that obstacle has vanished! She is as free as I am; she has broken with him. They are both trying to keep up appearances and act as if they are still together. How ridiculous! If you're a concubine, what's the point in trying to keep up appearances?"

"You're right: there's no point at all."

"There's the added element that she has since become a Christian. From the moment she became a Christian, she has to decide one way or the other: either she sanctifies their union or she makes a clean break. And then . . ."

"Then you and she . . ."

Her green eyes looked at me disenchanted, as if the outcome was too predictable. That disenchantment was cruel but even so I kept my self-possession.

Then I sighed like someone who feels released from a crushing weight: "Yes, my story is disappointing and would barely provide a plot for a sentimental story for twelve-year-old girls. But it's mine. I don't have any other. And I find it . . . quite beguiling. Just to think that one day I could be sitting next to her by the fireside on an autumn or winter's evening . . . Because one should sit so from time to time; man didn't come into this world simply to stay standing. Now both sides demand that we get up on our feet; both sides keep telling us to stand up: '*En pie, españoles!*' '*Dempeus, catalans!*' And yet one must sit now and then; a life standing up would be intolerable. Man was born to sit by the fire, on a winter's evening, accompanied by his beloved wife. As you can see, my story is naïve, the plot is on the thin side and soon comes to an end. But I find it enthralling."

"But she . . ."

"Now they've fallen out, shouldn't *she* decide to strike out for her freedom? You think it over. Their relationship can't be sustained indefinitely; it's a comedy that won't hold up. It is . . . foolish."

"I agree."

"There's one factor that complicates matters," I said, feeling my hands start to shake: "Namely that I'm a close friend of his."

Her eyes glinted, even more disenchanted. "What a coincidence!" she rasped sarcastically.

"And he's still in love with her and has never stopped loving her: he loves her more than ever and is very unhappy because of her."

"Yes, because of *her* – the mistress of the castle."

"Please, stop trying to make fun."

"Or is it the doctor's wife?"

"Stop trying to make fun," I repeated. "The doctor's wife? What's the doctor's wife got to do with this mess . . . ? The doctor's wife is a fool!"

"I agree entirely. Though she hardly needs to be Madame Curie for what he's after. Bottles of eau de cologne, packets of Camel – what didn't he bring her from no man's land?"

"Stop trying to make fun. I'm trying to be serious. My friend, like everyone else, has taken the occasional wrong path. But she won't forgive him. Yet she's a Christian, you know . . ."

"A Christian . . ."

"Forgive me: you've still not grasped how the whole of Christianity is contained within a single word: forgiveness."

"It's as well to know," and tears welled up in her green eyes that she had to wipe away.

"And do you think I'd be acting cheaply, that I'd be betraying my friend, if I were to reveal my feelings to the person I'm talking about? What should a man do in my position?"

Trini sobbed and wiped the tears away as she pushed away Ramonet who was pulling at her skirt again, wanting to show her a new drawing.

"Don't be under any illusion, Cruells. You can't imagine how much Lluís has made me suffer! And I only lived for him and his son . . . He had me by his side and didn't even see me; whole days went by when he said not a word" – Trini was upset and kept wiping her eyes – "weeks and months without writing a line . . . It's not that stupid affair in Olivel, as you seem to think. Let me speak and don't contradict me. What do you know about my life? You don't understand *my* situation at all! Forgive me for saying this, but you're always distraught, you're always coming out of a daydream; don't be offended, what I want to say isn't at all insulting; now let *me* be frank with *you*: you're way off mark, Cruells! Didn't you notice how he and the doctor's wife have been flirting for weeks? Yes, he and the doctor's wife . . . Do you think I let them out of my sight? Ay, Cruells, you don't know us women! In cases like this, we don't miss a thing, I can assure you. The lady of the castle, the doctor's wife and so many others I will never know . . . You've preached me a long sermon, Cruells; I found a way to swallow the lot; now it's my turn to have my say. So then, you're wrong about me. This rubbish you've come up with about Soleràs . . . yes, this rubbish . . . and you're . . . exactly like Lluís . . . like them all . . . Why do you all hate him? Why? Well, I'll tell you, because he's a thousand times better than the lot of you together, than this whole filthy brigade, than the whole universe . . ."

She started sobbing, much to the astonishment of Ramonet.

VII

Some of the country people began to return to the two villages in the middle of February. The peace had held locally for weeks, even months, encouraging them. They repaired their ruined houses as best they could to have a bed and a fire to cook their meals on; then they ploughed some of the terraces by the river, close to the village. They used donkeys for this because they'd lost their mules, requisitioned by one or other of the armies. They were more cautious that we'd been and didn't for the moment dare bring back their wives and children.

That was why we began to hear the almost forgotten sounds of peacetime among the ruins, donkeys braying, goats and sheep bleating and hens clucking; the beginnings of the resurrection, however halting, seemed like a dream and no doubt helped confirm a sense of profound tranquillity that events would soon shatter so brutally.

Teruel seemed further away than ever since the news, via the daily papers, reached us days late, often weeks, and moreover it came bowdlerised by the wartime censors. Our battalion – or rather what was left of it – kept body and soul alive in the back of beyond around those two villages as if nothing else existed. We scarcely had any contact with the rest of the army; weapons and recruits hadn't yet arrived. They never did. I later learned that this was true for many other battalions, covering large areas to our left and right that were also dubbed "dead fronts". Hundreds of kilometres of the Catalan front – the Aragonese front – were thus unequipped and the soldiers sank into even greater lethargy from the combination of an absolute lack of activity and the deep snowdrifts of a long winter.

Convinced that the children were much better off with us than in Barcelona, we kept postponing the date for Trini and the commander's wife to depart. The beginning of March was thus upon us, barely twenty days to the start of spring; we decided they would make the return journey on the fourth of the month, without fail. They'd been with us almost three months.

Then Ramonet woke up with a temperature. Nothing to be alarmed about – children get temperatures so easily!

"It's a straightforward case of flu," was Dr Puig's diagnosis, "but he'll have to spend a few days in bed. He can't go on such a long, difficult journey in this cold with a temperature of thirty-nine and a half degrees."

The commander's wife got into the Ford alone with Marieta; she didn't want to delay their journey any longer; she was all set to go. The day after, I went to Santa Espina to see how Ramonet was. I was on the point of opening his bedroom door when I heard Trini and Lluís arguing quietly with a latent violence they made little attempt to suppress.

"You are quite unable to understand," said Trini softly.

"And you have such a mania about being understood," retorted Lluís. "I expect that's why you wrote him so many long letters: apparently, he *did* understand you."

"Shut up."

There was silence for a second. I was going to rap at the door when I heard Lluís' voice once again: "What's the point in understanding? If you think you understand me . . . You imagine that we are having a ball at war cheek by jowl like this. If you only knew . . . It can be as numbing as peace-time!"

"What about me? I suppose you think I was having a ball starving in Barcelona while you were making heroic advances on every bit of feudal skirt that —"

"Every bit of feudal skirt? What are you prattling on about?"

"Not to say medical. Yes, feudal and medical!"

"Stop all this nonsense – it's gross."

"Gross, is it? Well, I wouldn't say any different."

"We've both suffered, Trini, each in our own way. Must we quarrel over this now? We've both suffered and it's not about apportioning blame: supposing I was entirely to blame, is that any reason to go on torturing each other for the rest of our lives? Can't one be husband and wife in this world, and yet love each other?"

"We aren't husband and wife," responded Trini unhesitatingly.

"We could be. It would be easy enough."

"It's too late."

Another silence descended.

"Don't build up your hopes around Soleràs," Lluís finally piped up.

"He's just a neurotic. I could tell you a thing or two . . . but you wouldn't believe me."

"Indeed I wouldn't."

"In the end he's simply a traitor."

"As you say so . . ."

"And I could point you to the exact fascist unit where he is right now."

"You're lying. Why would he want to be a traitor?"

"Why wouldn't he? That's what he's always been! He's always betrayed me, his companion and inseparable friend! How would you describe what he tried to do with you behind my back? And after he'd betrayed me, didn't he betray you as well? That first hope of marriage evaporated! Don't deny it: as a lover or suitor, or whatever you prefer to call him, Soleràs is remarkable from more than one angle. He is only interested in loves that are impossible! When they start to seem possible, he disappears, address unknown. If I didn't know him from years ago, his incongruous behaviour would make me suspect he is a . . . I mean . . . that he's lacking something . . . But I know him too well; I know him inside out. He's missing a screw or two. He's mad. And he never washes his feet; ask the machine-gun captain."

"It's all over between you and me," Trini interjected curtly. "There's no point indulging in all this slander, just as there's no point sending me your ambassador."

"My ambassador? Which ambassador might that be, pray?"

"Yes, your ambassador, Cruells."

I listened even more intently.

"I don't know what fool thing you've got in your head now."

"Well, you were the one who singled him out to me that Christmas Eve, when we were coming back from our stroll."

"I did?"

"Yes, you did. You noticed the light inside the church, and whispered to me: 'Let's go in and I bet you we'll find Cruells; we'll find him kneeling down at prayer, and you'll see he's so enraptured that he won't notice us.' And you insisted I go in; and I admit that I was impressed by the sight of him enraptured like that, so alone in a church that was dismally cold and dark. Yes, it made a deep impression; I was moved. I didn't realise at the time that you and he had engineered the coincidence to impress me, with a view to despatching him to me later as your representative. Because he did come from Villar that day, and when I saw him I felt like a good long conversation with him – but I didn't summon him. He took the decision to come; you'd gone off to no man's land with Picó: you know, yet another surprising coincidence . . . Then, when Cruells had performed his ambassadorial mission and delivered his edifying sermon, I understood what had happened. How disgusting. Yes, I understood why you were so keen for me to enter the church on Christmas Eve and see him at prayer; he acted out the farce so well and seemed enraptured in prayer as if he didn't realise that we were watching him . . . there were even tears streaming down his cheeks . . . an utter farce . . . so trite . . ."

"None of this is true. You're crazy. You imagine such abominable things, Trini; please, be your normal self. Try and calm down."

"It was all set up so I'd have to swallow his sermon, and a clever set-up at that, I have to admit. I fell for it hook, line and sinker! I listened to him to the bitter end."

"You don't know what you're saying, Trini; I don't know what sermon you're referring to. I don't know anything about *any* of this; I don't understand what you're implying. But what I do know . . . you can be quite sure . . . yes, quite sure that if ever Soleràs, if you ever gave yourself to anyone else . . ."

"What?"

"If you ever . . ."

"Keep your distance! If you touch me, I'll scream."

The sound of a slap rang out. I knocked on the door.

Trini's eyes were bloodshot. The boy's temperature hadn't gone down since the day before. He was amusing himself in his little bed drawing little people, not understanding why his parents were quarrelling. Lluís was looking out of the window.

"Make me a bandit leader," Ramonet asked me, "and a bandits' den so the leader can go in and out of the door."

I sat down by his bedhead with scissors and cardboard. "Mummy is behaving badly," he whispered. "She's hitting daddy like a stepmother."

"What do you think?" Trini asked.

"He's still got a temperature, but it's nothing serious. The flu has to follow its course. You know what children are like: they get temperatures at the drop of a hat."

But I felt vaguely uneasy. I thought I saw something in the boy that wasn't ordinary flu. I'd been particularly surprised by his voice: it had changed much more than it ought to have with a normal spot of flu. His voice wasn't simply hoarse; he hadn't simply lost his voice as you do with a bad cold. His had become an odd voice that I couldn't explain with my scant medical knowledge. I wanted to rush back to Villar, abandoning my friends who thought I'd stay for dinner and sleep over as usual. I wanted to consult the doctor immediately.

The moment I entered the medical store I heard the notes of "Voi che sapete" being played on a violin at the back of the cellar, muted as if they were coming from far away; he'd dug out his old violin the day after his wife left: evidently she couldn't stand the sound or sight of it. He'd play for hours and hours in the solitude of that cellar, sitting on a battered armchair we'd found in some attic and placed next to the wood stove. He played without a score; he had a wonderful memory when it came to music. There was always a bottle of Fundador within reach on the small table the other side of the stove. He'd been playing the violin and toping by himself for hours since his wife's departure, whereas the wife of the commander – his big drinking partner – was still in Villar. In any case, Commander Rosich couldn't stand Chopin or Mozart because he was the most fanatical Wagnerian I'd ever met. One morning, when Dr Puig and I were alone in the basement and he was playing the air "Cherubino alla vittoria" that I was accompanying – he'd sometimes ask me to sing the arias he played – the commander came down the stairs, barefoot so as not to make any noise, to the entrance to the medical store and threw a hand grenade our way: not *at* us, naturally, though close, into the corner of the cellar where we stacked empty bottles. The exploding grenade and shattering of broken glass resounded under those vaults as if the foundations were shaking. The commander ran back up the stairs shouting, "I'd do it again as long as he doesn't play Wagner like everyone else." The doctor gave him Cambronne's word by way of response. Such idiocy was part and parcel of our everyday life and made no impression.

At the time, my medical boss was so dependent on alcohol he only had to take a swig of cognac, glugged straight from the bottle, to be in a half-drunken state from early morning. He needed the drink to rouse himself into action; he'd reached the point where he could do nothing without alcohol – he told me as much. "I wake up," he said, "and feel that the whole universe is weighing down upon me and this lasts until the first swig of cognac puts me back on my feet." I can bear witness that he played wonderfully, with the greatest inspiration, when he was plastered stiff. Years later, I've often wondered how a man who was so refined, good-hearted and gifted could have fallen prey to alcoholism. I'm convinced that if that vice hadn't wiped him out he'd have become an excellent doctor, one of the best in Barcelona. I'd put two and two together and concluded he must have been one of those students, like so many nowadays, who enjoy a carefree youth and are incapable of adapting to the drab, unpoetic requirements of adult life. He'd first met Merceditas splendidly attired in an evening gown at a dazzling ball given by the guild of delicatessen owners on 17 January 1923, the night of Sant Antoni Abat, patron saint of the guild: I remember this date so exactly because he'd often remind me of what he called the most memorable night of his life. He then married her – he was deeply in love – when he was well past thirty, being fifteen years her senior, though he'd still not established himself professionally: he'd finished his degree years ago but had continued with his carefree giddy life as a bohemian student. He hadn't managed to build up a strong following of loyal patients. As his wife was wealthy, he allowed himself to lead a leisurely life at her expense, but it was all to mask the embarrassment of his lack of professional success. Perhaps it also explains why he decided to volunteer for the medical service in the army of Catalonia immediately after war broke out: at least that's what he suggested by often repeating a cliché which was also true: "I came to the war in search of peace." Nevertheless, I believe something else was throwing him off balance, apart from the frustrations he suffered because of his failure as a doctor.

But what was it? There was another frustration difficult to pin down and express in words, it was so elusive and fraught. If I attributed it to his failure as a husband, I think we'd understand and yet I'd have said nothing in particular. For all Trini's allegations – and I will say in passing that Picó was suspicious too, though he was prone to malice and you couldn't take him seriously – Merceditas had always remained faithful. Though she may not have been very bright, as a wife and mother she was beyond reproach and completely devoted to her husband and children. I even think that if she seemed to flirt with Lluís it was only because she was naïve; she wasn't double-dealing in any way, she was just very uninhibited. Lluís once admitted to me that he'd never known such a "soppy" woman, and he was someone who found it difficult to say such a thing about any woman who was at all attractive. The more I think about it, the more I imagine Dr Puig suffering from a frustration I myself found difficult to understand at the time, and not only because of what he called Merceditas' "frigidity": those famous "private secrets" he communicated to me alone had revealed that detail. No, that would have been too glib an explanation. Though what do I know of these subtle chasms that can destroy a man? In any case, this is what he'd complain about when he said, using language rather too picturesque, that she'd done "quite the opposite of making him a cuckold". I guessed this stupid expression hid painful frustration, but God alone can get to the bottom of the mass of contradictions and complexes each of us carries. What I can testify to is that he never, not even in his worst bouts of drunkenness, mentioned another woman; it was always Merceditas, cruelly and obsessively, as if she alone existed in the universe.

That day I'd travelled to and from Santa Espina in the Ford the commander had let me use because Ramonet was ill: it was early evening when I got back. As I said, he was playing his violin by himself, and a candle was flickering on the small table next to his eternal bottle of cognac. He stopped playing and gave me a drunken look.

"I thought you'd have stayed overnight in Santa Espina."

"Ramonet's temperature has got worse," I interrupted him. "I think there's something odd about him. His voice has changed, has gone."

"The flu's got to his tonsils; it happens so often when we think it's a straightforward infection: tonsillitis." He lifted his bottle up and took a swig. "It's tonsillitis, my friend. What a pity the lad can't take a good dose of this: it's ideal for tonsillitis!"

"Ramonet's tonsils have been removed."

"What are you on about? I saw them. They were swollen. It's such an everyday infection I didn't think it important; it's a straightforward sore throat."

And then he started to change the subject. He paid no attention to what I was saying, he was so sure he'd seen Ramonet's swollen tonsils. He whistled, hummed and talked about Merceditas: "Now she's not here, I dream about her every night. I drink in order to forget her, you know?"

"We should be talking about Ramonet," I insisted.

"Leave Ramonet in peace for a moment," he replied. "Don't start on about Ramonet now; we'll have all the time in the world to talk about him. Now I want to let you in on another 'private secret'. Only one, and I swear to you it will be the last. I won't burden you with any more."

He was very drunk that night; I could see that in his misty wandering eyes, in the way he couldn't follow the thread of our conversation. He kept jumping from one thing to another: "I don't know if I've ever told you about a particular beauty spot. Merceditas is justly proud of it, but as she's convinced herself she is too sensitive a soul and suffers from nerves, she can't go to bed without first drinking a cup of lime tea with a few drops of a sleeping draught. 'I'm suffering from nerves, I'm sensitive to the point of being ill,' she assures me. 'I couldn't bear it without my sleeping draught.' But I can assure you that what she's suffering from is quite the opposite; she's a clear case of female frigidity! You know, if you add in the lime infusion and the sleeping draught . . . if you pour a lime infusion on frigidity . . . ugh, it's the North Pole, I can tell you!"

"And I can tell you that Ramonet's tonsils *were* removed," I repeated. "His mother had them removed more than a year ago. I'm positive about that. I beg you to listen to me, Dr Puig."

"We were talking about beauty spots, not tonsils. A fellow student at university, a psychiatrist into the bargain, once advised me to find a distraction. 'You've got a beauty spot complex,' he told me. 'I'm sure,' I replied. 'You should rid yourself of your complex.' 'If only I could! How do I do that?' 'Well, you know . . . try other women.' Try other women! How stupid! As if I could want anyone apart from Merceditas! I tell you, Cruells, these psychiatrists are a fine pack of charlatans . . ."

There was no way to make him focus on Ramonet; he was about to lift the bottle to his lips again, but I snatched it away.

"I beg you, Dr Puig; make the effort to listen. Ramonet can't possibly have tonsillitis because he doesn't have any tonsils."

"What do you mean – he doesn't have any tonsils? He must be a monster. All children are born with tonsils. Like bulls are. Bulls are born with them and that's why in this brigade we say 'he's got tonsils like a bull' of someone who's very frisky."

He'd got up from his armchair and was groping in the cupboard for the bottle I'd hidden among the medicine; I put my hands in and led his to a bottle of cough mixture.

"There should be more solidarity, more camaraderie among husbands; it's not right for Lluís, who is a member of the club, to try to be on Merced-itas' back all the time. 'Husbands of the world's innocents, unite!' should be our slogan. It's what Soleràs used to say. He always used to say, if you remember, that the two fronts should unite against the two rearguards, and that may not have been a bad idea. Hey, why is this cognac so thick and sweet? It gives you one hell of a cough!" And in effect he started to cough until he was hoarse. "Hmmm, the two fronts . . . on each front . . . you can see a fine pair of horns . . . What's wrong with this Fundador? It was a topnotch fascist cognac and now I want to spit it out. Do you reckon it's gone over to the republic?"

He stumbled over his violin that he'd left on the ground; the sound box resounded like a long almost human moan. He suddenly stopped his flow of nonsense: he piped down and looked at me, as if suddenly beginning to grasp the situation: "Did you say something about Ramonet?"

"He has no tonsils!" I shouted. "For the simple reason that they were taken out more than a year ago! His mother told me!"

"No need to shout, I can hear you. He has no tonsils . . ."

"His mother told me ages ago," I lied, since I knew that was the case, not from her but from the letters. "They operated on him at the beginning of the war. Please pay attention to what I'm saying; make an effort, Dr Puig, I beg you! For the sake of God who is listening to us right now! You are the only doctor in these parts!"

He stared at me again and again with those alcoholic eyes, as if he felt vaguely haunted. He looked at me and said nothing; his eyes had gone blank as if seeing something horrendous on my face. He flopped back into his armchair.

"Oh," he said, "are you sure? They're not tonsils?"

A fearful silence. Then he looked down and added: "The inflammation that at a glance I'd taken to be swollen tonsils . . ."

He hesitated before blurting the word out: "Diphtheria."

"Diphtheria?" I exclaimed. "That's impossible. There are no children for miles around. How could he have caught it?"

"The cow," he replied drily.

Soon after the wives arrived, Picó brought a cow from no man's land with her two calves: "Home-produced milk," he announced triumphantly. The acquisition of that cow was greeted in the way such a timely event deserved: thanks to the cow, wives and children would have plenty of fresh milk throughout their stay with us.

"That wretched Picó with his mania for cow's milk," Dr Puig rambled on. "Was it Napoleon or Pope Borgia who bathed in cow's milk every morning? I'm quite sure that cow was suffering from diphtheria. Don't you remember how it was slavering and finding it hard to breathe? I'm no vet, for Christ's sake; one can never know everything! I think one of the calves was also whistling when it breathed; I couldn't keep it under observation because we soon roasted and ate it like greedy country bumpkins."

"Diphtheria is very serious."

"It was. There's a serum now," and he continued in a chirpier tone as if he found the idea of the serum soothing: "It is an illness defeated by science."

> Today sciences progress
> like no-one's busi-ness.

He hummed that, winking at me, as if he suddenly felt strangely euphoric.

"Cruells, diphtheria belongs to history! I have no doubt that cow had diphtheria. Unfortunately I didn't pay it enough attention, you know – we can't do everything! And in the end the cow died and took its secret to the grave."

"But are you sure the boy . . ."

"I am now. Absolutely sure! As is well known, the false membranes caused by diphtheria sometimes look as if they are tonsils. If I'd listened properly – something I didn't do, being an idiot – I'd have heard the air whistle as it struggled to get through."

His glazed eyes gave me a knowing look, as if he was struggling to co-ordinate his thoughts.

"Before we had the serum, you know, the false membranes obstructed the respiratory channels and children were asphyxiated. Some didn't die; anything is possible. In this case, they were left with the paralysis caused by the toxins that spread through their system. Ours is a filthy trade; there are always toxins and filth."

"We should alert Lluís."

"Bah, Cruells, what's the point of alarming him? Today diphtheria amounts to nothing. It's less dangerous than flu! There is a serum: ours is the century of science. You must take the Ford and go to Barcelona imme-diately."

Two days later, I sent a telegram to Dr Puig from Barcelona that the military telephone line had to retransmit to Villar: "No serum in the entire zone."

VIII

I went everywhere in Barcelona, from Hospital de la Santa Creu to Sant Pau, from military to civilian hospitals, and then made a pilgrimage to all the private clinics. In one of the latter, after listening to me and not saying a word, the director took me to the bedhead of a three-year-old girl. She must have been pretty once with her light brown hair and large brown eyes; now she is . . .

Her parents were sitting by her bedside listening in silence to her wheeze through her blocked larynx.

"She sounds like a train," murmured her father.

At the time, trains still ran on steam. The man's face wore that foolish expression we all adopt when we confront the absurd. The mother was stiff, as if frozen; I thought she was absorbed in prayer, but when she realised the director and I were there, without moving or ever looking at us she said: "There are so many children in the world. Why did it have to be ours?"

"Are you going to let this girl die?" I asked the director once we'd returned to his office.

"I can't work miracles."

He was in his fifties, lean and energetic looking, with white hair on his temples. He probably had problems with his liver.

"I can't work miracles. We have been ordered to hide this and say nothing to anyone, but I don't want to deceive you: there is no serum in the republican zone. I've even approached the minister; we're friends and studied together. All to no avail. You won't find any anywhere! Don't waste your time looking. It's a bastard of a situation, believe me!"

When I left the hospital, it was pitch black. The beams from the searchlights on Montjuïc met those from Tibidabo to form an illuminated cross that stood out against the low, rainy sky. They didn't pick out any bombers. They flew so high you could barely hear their drone. It was the third consecutive night they pounded the city.

I was walking through the dark, where hundreds of other phantoms were groping their way. All traffic had been halted; you had to go on foot.

As I walked across the empty building plots alongside the rail track, I heard invisible trains pass by in the dark. At times I felt I was flotsam adrift on the high seas; at others it was like walking on a huge body in its death agonies; the aeroplanes were like bluebottles coming to lay their eggs on a moribund city that was about to start stinking like a rotting carcass.

I wandered down main roads in that deathly dark, bumping into telephone or electricity posts and sinking into piles of rubbish that gave off a strangely sweet smell in those shadows. I felt excruciating sadness: that mother's face kept coming back to me and I could see she wasn't deep in prayer but frozen in a state of shock. Her stare accused the whole universe. Was she perhaps even accusing God? The eyes of the Virgin Mary at the foot of the cross stared less icily . . . and then I thought: Even the minister! Though strange things can happen, I thought; everyone says they do. They say there are very powerful ministers; they say the government of Catalonia has no power, like the republic . . . They say that. Everyone does. Why not try? He is his uncle!"

And suddenly I was in the great man's antechamber, though I never knew how I'd got that far. The great man came out to usher me into his presence in front of everyone else waiting, and patted me on the back in a reassuring gesture. We went into his office.

It was an imposing office, worthy of a great man; I felt awestruck. He was young and handsome, dark, strong, friendly, optimistic, dynamic and self-important. His dark eyes shone with an emotional gleam that softened their fire; it was well known that his eyes were quick to water when he was haranguing the masses, something that contributed in large part to his success as an orator, together with the quivering inflections he could bring to his voice. A magnificent baritone voice, a powerful voice that could curse and bawl or quiver according to the needs of the moment; this is a great man, I was thinking, at last a great man. I hadn't met him till then, it was the first time I had entered his office. The walls were hung with the most famous of the masterpieces that had been created thanks to his initiative, the "Make tanks", the "Battle of the egg", the "And what have *you* done for victory?" Dozens and dozens of huge, vivid, lurid, loud posters. The moment I walked in, two impeccably uniformed young men spread the still-wet proofs of a new poster on a vast table. It showed a four- or five-year-old boy in a republican soldier's uniform cheerfully aiming a sub-machine gun. The great man smiled at me patronisingly; he listened and spoke to me at the same time as he examined the new poster and gave instructions to his subordinates: "This red needs to be darker, it looks pale; make sure the ink is as red as possible when you start printing..." He smelt of eau de cologne and his half-military, half-civilian uniform was made of the finest wool and the last word in elegance. Once he'd scrutinised the new poster, he pointed to his desk: "I'm always so busy ... but I *am* listening."

While he spoke, he continued to open letters and telegrams, consult figures and notes. Yes, he was very busy, the sheer range of his responsibilities weighed him down; but he was everyone's mate, his highly important duties didn't prevent him being a friend and comrade to everyone who paid him a visit. He kept saying "comrade Cruells" and treating me like a lifelong mate, when in fact it was the first time we'd met. It was equally true that each time he addressed me by my surname he had first to glance at a page in his diary where his adjutant had written my surname alongside the reason for my visit and the likely length in minutes of our exchange.

"He's my nephew, do you see, and I can do absolutely nothing for him. For him or for so many thousands of other proletarian children! Comrade Cruells, it's most distressing." For a moment he abandoned his documents, statistics and telegrams and looked at me in the warmest, most tearful way possible. "I find it most distressing. I have sacrificed the whole of my life on the altar of the proletariat and can now do nothing for the children of the proletariat who are afflicted with diphtheria. There is no serum! The frontiers are closing, foreign powers are forsaking us; we face the most serious problems. I'm working myself to death, as you can see, but we are receiving no help from the world outside. None at all! No fertilisers for our agriculture, no forage for our animals, no sulphur for our chemical industry . . . I am a chemist, comrade Cruells, and I could show you the statistics for the last few weeks: production has plummeted . . ."

"I'm only asking you for a few drops of anti-diphtheria serum," I mumbled.

"But, comrade, didn't I just tell you that absolutely nothing is getting through at the moment? They have shut the frontier along the Pyrenees;

they are sinking every vessel that tries to reach our shores. They are isolating us from the outside world as if we had the plague. Ours is one of the greatest tragedies of history. In comparison, what is the tragedy of these little children? What are their tiny tragedies? Our struggle is being fought at a cosmic level; we must resign ourselves to our private misfortunes because they are the price to be paid for the redemption of the proletariat throughout the universe. He is my nephew, as you know, and I cannot stop my tears" – the great man's magnificent eyes began to water and his seductive baritone voice wavered slightly – "but we must be manly, overcome our weaknesses, sacrifice our own selfish interests and see the big picture!" His voice now surged, heroic and energetic. "This is the advice I would give every comrade: ignore what is befalling every individual proletarian and simply consider the proletarian masses as a whole. I don't know if you comrades at the front grasp the dangers we face in the rearguard; luckily we are here to deal with everything that comes at us. While you resist the enemy at the front, the enemy in the rearguard would stab you in the back if we weren't here to mount a heroic challenge against them. You should know that at this very minute we are facing the greatest of dangers in Barcelona: a clerical conspiracy. Yes, indeed, there are conspirators bold enough to dare ask that we reopen the churches. And however incredible you may find this, you will see among them members of the autonomous government and ministers in the republican government. From the expression on your face I see you find that hard to believe: well, it is true enough. That conspiracy exists. Luckily, we are ever vigilant; luckily, we never sleep. Reopen the churches? All our heroism would have been to no avail! Our sacrifices, the rivers of blood we have shed, all to no avail! However, no need to be fearful, comrades at the front, no need to be fearful, comrade Cruells . . . We are here, and we will meet every threat head on . . ."

"Comrade Cruells, comrade Cruells . . ." I felt a deep and dark desire to weep and to go for a pee.

IX

I called Lluís to one side; he'd not understood.

"I imagine it's some kind of joke . . ."

He looked at me with hate in his eyes: "So the great Llibert . . ." He gripped my arm and dragged me outside the village. The snow had begun to melt over the last few days and our boots sank into the mud. We reached the palisade where they kept the infamous brougham; he harnessed the mule without saying a word.

"What are you going to do?"

"Jump in."

He lashed the animal and it galloped in the direction of the deserted valley. Did he hope to find anti-diphtheria serum in one of those deserted villages? Apart from cursing our steed, he said nothing through the entire journey. His whip hissed through the air like a sheet being ripped. He spoke to me just once and that was to repeat with hate in his eyes: "So Llibert . . . our brilliant comrade . . ."

The cart track climbed steeply for a couple of kilometres; when we reached the ridge, where the other abandoned valley – no man's land – suddenly came into view, the mule, goaded by curses and lashes, launched a kind of cavalry charge and hurtled downhill; it was a miracle the old carriage didn't fall apart on the rocky track. We reached Cruyllas past Nogueras in under an hour. I'd never travelled so far into that valley, not having set foot in it for months – not since brigade headquarters had restricted travel permissions to Picó and Lluís. There was a wood near the village and halfway up the mountain the barbed-wire fences glinted through the tree trunks as they were hit by the slanting rays of the rising sun.

We left the brougham and mule in the church square and walked silently along the main street.

It wasn't a village that had been laid waste. It was intact. Though it hadn't been bombed or razed, its inhabitants had clearly abandoned it when they discovered they were caught between two fronts close to enemy positions. Its houses undamaged, the village seemed ghostlier than Villar or Santa Espina. The rising sun spread across the snowy rooftops like honey on a slice of fresh bread and the air on the streets smelt like a large empty house. Unscathed yet empty, it made a weird impression, a body living on after losing its soul. The fact that the houses, even the humblest, were a brilliant white added to the eeriness, as if the inhabitants had decided to whitewash them just before the battles had unexpectedly forced them to depart.

We left the village behind and climbed the slope in the direction of the fences. Lluís took long strides and I found it hard to keep up. After a quarter of an hour of walking between box and kermes oaks he waved me to stop; the barbed wire was a hundred metres in front.

"Don't be afraid," he said. "We pinched their cow, but they are generous folk."

Cowbells of every kind and size hung on the barbed wire and goat skulls and human skulls alternated on the tops of the stakes. It wasn't the first time I'd seen skulls, polished like ivory like those, stuck on the posts of barbed wire fences. Our soldiers, like the enemy, had this custom of collecting them wherever they found them – on fields where a battle had been fought months before – and displaying them in this way. I don't believe the intention was to make fun of them; on the contrary, it was more a homage to the anonymous dead, whether friends or enemies. The acclaim was eccentric and difficult to fathom, but I believe in their eyes that was what it was meant to be. The novelty on this occasion was that goat and human skulls alternated, something I'd not seen previously. Cardboard signs were nailed to the stake under each skull: "From the top of these pyramids forty centuries of history look down upon us", and other such renowned sayings. I'd still not understood – though I was getting an inkling – why Lluís had brought me there, and I stared at those signs and goat skulls in amazement; he didn't, as if they were nothing new.

"They are his ideas," he told me.

"The old guard dies, but never surrenders" said another sign; the rising sun projected its rays obliquely, endlessly elongating the shadows of the posts on which the skulls seemed to grin. I discovered one that was very small, like a toy that could have belonged to an eighteen-month-old baby; it had its own sign: "Suffer the little children to come unto me".

Lluís cupped his hands into a megaphone and shouted. As his shouts brought no response, he started shaking the wire; some of the skulls fell and the bells tinkled grotesquely. Still nobody appeared; we could have cut through the wire and advanced. He stood in full daylight so they would see him, creating a terrific din with his shouts and the bells, like a madman. I stayed hidden among the bushes though I called out to him, afraid that at any moment he'd be hit in the guts by a stream of machine-gun fire. He didn't even hear me.

Finally, four sleepy, bleary-eyed soldiers in tattered uniforms appeared, clearly annoyed their sleep had been disturbed. Lluís bawled at them in Spanish, saying he wanted to speak to their lieutenant; one of the four went off and came back minutes later with a man as ragged as his colleagues. Two small golden stars gleamed on the front of his sheep's fleece coat.

It was Soleràs.

"There's no serum," Lluís shouted at him. "Can you hear me? Cruells will tell you all about it . . . I don't understand, a cure for diphtheria . . ."

I was a few paces behind him and felt calmer now, but not entirely; we were still two against five. Lluís gestured to me to come nearer; I stood my ground.

"You want serum now?" said Soleràs. "You're such a whimsical fellow! You ask for the oddest things . . . So it is serum now, is it? Who do you want that for? For your latest bit on the side, like the eau de cologne? Don't tell me the doctor's wife has caught diphtheria?"

"There is none in the whole republican zone. Cruells will tell you. It's for Ramonet!"

Soleràs looked at him in amazement: "Ramonet is here?"

"They were having a quieter time here than in Barcelona. Ever since your people started dropping bombs . . ."

"Do you mean . . ." Soleràs couldn't get over his amazement: "Do you mean that Trini is with you as well? Did you have her accompany the doctor's wife? She and Ramonet? Are you mad? Tell them to leave immediately! Something nasty might happen to them!"

"I'm not asking for your advice."

"Something nasty might happen to them!"

The sea breeze had swollen and gusted fiercely past me towards them; it prevented me hearing what they were saying. I could see them gesticulating and opening their mouths and when the wind dropped I could hear them again: "Something nasty might happen to them!" Soleràs repeated for the third time, shouting into the wind. "You must send them away immediately, before tomorrow!"

"I didn't come here to be ordered around by you."

"And you say I'm the madman around here! You'll force me to tell you . . . I'll do so later. First let's speak about the cow. We'd persuaded you not to pinch it; you broke your word."

"Now's hardly the time to remind me of that fucking cow."

"You're obviously a generous man, Lluís: you'll forgive me the cows you steal from me as magnanimously as that punch you threw my way."

"A fine time to bring up that punch . . ."

"Do you think I can work miracles? Do you imagine me making anti-diphtheria serum here in the trenches? Maybe you think I make it from dry shit?"

"And maybe you could imagine, you moron . . . If there's no serum, the doctor will have to apply a red-hot brand!"

Dr Puig had told us that before the invention of the serum they tried to destroy the false membranes with boiling water or better still with a red-hot brand; Goya has a painting depicting that: at the time, it was the only way to stop children suffocating . . . Goya painted absolutely everything! The sea breeze blasted away for a while and I couldn't hear a word of what they were saying.

"You're always the same: you throw yourself in head-first when you want something and never stop to think; that's why you have so much success with women . . . Why didn't you tell me that Trini was in Santa Espina?"

"Why do you think . . .? After the game you played with the letters . . . Bah, let's forget that for the moment – it's hardly the time! I'll only punch you again like I did the other day and that's not what's on my mind now – I'm worried about something else. Let's forget that!"

From what they were saying, I assumed Lluís must have landed him one a few weeks ago. Why? I'd never find out; I'd never ever have an opportunity to ask him and now, all these years later, I really couldn't care less. He must have had good reason, not because of Trini and his letters, but perhaps some impertinent remark Soleràs may have made about the doctor's wife, since, as I was discovering, he was the one supplying Lluís with the bottles of cologne and packets of Camel destined for her while she stayed with us in Villar. That's how he knew she existed and even that we called her "the doctor's wife", but none of that was worrying me at such a tense time.

"Come a bit closer and I'll let you in on a secret that's strictly for the two of us. I don't want Cruells to hear. Yes, it's a secret; they could execute me for telling you, but I will tell you all the same."

"Can't you see the barbed wire?"

"Be patient. There's a gap, the one you used to get to the cow. You pinch our cows and still want . . ."

He disappeared, only to reappear immediately on our side of the fence. Tired of listening to a conversation in Catalan which was a total mystery to them, his four men had stretched out on the ground and seemed to be asleep. Soleràs was now whispering into Lluís' ear and from the latter's expression I guessed it was big news.

"What did you think then?" Soleràs shouted. "That this would last for ever?"

"You once told me there would never be any military activity on this front."

"And you believed me? Don't act like such a fool. Men always turn out to be bigger fools than they appear; women, on the other hand . . ."

He started whispering again; Lluís suddenly exclaimed: "You're not trying to make me believe she's a spy!"

"If I am . . . I personally couldn't care a damn! She's trying to look after herself, that's all I can say: she's more clued up than you and I and everyone else. This kind of bird has it in their blood; you can't keep track of them. But you should take precautions with a view to a possible change. A spy? What does being a spy mean? What she wants is the land and the castle; she doesn't lose a wink of sleep over anything else. The change, on the other hand, will suit her down to the ground; it will be like a dream come true. As if you only had to put the pot out and the partridges flew in of their own free will, plucked and gutted! Perhaps you heard that Turdy was killed not long ago in a skirmish."

"Anyway, Trini is bound to refuse."

"O man without imagination," retorted Soleràs, "why would she refuse if it's all about saving Ramonet? And even if there wasn't the boy, you're rather ingenuous to think that she and Trini wouldn't want to meet up . . . Even if there wasn't the boy, Trini would jump at the idea: 'Delighted to make your acquaintance, senyora.' I find it incredible that you understand so little about them: you can be sure they're both dying to meet. They are women: inquisitiveness is in their blood. Besides, there *is* the boy, and they're going to fuck him up! 'Suffer the little children to come unto me.' I suppose you're familiar with those words; I suppose you saw the sign . . ."

Soleràs took a deep breath, as if he wanted to fill his lungs in order to exclaim with all his might: "The whole universe isn't worth the life of a single child!"

And he continued without pausing, in a matter-of-fact tone: "Turdy was another matter. The great Turdy was tumbled some time ago. His death was a devious business, of course – a death that stinks to high heaven. An enemy bullet? Obviously! Any bullet that penetrates our head must be considered by definition to be an enemy bullet, particularly if it goes in through the nape of the neck. Yes, I can assure you it hit him in the back of the neck. This lady is really clued up, believe me. You are an innocent abroad and think they are less worthy of a romantic novel than they really are. She will do whatever it takes because she is grateful to you. You did her a big favour and she doesn't hold it against you; it's the first time I've met such generosity. She is magnanimous and more scheming than ever, set never to leave the castle come what may! She'll become the lady lording it over that whole area. They are already talking about her in these mysterious terms: 'A great dame, from the oldest branch of the princes of Aragon, orphaned by a hero and widowed by a martyr.' A legend is beginning to spring up around her. So what do you think? That this is beside the point? That you're no longer interested in the lady of the castle? That you're only interested in anti-diphtheria serum? My dear fellow, have you still not understood what I'm saying? I'll see to it: you'll find some in her castle. I couldn't be more explicit! Not everyone wants to becomes a legend, believe me, and nowadays you can go a long way with a little bit of legend and that's the kind of person who will soon be dividing up the cake. What about us lot at the front? Yuck! They'll all avoid us like the plague. Poor Lluís, you're in cloud cuckoo land, more or less as I am. Yes, more or less, because however hard you try, don't delude yourself: it's not easy to turn into a right bastard . . . No, it's not! There's always a learning curve."

He was no longer bothering to keep his voice down, as if he hadn't noticed I was there. Lluís said something I didn't catch and he quickly retorted: "The cow? So it definitely had diphtheria? You can't really blame me, my son; how could I ever imagine you would pinch it, or that you had Ramonet with you . . . No, better forget all about it; let Daisy rest in peace. After all, what can one expect from a cow? On the other hand, *she* will go far; her life starts now! This kind of lass doesn't get going until she's well past the fifty mark."

"Past the fifty mark? You're way off target."

"Is it beyond you to get the age of these charmers right? A few weeks ago I asked her for her baptismal certificate with the excuse that I would need it if the business of her marriage *in articulo mortis* was to be of use if the situation changed. She was born in 1888, that's a date easily remembered; do your sums, use your fingers if it's the only way you know. And you'll get a round fifty and almost to the day because she was born on 1 March. Fifty – the golden age for these charmers! She'll be thunder and lightning – everything's falling into place for her! It's not easy to be widowed by a martyr . . . some husbands aren't up to it, they need a little push on the sly. Llibert is another who will go far. There are no flies on him! Our brilliant comrade! What's that? What did you ask? Of course! Him too! If I never said anything it was because I thought you must have had some idea . . . Yes, of course! What did you think? You refuse to believe me? Have you ever believed me, my son? . . . 1888 is a date easily remembered: the First International Exhibition in Barcelona! The big attraction at the time was the captive balloon: everyone was queuing up to climb aboard . . . What? You'll never believe that the lady of the castle was born in the days of Rius i Taulet? Well, my boy, I swear it is true: I saw her baptismal certificate! It's hardly my fault if you always refuse to believe me. Alright then, I'll repeat my prophecy so you'll remember it one day:

these are the people who'll be dividing up the cake. You and I won't! We've swallowed too much dirt; we've smelt too much burnt flesh; we've scratched too many itches; the trenches leave a mark that never fades; everybody will avoid us. On the other hand, our brilliant comrade Llibert . . . and if I were to tell you that, already . . . You've never believed in my prophecies; time will make you change your mind. When you see the shop windows in Sant Antoni full of Queen Isabel furniture . . . yes, I've made this prophecy several times: after the end of the war, the Queen Isabel style will be back in fashion. What does that have to do with the war? How should I know? I prophesy, full stop. Queen Isabel furniture and the complete works of Eugeni d'Ors! Yes, once the war is at an end, you'll see the complete works of Eugeni d'Ors everywhere! You'll find them in your soup! Why are you pulling such a face? Have you never heard of one Eugeni d'Ors? Does he have nothing in common with diphtheria? But, my dear, we can't spend our lives talking about diphtheria; now I'm talking about Eugeni d'Ors, that scumbag . . ."

*

Back in Santa Espina, Lluís closeted himself with Picó. Then I helped him pack his bags. Trini sobbed uncontrollably.

"They'll act as if they saw nothing," said Picó, who'd just made a call on the field telephone. "We'll report you as missing. But you need to look lively."

Carrying the boy swaddled in her arms, Trini climbed into the brougham; Lluís hugged Picó.

"You know how much . . ." He didn't finish his sentence, perhaps for fear he might add something trite. He jumped into the brougham and gripped the reins. Picó and I had walked out to the cart track, but Lluís said nothing. He didn't even give us a glance. Nor did Trini, wrapped in a large blanket with the boy pressed against her bosom. The brougham rattled furiously downhill and disappeared out of sight round the first bend.

I slept the night in Santa Espina.

A hellish din woke me in the morning just before the first light of dawn. It was 9 March 1938.

Enemy artillery had opened fire across the whole of the dead front that was occupied by our brigade and the brigades to our north and south. At least that's what it roughly looked like from one of our observation posts; Picó had hardly slept that night, preparing the ground and telephoning battalion headquarters; he'd loaded the machine guns onto our mules and taken up positions with the entire company along the ridge. He'd instructed me to sleep, then headed to Villar at dawn and joined my lieutenant, but rather than take the track to Villar I'd taken the track to their positions.

I found Picó on one of the crags they called observation posts from where we could see a string of explosions along the curling front line of republican troops, far to the north and south; the artillery shelling was heaviest to the south and was supported by small squadrons of aeroplanes that flew back and forth in growing numbers as daylight broke.

"That lot is hitting the flatfooted brigade," he said in an unfamiliar voice; he wasn't wearing his dentures.

An hour later the commander arrived and trained his big binoculars on the massive bombing raids attacking the flatfooted brigade; he was soon joined by the doctor and sergeants and soldiers belonging to the general staff. For the moment not a single shrapnel bomb had fallen on our battalion's trenches, as if they'd been forgotten; we watched the line of dust and smoke curl and heard the blasts as if they didn't affect us.

"*La loca*" was the nickname our soldiers had given to the latest ultra-rapid field gun the enemy was beginning to deploy; it wasn't heavy calibre, but shot at a rhythm similar to a machine gun. Needless to say, after demolishing the barbed-wire defences and parapets of the flatfooted brigade, "*la loca*" and their aircraft came to devastate ours. Bombs and shells pummelled our trenches, which collapsed in places as the survivors, splattered with mud, fled them. The enemy aeroplanes flew very low – we had no anti-aircraft guns – cluster-bombing and shelling our barbed wire fences and sandbags to bits. They'd finished the job before noon.

Our fortifications had been totally destroyed: parapets devastated, machine-gun nests blown up by mortar fire and bombs. Our men were still holding up on the ground, protecting themselves behind what little cover they could find: tree trunks, rocks, scattered sandbags. They thought that when the infernal artillery fire stopped and the enemy infantry finally appeared, they'd be able to fight them off with hand grenades. They'd fought them off so often in the past, before they'd encountered these new elements.

Now the fire from "*la loca*" and the squadrons of bombers shifted north; bombs and shells suddenly stopped raining down on us. It was the silence that preceded the enemy infantry attack; we took advantage of the lull to collect our wounded. The doctor, stretcher bearers and I were engaged in this when the enemy appeared.

Their tanks came first. A mass of small mountain tanks supported the advancing infantry, surprising us completely: at the time we didn't even know of tanks so light that they could scale mountains.

And the rout . . .

I ran as fast as the next man. There was a heady smell of dense forest, sweat and gunpowder. Groups of fusiliers were fleeing in utter disorder. Someone next to me shouted: "A mortar shell blew his head off," another said, "Did you see those tanks?" I'd lost sight of the doctor; I'd lost my way and didn't know where the doctor, stretcher bearers and wounded were. It was a ghastly shambles, a senseless endless nightmare. I sat down, suddenly wanting to weep, because I was thinking of one of the wounded we'd had to abandon, calling out to his mother.

A tiny tank suddenly appeared in front of me, perhaps one of those small ones that had advanced quicker than the others and lost its way in the woods. It moved along the small ridge in my line of vision, slowly, like a caterpillar on a precarious branch; I looked at it as if bewitched. It seemed so peculiar against that landscape, as surprising as a tram might have been. It was then I realised that I was alone – just me and the armoured vehicle. To my right a tall almond tree in blossom was a splash of bright white on a small patch of earth; the tank's toy cannon released a shell that sped above the ground, uprooted a bush of rosemary by my feet and exploded in the distance. The tank was less than fifty metres away. I broke into a run.

I ran and ran, until I was out of breath. Then I collapsed on the grass.

"See how they run," said someone behind me. "Their tanks have sown panic. Why are they such a big deal? They're only machines! If we'd kept our cool we could have turned them over, if we'd put bombs under their transmissions. If we'd had a bit more culture . . ."

Without his dentures, his face wore the expression of a sardonic old farmer; he was quietly filling his pipe. Then I spotted the mules at the bottom of a ravine, the machine guns already mounted on their saddles.

"There's not a soul left on the ridge," he added after a few puffs of pipe smoke. "Only corpses. The fusiliers didn't give us any cover. They beat it in total disorder. Every man for himself! We must establish contact with the commander, supposing he . . ."

Then we saw the armoured vehicles once again; six or seven had just appeared, silhouetted against the sky. They opened fire against the column of mules; it was time to retreat.

Finding the commander was no easy matter. It was as if the earth had swallowed up the routed battalion. Men and mules, we walked for hours and met no-one. Hour after hour after hour. Night was already falling when we heard mutterings in a cave near a village called Castelfort; it sounded like a community of monks at their rosary prayers.

We found the commander inside. He was sitting on the ground, surrounded by the doctor and soldiers of the general staff; an oil lamp illuminated the weird scene. It *was* very weird, given that they were in fact at their rosary prayers while, in the distance, to the north, you could hear the dull, interminable thunder of cannon fire.

"Do you know the *ora pro nobis*?" the commander asked by way of a welcome, and without waiting for our reply, he continued the loud litanies.

Picó pushed me out of the cave. He said nothing, but you could see he was annoyed. He led me to the top of a small outcrop of rocks, from where we could see, in the distance, to our south, a line of dust about seven or eight kilometres long that wasn't raised by cannon fire. In the last glimmer of twilight I managed with the help of my telescope to make out a motorised column inside that dust cloud being transformed into a magical halo by the dying light.

It was an interminable convoy of troop-carrying trucks, like small toys in the distance. Toy trucks full of lead soldiers . . . They were crawling along.

"This bold advance would cost them dear if our brigades were able to get their act together; it would be so easy to cut off their retreat! But you've seen the state they're in, plastered out of their minds . . ."

The commander shouted to us from the entrance to the cave: "Orders from the division, on to Lomillas!"

The field telephone line was still working and we were managing contact with the division. Lomillas was a village far to our rear and we headed straight there.

We'd just fallen asleep when we were rudely woken by reveille. Commander Rosich wanted to dig out a trench before dawn and he'd climbed up to the belfry of the village church to get some idea of the lie of the land; he was accompanied by the doctor and two of the clerks from the general staff. The four of them – the commander, doctor and two clerks – reeked of rum, talking and gesticulating excitedly.

I stayed with Picó, who was looking for a good spot to set up his machine guns. The sun was beginning to rise; there was a plain before us, its far boundary an advancing cloud of dust.

"Their cavalry," said Picó, looking through his binoculars. "If they give us time to set up our machine guns, we'll mow them down – like clockwork!"

He started giving out orders; it was already too late. The Moorish cavalry had begun their charge – they were Moors we could now see perfectly well without binoculars. Our men were in flight yet again; it was all screams, clouds of dust, confusion and contradictory orders. Groups of soldiers ran to and fro and we couldn't tell whether they were ours or the enemy's. I'd have run off like everyone else if it hadn't been for the presence of Picó, whose calm demeanour steadied me. He ordered them to load the machine guns back on the mules as if he were solely worried about not losing a single weapon.

Once again we hadn't a clue where the commander was. Picó and I marched at the head of the column of mules and argued that we couldn't believe he'd stayed in the belfry since he must have caught sight of the Moorish cavalry in plenty of time from up there. As calm and canny as ever, Picó let his instincts guide him: he found a deep narrow ravine where we slipped down and hastened away from Lomillas, "away from their line of sight and fire". Scattered groups of fusiliers kept joining us; they shouted out incoherently and nervously: "They've killed the lieutenant", or, "They cut us off", or "Nobody lived to tell the tale". Picó took it all calmly: "If they'd cut you off, you wouldn't be here now." He listened to the most catastrophic news those fugitives brought us as if he knew it all and it even formed part of his plans. He issued curt orders in a most deadpan voice and if you'd looked at him and heard him you'd have said he'd anticipated everything well in advance, that nothing ever took him by surprise. His sense of calm was contagious; the wandering, panic-stricken bands of men we found on our way soon became disciplined and self-confident simply by seeing and hearing him. They let him scold them like schoolchildren being nagged by their teacher and kept joining our column, which grew in number by the hour. A battalion stricken by panic is as chaotic as the delirium you're in when your temperature reaches forty degrees: Picó gradually managed to bring a little coherence to that chaos. His instinct hadn't played tricks on him and never did. The ravine turned out to be really long and not the impasse I'd dreaded: it was a genuine covered path, as he had predicted. When we reached a good spot he divided up the men following us – a hundred or so – and positioned the machine guns: "We badly need a rest. We've been on the hoof for twelve hours and didn't sleep last night. But rest has first to be earned."

In effect, the enemy soon reared its ugly head, though it can only have been a scouting party: it only needed a brief skirmish, a short barrage from our machine guns to see them off and leave us in peace for a few hours.

Picó wanted to continue our retreat as soon as dawn broke.

"We'll catch up with the commander in Malluelo," he said. "That's where they must have concentrated all the battalion's remaining strength."

There wasn't a single soul, military or civilian, alive in Malluelo. The middle of the street was strewn with a pile of random objects, including a huge, surprising electric pianola; the houses were empty and open to the world. While we searched them for any sign of food, heavy-calibre shells began to fall on the village; the poorly built houses collapsed around us. Picó gave the order to evacuate, though the soldiers protested – wracked by hunger, they wanted to continue raiding pantries.

When we were leaving the outlying houses behind, a crazed man in tattered rags stumbled out of an animal pen and threw himself at Picó's feet: "Captain, in God's name!" he shouted. "Some faces I recognise at last! I was hiding in there under a pile of dung . . ."

It was one of the clerks in the general staff who'd climbed up the belfry in Lomillas with the commander.

"Where's the commander?" Picó asked him.

"Done for!"

"What do you mean 'done for'?"

"Percolated!"

He was frantically scratching himself, as if he'd caught a whole brigade of lice and ticks in the dung within that pen.

"Percolated? Speak plainly for once! Who are you talking about?"

"Him, the commander!"

"Fuck off," retorted Picó, who couldn't stand clerks, particularly that character, a sergeant who had been, back in the day, a stalwart of the "republic of the baby's bottle"; the man looked deranged, he had turned a bright red. His days' old beard was black and prickly.

"They trapped us; they surrounded the village," he shouted nervously. "Lomillas, you know the village I mean. Their cavalry, you know which I mean, the Moorish cavalry, those bastards . . . We were up in the belfry . . . What a racket! What scum! The other clerk and I stretched out flat, but the commander poked his head through the arch and was firing his pistol; so was the doctor. The others responded from down in the square with their Mausers and the bullets ricocheted off the bells, which rang with festive chimes!"

"What happened to the commander?"

"He soon used up his ammunition."

"What happened then?"

"He stood up on the ledge" – at that very moment the man managed to extract a fat tick from his hairy chest – "and climbed up holding onto the bell clapper and . . ."

A frenzied burst of laughter stopped him dead; he was splitting his sides and tears were rolling down his cheeks. . .

"What's so funny, you idiot?"

For all Picó's disapproval, he couldn't stop convulsing; he barely managed to mouth these words: "Vintage 1902."

Picó looked at me and pointed a finger at his forehead.

"Vintage 1902? What nonsense is that?"

"Sauternes, captain! Vintage 1902 Sauternes! I swear! As he'd used up his bullets . . . he kept bawling 'From the top of these pyramids forty centuries of history are looking down upon us,' until he fell down with his hands clutching his belly."

Picó glanced at me silently once again.

"What about the doctor?"

"I haven't a clue; he stayed up there. He and the commander had downed a bottle of rum for breakfast between them; a shell burst among the bells, as the other clerk and I crawled down the spiral stairs to the sacristy; concealed in the cupboard among the communion wafers we found —"

"No more nonsense."

Night after night the remnants of the 4th Battalion beat a retreat through deserted village after deserted village following the machine-gun captain. We had no sense of the situation in general; we didn't know where the other forces of our brigade, of our division might be; it was possible for us to conclude that the entire republican army had evaporated and that the hundred men following us were all that was left. We did know it must have been a sudden, general rout across the entire front; for example, we found bridges that were intact. Unless it was a case of incredible carelessness, there could be only one explanation: the sappers had had no time to blow them up – our lines must have melted away in a moment.

We guessed that a large-scale disaster had broken the Catalan–Aragonese front at its weakest points; the dead fronts had been numbed by long hibernation; we guessed that, but wandered like a handful of ants lost in an interminable desert and nowhere did we find a trace of the other forces in our army. We walked by night, slept by day. One morning we camped dead tired outside a hamlet, as deserted as they all were, near an ancient bridge with many arches. Dawn broke and we wanted to sleep on for a few hours among the poplars on the river bank, we were so exhausted. We'd barely nodded off when Picó called for a blast on the bugle.

"Just a hunch," he whispered to me.

We walked uphill for almost half an hour to a vantage point among the pines from where we could see the hamlet, bridge and riverside poplars. The sun's slanting rays illuminated the whole scene: the red stone castle and collegiate church stood out against the intense blue of the western sky, spotlit by the rising sun. We had only just lain down among the pine trees when we heard a distant hum that drew ever nearer. We didn't see them, we only heard them; they must now have been overhead.

Suddenly, a column of black dust rose silently from the bridge, towering high above poplars, hamlet, castle and church. Then we heard thunderous explosions. Fresh columns of smoke, fresh explosions: now we could see neither hamlet nor bridge nor poplars. Everything was immersed in a repugnant, dense black haze.

"They're shitting right where we were sleeping," was Picó's only comment before he went back to sleep.

At dawn the next day we were walking along a high, bare plateau, searching for camouflage before the sun was too high in the sky, when a snitcher – the name soldiers gave the reconnaissance aircraft – appeared and circled above us. "We must find a wood before the fighters get here," said the captain. They came quicker than expected. Three all told: more than enough to despatch a hundred straggling soldiers if their machine guns strafed us. At that very moment a sea breeze blew up and covered the plateau in mist; we walked for a long time, perhaps hours, in a mist that made us invisible and soaked us like cold drizzle. Not a single man lost his way.

For food we collected everything we found in deserted villages. We were sometimes lucky and stumbled upon a communal bakery packed with dry bread, the last batch that the inhabitants had been forced to abandon in a rush. The houses were always empty; everyone had fled taking everything they could carry. There was also the last harvest of olives we found heaped under the trees on burlap sacks, or half sacked. They were large black bitter-tasting olives, and very nutritious.

Then we came to the steppe. First we'd left the mountains, then the woods and finally the olive groves; we were now on vast, barren monotonous plains, the only vegetation as far as the eye could see being scant, spindly bushes of gorse and thyme. During the day we stayed as still as we could under the few shadows the treeless flatlands had to offer. Enemy aeroplanes passed to and fro overhead but never spotted us, we were such camouflage experts, and they never would have if it hadn't been for the mules.

Picó had decided to save the mules whatever the cost – they were vital for transporting machine guns and boxes of ammunition – as if his honour depended on it. One day at noon when the sun was almost at its zenith, aeroplanes appeared unexpectedly; we hadn't heard the approaching drone and by the time we had noticed they were already overhead. I curled up into a ball as best I could under a solitary hawthorn bush. No part of me lay outside its shadow, while the machine gunners forced the mules to lie down and stay still under other scant shadows the landscape provided. Frightened by the whirring engines, one animal got to its feet and started to trot towards my hiding place; it stopped next to me. In the full light of the sun that animal caught a pilot's eye; he started "telling the time", as we called it, and was followed by the others. They zoomed down level with the ground and sprayed us with machine-gun fire, then immediately climbed back towards the horizon, described a circle, and returned – time and again – until they ran out of ammunition. On that occasion they "told the time" for a couple of hours that felt like centuries to me.

However much their airpower chased us, we'd lost contact with the enemy on the ground days previously as much as we had with our own soldiers. Without the constant buzz of Junkers and fighters we'd have imagined we were the universe's sole survivors. The steppe was never-ending; we didn't march in a straight line but zigzagged wildly, following Picó's inspired hunches. We walked – always at night – six hours to the north for example, then four to the east. The day after, when night fell, we resumed our march and would go five hours to the south, and another five eastwards. Sometimes we even turned back and headed west, never once fathoming what drove Picó's topsy-turvy orienteering. If I asked him, he simply shrugged his shoulders and said "hunches". All I can say is that his instinct never erred. He always managed to prevent his band of a hundred men being encircled and exterminated, men who trusted and followed him like a father; we forded rivers far from well-trodden paths and bridges

448

that Picó avoided as much as he could. We'd sometimes see an intact bridge in the distance. Now and then we'd find piles of abandoned material, random items such as heliographs, angle gauges and other items we didn't recognise at all; and often heaps of intact fragmentation grenades, their pins gleaming in the sun; and one day a huge, solitary 15.5 cannon in the middle of the bare plain.

We skirted this jetsam from the vast shipwreck; it left us cold and we clearly couldn't salvage it. Bits of human bodies would be quietly drying in the sun, scattered around that cannon, some a considerable distance away, apparently the bones of those mounting the gun that a bomb from an aeroplane had blown to pieces. Soon after, we came across a pile of bundles tightly wrapped in paraffin waxed paper we could easily have mistaken for bars of luxury soap. Picó picked one up: "TNT," he said. "This is the stuff those bastard sappers should have used to blow the bridges up before they scarpered, but there you have it, cast aside like so many lumps of shit!"

And lo and behold, a few days after we found the TNT our path was blocked by one of the widest rivers in Aragon; it was too deep to ford and Picó sent scouts upstream and downstream to look for a bridge. They returned to report that there was a wonderful bridge about four kilometres away and that they'd even found a contingent of sappers.

"They told us to get a move on. They've been working on it for three days and expect to blow it up today."

It really was a magnificent modern bridge, and intact like all those we'd come across so far. Twenty or so men were working on it up to their waists in water under the orders of a lieutenant engineer. A couple of kilometres on the other side of the river we could see a hill covered in spindly juniper and pine, the only trees in that grey expanse stretching out before us. After talking to the lieutenant Picó told me to take our troops to that small wood we'd seen while he and five veterans stayed behind and helped the sappers with their taxing work. In fact the sappers had no need of assistance, as he knew very well, but he was dying to see how one blew up a big bridge from close up. He'd not have missed that show for anything in the world.

The dawn light began to glow on the horizon to our east: from that isolated peak the surrounding plain seemed endless, the peace profound and the solitude absolute. Picó had instructed me to scrutinise the horizon to the west with my telescope as it was much more powerful than his binoculars. I could only see a stretch of land grey and monotonous as our despair, crossed by the deserted road. Suddenly I thought I heard a very distant rumble. Daylight was still too dim for me to make out any precise details through my telescope of what was happening twenty-five or thirty kilometres from my vantage point. I didn't want to prompt Picó's sarcasm by alerting him to what was mere anxiety on my part – anxiety that nevertheless I felt was gathering strength.

The sun came out almost immediately, huge and red like a watermelon split down the middle, and I spotted something moving in the distance almost on the horizon.

It was impossible to make out what it was; through my mariner's glass – which I rested on a branch for stability – I could only discern small blobs moving forward very slowly: they brought to mind the almost invisible bacilli one can see under a microscope. I tried not to lose sight of them, but they disappeared for long periods as if they'd never existed. While I concentrated on seeing what I could, the twenty men in the contingent of sappers had emerged from under the bridge and were now calmly walking cross-country in small scattered groups. The affable lieutenant came to inform me that Picó and the five soldiers had stayed under the bridge: "They wanted to make sure the bridge was blown up at the right time," he told me. "We've left everything ready – they only have to activate the electric wire to detonate the explosives." "Isn't that difficult?" "No, it's easy," he replied. "Very easy. And we must move on because we have work to do on the other side of the river."

I returned to my telescope and was surprised once again by the sight of those blobs I'd found so intriguing that were now still. So still I doubted they had ever moved; they were too far away for me to decide whether they were simply patches of tar on the asphalted road or shadows – but shadows of what on that bare steppe? While I was engrossed in my telescope, the five veteran machine gunners walked up; Picó was now alone under the bridge. He'd scribbled a message for me on a scrap of paper: "Stay there with the troops; don't move; tell them to get some shut-eye. Keep looking out and let me know what you can see. With culture and patience, we'll execute a most splendid action here." They told me he was hiding in the rushes near the bank, two or three hundred metres from the stanchions of the bridge, and that the top of our little hill was all you could see from down there. I got very weary continually focussing on those blobs or shadows that refused to stir; they didn't start to shift until after midday. There were about a dozen, but a dozen of what, exactly? They were in the far distance and continued to crawl along. They disappeared for a while in a great dip in the terrain and reappeared at about two o'clock.

Then I saw what they were: ten or twelve ugly armoured trucks that seemed to be advancing at walking pace.

I was struck as before by how much those vehicles seemed like toys in the distance: a column of ten or twelve toy armoured trucks advancing along the road, not taking any precautions whatsoever – who did they need to be wary of? And now I could see men who really did look like lead soldiers. Another couple of hours went by; I informed Picó via a messenger who kept coming and going; I trained my eye and telescope on the trucks. The messenger returned with very precise instructions: "When the first truck reaches the bridge, light a small fire of dry undergrowth so I can see the smoke." They'd stopped again for a good half hour; then they resumed their lethargic procession. They were half trucks half assault vehicles and were big, ugly and probably antiquated: the contingents of men aboard relaxed without a care in the world, and were now very visible from the waist up on their nasty iron beasts. At the age of six or seven I'd had a model of that armoured truck, with soldiers seated on benches, the top half of whose bodies were visible; the benches had holes in them where you inserted the catch each soldier carried on his back . . . They suddenly disappeared into the grey undulating plain, then reappeared closer to the river. "Wait for me until nightfall," Picó wrote on the last scrap of paper the messenger brought me. "If I'm not with you by the time it's dark, go on with the troops and don't wait for me any longer."

The dry half-rotting grass I heaped up and the smoke, thick and white then black and acrid, which made me cough, now seem like a dream, as do the men waking up and looking at me as if I'd gone mad – they didn't know it was a sign agreed with the captain: they didn't know what was happening; yes, as if I were mad. Who'd ever think to light a bonfire and betray our presence to possible aeroplanes? And their eyes suddenly opened wide in amazement when they saw the armoured trucks on the bridge – the first was about to roll off the other side while the last had just rolled on, as if that bridge had been tailor-made to accommodate an armoured column that size! It was late afternoon with the sun low in the sky when that cloud of thick black smoke rose silently from the arches of the bridge with bits of lead soldiers and scraps of metal and stone congealed in the air. All was silence, a few seconds of silence followed by a tremendous thunderclap and an extraordinary blast that shook our little hill and the branches on the pine trees.

I remember like a dream the jubilation we felt at the sight of those fragments blown in every direction by the expansion wave – what a bang! – those dreamlike bits that didn't belong to lead soldiers but to men whose friend and comrade I might have been, whose friend and comrade I'd wanted to become and almost had become at a given, recent moment in my life. Yet I felt wildly elated when I saw them being blown to smithereens. "What a bang!" muttered the soldiers around me ecstatically. "What a big fucking bang!" And then I did have a strange hallucination, wide awake with my eyes wide open: everything suddenly disappeared, the blown-up bridge, the soldiers around me, shouting as if stunned in admiration: "What a big fucking bang!" the endless steppe and the setting sun. All I could see was the face of Dr Gallifa that seemed to fill the horizon.

His sad smile was reproachful, but his face faded into the bright lights of sunset and all I could see was a dungeon; and that dungeon was dismally dark – and lo and behold the sun touched the horizon and there was that red watermelon again and he was at the back of the dungeon because it was that red blotch that was changing into a pitch-black dungeon at the back of which I could still see his face, now splattered with blood.

And men were moving about in one corner of the dungeon like a pack of rats scurrying around a carcass, and I saw and recognised *him* among them, trying to pass unnoticed. Yes, I could see Lamoneda, his face half hidden under a red and black scarf; I could see him in such exact detail, I'd never ever seen anything so exact, and that was when Picó shook me and woke me from my dream: "Come on, that's enough sleep; the sun's set, forward march!"

On another evening, during another glorious twilight on the endless steppe, we spotted a leafy bower, a desert oasis in the distance. After so many days on the road we were about to meet up with a civilian, a solitary civilian and such a peculiar one! Perhaps he was a lunatic, or a ghost. A large building was concealed among maple and laurel, magnolia and cypress trees, a park and building so unexpected we thought it must be a mirage. The civilian we met informed us that it was a spa: it possessed a famous mineral-water spring. We were amazed when we went in. It was a kind of huge Swiss chalet and everything was so neat and tidy as if they were expecting their usual clientele, though of course there were none; only that gentleman.

That well-dressed middle-aged man, alone behind the bar in the dining room, didn't seem at all surprised, in fact seemed to be expecting us: "Please do come in. Take a seat."

It was grand and welcoming; the tables were arranged and laid: best crockery, silver and glassware, like the tablecloths and napkins. It was a luxury spa that had once been famous and we exchanged astonished glances across that vista of order, cleanliness and luxury. Through a large window you could see dark overgrown gardens in the ebbing light. As that gentleman was so insistent, we sat down in groups of four or five per table. He switched on the lights; the bright electric glare seemed magical in the circumstances; he explained how the current was driven by a weir and went into detail about how the dynamo worked. Picó looked at the man and nodded at me and couldn't stop himself bursting into laughter: "Home-produced electricity!" he exclaimed, though he then immediately shut up. We found it too sad to remember the commander and sat awkwardly in our rags and tatters in that elegant dining room, suddenly realising that our beards were long and dirty, our shirts torn and stiff with sweat, and our hair and armpits crawling with lice: suddenly realising we reeked of sweat many weeks old. But that gentleman noticed nothing: "Senyors, do please eat. Don't stand on ceremony."

And he spoke in Catalan! A civilian who spoke Catalan heightened the sense of unreality in that whole scenario.

"Eat," he insisted. "The crockery is national and the menu republican."

That was the first time we'd heard the word "national" used rather then "fascist". Naturally the menu never came, didn't exist; that must be why the master of the spa said it was a "republican menu". Picó signalled to us and we took out of our haversacks bread that was harder than stone and wrinkled olives and lo and behold! – the gentleman sat down at the table with Picó and myself and shared in our provisions. He wolfed his food down and rattled on incoherently, a tad pompously. We, the soldiers included, had emptied all our supplies on the tables, but that didn't amount to much: the dry bread and olives we had left. And we were so astonished to be eating on such beautifully set tables that we silently devoured those hard crusts and those olives like goats' droppings and stared at each other in amazement. A large shell exploded in the gardens and interrupted that peculiar dinner; another shell soon followed, and another, and another.

"Four: a complete round from a 15.5," announced Picó. "Please switch off all lights."

But the man ignored Picó and went on talking to us in that posh voice as if he thought we were part of the spa's usual wealthy clientele: "Well, you know, I have nothing to fear," and he smiled ineffably. We quickly swung our haversacks on our backs before the second round of shells started to fall, which would more than likely make direct hits on the Swiss chalet.

"Come with us," Picó told the owner, but he stood straight-backed in the fully lit entrance to the dining room, at the top of the three steps leading down to the garden. "Off you go, gentlemen. Please don't stand on ceremony," he repeated most affably. "Gentlemen, please don't stand on ceremony."

A perplexed Picó glanced at me as the second round exploded, this time on the other side of the spa. The soldiers were waiting in the pitch-black overgrown gardens for the captain to give them their orders. The column marched off; the gentleman in that brightly lit entrance waved us goodbye: "Good night, republicans. Never forget what I said: national crockery, republican menu . . ."

He didn't finish his sentence; the third round fell right on the spa and blew up windows, tables, doorways in a shattering din, though the lights were still working as we rushed to leave the chalet far behind us. We could still hear the man's voice cheerfully calling out to us after that racket, "Don't you worry about me: I'm one of theirs, not one of yours. They don't want to do me any harm!"

Four fresh explosions and all that had remained of the building collapsed. Then there was a sudden and absolute blackout followed by flashes and crackling flames. We put all that quickly behind us; we were back on the bare steppe. It was a cold refreshing night with no moonlight; the spa and its owner, probably blown up together, were soon forgotten. The following evening, after a day spent sleeping in a ravine, we came across a large farmhouse.

It looked abandoned, which was hardly surprising given the situation. We began to search for food. The pantry was a real joy: a ham, tripe and four huge sausages were hanging from the ceiling beams and in one corner was a pitcher of olive oil awash with pieces of preserved pork. Picó gave out orders and fair shares of the booty. I acted as his secretary. The apparition took place just as we were about to carry the pitcher of pork into the farmhouse entrance – it was huge and required four men – where we intended dividing up the contents among the hundred or so men.

Shocked to the core, we put the pitcher on the ground. It was only a girl, perhaps fourteen; she was tall, skinny and pale-faced, with dark eyes and hair, dressed in mourning black. She stood silently at the top of the steps into the house and stared reprovingly down, holding an oil lamp which lit up her face with its dim glow. "Aren't you ashamed of yourselves?"

Her voice seemed remote; she spoke in Catalan, like the gentleman in the spa: Aragonese Catalan. We stood stock still, listening to her, intrigued.

"You're such cowards and hopeless fighters, and on top of that will you steal from us? What's more, in land you should think of as your own? We waited for you as our brothers and you came; but what did you do? Where is our Virgin Mary? Where are our saints? Who can we turn to, you wretches? Everybody flees you like the plague; I'm alone in the house. You can steal everything – it's you lot against me all alone . . ."

That night we marched on empty stomachs.

Just before daybreak we came to a river much bigger than any we'd crossed up to that point. We didn't know then but it was the Cinca. Picó didn't want to look for a bridge, "because now, more than ever, we must avoid bridges and roads. We're getting close to the new front." While we attempted to ford it, with the water up to our necks, we saw groups similar to ours drawing near from upstream and downstream; small contingents like ours, wandering at a loss, drawn to the few kilometres where the river wasn't too deep to cross. After the solitariness of our long wanderings, we were encouraged by the sight of other Catalan forces: we no longer felt alone in the world! The strong flow of the river swept away a mule and a few men. The bank opposite was steep and high.

We finally found troops in trenches across the Cinca, on a high bank. They'd quickly established trenches, barbed wire fences and a few machine-gun nests to prevent the enemy from fording nearby; it was the first line of trenches we'd seen in three weeks of the rout. They said our army was beginning to rebuild behind that improvised line of fortified defences – rebuilding in preparation for the counteroffensive. In effect, scattered bands like ours were being re-formed and incorporated into new units that were being put together as they arrived.

We could see a large hamlet on a hill, about three kilometres behind the line, towards the east, overlooked by an ancient church, with a belfry that you could have mistaken for a castle tower. It was silhouetted in black against the eastern sky and was beginning to glow like the background to an altarpiece. There was a storks' nest on the belfry; I could see it clearly, big as a cartwheel, through my telescope. Mother and father flew from nest to river and from river to nest; their beaks carried to their brood fish that glinted in the first rays of sun, waving tails their little ones greedily devoured.

"Spring is here," said Picó, "spring has come. The storks are the first to go and the first to return. The good weather is back."

I thought of the storks Lluís and I watched at the end of summer when they were preparing to migrate. So much had happened since then!

One afternoon, taking advantage of a lull at the front – the enemy offensive had finally stopped – I walked to the nearby hamlet. It was full of stray soldiers from the most diverse brigades and divisions as well as civilians, particularly country people who had fled from the area affected by the offensive. It was a very motley band that had gathered around the hamlet, sleeping in huts they'd thrown up, in caves or in the open air: old men, women and children, the sick and the wounded. Enemy aircraft had bombed and strafed them as they walked with their carts – poor people who knew nothing about the rules of camouflage. They had walked by day, taking no precautions, always along roads across treeless plains; they had left in their wake, so they told us, a string of blown-up carts, disembowelled nags, corpses and the sick that couldn't go on.

My God, they were so wretched! They lived on the leftovers of food meant for the soldiers.

Picó never mentioned Lluís again; we did not speak of him in our conversations; we had no need to speak of him. An old woman from Castel de Olivo recognised me. She was queuing with many others outside the military kitchens begging for a bowl of soup.

"We saw lootenant Don Luisico the day before the trouble started," she told me. "'e didn't see us, 'e didn't look at nobody; 'e were driving a woman in a cart, wrapped in a blanket and looking like the Virgin of Sorrows. They went through Castel, but didn't stop. They took the track to Olivel de la Virgen."

Olivel fell on the first day of the enemy offensive, a few hours after it had begun. It put up almost no resistance.

OTHER NEW YORK REVIEW CLASSICS

For a complete list of titles, visit www.nyrb.com or write to:
Catalog Requests, NYRB, 435 Hudson Street, New York, NY 10014

J.R. ACKERLEY My Dog Tulip*
J.R. ACKERLEY My Father and Myself*
J.R. ACKERLEY We Think the World of You*
HENRY ADAMS The Jeffersonian Transformation
RENATA ADLER Pitch Dark*
RENATA ADLER Speedboat*
AESCHYLUS Prometheus Bound; translated by Joel Agee*
LEOPOLDO ALAS His Only Son *with* Doña Berta*
CÉLESTE ALBARET Monsieur Proust
DANTE ALIGHIERI The Inferno
KINGSLEY AMIS The Alteration*
KINGSLEY AMIS Dear Illusion: Collected Stories*
KINGSLEY AMIS The Green Man*
KINGSLEY AMIS Lucky Jim*
KINGSLEY AMIS The Old Devils*
KINGSLEY AMIS Take a Girl Like You*
ROBERTO ARLT The Seven Madmen*
U.R. ANANTHAMURTHY Samskara: A Rite for a Dead Man*
WILLIAM ATTAWAY Blood on the Forge
W.H. AUDEN (EDITOR) The Living Thoughts of Kierkegaard
W.H. AUDEN W.H. Auden's Book of Light Verse
ERICH AUERBACH Dante: Poet of the Secular World
EVE BABITZ Eve's Hollywood*
EVE BABITZ Slow Days, Fast Company: The World, the Flesh, and L.A.*
DOROTHY BAKER Cassandra at the Wedding*
J.A. BAKER The Peregrine
S. JOSEPHINE BAKER Fighting for Life*
HONORÉ DE BALZAC The Human Comedy: Selected Stories*
HONORÉ DE BALZAC The Unknown Masterpiece *and* Gambara*
VICKI BAUM Grand Hotel*
SYBILLE BEDFORD A Favorite of the Gods *and* A Compass Error*
SYBILLE BEDFORD A Legacy*
SYBILLE BEDFORD A Visit to Don Otavio: A Mexican Journey*
MAX BEERBOHM The Prince of Minor Writers: The Selected Essays of Max Beerbohm*
STEPHEN BENATAR Wish Her Safe at Home*
FRANS G. BENGTSSON The Long Ships*
ALEXANDER BERKMAN Prison Memoirs of an Anarchist
GEORGES BERNANOS Mouchette
MIRON BIAŁOSZEWSKI A Memoir of the Warsaw Uprising*
ADOLFO BIOY CASARES The Invention of Morel
PAUL BLACKBURN (TRANSLATOR) Proensa*
CAROLINE BLACKWOOD Corrigan*
CAROLINE BLACKWOOD Great Granny Webster*
RONALD BLYTHE Akenfield: Portrait of an English Village*
NICOLAS BOUVIER The Way of the World
EMMANUEL BOVE Henri Duchemin and His Shadows*
MALCOLM BRALY On the Yard*
MILLEN BRAND The Outward Room*

* *Also available as an electronic book.*